NO COUNTRY
FOR OLD MEN

ALAN SCHWARTZ

NO COUNTRY FOR OLD MEN

NEW AMERICAN LIBRARY

TIMES MIRROR

PUBLISHER'S NOTE

This novel is a work of fiction. Names, characters, places, and incidents are either the product of the author's imagination or are used fictitiously, and any resemblance to actual persons, living or dead, events, or locales is entirely coincidental.

NAL BOOKS TRADEMARK REG. U.S. PAT. OFF. AND FOREIGN COUNTRIES
REGISTERED TRADEMARK—MARCA REGISTRADA
HECHO EN CRAWFORDSVILLE, INDIANA, U.S.A.

The author wishes to thank the following sources for permission to quote material in this book:

Random House, Inc., for material from THE SOUND AND THE FURY, by William Faulkner. Copyright 1929 and renewed 1957 by William Faulkner. Reprinted by permission of Random House, Inc.

Macmillan Publishing Co., Inc. for excerpt from "Sailing to Byzantium" from COLLECTED POEMS of William Butler Yeats. Copyright 1928 by Macmillan Publishing Co., Inc. renewed 1956 by Georgie Yeats.

SIGNET, SIGNET CLASSICS, MENTOR, PLUME, MERIDIAN and NAL BOOKS
are published by The New American Library, Inc., 1633 Broadway, New York, New York 10019

Designed by Julian Hamer

Library of Congress Cataloging in Publication Data

Schwartz, Alan.
  No country for old men.

           I. Title.
PZ4.S3978No   [PS3569.C5648]   813'.54   80-15496
              ISBN 0-453-00390-7

First Printing, November, 1980

1 2 3 4 5 6 7 8 9

PRINTED IN THE UNITED STATES OE AMERICA

For Nancie, Erica, Jennifer,
and the crew of the Chinese Soup Wagon,
whose unrelenting pursuit of the
Evil Fong led past the Great Wall
to this book.

... and gather me
Into the artifice of eternity.
　　　—W. B. YEATS

History hath triumphed over time
which . . . nothing but eternity hath
triumphed over.
　　　—SIR WALTER RALEIGH

PROLOGUE

July 5, 1943

34° 12′ N. Lat. 68° 16′ W. (off Bermuda)

RAVEN STOOD on the afterdeck of the *Libertador* and watched the phosphorescent wake. He looked at the time. Almost midnight. Stars but no moon, and the sea an infinite expanse of black. "Good," he said aloud. He removed the band from a Havana cigar he was holding, tossed the adornment overboard, and took a small box of matches from his pocket. Suddenly tense, sensing a presence behind him, Raven turned around. But no one was there, only the lounge chairs lashed down for the night. No lovers or midnight strollers idled by. He lit a match, but the wind took it, another; and then cupping his palms around the third, held the cigar to the flame, which lit his face with its flicker as he drew on the tobacco until the tip glowed.

As he turned to look at the wake once again, a white-coated steward stepped up to him.

"Senor Raven?"

Raven turned to the man, muttered acknowledgment.

"Will you please follow me?"

He led Raven to the companionway, and up the stairs. At the top a door marked FIRST CLASS PASSENGERS ONLY had been wedged open, and they stepped through into the carpeted corridor.

* * *

In Cabin 14 Captain Novaes, the ship's commander, sat facing the man in the wheelchair. On the small mahogany table between them, there was a briefcase and the bottle of cognac the steward had brought in a few minutes earlier.

"Well, Senor mío, I think we can drink to the successful conclusion of a highly delicate operation," the captain said as he filled their glasses.

The man in the wheelchair nodded approvingly.

"Prosit."

They lifted their glasses and touched them together. Captain Novaes hesitated before drinking; the other tilted his head back in a quick swallow. When his eyes returned to the captain's face, Novaes had not yet touched his drink.

The man in the wheelchair started to say something, but could not speak. Then his body slumped forward, head banging on the table, mouth open, eyes wide in amazement on the leather briefcase.

Captain Novaes reached forward and felt the faint pulse. He hissed the one word "traitor" through his teeth and then laughed aloud. He felt pleased with himself. So far, so good. He got busy with the bulky form.

When the steward knocked on the door, Captain Novaes was sitting alone. The table was empty.

"My dear Senor Raven," said the captain, "now we can talk."

Captain Novaes glanced at the steward, indicating the door to the sleeping quarters with a motion of his head. The steward nodded and stepped through the door. Raven, seeming relieved to relax in the cabin's safety, sighed and sat down, taking off his rumpled and dirty white dinner jacket. The steward returned and took it.

An hour later the captain and the steward accompanied a drunk out of the cabin, each supporting him with an arm around his waist and one of his arms held over their shoulders. In the corridor, the steward stumbled slightly against the door of Cabin 7, and as the trio eased themselves through the companionway, the cabin door opened.

"Que pasa allá?" asked a bleary-eyed elderly man, squinting in the sudden light of the corridor.

"O, Senor, disculpeme," said the steward, apologizing for the disturbance. "Este caballero, el poeta Raven, esta borracho denuevo, y estaba peleando con los marineros. El necesita aire."

The sleepy man shrugged his shoulders and closed the cabin door. He had seen the poet drunken and quarrelsome since boarding ship in Havana. He had probably got what he deserved in a fight with the sailors.

Just before dawn, Becari, the ship's engineer, went off duty and climbed to the afterdeck to smoke his customary pipe before turning in. It was against regulations for the crew to use the afterdeck reserved for first-class passengers, but Becari didn't care; he never saw any passengers there at this hour anyway. And he enjoyed a quiet smoke before turning in. As he stepped out of the engine room companionway onto the portside deck, he looked aft to make sure no insomniac passengers were at the rail. Indistinct in the starry darkness he saw two figures, one in a white jacket, the other in dark clothes. Then he heard a voice he knew was Captain Novaes'.

"Senor, I beg you! Don't do it!"

The engineer realized that the figure in white was outside the rail. Suddenly there was a flailing of arms and the white jacket disappeared.

The captain yelled "Help," and Becari ran towards him.

"It's that crazy drunken writer," the captain shouted in his face, grabbing a life ring and throwing it into the water towards the white-coated figure.

"You stay here and keep watch, I'll go sound the alarm. Drop a floating flare from that locker."

Captain Novaes handed Becari a powerful searchlight and ran forward. The engineer leaned over the rail, and turning on the beam, tried to follow the white coat rapidly slipping astern, floating face down in the wake. The light danced for a moment on the back of the prostrate form, gleamed on the life ring floating nearby, and then lost them both in the darkness. Becari lit a flare and dropped it, watching it pass astern rapidly.

Summoned by the captain, the second mate sounded the crew emergency bell for the forecastle hands and hurried to the afterdeck to find Becari at the rail, playing a searchlight in the wake.

"Where is he?"

"Can't see him anymore; must be almost a mile back, past the flare."

They both felt the old ship shudder through the decks as the engine screws reversed.

In a clatter of running feet the crew appeared on the afterdeck. The second mate assigned ten each to two lifeboats, put the bosun in charge of one, stepped into the other himself, and ordered the boats lowered by the remaining hands. Becari watched the boats fall away into the ship's wake and then disappear in the darkness toward the pinpoint of flickering yellow flare.

* * *

The first shark, drawn by the huge slab of bloody beef liver wrapped around the corpse's leg, nudged the body with his hammerhead, passed by, and making a quick turn, rammed the body hard, lifting it from the water. Another turn and the teeth ripped into the bleeding beef, taking half the flesh off the man's thighs. Almost instantly the water was filled with wild thrashing as dorsal fins and the dull white bellies of striking sharks rabbled in the gore.

In the east the sky was getting light rapidly when the lifeboats reached the dimming flare, where they parted and moved in overlapping semicircles, their lights crisscrossing each other in the gap between and ahead. When the bosun spotted the life ring and reached with a longboat hook to pick it up, a four-foot shark, alerted by the movement, surfaced and darted in, belly skyward, taking a chunk of the doughnut-shaped preserver away with him.

Almost half the sky was gray; the rest was black, and the long lifeboats continued slowly. No longer necessary, the searchlights were extinguished as the light increased steadily until the entire sky was bright and a faint glow of the rising orange sun was just below the eastern horizon.

Dozens of dorsal fins were moving blackly through the water, and the area surrounding the boats was thick with bits of cloth and pieces of bloody flesh attached to human skin, a slick of blood and gore extending in all directions. One sailor began to reach over the gunwale toward a small leather object floating by, but the mate stopped his movement with a shrill cry, and reached over with the net. It was a cigar case with the initials H.R. embossed in faded gold.

The *Libertador*, its speed reduced, had turned in a wide circle and was now approaching the lifeboats. The liner's rails were crowded with passengers in pajamas and robes, frowsy and curious. Captain Novaes stood on the bridge with a megaphone in hand.

"Have you found him?" he shouted at the lifeboats.

"No!" bellowed the second mate through cupped hands. "Sharks! Nothing left."

"Keep circling the area," replied the captain. "Pick up what you can."

He turned toward the chart room, handing his binoculars to

the first mate, who took them and scanned the western horizon to starboard. Nobody else had looked in that direction, so engrossed were they in the lifeboats and the gossip.

He caught a flash reflected from the red ball now clearing the eastern horizon.

"What the hell!—"

The man rubbed his eyes and refocused the binoculars.

The periscope was still there, not more than 100 meters off the starboard bow. As he watched, it turned around slowly in a complete circle and then withdrew beneath the surface. He ran from the bridge into the chart room where the captain stood at a high table, pouring over a chart of the area south of Bermuda.

"Captain, there's a submarine out there, watching us!"

Novaes reached for his hat.

"Where is it?"

"I saw the periscope about two points off the starboard bow."

Novaes was already through the door of the chart room into the wheelhouse. The mate ran ahead of him and opened the door to the bridge.

"Show me where you saw it!"

The mate pointed, and the captain looked through the binoculars.

"You're sure? Perhaps the strain of the past few hours is affecting your vision!" His eyes came about terse, narrow, yet his voice took another tack: flippant, sarcastic.

"I don't think so; I saw a scope describe a circle and withdraw."

"Nationality?"

"No way to tell."

Captain Novaes looked at the first mate curiously. "It may have been a water-logged timber floating vertically." He turned toward the wheelhouse door.

"Look!"

The dark gray conning tower broke the flat surface of the ocean where the mate had pointed a minute earlier. He seemed relieved not to have the captain think that he had hallucinated. The captain stood gripping the rail, his knuckles showing white against the pressure of his hands.

They could both clearly see the Iron Cross insignia painted on the side of the tower. On the submarine deck, still slightly awash in the turbulence of surfacing, a hatch opened, and a sailor in fatigues stepped up, climbed a ladder to the conning tower bridge and flashed a semaphore lamp.

"STAND BY FOR MESSAGE. IDENTIFY VESSEL," Captain Novaes read aloud as the light flashed the international code.

"Call the radio operator," he said to the mate who scurried along the portside catwalk to the radio room aft of the bridge.

The signalman hurried forward to the bridge, where the captain had readied the semaphore light.

"Identify us to that submarine."

Perspiring and awkward with fear, the signalman fumbled with the lantern shutter and then flashed across the water: LIBERTADOR, ARGENTINE REGISTRY, OUT HAVANA, BOUND NEW YORK. CAPTAIN SERGIO NOVAES.

A uniformed naval officer appeared on the conning tower bridge of the submarine and spoke to the crewman at the semaphore.

"WHAT PURPOSE YOUR SEARCH OF THIS AREA," the radioman read off as the message flashed from the Germans.

"Tell them we have lost a man overboard and are looking for the body," said Novaes. "Indicate a passenger suicide."

The signalman flicked the shutter rapidly: RETRIEVAL BODY. PASSENGER SUICIDE.

With no hesitation the submarine flashed back; MUST ABANDON SEARCH IMMEDIATELY. PROCEED ON COURSE. IN WAR ZONE. WE RESPECT ARGENTINE NEUTRALITY. LIBERTADOR CONTINUED PRESENCE IN AREA CONSIDERED ACT OF BELLIGERENCY.

"Goddamn Nazi bastards," muttered the mate. "Do they own the fucking sea?"

Captain Novaes seemed lost in thought.

"The search is hopeless in any case," he answered, "and I can't risk the safety of the ship because some lunatic drunkard decides to feed himself to the sharks."

He spoke now to the signalman: "Tell them we will abandon the search under duress, and proceed on course if safety is assured."

The blinker from the submarine flashed back one word: ASSURED.

With that the German officer raised his right hand to his peaked cap in a formal salute, and disappeared below. The crewman climbed down the conning tower's outboard ladder, eased into the open hatch on deck, and closed the cover over him.

Captain Novaes watched the hatch close on the submarine, and turned to the first mate.

"Recall the boats!"

While the first mate hurried aft with a megaphone in his hand, Captain Novaes entered the wheelhouse and lifted the main intercom microphone; he addressed the knot of passengers and crew who had crossed to the starboard rail and were watching the interchange of signals with curiosity and fear.

"All passengers must now return to their cabins. We will resume course immediately. There is no danger to us. I repeat: there is no danger to us. Your captain and crew are most sorry for the inconvenience and unpleasantness of this interruption, and hope you will enjoy the remainder of our journey. Our speed will be increased to make up for lost time, so we should arrive at New York tomorrow afternoon as scheduled."

Lifeboats aboard, passengers shuffling back to their cabins, Captain Novaes gave his orders to the man at the wheel and the huge liner turned slowly to port and then straightened its course to the correct heading. As the white ship moved northward, its speed increasing, he watched the German submarine just sitting in the water, its hull almost invisible now, only the conning tower showing above the surface of the sea like a huge dorsal fin.

A few minutes later, in the chart room behind the wheelhouse, the second mate handed Captain Novaes a small canvas bag containing some tatters of white cloth, a few pieces of bloody flesh and a cigar case; the last remains of the poet Harry Raven.

PART ONE

1

New York, November 1973

FED UP WITH staring at the dirty glasses, open books, dog-eared quarterlies, and last week's newspapers on his coffee table, Professor Eric Newman shoved the Xerox copies of the old newspaper stories he held into the briefcase he was taking to Columbia today. He poured a second cup of coffee, opened a recent *New York Review* lying atop the rest of the litter and turned to a vitriolic review of a new biography of Orwell. The reviewer was attacking Orwell rather than discussing the book, and Eric Newman wondered what they would do to his book on Harry Raven, when and if it was published, when and if he stopped amassing data and finally finished writing the damned thing.

Could he do it? Could he really bring the project to its long overdue completion? Afraid of the critical reception he would have to face, of what "they" would say, he saw himself ripped open by the critical sharks and left to sink in the gray ocean of academic hopefuls, a mangled and forgotten might-have-been who never fulfilled his early promise. Like Harry Raven. He opened his briefcase, retrieved the photocopies he had just shoved in and reread the thirty-year-old stories for the fifth time that morning:

New York Times:

POET LOST AT SEA; APPARENT SUICIDE
SHIP ABANDONS SEARCH AFTER U-BOAT THREAT
New York, July 16, 1943

Prize-winning poet Harry Raven was lost at sea early yesterday when his recovery after a leap from a cruise ship was curtailed by the presence of a German submarine. . . .

Daily News:

LEAPS FROM SHIP TO SHARKS
SUB SCARES SEARCHERS
New York, July 16, 1943

After a lover's quarrel, poet and critic Harry Raven jumped off a ship into the shark-filled waters near Bermuda in the small hours yesterday morning. The search for his body ended quickly when a German submarine threatened to torpedo the ship if it remained in the area. . . .

P.M.:

SPANISH CIVIL WAR HERO COMMITS SUICIDE
NAZIS THWART RECOVERY OF BODY
New York, July 16, 1943

Harry Raven, progressive poet and hero of the Abraham Lincoln Brigade, was lost at sea early yesterday when a Nazi submarine prevented the crew of the Argentine ship *Libertador* from recovering him. . . .

His eyes skimmed the familiar stories, hardly seeing them. Why was he looking for the answer here, at the end of Raven's brief life? What Eric Newman needed was a beginning for his book, an eye-catching, interesting opening. A handle for organization.

That was the major problem. Was he writing the biography of Harry Raven from the womb to the tomb? He didn't want to do that. Raven's childhood friends, the acne years, and shoe repair bills bored Eric Newman. What interested him was Raven's sudden ending, the truncated potential of this great writer, and the agony he had suffered in a world where he saw the ideals he lived for overshadowed by the frenzy of World War II and the mania called totalitarianism.

No answer in view and filled with self-pity, Eric sighed his way into the bathroom and began lathering his stubbled chin. Shaving done, he turned on the worn porcelain shower faucets and pulled the plastic curtain across the tub, waiting for the warm water to come through. Ass-backwards, he thought, you don't start by . . . He stopped, one foot in the tub. *That was it!* Backward! Start from the end. The suicide, and then flash back to the formation, but *only* the intellectual formation of the man who leaped into the sea.

The warm water sluiced down Eric's back and he felt better, as though a load had been lifted. Somehow it had fallen into place, after all the agonizing—a solution in the shower. He liked the idea, and thought of openers. . . . In a flash he saw the whole book in his mind's eye. Now to work out the opening, and his long struggle was over. He finally had it.

Whistling, he had just started to soap his head when he heard the ringing. He let it go at first, but when it didn't stop after five or six rings, he got out and ran to answer. "Schmuck," he muttered as he tracked wetly across the dusty floor. At 8:15 in the morning it had to be his ex or other bad news.

She was friendly enough, asked about his recent trip to Mexico and Cuba, thanked him for sending the check on time, then shifted gears into the old children-need-new-clothing road.

"Elly, I don't want to argue."

"This isn't an argument, Eric, it's a conversation about your— our children. How do you expect them to go to school without any clothes?"

"They'll be very popular, real hits."

"Very funny. You're always so dependable for half-witted remarks when I'm trying to be serious. I didn't call you, which is hard enough for me because *she* might answer, so that I could play straight man for your act."

He hated her for kicking his nice morning in the teeth. Why couldn't he make enough money just to send her a check and shut her up?

"Straight *person*, Elly; eliminate sexism in even its smallest manifestations. And who is *she?*" He couldn't let the provocation go. The old tit for tat didn't end with divorce.

"Don't play with me, Eric. *She* is that Puerto Rican adolescent you . . . you left me for."

"That's your mythology. I got involved with Lucia months after you threw me out, and she's twenty-eight years old and Venezuelan. Look, I won't continue this. If you want to argue and rehash, forget it, I'll hang up. Besides, she doesn't live here. I'm alone."

She didn't say anything for a few seconds, and then turned

down the volume. "The kids need fall 'outfits,' " she repeated.

"I can't do it, Elly. Just paid Mike's tuition, and Nina's ortho-dontist. I'm flat broke until the end of the month. Can it wait a few weeks?"

Sweet reasonableness wasn't her forte. "Didn't you save any money from the research grant?"

"The money is itemized and budgeted. I've got to account for every penny, and there is no allowance for my children's clothes for school. Anyway, it cost me a bit more than I got."

That was the red cape: she came in charging hard, hooking her horns at his kidneys.

"For three years now you've spent all your money and time on that damned book. I don't think you'll ever finish it. You get a perverse pleasure in letting it hang over your head."

"Thanks for the two-bit analysis, Elly. I can't send you any money now." He sidestepped, the muleta drawing her energy.

"Sure—because you spend all your money gadding about, pre-tending you're writing a great book, a real contribution to human knowledge—which nobody cares about and no one will read. Professor Newman the expert! But when it comes to your basic responsibilities, you don't know shit! I'll bet you have plenty for your whore!"

"Goddamn it!" he shouted, dropping protective metaphors with a clang, "you're out for blood, and I really don't want to bleed. What the hell do you want from me? You've got the house, the car, the kids; I send you half my monthly paycheck and you make as much money in your job as I do; I live in this dumpy furnished apartment like a fucking pauper, and I don't need the fighting. One reason I'm here is that I couldn't stand it before."

"And the other reason is *her*?"

"Oh shit, that's enough. The answer is no. The kids will live without new clothes. If it's so important to you, you buy them, or take me to court."

He didn't give her a chance to answer, said good-bye quickly, and hung up the phone, sorry that he had given her the last idea. She had managed a wipeout once again, touching the sensitive and guilty sores in his psyche. He didn't see the kids very often—once every two weeks—for a day when they kept busy doing things: basketball games at the Garden, Museum of Modern Art, movies, restaurants; always on the run so they wouldn't have to confront each other, deal with the resentment and loss they all felt. He put distance into the already existing distance; and in her own borschty way, Elly intuited his guilt and clobbered him with it. Even when Eric won, he lost. Sweating, he got back into the shower, then dressed in a rush, watered the plants, fed Horace the cat, forced the scuffed briefcase to close, and left.

As he was stepping out of the apartment door, the telephone rang again. Hesitating for a moment on the threshold, he decided to answer it, hoping it wasn't Eleanor with a coup de grace. It wasn't.

"Oh, Eric, this is Lee Winkler. I hope I didn't wake you."

"Not at all; I was just leaving."

"Good; I wanted to speak to you because, umm . . . something that may help your book along." Lee had been Raven's lover at the time of his death. Her husband Ben had been Raven's closest friend, and Raven had wounded them both, with love and betrayal.

"What is it?"

"Something of Harry's that I didn't mention to you before, for various reasons, but if you'll come over I'll tell you all about it."

Puzzled why she had withheld something and then called out of the blue, Eric asked her what it was.

"Some writing . . . sort of, that *no one* has ever seen!"

He felt his heart pound. Fright? Joy? Both! A peak in Darien.

"When can I see it?"

"Can you come over for a drink tonight? Ben won't be here, and we can talk."

He said he was free that evening.

"Good, I'll expect you at about five."

He closed and double-locked the apartment door and rang for the elevator. Mrs. Macintosh was inside when it arrived.

Every day the same question.

"How's Horace?"

Every day the same answer.

"Fine, autumn weather makes him frisky."

In the winter, he varied the answer saying that the cold made the cat drowsy; in the summer the heat made him listless.

"Well, I can't blame him. Sasha and Maude won't even touch their food, and when I try to change their diet . . ."

7

The elevator stopped and he held the door while she wheeled out the shopping cart, coupons torn from the newspaper clutched in her bony hand.

"The vet said . . ."

Eric kept nodding with all the sympathy for the cats he could muster and then when they reached the front door, stepped out onto 113th Street, and walked quickly toward Broadway, stopping at Nagle's bakery on the corner to buy some brioches to take to the office for breakfast.

It was a nice day, sunny and crisp; a football day, and he felt good inside despite Elly. His doubts were banished, at least about the book. Lee Winkler's sudden need to reveal something must be outside of Ben's knowledge. Eric had thought that Lee's love affair with Harry Raven over thirty years ago wouldn't be a sore spot anymore, but what the hell, the male ego is always vulnerable.

* * *

"One for you, two for me. Is there any coffee?" He dropped the bag from Nagle's onto Lucia's desk.

"Drake wants to see you," she said, nodding her head toward the chairman's closed door, "but somebody's with him now."

Why today? Eric didn't need the finish-the-book-for-tenure-and-promotion-or-else routine just now. But you don't argue with Caesar; you humor him.

"Is he foul or fair today?"

She shrugged her shoulders. "Quien sabe con el?"

Lucy took a Styrofoam cup out of her desk drawer and handed it to him.

"It's set up in the conference room."

"Our meeting?"

"No, dummy, the coffee!"

Her black Latin eyes studied his face, and he caught a whiff of the jasmine perfume she wore.

"I'll ring your office when he's free."

She reached over and patted the back of his hand.

"Eric. I miss you."

He smiled feebly and stepped away toward his office door, two brioches and a Styrofoam cup in one hand, heavy briefcase in the other, keeping Satan behind him.

For three years Eric Newman had been working on this biography of Harry Raven. He knew as much about Raven as he did about himself. Interviews with contemporaries, careful study of all the poems, letters, essays. He had read all the manuscript material in the Rare Book and Manuscript collections at Columbia, Yale and the New York Public libraries, and all of the critical papers and analyses of Raven's work by other scholars. Any book, memoir, collection of letters that mentioned him. He had traveled to Latin America, where Raven had been well received during the 1930s, and read all the old newspapers and magazines in the libraries to find any smatter of information which helped to clarify how Harry Raven's contemporaries had seen him. Interviewed everyone he could contact who had ever known the poet. There were many new insights. Ben Winkler, for instance, had told him how vehement a partisan fighter Harry was during the Spanish Civil War. No other researcher had the information Winkler had given him. Tasting victory's sweet fruits in advance, Eric pulled the taped Winkler interview out of the cassette file and popped it into the tape machine on his desk. He pressed the "fast forward" lever and kept his finger on it, listening to the high-pitched sound. Here was the place, around the middle:

"You should have seen old Harry in Barcelona. Fierce, and a damned fine shot. Handy with all weapons. Once, chasing an Italian patrol down the Ramblas . . ." (Eric interrupted the anecdote with a question about Raven's politics.)

"Too far left for me. Really committed to international communism. You know, I fought for Spain today—I mean then. He fought for Russia, for world revolution tomorrow; it happened to be in Spain." (Winkler had fallen silent. The tape hummed on while Eric had waited, wanting Ben to follow the curve of his own idea . . .) "He was behind some of the purges, you know."

Eric hadn't known and said so; he had never read about it anywhere.

"Oh yes, Harry fingered the deviationists—revisionists. And they were shot for treason. Trumped up charges—but before a court martial—it was open and shut. I lost some good friends because of him. Surprised they never got me too . . . And everyone knew that Harry had a direct line to Moscow, but nobody said anything. Isn't that strange. There we were, fighting and dying for the Span-

9

ish Republic, and our own partisans were knocking us off for ideological distinctions.

"Of course, I found this out later. Hemingway told me. He knew at the time what they were doing because Regler, the political man in International, told Hem who was getting the lead in the back of the neck, but he kept his mouth shut. There's a lot of dirt there; it broke up Hemingway and Dos Passos, but that's another story . . ."

Eric turned off the machine and put the tape back in the cabinet. Now he had it all. He had only needed the handle of the opening. *Eureka!* The shelves of his office were jumbled with books and papers, his files full of carefully annotated index cards, and the tape cabinet held one hundred and seventy cassettes of taped interviews. This book was going to be *the* definitive biography of Harry Raven, great American poet and critic. It would make Eric Newman's career in the academic world.

What is it that absorbs one man in the life of another? He thought about that a lot, but was still not sure, although he had some good guesses. Creative work one would like to do but fears he never will? A kind of magic for him in Raven's poetry, which he had first read as an undergraduate when he fancied himself a misunderstood poet? He remembered the thrill, the visceral tingling when he first read "The Water Dance" . . .

. . . the green current cluttered with the wreckage of yesterday's love, a cargo of despair for the sea.

Eric had imitated Raven, written poems in his second year at college full of disillusionment and pain, dedicated to girls he knew, and they did what they could to relieve the pain. Eric was the high scorer in the dorm. That always bothered his roommate Nicholas. Serious, high-minded Nick, who worried about the state of the world, and always beat him on the tennis court or in one-on-one under the backboard, took little comfort in those triumphs. He used to call Eric the little politician of the pen. Nick was right, in a way, until Eric really got hooked.

He got caught in the magic of words, an absorbing play of language and form, a hermetic symbolism which left him feeling like the priest of a religion which had no acolytes, no laity but himself. He published a few poems in an obscure literary magazine and was told, "I saw your poem and liked it," by at least three friends and two professors, but that was that. Knowing he was no great verse maker, poetry became for Eric a collector's passion, as one might gather beautiful stamps or shells or master drawings or butterflies. Volumes of verse, first editions of T. S. Eliot, Hart Crane, Wallace Stevens, even a Keats. He loved possessing the images, these fragments of worlds, and was happy just to own such beauty. He continued to write poems, but confined himself to a notebook, never exposed it to the wary eyes of editors or the barbarism of rejection slips.

Then, in graduate school, studying comparative literature, he came across the supreme collectible: another person's life. First editions were one thing, but a whole life! To possess the day-to-day doings of another person, to assimilate the ideas, the habits, the concerns, the loves, hates, neuroses of someone else—and to know more about him than you did about yourself—that was collecting; that was possession with a passion!

An entire life could be seen from start to finish; it formed a whole, a definable entity. In the case of a creative thinker, the patterns, the movements could be understood, grasped, and the relationship between life and creativity made clear. The biographer pulled it all together, made the dead come alive, *and he owned the life breathed into his subject.*

Now the written, spoken, printed records of Harry Raven's life surrounded him, filling his shelves, his file drawers, his mind: all he had to do was revise the first draft and tie all the loose ends together, filling in the gaps with the material he had gathered in the past few months. Now that he had a handle on his opening chapter, and had decided on the flashback narrative, it should be a cinch. Then just final revisions.

Lucy walked into the office as Eric was changing the typewriter ribbon.

"Professor Drake wants to know if you can have lunch with him today."

He could, and they set it for 12:30 at the faculty club.

She picked up the brioche on his desk and bit into it.

"I don't get such privileges," she said with the half of her mouth that wasn't filled with the roll, "and I would *make* lunch for you, not buy it, with a dessert you would remember a long time."

She stood in front of the desk, her almond-shaped eyes flashing, her tongue searching her teeth for bits of brioche, and he wanted to step around the desk and kiss her. But he didn't. With the twisted spiral of the old typewriter ribbon dangling from his hand, fingers all sooty from the carbon, he tried to smile.

The smile simply aggravated her annoyance, and swallowing, she narrowed her eyes and said, "And don't give me all that baloney about still being good friends. For three months you go away and not even a postcard. Then you avoid me since you're back. No calls—nothing. So maybe you got another woman; okay! I can handle competition. But I got feelings too; maybe it's something you can't understand. Why should I still feel a passion for you? And let it show in public? Because I'm a Latin woman, and the American women don't act as if a man they love is so important. It might be embarrassing, like this. I still love you, Eric . . . but you know what? You're a selfish shit!"

She turned and walked out of the office.

He watched her hips wiggle through the door, wanting her in that moment, wanting to get up and grab her, pull her back onto the couch, but he didn't. Couldn't. He sat there with the black ribbon dangling from his hands, trying to keep his pants clean.

* * *

Drake was already at a table in the Faculty Club when Eric arrived. He was nursing a martini and sucking meditatively on a large curved Danish pipe.

"Good to see you, Newman, m'boy. We haven't had a chance to talk yet this semester. I hope you had a good trip this summer, productive?"

"Very," Eric said. "Lots of untapped source material. How about you?"

Drake nodded and shifted in his chair.

"The Chilean situation is so depressing that I can't think of anything else for long."

"What's the latest you hear that isn't being printed?"

Drake smiled at the salute to the reviewing stand of his vanity and began to talk. "Pinochet is claiming Allende killed himself, but according to my information . . ."

Drake had his "inside" sources for information on South America, and his early training and career as a reporter, then as foreign correspondent for the *Times* conditioned him to a style of secretiveness, of being privy to the inner councils. His present authority reinforced the need for having an "inside wire" and having it, in turn, reinforced his role. The tendency to be officious irritated Eric, who hated to acknowledge that Drake really did know something not yet public, but he usually did. ". . . and the state of siege is going to last a long time. The junta had to pass down the police hierarchy umpteen positions till they found a carabinero to make jefe. The loyalty to the legal government was that strong. And a lot of the military wheels are being rolled into the clink, because of 'wrong attitudes.' "

"Sounds bad for a long time to come," Eric ventured.

"No doubt," Drake said, "the eleventh of September will be a mournful anniversary for Chileans forever."

"No doubt," Eric echoed, then steered elsewhere. "What have you been working on?"

"Nothing unusual; I spent the summer with the family at the house in East Hampton, lots of beach, sailing, a little work, mostly on a review essay for APSR."

"Of what?"

He wiped some Martini off his bushy white mustache, put down his pipe in the ashtray, and talked all the way through the tired salad and goulash facsimile about Horblick's book on the Venezuelan land reform movement.

With an occasional monosyllable of commentary, Eric listened as Drake sharpened his spears in poor Horblick's back. This is how the critics would do it to me, he thought: roasted over lunch. After Eric had exhausted the possible permutations of "H'mm," "of course," "oh, yes," and "really?" coffee arrived.

In the sanctified protocol of lunch and "business," now was the time for Drake to open fire, and he did.

"Eric, you know, I thought it would be good to talk of your future now, before the momentum of the semester catches us up completely."

He divided his attention between Eric and the Danish pipe which he had emptied and was now filling from a soft, black leather pouch.

"We're all very fond of you at the institute . . ." (especially

Lucy, Eric thought he was going to say, and then wondered if Drake tumbled with her sometimes too) "but this magnum opus of yours is taking a bit longer than we had thought it was going to. I thought that maybe you were dragging your heels a bit because of the . . . um, emotional setbacks . . . recently . . . um, the divorce etcetera.

"Let's put it this way," he continued, then paused, struck a match and filled the area with clouds of smoke that hid his face for a moment. "We took a long shot on you. Solid dissertation, a few good articles, a brilliant first book, eight years of solid teaching experience at the state university, and a really fine project for a new book."

He patted his jacket pockets until he found some more matches, relit his pipe, and then continued.

"It's just this, lad; tenure review comes up for you in the spring—in April, and if I can't tell the committee that the book is finished with a publication date certain, you'd be wise to look for another job. Maybe start looking now, if you can't do the writing by then. With the book done, I can practically assure tenure for you. Without it . . . well, there are other *promising* people out there. I know it sounds harsh, but I thought I had better give it to you straight, and early enough to do something about it. Finish the book, *soon!*"

Eric told Drake that he could understand the situation and thanked him for his forewarning. They left the club and parted in the corridor on the ninth floor of the International Affairs Building. Eric had a seminar to conduct; Drake had other lives to run, and ran trailing clouds of gray smoke down the corridor to his office. Eric felt like a little kid who had just been spanked and knew he deserved it, but still hated Daddy for doing it.

"Change your mind, michito?" sloe-eyed Lucia asked as he passed her desk. Her face was an open bed.

Suddenly the idea excited him again, her raw sex. He needed a warm body—one that needed him. And he told her he'd see her Wednesday night, the eve of Thanksgiving.

"I'll show you what lovin' is," she said, squeezing his hand.

That's what he was afraid of.

* * *

Lee Winkler was short, with an olive complexion and a narrow aquiline nose, green eyes, and long dark hair pulled back over

14

the temples and wound into a tight chignon. She was wearing a long red African muumuu and a heavy medallion on a silver chain.

"Scotch?"

"That's fine. I drink it neat—" Eric told her, then added, "without ice."

Lee rolled her eyes upward as though appealing to God.

"You think I was born yesterday? I know what *neat* means, and even if I didn't, you tell me every time you're here."

She poured two fingers of Teacher's into an old-fashioned glass for him, then dribbled some over ice for herself and filled her glass with water. Her hand shook as she lifted the pitcher.

"I feel jittery and upset, because in doing this, I'm breaking my word to Ben. I promised him I wouldn't and here I am doing it."

She looked away; not before he could see the tears in her eyes. Then she got up from the brown leather couch they sat on and walked over to the Beckstein. She played one chord, lit another cigarette from a pack lying next to the pile of music, put it into a long amber holder and blew a cloud toward the ceiling.

"Lee," he said, "I don't know what you are talking about. I don't like to see you upset, but I'm confused and don't know what to say."

"I'll be right back," she said, and left the room.

He imagined her bringing out some dull memorabilia hoarded like a secret sin: maybe some love letters. That was it: she had said a manuscript. Maybe it was some letters she had treasured for thirty years, letters which made Ben angry whenever he heard about them because they reminded him of her affair with Raven, how she ran away to Cuba with him, how he took her back after Harry killed himself. She'd felt guilty about them since Harry's death, and now would be making it worse by underlining Ben's cuckoldry in a book about Harry.

Eric had the whole story worked out until she came back into the room not with a lavender-scented, ribbon-tied bundle, but with a small, black, looseleaf notebook, soft-covered in the 1930s style. His nasty fiction ended there.

"The night of Harry's accident," she said after taking a long pull at her drink, "he left this in my cabin. It must have fallen out of his jacket. Later, when Ben was organizing the manuscript collection for Columbia, he said that it was too personal, and I should keep it as a memento."

"Is it personal in a way your husband would have wanted to suppress—I mean embarrassing?"

"I can't see it that way. Harry used to write in this sometimes, make a note, scribble down a line that came to him at some odd time, put down an address, and so on. He had it with him most of the time; he kept it in his pocket."

"What was in it that bothered Ben?"

"There are some lines, or notes . . . whatever, Ben thought were derogatory toward him, and, um . . ." she hesitated, "even anti-Semitic. And, you know, Ben was such a good friend to Harry, even though I left him to be with Harry and would have married eventually, I really believe that Ben would have forgiven us and continued to be his friend."

Eric didn't say what he thought about her supposition. She opened the notebook to the middle and put on a pair of half-lens reading glasses. Turning a few pages, she stopped her finger in the center of a page and said, "Here's the sort of thing that bothered him:

> This beaked flock of scavengers,
> Moneylenders who become cuckolds
> While guarding their purses.

"It's just nasty and trite. Harry wasn't like that. He had lots of Jewish friends. Ben and I, Goldfeder the scientist . . . Maybe these lines were for a character in the novel he always talked about doing someday, or in the play he was working on when he died. But I couldn't convince Ben. He said that someone would exploit it and that Harry should be remembered for his great contribution to literature, not for some offhand remarks or moral lapses."

He didn't know what else the notebook contained, but was wary; maybe she wasn't aware of the niceties of copyright law, but in effect, she owned the manuscript, no matter who wrote it. After all these years with no claimants, he would need her permission to quote it or use any information based on it. If he found something there that would really contribute to the biography and she didn't want that information or quotation in print, she could control its use. Half of him wanted to see the notebook, and the other half didn't want to make waves.

"What else does the notebook have that you think is important for Harry's biography?"

"Some unfinished poems, jottings, notes on travel, books he wanted to read, titles for poems or books that occurred to him—you know, the sort of stuff writers always scribble down for later use. And I think it may give you truer insight into how Harry felt about certain things, what his plans were, and so on."

"Tell me how you got the notebook."

"Oh, there's no mystery there. As I told you, he left it in my cabin the night he committed suicide. I didn't notice it then, because we had been arguing, and after he left the cabin, I dropped onto the bed and cried myself to sleep. Sometime the next day—I think it was after I heard the news—I found it."

She looked away and wiped her eyes. "I *know* it'll be a great biography, Eric. He was a great man. I didn't think he was so upset that night, otherwise I never would have let him leave my cabin. He was the single great passion of my life, and though the scars healed, I still feel the pain now and again."

She began to cry again; her shoulders heaved and the tears ran in splotchy streams of mascara down her cheeks. Moments like these he couldn't handle very well. Dumb before crying women. Finally he said, "Everything you've told me suggests that you were very important to Raven, and probably *the* real woman, the great love of his life. The biography will make that clear."

Two lovers of Harry Raven, they sat there and looked at each other, and he felt drawn to her. He wanted to reach out and touch her, embrace her, reassure her. At that moment, Eric would have made love to her, this woman old enough to be his mother, just to comfort her and touch what Raven had loved. He saw her beauty, her helplessness before the ravages of time and he cursed himself for being a critic, for being accustomed to examining everything with a jaundiced eye and a well-defended heart. If he could have changed anything, made her happy, he would have done it. But the futility, the bits of paper blown away by the wind, made it impossible. He looked at her, and restrained his impulse to take her in his arms. She sensed it all; he could swear she did, because she reached her hand across to his and squeezed it hard as if to say, "I know how you feel. I do too. Thanks." There was an instant bonding, a crazy-glue of souls. Then she pushed a smile onto her tearful, makeup-stained face.

"I made his life whole again, I know it; he told me, and some of these unfinished poems will tell you too."

There was the sound of a key turning in the lock, and Lee's face became fearful. "Oh my God, it's Ben. I didn't expect him for another hour," she gasped, looking around furtively. "I've got to hide the notebook . . ."

One would have thought that they were adulterers caught in flagrante delicto, and she was looking for a closet to shove him in.

"It's no crime," he said, but she didn't hear. She was staring at the doorway to the living room, where Ben Winkler stood with his coat on, looking at both of them. There was a twinkle in his light blue eyes, and a curious expression on that face with the bushy mustache and soft white hair that made him look like a stereotype, a Norman Rockwell portrait of the country doctor. Tell anyone he had been an ardent socialist in his youth and now was one of the country's most esteemed left-wing journalists and social critics, and they'd find it hard to believe, just to look at him.

He saw the notebook immediately, but the smile didn't leave his face. Only the eyes became flat and hard.

"Good to see you, Newman," he said, advancing toward Eric with outstretched hand. "And you, my love," kissing her cheek. "It looks as though I barged in at the wrong time."

"No, I was just leaving," Eric said, annoyed that he had been led into a family conflict. He didn't want to be a chip in Lee's poker game.

"Oh Ben!" Lee blurted out, starting to sob again, "I know . . . I know you'll be angry . . ." She got hold of it then, and dried her eyes with the pocket handkerchief he held out to her.

"I'm not angry, just disappointed," he said, tugging on his mustache. He walked over to the liquor cart, poured some whiskey into a glass and knocked it down in one shot. *L'chaim.*

"I wish you had discussed it with me first, that's all," he continued.

"But I knew you'd say no; you want the story of Harry and me buried, I know that," Lee said, her eyes dry and her voice getting tense. "After thirty years, you're still jealous of the love we had."

"JEALOUS?" he asked in a voice that jumped up an octave. "NO, you have it wrong, my love. Eric here knows the story of that affair, and so do most people who are interested. I'm sure the biography will deal with it, and frankly, I never expected otherwise. I'm not so vain as you think."

Eric thought he could risk a question. "Why did you keep the notebook out of view, then, for all those years?"

Ben smiled cautiously. "It was Harry's reputation I was protecting. There's a carping tone, a hint of anti-Semitism which he never showed in public, and as his closest friend, a Jew no less, I didn't ever see. What's in this notebook is an aberration, an exception, and I wanted to make sure he was remembered as the passionate liberal he was, even though his passionate liberalism spilled over and flooded away my wife."

"Maybe you're protecting *his* memory," Lee snapped, "but I'm trying to preserve mine. I played an important part in his life and want the record to show it."

Ben took two cigars from his jacket pocket and offered Eric one. He declined and took one of his own cigarettes instead. Ben held a match for Eric and then got his own cigar lit.

"The problem, Lee," Ben went on, "is that Eric is writing history, not romance, and though you think you are reinforcing the role you played in Harry's life . . . and it's true, it still hurts to talk about it . . . at the same time, you are giving evidence to a side of his character which was so private that I, his best friend, didn't know about it. I suppose I'm building my own kind of monument to the friendship by keeping his myth untainted."

She turned down her mouth in a frown that said paragraphs. Eric was caught in the middle now and wanted to squirm out. It all seemed like a tempest in a teapot. He had enough domestic squabbles and didn't need the Winklers' to add to his own.

"Why don't you let me draw my own conclusions from examining the notebook? I hope you're not going to hold it back now that I know about it. What you are worried about may be so inconsequential in relation to the whole picture that it isn't worth mentioning," Eric said to Ben, and turning towards Lee, added as kindly as he could, "You can be sure I'll mention anything in here that emphasizes how important you really were to Harry."

He hoped that would satisfy them both.

Ben shook his head in silent agreement, sadly it seemed to Eric, and Lee put her hand on his arm with a thankful look and squeezed.

Eric thanked them both, said he'd call, took the notebook, and left quickly.

2

Paris

NICK BURNS looked out of the Embassy window at the dripping sycamore trees on the Champs-Elysées. He hated Paris in cold weather, despite popular songs about its beauty in any season. A discord of horns drifted up to the fourth floor where he stood watching as the motorists coming across the Seine into place de la Concorde were challenged by the cars just disgorged into the ring by the slick tongue of the great boulevard. Each change of traffic light brought a new cacophony.

He had agreed to meet Odette in the Tuileries without thinking about the weather when she called that morning. Her invitation took him by surprise. She had made it sound so urgent, he hardly thought before saying yes.

Nick watched a bus entering the traffic circle, inching its way across from the Champs, hugging the left lane, and then cutting out right to head up the rue de Rivoli. More car horns swelled the chorus.

She wanted him back? Wishful. It was over for her years ago. But for him her husky voice on the phone still evoked long nights of loving in her apartment on avenue Charles Floquet in the shadow of the Eiffel Tower, early morning walks along the shuttered boulevards for coffee and croissants at their favorite bar on the quai Voltaire before crossing the bridge and separating for office days, or quiet drinks after all was done, in sidewalk cafes at *l'heure bleue.*

How he had loved her then: the long dark hair she pushed away from her face with a shake of the head, the faint smile always at the corners of her deep blue eyes, the confident way she walked down the street.

She had been hurt, badly, by his refusal to consider marriage. "Is there something against diplomats marrying . . . or maybe your government would find me too far left?" Sharply spoken, after he had given her a "no" answer to a question never asked; a rhetorical point he raised himself, a nip in the bud.

How could he have told her that the press liaison job was a cover, that he was with OMEGA?* Marriage wasn't fair. The rules said nothing, but he knew that he could only be responsible to himself. No more hostages to fortune . . . he didn't even keep houseplants; there was no room in his career for possible widows and orphans; once there had been, but never again.

He had tortured himself for weeks over the choice he had to make between Odette and OMEGA, a choice he alone dictated to himself. She had intuited the dilemma behind his pain and tried to soothe it; "It's all right, my love, we'll just go on this way, and be happy the way it is." Very French, very stoic; but Nick was neither.

One summer evening, the long blue Paris twilight slowly darkening around them as they walked along the Seine embankment toward her apartment, he told her that he couldn't go on; it was tearing him up. He couldn't risk loving her anymore.

They stood and watched a bateau mouche filled with tourists glide by on the river. A long embrace, then silent tears, and she turned and walked away.

A few days later a brisk note told him that she was going to Vietnam for *L'Express* and she hoped his cloaks and daggers would keep him company. That was seven years ago, years of casual affairs for him, just indoor sports, and a movement up toward the top of OMEGA. He followed her career as a journalist from staff correspondent to star reporter to free-lance interviewer whose by-line was sought by every European magazine and newspaper of the liberal left. Heads of state and stubbled

---

* The Office for Management and Evaluation of Government Agencies was formed in 1948, as an overseer, a supra-agency coordinating all intelligence operations by other agencies and preventing conflictive duplication of activities.

OMEGA's small Washington staff is housed in USIA headquarters. A town house on New York's Washington Square serves as operations center, and contains the computer and international satellite phone hookup; OMEGA's budget is concealed in the administrative appropriation for the General Services Administration. OMEGA almost doesn't exist, certainly not as a matter of public record. All of its active staff are on the payrolls of the sundry agencies which employ them and act as continuous cover. Service in OMEGA's respected elite is an honor for which very few are chosen. No one has ever refused.

insurgents in the hills opened up to her and were treated alike with critical candor. Nothing escaped her barbed pen. To be interviewed by Odette des Chavannes was to be honored and roasted alive simultaneously.

Probably, he was now just another source for her; not only the official "flack" for USIA that he was for her colleagues in the fourth estate, he was her opening into the shadow world of counterintelligence operations. Where once they had washed each other's body in love, now they washed each other's hands in information: this was the prize passion had won.

Half an hour later the rain had stopped, but the wind still gusted damply as Nick crossed the avenue Lemonnier from the rue de Rivoli and walked on the wet reddish dirt path toward the little arch, l'Arc de Triomphe du Carrousel near the Louvre. He turned his collar up against the wind. The car park was filled with waiting chauffeurs in black official Citroëns, and a gas company van had pulled up onto the path where some workers in coveralls were opening up a manhole cover.

He could see her already, standing near the little arch he had been so disappointed with many years ago, when he first visited Paris and thought that *this* undistinguished piece of sandstone was *the* Arch of Triumph. The world had gotten a lot smaller since that day of green years past, but at the sight of Odette striding toward him, her dark hair blowing out in the wind, her open raincoat showing one of the tailored Chanel suits she favored, he was reduced to emotions he smothered for a brief moment, pulled backward in time with a longing for innocence, a wish to start all over.

"Nicholas, mon cher, you are looking so well, so handsome . . ." They hugged briefly and she held him at arm's length. "If I didn't know you were an American diplomat, I would think you were a well-dressed Frenchman, and fall madly in love with you." Nick had forgotten how effusive she could be; her compliment embarrassed him.

"New tailor, new barber, same Burns," he said. "You're the one who is to be fallen in love with, looking so chic." As he said it he knew that he had never stopped loving her . . . but no, it was impossible now, impossible. The die was cast for good.

"But why do we have to meet out here in this weather?" he asked. "Are you afraid to be with me in closed places?"

She smiled wickedly and said, "No, *that* was always my wish and *your* fear. I asked you to meet me here because I didn't want to be overheard. Let's walk around here."

She closed her trench coat, knotting the belt casually, and took his arm. They strolled away from the tourists who had emerged from the Louvre with the end of the rain and were busily snapping photographs of the Arch and each other. Nick and Odette walked toward the dozing official chauffeurs. He said nothing, waiting for her to begin.

She dropped his arm, stopped walking, and facing him said, "I wanted to speak to you because I have heard a horrible story from a Chilean political refugee about torture of political prisoners, and I thought you might be able to give me some information."

Nick was surprised. "What do I have to do with that?"

Odette laughed sardonically. "Whose government supplies those animals in the military junta with their means of destruction?" she asked.

He didn't hide his disappointment that she held him responsible by association. The grapevine was full of rumors; the agency had helped the generals to trounce Allende, that much was certain. How, and who was involved, and why it was so important to hemispheric policy was not clear. But the multinationals had been scared and had leaned on the secretary of state and the president for a long time. September 11th had been the result.

To him it was unlikely that Chile would have become another Cuba. But second-guessers like Burns were disregarded by their colleagues in the intelligence community as "idealists."

In any case, it was over now. The generals and their secret police ruled the country; Allende was gone, and the constitutional rule of law was dead for a long time to come. At least they hadn't asked Burns to participate in its demise.

"My feelings haven't changed in that regard, Odette," he answered, feeling a bit miffed that she too was won over by the left's myth that all American officials agreed with every foreign policy decision coming from the State Department and the White House. "Personally, I wanted to see Allende make it, but he did make some big blunders—"

She cut in abruptly. "That is all beside the point now, mon

ami. The question I want answered is more complicated. I have heard that the secret police are using an interrogation device which could only come from the Americans. A torture so diabolical that even the filthy *boches* didn't think of it."

Nick waited for her to go on, to get beyond her classic French left prejudices. They were walking again, and had reached the street where the chauffeured cars waited for their bureaucrats; now they turned back toward the arch.

"They have a mind-reading machine!"

"A *what*?" He found it hard to believe that she had said it.

"It sounded to me like a lie detector, electroencephalograph, and one of those alpha wave scanners hooked up to a computer," she continued. "When you are asked a question, the machine reproduces on a readout scanner the actual thought in your head. If your spoken answer disagrees with what it says on the screen, you get a severe shock."

Nick started to laugh aloud; he couldn't help it. The idea was ridiculous. She looked offended at his laughter.

"You don't take me seriously, and act as if I were a fool . . . and now I feel more like a fool for thinking I could confide in you." She sounded angry and hurt.

"I could never think you that, Odette," Nick said. "It's just that it all sounds like something out of a science fiction movie. Where would an underdeveloped country like Chile get such sophisticated technology? I don't even think such a machine exists. If it did, I probably would have heard. Anyway, such a device would be a Russian or East German kind of thing, not ours." The tacit admission of how well wired for sound he was passed, apparently unnoticed. "Besides," he added, "drugs do *everything* today."

She pulled her eyeglasses, large tinted lenses, down from their habitual perch atop her head, and took a notebook from her handbag.

"One of the victims noticed the logo of a well-known American company on some of the machine parts," she said, showing him a design drawn on a blank page; a globe with the Atlantic hemisphere visible and the letters ICO superimposed.

"Odette, it proves nothing! I could put an English battery in a Japanese car along with a French generator. Any machine could be a combination of parts, you know that, and it doesn't prove that the company whose parts are used makes the machine in question."

"I can't argue with your logic," Odette said, with a trace of resignation in her voice, "I never could. But if International Communications Organization has nothing to do with this torture machine, why have I been followed for three days now, ever since I interviewed John Fleming, the president of ICO, and asked him about the torture machine in Chile and his company's support of the coup d'état?"

Nick wondered if Odette's left leanings had finally brought her into the camp of the conspiracy theorists who saw imperialist plots under every stone. This couldn't be the broad-minded woman he had loved.

"What makes you think you are being followed?" Nick asked, trying not to sound incredulous.

"That gas company truck. You saw it?"

Nick nodded, knowing better than to look at the vehicle.

"It has been wherever I was for two days . . . that's why I wanted to meet you in the open, and didn't want a closed place prearranged over the phone," she said. "This has never happened to me before, and it frightens me. I wanted you to see it too, for confirmation. You know about such things." Odette laughed, then shuddered involuntarily.

"Maybe gas mains break when you're near," he teased.

She frowned. "Silly man!"

"Okay," Nick said, taking her arm, "let's see what they do now. How about some coffee?"

"That would be nice," she answered, smiling, "and I could smoke a cigarette, which I really need right now."

Odette, he remembered, would not smoke while walking in the streets. It was *de trop*, as she would say.

There was a cafe he liked two blocks away. As they reached the door the rain started again. Nick looked around for tags, but didn't see any. The gas truck stayed put. He sat where he could see the door and the street.

". . . and she said that the day after her interrogation with that machine, all the members of the MIR* cell she knew were

---

* MIR = Movimiento de la Izquierda Revolucionario (movement of the revolutionary left)—a political group of radical socialist philosophy.

rounded up by the secret police and sent to prison camps,"
Odette continued, after she took a sip of the steaming espresso
coffee a bedraggled waiter brought to their table. She lit a Gitane
with a gold Dunhill lighter.

"Maybe she did betray her friends," Nick said, "and concocted
this story of a hocus-pocus machine to avoid being held responsible." He refused the cigarette Odette offered him and filled a
darkened and scarred old briar pipe instead with some caporal
tobacco he had just bought at the bar.

"I don't think so," Odette answered. "This is a very reliable
woman, a journalist, and a good observer. I believed her, and
there were others."

Nick breathed out a smoke cloud. "Others?"

"But of course, mon chou. You don't think I would chase a
story on one person's say-so? At least five other Chileans who
managed to get out and are now in Paris have told me similar
stories—if not the betrayals, at least the interrogation part."

"Well, *this* time, Odette, I can't be of any help to you. I
honestly have never heard of this interrogation device."

"You could ask," she said. "Look, I don't want to spy on your
government, just to confirm this device's existence. It horrifies
me. And if for once the CIA has nothing to do with it, I'd be
surprised. Disappointed because of my story, but happy to believe that you didn't lie to me."

"Frankly, I doubt that my government has anything to do with
such a device; it sounds harebrained, out of a comic book." He
didn't bother denying the CIA connection, because he knew that
she would take it as a confirmation. OMEGA didn't exist officially; it was only known within the intelligence community as a
watchdog over the interagency rivalries. A dog which could bite.
As far as anyone outside was concerned, there wasn't a kennel or
even an audible bark.

"But you *will* look into it and let me know? I am working on a
story, and it will help to have all the information I can before I
go there," Odette said, lighting another cigarette.

"Where?"

"Santiago. If I can get in. My credentials may be the wrong
color," she answered.

"Depends on what I find out," Nick said. "The rules of the
game still apply."

They both understood the standing conventions between reporters and their sources. "Deep background" and "not for attribution" were not to be violated if you didn't want your source to dry up.

"Un coup sûr," Odette said, stubbing out her Gitane and getting up. "I must go now. Have you noticed anyone following us?"

"I don't think so," Nick stalled, watching the woman in the blue raincoat who had come in after them get up as Odette did, put some coins on the table, and leave the cafe. He didn't want to alarm Odette unless he was sure.

"You go, and I'll stay a few minutes. Call me later."

Odette squeezed his hand and left.

Nick watched the woman in blue cross the street and caught the almost imperceptible nod she gave to a teenager with a transistor radio who had been thumbing through the record albums at a disque stall across the street ever since he and Odette had arrived at the cafe fifteen minutes ago.

Odette passed through the door, opened her umbrella against the steady rain, turned and waved to him, and walked off to the right. Nick saw the teenager turn up the collar of his leather jacket, and start off in the same direction. Not very professional, Nick thought, as he saw the boy speak quickly into the radio, evidently a transceiver.

He beckoned to the waiter, paid for the coffees, and left. The gas company van idled at the curb, half a block away. Nick turned and walked toward it. The van made a sudden U-turn and rolled away from him, but not before he made a mental note of the license plate. After he had walked a block, he stopped to light his pipe and checked for tags, didn't pick up any, and continued to walk through the darkening wet streets toward the American Embassy a few blocks away.

* * *

"Cattle prods, the water barrel, no sleep, some beatings, and maybe sodium pentathol," the CIA station chief told Nick. "That's what I heard, and they don't need us for that. The other thing is pure Buck Rogers. Why do you ask?"

"Visiting American journalists riding a sensational lead for a story, and bugging me as official flack," Nick answered, wondering why he was dissembling. He automatically moved to protect

Odette. He remembered why he **was afraid of** emotional involvements; they always got in his way.

"I'm sure those guys can put you up a tree. Your cover would drive me nutty, I don't see how you do it," the station chief said, shifting his bulky frame in the desk chair and shuffling the papers on his desk.

"It's useful," Nick said, stood up, thanked him, and left the small windowless office in the embassy's Political Section.

* * *

Barnwell, OMEGA's director, was in Paris for a few days of meetings and Nick had left a message with the ambassador's secretary for the director to call him when his conference was over. Sitting now on a Barcelona chair in Nick's office, he stretched his legs out under the glass coffee table, put his hands together to make a cathedral with his fingers and blew his breath down the nave. His laconic slouch, close-cropped gray hair and tweed jacket reminded Nick of how professorial he thought Thad Barnwell had looked the day they had met at Yale sixteen years ago. The director had been sitting in Professor Fauna's office the same way—maybe it was the same jacket, Nick thought —when Nick came in for his weekly political science tutorial. . . . He snapped back to what the older man had just said.

"A marvelous fantasy, Nicholas," he continued, "but without any substance in present-day reality. Actually . . ." He hesitated, put his cathedraled fingers up to his face once again and knocked the spire against his lips a few times. "Actually there once was such a device, or at least it was being developed, but that was way back during the Second World War, and I think that the whole damned project aborted when the scientist in charge died. I was with OSS at the time, one of Wild Bill Donovan's cowpunchers, and I thought the whole thing was ridiculous then," he snorted. "But the money had been appropriated, and the work went on—up at Columbia, I think. What was the guy's name? Let me see . . ." He looked as though he were reaching back over thirty years of canned information with a grocer's tongs. Nick said nothing but sat and watched.

"Godfein . . . something like that . . . Goldfeder! That's it. Leon Goldfeder."

The director looked pleased with himself, so Nick complimented him for remembering.

"Just for curiosity's sake," said Nick, "I'd like to run a check on this Goldfeder's work, to see what happened to the machine or the plans—whatever—after his death."

"Feeling your oats, aren't you now?" asked Barnwell. "I thought only the director, and that's me," he added sarcastically, "instituted inquiries which were project related."

"I'm not trying to tread in your bailiwick," Nick assured him, "but I got the lead on this from a reliable source and would like to verify it or disprove it before the press gets in and gives us a blacker eye in Chile than we already have."

"Do I detect some quibble with the policies of our fearless leader and his leading knight?" asked Barnwell, eyeing the obligatory picture of the president on the wall of Nick's office.

Nick shrugged his shoulders, a valuable gesture he had acquired during the years in Paris. "I just want the information. I know who makes administrative decisions," Nick added, to placate the director if he was *that* sensitive.

"I'm kidding you, Nick," Barnwell ventured. "It's good training for you to start the ball rolling sometimes, even into a dead end."

Then the director stood up. "I'm leaving for New York tonight; get back to you as soon as I know anything."

He hesitated as he reached the office door. "Your home-leave coming up?" he asked.

"I'm taking the month from Thanksgiving on. I want to be back in Paris for the Christmas and New Year's rounds," Nick answered. "I'm leaving here Wednesday afternoon."

They shook hands at the door and Nick turned back to his desk. He sat there for a few minutes and looked out at the driving rain and the bare branches of the plane trees on the Champs-Elysées whipping back and forth, glistening blackly in the light of the streetlamps which had just come on. He thought about Odette. Seven years ago it had been. His first major cover post, and she had been new to her job at *L'Express* after a few years on provincial papers. They met at a press cocktail party and were drawn to each other immediately.

His decision that summer night on the embankment had been to go it alone, to be solitaire, freewheeling, able to pack a bag on a moment's notice and be off to anywhere, either on assignment or to please a whim. And there was something in that attitude of his that women found attractive; he was elusive. Loving but non-committal, he put distance between himself and anyone who demanded constancy.

One of those paradoxes, Nick thought; women found attractive in him the very quality that a permanent attachment would destroy. Yet with Odette, the only woman he had ever known who didn't want to clip his wings in the service of love as an institution, he also flew away, toward his career, his *own* race.

And he was winning consistently, he knew. Didn't Barnwell just hint at that: get practice in initiating investigations. What wasn't said was that Nick was in line for the director's job. Of course that was years away, but still, that was the glittering prize.

And yet . . . and yet, whenever he saw Odette, he knew that he had lost something too, something of incomparable value that he would never regain. It would require changes in his priorities that he was less and less able to make as he got older and more entrenched in his work, more distinguished in his profession. Yet how lonely it was because there were no recognitions except within OMEGA, among the handful of other intelligence operatives who knew that he existed as one of them. For the rest of the world he was a middle echelon information manager, a press and PR guy who chose the security and foreign postings of USIA rather than the Madison Avenue razzmatazz.

Seeing Odette always helped to orchestrate the theme that his daily life struggled to suppress, a theme of longing and regret for what never was and now never could be. He was what he did, the consequence of his acts, he thought; the existentialists were right. A bureaucrat and a spy—no more.

With a sigh, he lifted the receiver from the hook and dialed Odette's number.

"Allô . . . ALLÔ?" she repeated loudly when he didn't speak.

"Can you call me back from another phone?" he asked, without identifying himself. She knew the voice.

"Of course. Two minutes," and she hung up.

His private line rang a few minutes later.

"Where are you?" Nick asked.

"At a neighbor's. It's all right. Go ahead."

"Can you meet me at the Overseas Press Club in an hour?" he asked.

"For what?"

"A drink, some information, and maybe dinner," Nick said hopefully.

There was a pause. "The first two, yes. The last no. I can't, I already have a dinner date," she said matter-of-factly.

"Can't you break the date?"

"I can, but don't want to . . . unless that is the price of the information, and I *must*. Have you changed so much?" She seemed genuinely shocked.

"No, Odette," Nick responded, piqued by her implication that the information had a price, "I haven't changed at all. Just meet me for a drink in an hour. And be sure you take a taxi, not the métro." He rang off without any further comment.

He wanted to be sure that any car following her could be observed easily.

Then Nick phoned his friend Benoit at the Metropolitan Police force and called in a favor voucher.

A few minutes later, when Nick walked past the young, bored Marine guard at the embassy door, he felt the tingle at the nape of his neck, that uncanny visceral feeling which told him he was being watched. Looking out of the wet and dirty rear window of the taxi as he settled himself and gave the driver the address of the Overseas Press Club, he saw headlights go on at the curb fifty yards behind him, and watched the cream-colored van with the gas company emblem pull into traffic two cars behind him. Then he knew the game was afoot.

* * *

After she put the telephone down and thanked her neighbor, an elderly spinster in the apartment below for whom she shopped in bad weather, Odette wondered why Nick had called her so soon after she had asked the favor of him, and what all the business of "safe" telephones, taxis, and last minute meetings was about. She had started the whole thing herself, she thought, by calling Nick and meeting in the Tuileries. He didn't seem to take her seriously, and even after his promise to look into the question that afternoon, she thought he was just placating her, looking to brush her off. Maybe the gas company van was just coincidental, and she was cultivating a paranoia about the whole thing, lending her story more importance than it had by imagining that a company such as ICO would trouble itself over a reporter in search of a possibly embarrassing story.

But Fleming had been a bit too vehement in his denial, too heated in saying that ICO was interested in profits for stockholders, not political systems. "Look, we deal with Russia and Israel, South Africa and Yugoslavia. We don't care how they are governed as long as they buy, and don't interfere with us. No matter who's in power, they get their piece of the action, believe me, both in taxes and other niceties. You know that, Miss des Chavannes; you weren't born yesterday. We lobby, we pressure, we court people who look out for our interests, but it stops there. We sell, rent and develop communications systems, not science fiction torture machines; that is absurd. Most ridiculous thing I ever heard."

Then why, she thought, as she let herself back into her own apartment, was he protesting too much? And why was she so sure she was being followed since she had questioned Fleming?

Nicholas must have discovered something, she thought, or else why would he summon her so soon? And why did she respond to his dinner invitation by implying that he had his price? She knew he wasn't like that, or at least hadn't been before this. She had hurt his feelings. Damn the man. He was as attractive as ever, maybe more so. Age improved his good looks. The almost black hair was longer, fuller, and his face was thinner. The green eyes glistened passionately when he spoke, but something had changed in him; there was a hardness, a self-sufficiency, a sense of secrets buried behind the eyes, an impenetrable core which wouldn't yield to any woman.

And she didn't want that; it was too much like herself, or at least what men told her she was like. It attracted and repelled her. She wanted a man who was available to her, emotionally open, even vulnerable. Someone who could operate from the heart, not just the head. Once that had been a conflict in Nicholas, but he had resolved that one when he made his decision to leave her, and she wasn't going to participate in a new tug-of-war for anybody. No, she'd keep her dinner date with Georges; he was comfortable to be with, full of interesting back room political gossip, and emotionally safe; he'd never leave his wife. At this point in her life, *that* was a major attraction.

Odette went to her closet, pushed aside the dresses and opened the wall safe. From under some papers she took the snub nosed .32 caliber Baretta in a soft leather case, and a small razor-sharp knife which lay in a closed plastic tube, sealed and smoothed at both ends, with a short cord fused into one end.

She dropped both weapons into her handbag, knowing that it was a false sense of security they gave her, but nonetheless feeling better for having the possibility of defense rather than the certainty of helplessness. She didn't even know if in a crisis she'd have the courage to shoot or stab. She rather doubted it.

Half an hour later, Odette double-locked the door behind her and left the house. She looked up and down the street but didn't see the gas company truck, and feeling that perhaps it had been her imagination after all, she walked around the corner and up the short block to the avenue de Suffren where she knew she'd get a taxi. She didn't notice the unremarkable gray Simca parked across the road near the corner. Inside, a woman in blue sat with a teenager in a leather jacket and watched while she hailed a passing taxi, then they pulled away from the curb to follow.

* * *

"Okay, let's see what happens now," Nick said, and led Odette to a window of the third floor lounge at the Overseas Press Club where they could see the street.

The gas company van was parked across the street opposite the entrance to the club, amd below the window where they stood was a gray Simca.

Odette let out a brief "merde" at the sight of the van.

"They switched to me, and there's the one that was on you," Nick said, pointing to the gray car. "Now watch."

Four black cars, all identical large Renaults, drew up quickly on either side of the street, blocking any escape for the van or the gray sedan. All the doors of the black cars opened at the same time and eight men stood with drawn pistols around both the van and the sedan. Their doors were yanked open and the occupants emerged, hands in the air, and were shoved into the waiting open doors of the black cars, which drove off without delay. One man from each of the pickup details stayed behind and, as the black cars pulled away, got into the van and the Simca and followed. It was all over in a twinkle.

"Who were those men? Did you arrange that?" Odette asked, amazed at the speed with which it all happened.

Nick nodded his head solemnly.

"Police," he said. "Now we'll find out what all the surveillance is about. At least they're off our backs for a while.

* * *

Nick watched Odette sip her vermouth. She looked a little shaken to him. He toyed with the ice in his whiskey.

"You may be onto something or not; that I can't say," he continued after a moment. "All I know is that those who would know something about this mind-reading machine, don't. And that's the truth."

"I believe you, Nicholas. I have no reason not to, but is there nothing else?"

"Only that there was such an experiment being developed way back in the forties, but it was scrapped when the inventor died. That I have on good authority—and it's not for attribution."

"What was his name?"

"I think you should drop it!"

"Nicholas!" She sounded exasperated.

"I guess there's no harm," he said grudgingly. "Leon Golfeder."

Odette wrote it down in her notebook. "That's all?"

"Uh-huh. Look, what good is all this? Can't you do a story on torture in Chile without digging up the past? What a waste of effort."

"I don't tell you how to do your work, do I?" she retorted. She resented his attempt to control her, and became even more determined to investigate the truth behind the horror story she had heard.

"No you don't," Nick answered, "but—"

"No buts," she said. "I do appreciate your help, and will return the favor if I can, but I do things my own way."

"Are you having dinner your own way too?" he asked, to change the subject.

She laughed, the tension broken. "Yes, I didn't want to break the date and disappoint a very nice, kind man. I'll bet you didn't change your plans either," Odette teased him.

He smiled and shrugged Frenchly.

"Nicholas," she said, standing up to leave, "I'm not the impetuous young girl I was eight years ago. When you made your choice, it forced me to make mine. Oh, it was difficult for a long time to see that, but I made the same choice as you did. My work is my only passion now. The rest is convenience and the pleasant company of men to enjoy when *I* want, men who don't get in the way. I'm afraid of you, Nicholas. What I want from you, you can't give me, and another fling is not it. I can't afford to be left raw and bleeding again, so I'll play it safe—as you Americans say—until the right man comes along. For him I'll change, no one else."

"And if he doesn't?" Nick asked, walking with her toward the elevator.

"I'll manage," Odette answered. "I don't do badly, and neither do you, judging from appearances. We're too much alike, mon cher; I don't need any more pain in my life, and I don't think you do either. Just friends, eh?" she said, kissing his cheek lightly. "Thanks for looking after me."

He waited while she took the first taxi, and was pleased to see that there were no tags. When he got into the next cab, he watched carefully, but he was clean too. Then he let out his breath in a long sigh. He felt caught between the Scylla and Charybdis of disappointment and relief. He leaned back, resting his head on the seat, and decided to leave his car at the embassy garage. He'd spend the night with Gabrielle.

* * *

It didn't take long for OMEGA's director to get back to Nick. Late the following afternoon the red telephone on Nick's desk rang.

"Are you on 'scramble'?" asked Barnwell.

"One second," Nick answered, and pressed the combination of unmarked push buttons on the instrument which made the call impervious to interception and rendered the conversation unintelligible to anyone else.

"I got 'curiouser and curiouser,' as the little girl said, on the flight over here last night," Barnwell began, "and stopped at the office before I went home to start the information retrieval going on the . . . fantasy question your source unearthed."

Nick knew that Barnwell was being circumspect because he had a healthy dislike of telephone communications, however safe they were supposed to be, a quirk Nick himself had picked up.

"Suffice it to say," continued the director, "that there's more on the other side of the looking glass than we thought. To our knowledge, the person whose name I remembered yesterday didn't die, but disappeared mysteriously, and oddly enough *you* have the contacts to follow through, when you get here."

Nick said nothing. Damn the man. He would manage to screw up his home-leave with an assignment. Nick decided to play innocent. "But I'm not going on assignment. I'm seeing my family in New York." He might have saved the breath.

"Fine," said Barnwell, "that's where I want you. The work is there. And whatever time it takes from your leave, you can have compensatory time for, or an additional per diem. When do you arrive?"

Nick realized that Barnwell was only couching the order as a polite request. There was no possibility of refusal.

"Wednesday night." Nick decided to test the urgency. "Thanksgiving Day is family," he said firmly.

Barnwell chuckled. "It's not a national emergency . . . yet. Friday will do. That will give me a chance to see Sir Galahad and establish our priority. I don't want too many hounds in the field. By the way, will you see your friend at Columbia?"

Nick wondered what Eric Newman had to do with this. "Yes, of course, I planned to."

"Wait until after we speak. New York office, Friday at ten o'clock."

Nick sat and stared at the phone. Eric? And clearance with the secretary of state? This was more than the Thanksgiving turkey he had bargained for. It was beginning to sound like a mission. He almost regretted opening his mouth to Barnwell yesterday.

* * *

"We had to let them go," Inspector Benoit said. "There were no real charges, because they didn't molest anyone."

"Who are they?" Nick asked.

"Security team for a private company; they protect the president from kidnappers, and they say that they were near the Louvre yesterday because he had a meeting at the Ministry of Labor across the street, and at the Overseas Press Club for the same reason. They are in touch with his limousine by radio and always hover nearby."

"Thanks anyway, Benoit," Nick said, not wanting to encourage further curiosity in the policeman. "At least I can lay my paranoia to rest for the weekend. Which company, by the way?"

"The only one in Paris whose president is worth literally millions to kidnappers," the police inspector said. "ICO!"

Curiouser and curiouser, Nick thought as he drove his silver Maserati up the ramp of the embassy garage and eased into the traffic on the Champs-Elysées. He filled and lit his pipe while waiting for a traffic light, and tried to banish the hodgepodge of details from his mind. Gabrielle was waiting to be picked up, and the rest of the world, dammit, was just going to sit tight until tomorrow. To drown out the horns, he pushed a tape into the cassette deck and filled the air with the hard-edged bitter longings of Jacques Brel, as he drove quickly toward the Arch of Triumph—the real one.

3

New York

THE NEXT MORNING in his office Eric took Harry Raven's note-book out of his briefcase, lit a cigarette, and began to read. It was pretty much as Lee had said: a few finished poems, addressed to a lover, filled with alternating sentimentality and bitterness, even rancor disguised as admiration, and a lot of notes. One labored sonnet, titled "Song for Lee," seemed to justify her idea that she had "saved" him, and given him a new direction in a disoriented life. It had gone through several changes, and all of the versions were in the notebook, with crossing out, revision and so on, up to a fair copy of the final version. Eric hadn't seen the poem before in any of the manuscripts, and this was authentic: in Raven's own handwriting. The poet *had* felt strongly about Lee's effect on his life.

> You were a wild flight of southward birds
> Plunging past my tired eyes, incendiary
> Golden darts in the cold sun of ancient words,
> Or a flood river dragging old roots to the sea.
>
> You were a wind shift that jibes the running sails
> Straining sheets in blocks set carefully,
> That wets a sunning crew with sudden gales,
> Or hail smashing blossoms on a tree.
>
> You were an ice cream vendor on a winter beach,
> When the weedy sand is abstract and free
> From bodies, bottles and bits of peach,
> Or ebb-tow tumbling swimmers like debris
>
> And my craft's course changed, the plotted chart away
> Your laugh [word illegible] the pinch of drying clay.

There were some other poems, not addressed to Lee, at least not directly, which were angry and rejecting. Whom they were written for might become evident when Eric was able to date them and make a judgment according to the biographical data, but he could see why Lee didn't want to even allow the thought that they might address her.

For the opening of an essay, "In Defense of Destiny," Raven had written a fragment dated June 1935.

> Let it be said that the political world as we have known it cannot be sustained much longer. Democracies are weakened and moribund, and communism is a quack cure, proposed by charlatans who induce the weak to believe they have power only if they join together their feeble wills. . . .

Surprising stuff, Eric thought, for a left-wing liberal who then supported Earl Browder for president in 1936 and fought on the Red side to save the Spanish Republic from Franco and fascism.

The book served Raven for commonplaces as well. " 'History hath triumphed over time, which beside it nothing but eternity hath triumphed over.'—Raleigh, A History of the World, 1614," he had written on one page, underscoring it several times. Later on, he had copied out a section of Faulkner's *The Sound and the Fury* which he had read in 1939.

> I went to the dresser and took up the watch, with the face still down. I tapped the crystal on the corner of the dresser and caught the fragments of glass in my hand and put them into the ashtray and twisted the hands off and put them in the tray. The watch ticked on. I turned the face up, the blank dial with little wheels clicking and clicking behind it not knowing any better . . .

And underneath:

> Not that you may remember time, but that you might forget it now and then for a moment and not spend your life trying to conquer it. Because no battle is ever won . . . They are not even fought. The field only reveals to man his own folly and despair, and victory is an illusion of philosophers and fools . . .

There were also some names or notes to himself which puzzled Eric. In 1941 Raven jotted: *Goldfeder's illusions, Xeno project*; and 1942 had many obscure references.

Castelli Bravo, editor of *Pampero*
H. Villacampos
R. Montenegro
K. Immerman
Novaes, Vicente Lopez' 391 B.A.
July 15, 1943?
Hartman's timetable?
Herman Graf, mil. attache, Santiago
Joaquin Saenz, carabinero, Stgo
*Goldfeder fears tragic implications of his machine for human free-
dom. Sentimentality of the wandering Jew.*
Ordoñez, H. Yrigoyen 2240

And in 1943 another poem fragment:

> *The wind rocks the crusty buoys.*
> *Cold, teetering like drunken sots,*
> *Past Gravesend Beach, over lobster pots*
> *And gangster bones in concrete molds.*

July 15, 1943 Midnight
What if we are wrong?

was the last entry.

Befuddled, Eric sat for a long time after closing the notebook, staring out the office window. It was a drab day of indeterminate season. From his window he could see the gates to the small courtyard fronting Barnard's Johnson Hall dorm, and the coeds, hip frizzies in jeans, long-haired, skirted preppies, flowing in teams of two or three through the gate.

The manuscript made his mind race around and he tried to stop, to repossess himself. After all, he had studied Raven's life closely for years and could fit many details of this notebook into what he already knew. The love affair with Lee was established fact. So was the homosexuality. But the repudiation of liberalism by a known "fellow traveler"? The worship of power? Obsession with time? Nothing in the data Eric had collected previously reflected such an attitude. Then the names; there was no record of correspondence with any of them, and Eric had no idea who most of them were. There had been no evidence in Eric's earlier research that Raven had any contacts in the southern cone of

South America. Most puzzling of all was the date, the date of his death! Entered twice, he realized! The last entry, conceivably made on the eve of his suicide, was understandable, but the earlier entry of the same date followed by a question mark? And why the focus on Chile?

How could his death, the wild act of a desperate, drunken, frustrated man, have been known to him almost two years earlier? Unless he had a prescience, a mystical power of ESP which no one had ever known about.

* * *

"So, what do *you* think of the stuff in that notebook?" Lee asked when Eric called a half hour later. "You know I had a big fight with Ben after you left," she added, as though it were his fault. Eric's ex-wife had taught him well and he recognized the free trip on guilt, the prize won by any answer; so he said nothing.

"Do you like the poems to me, at least?" she asked to break the silence.

Her voice sounded edgy, and he heard her lighter click, then a long exhaling. Somehow he had to be politic.

"The poem to you," Eric said in his most soothing professorial tone, "is . . . is very interesting, because he was hardly a formalist and yet it's so clearly a classical English sonnet. I didn't expect it."

That was noncommittal enough. He continued before she could answer. "Lee, I . . ."—hesitating—"I'm confused about some of the entries, mostly names and addresses, and the date—"

"I don't know about any of that," she snapped impatiently, interrupting him. "Don't you have any idea?" she asked carelessly, implying that anything but recognition of her role in Raven's life was insignificant, the province of pedants such as Professor Eric Newman.

"No, I looked through the letters and other material at my office this morning, but I can't find a single reference to the names anywhere," he answered calmly, wanting information, not ire.

"Well," she said triumphantly, "I never paid attention to *those* details. I assumed they were personal, some of his 'gay' friends from before I converted him, and I didn't wish to know who they were. Maybe Ben might know."

"But I don't want to antagonize him more," Eric said, "that's why I'm asking you."

"Okay, I'll ask him. Just give me the names. I can handle that sentimental dope." She laughed, but it seemed forced. "Imagine, jealous after all these years of a dead man's notebook . . . ridiculous." She sounded determined, and Eric was glad she would help.

"You know who might help you?" she went on. "Max Hartman—he was Harry's literary executor. He claimed all the manuscripts, even his private library, and then made a big profit selling them off, the bastard."

"And the notebook you gave me?"

Silence. Finally she said, "He never knew about it. Ben insisted that Hartman was low enough to sue and, as executor, would probably gain custody. So I kept quiet. For once, I listened," she added coyly. "I owed Ben at least that!"

Eric avoided an answer. Again, silence.

"Eric?" she pleaded. "Be fair to me in the biography. The memory is all I've got."

He mumbled something acquiescent, and said he'd let her know what Hartman said. She promised to speak to Ben again.

* * *

His head ached with possibilities, and Eric was becoming annoyed with it all. What had seemed so simple yesterday, when he had thought of how to begin the book, was now a fine muddle. The circle he had closed was open again. He locked the manuscript in his desk drawer and left the office for some lunch.

It was not yet noon, so the West End Bar was empty except for a few of the serious drinkers who stood alone eyeing the big TV up in the corner, and three early tarts who sat together talking at the end of the polished mahogany.

"What'll it be, buddy?" the fat barman asked over his shoulder, without stopping his glass wiping.

"Heineken."

"Out of it."

"Do you have any ale?"

"Ballantine or Halbatt?"

"Ballantine."

He snapped the cap off the bottle and poured half a glass. Eric carried the glass and bottle to a booth in the corner after buying a corned beef on rye from the food counter.

Halfway through the second bottle and second cigarette, Eric was sure that he would simply include the poem fragments and the political statement as footnotes. He wouldn't take the responsibility for vindicating Lee as Raven's Earth Mother. She was a fling, Raven's attempt to be part of the straight world. Nobody could possibly know how Raven would have responded once back in New York, if he had ever made it alive. Because no relapsing was ever to become possible, his first female lover could now take credit for a grand conversion. Lee wanted to be pictured as the woman who "saved" Harry Raven . . . his muse. It was her grandstand play for notoriety: "How I became famous lying down."

As Eric saw it, beginning on his third ale and pulling the Camel plunger on the cigarette machine, he would cite all the information and let the reader draw his own conclusions. It was a big pain in the ass, he thought. Who needed it?

Depressed, he returned to the office; this notebook could be his nemesis. He couldn't just add some footnotes, that was the ale speaking. Eric had a reputation for thoroughness to protect. But tracking down the information would affect the time needed to complete the book. He was risking losing his job, therefore, if he pursued the information until he snared it. On the other hand, if he ignored or somehow subsumed the information in largely unread footnotes, relegating it to some industrious graduate student for a future doctoral dissertation, he was risking professional embarrassment. Overlooked information with any significant bearing on Raven's biography would make Eric's book *not* the definitive study he had intended.

Swiveled in his chair to face the windows—a habit when he wasn't actually reading or writing—he turned back to the desk and knocked over his ever-present coffee cup. The milky brown liquid went sloshing across the desk and had just reached the edge of the Raven notebook as he grabbed it away.

His heart pounded with the sudden infusion of adrenaline. And he stood there, the coffee dripping off onto the rug, holding the notebook above his head as though the coffee would jump up and attack it momentarily.

He threw some paper towels onto the coffee, wiped up the

mess, took the notebook into the corridor, and made three Xerox copies of the manuscript. Then he took the original and one copy back to his office, locked one copy in the drawer, and inserted the other two copies in a brown manila envelope to take home.

Lucia, typing in the reception area out front, looked sourly at his coffee-stained pants.

"Couldn't hold it in, little boy?"

"Lu—I'm in no mood for games," he said. She cowered mockingly.

"I need a favor," Eric said, ignoring her teasing. "I want to see Drake—soon."

"He's busy now."

"You can do it, use your influence." He blew her a saccharine kiss.

"I'll take it out on you," she said, a wicked smile glowing, "in trade." And left.

Eric's intercom buzzed a few minutes later. "Professor Drake will see you now," Lucia purred, the tigress biding time before the kill.

He took the Raven notebook, put it in his jacket pocket and walked over to Drake's office. He *had* to see it Eric's way: more time for the biography, tenure review or not. Maybe an extension, a six-month postponement before Eric's name came up. After a review, it was on and up in rank from associate to full professor—or out. All he wanted was time to research, not to have to look for a job and even move again.

Through the miasma of pipe smoke he could see Drake at the desk writing something on yellow legal sheets.

"Bob, I want you to see something, and need your opinion."

"Sit down, Eric, and wait a minute." He scribbled furiously. Finally he stopped, called Lucia on the intercom, and after she gyrated out of the office with the letter in her hand, he said, "Okay, Eric, I'm all ears, shoot!"

Eric pulled Raven's notebook out of his pocket and put it in front of Drake. "After we spoke yesterday, I came across an unknown notebook of Raven's. There aren't any listings of it anywhere, and it is authentic: it's in his handwriting, I can verify that."

"Why should the notebook make any difference in what you're doing?" Drake asked, pulling on his mustache.

"Well, there are a couple of poems addressed to Lee Winkler, his onetime mistress, and that merits at least publication, but—"

"So what!" he interrupted. "A footnote, a page or two."

"Yes, but listen, Bob. There are all sorts of names and addresses in here: people I never knew Raven knew, such as a Nazi diplomat in South America—and, finally, the date of Raven's death!"

"All that proves is that he had thought about suicide and was fanatic enough to plan it, date and all," Drake said, looking exasperated, as though he thought Eric thickheaded.

"No, Bob; there's something in this I can't figure out. Almost as if it were the work of another man, a different personality, a different sense of the world than in the published writing—a whole different ballgame." Eric disliked his own metaphor, but used it for his point.

Drake picked up a pipe on the desk and began the filling ritual. "Let's say there is a different person," he said. "Maybe he *was* schizoid; I can't see what your problem is. You mention it and that's that. Jekyll and Hydism; it's common enough."

"But, Bob, I want to track down *all* this stuff, I want to be so thorough that my book will be the *definitive* biography."

"Still doesn't change things," he said, striking a wooden match on the sole of his shoe and waiting until the sulfur burned off before he began to draw the flame down into the bowl of a large Meerschaum darkened to a deep rich brown with years of use. Through the billows of smoke he said, "It seems to me that you're just finding more reasons not to get going." He took the pipe away from his face. "And I'm not about to change my opinion because you find Raven's pocket memo book with some names in it. You could go on doing that forever and never put pen to paper. Collect memorabilia and open a Raven museum! Find Raven's favorite spoon, his shoe laces, his underpants, collect all the books he owned, his laundry tickets and spend your life as a curator. Collect, collect—and charge fees for viewing the wonders. You'll need the money because you won't have a fucking job."

His face was red and the veins bulged in his neck.

"Hey, hold on," Eric objected. "You don't have to get so angry. All I did was to tell you about a notebook I came across. It puzzles me."

Drake was still livid, but a little less so.

"So what can I do?" he asked.

"Look at it and tell me if you think, aside from the whole business of finishing the book, whether as a biographer you would find the stuff in here of any importance, whether it forms a part of the man's work, or if it should be treated as an interesting curiosity, with a footnote and no more."

"I told you what I think already . . . um . . ." He hesitated. "Okay, leave it with me for a while."

"I tried to contact Max Hartman, Raven's literary executor, to find out what he knew, but the phone had been disconnected."

Drake's eyes widened. "His executor! That old thief. I didn't know he knew Raven."

"Well he did. My information is that they were in the same 'fraternity.' "

"I don't doubt it. But Hartman is a conniving bastard. I wouldn't believe anything he said."

"How do you know him?"

"When I wrote that biography of Getulio Vargas, he was brokering a collection of letters Vargas had written. He wouldn't let me take notes—only look briefly. Not a principle in his body. No respect for the material he sells; it's just a commodity for him, like stock or pork belly futures."

He stopped and drew out a white handkerchief from the breast pocket of his suit jacket and wiped his forehead, still sweaty from his apoplectic outburst.

"All I want," Eric said before Drake could start talking again, "is to ask him about some names in a notebook."

"You're really too obstinate for your own good. You're already chasing the wind here . . ."

Drake stood up, indicating that the interview was over.

"Leave the notebook and I'll give you an informed opinion." He was suddenly the diplomat again, the senior statesman, judicious, smiling, and deadly with the concealed power of his office. "I'll have it back in an hour or two."

"Thanks. I appreciate it."

He waved Eric off, the king's pleasure.

* * *

When Eric came back to the office after class, the Raven notebook was sitting on his desk, unholy in the midst of the papers and used Styrofoam coffee cups. A note from Drake was clipped to the cover: "Interesting, but trivial. My opinion is confirmed now. A footnote, maybe a spin-off article on some 'undiscovered-until-you-came-along' poems of H.R. But the rest is of no import. Let it go. Write the frigging book and stop looking for—and finding—excuses. R.L.D."

So Drake had spoken. Well, Eric *did* respect his opinion. Drake was a fine scholar and biographer. But Eric still wanted to see Hartman to satisfy his own curiosity. He promised himself that if there was nothing Hartman could tell him, he'd take Drake's advice and get on with it.

4

Santiago

As THE BLACK limousine with its motorcycle escort moved swiftly up the Alameda on its return from the airport, the thin-lipped man sat and looked out the window at the deserted midnight streets. He preferred silence to any further attempt to make conversation with General Pinochet. Surprised when the jefe himself had met the private plane which brought him up from the south, he assumed that the military man wanted to speak to him alone, *before* the meeting.

Don Enrique, a silver-haired man in his sixties with pale skin, an aquiline nose, and a look of bored indifference about his aristocratic features, glanced over at the general, who reminded him of a well-groomed baboon, and thought of an old Chilean proverb: *Lo que crece por el día el gobierno lo roba por la noche* ("What grows by day the government robs at night"). Pinochet and his gang had overthrown President Allende in the name of anticommunism, and now the battler of the red menace was mostly concerned with lining his own pockets.

"They have met the payment schedule before," he had answered the general's only real question fifteen minutes earlier, "and there is no reason to assume they won't now. Your money will be delivered as I told you, half tonight and half in two weeks when they take delivery of the machine." The gluttonous look of delight which had played over the anthropoid features revolted the aristocrat. What had Pinochet done to warrant payment? Nothing. He was just a gangster in uniform running a protection racket. Not that the general's two predecessors, both elected promisers of reform, were any better, but at least they were gentlemen, men of wide culture with whom the aristocrat was comfortable. He could converse with them and they were clever at dissembling their greed. The general was honest about his, but

---

Don Enrique resented his crude directness nonetheless, the peasant cunning about the man.

The motorcycles ahead signaled a left turn and the limousine followed, entering a street near the bomb-ruined Moneda, the presidential palace in the Plaza Constitucion, the heart of the city.

Because of the early curfew in effect since the military junta's takeover, the streets were empty, the place a corpse of civic normality, the state of siege its pall.

In front of the Directorate de Intelligencia Nacional (DINA), secret police headquarters, two unmarked blue vans disgorged a dozen or so political prisoners—young men and one woman, looking like university students, and hustled them into a single line.

"Stop for a moment," the general said to the driver. "See what your work has helped us do?" he continued to Don Enrique.

A tall youth began to sing "Venceremos" and the others joined in. One soldier stepped forward and smashed his rifle butt into the young man's face. He fell to the ground, blood gushing from his nose and mouth, his hands covering his face. The soldier, laughing, kicked hard into the boy's groin. The singing stopped. Now, at a word from the general, the driver accelerated.

"Communists," sighed the general.

"How do you know?"

"You heard them sing! Who else sings such songs?" the military man replied, indignant.

"Students, ordinary people who voted for Allende," answered his companion, playing devil's advocate.

General Pinochet wasn't taking the bait. "They're all communists. We'll teach them a good lesson and good riddance to the vermin."

Don Enrique decided not to continue the conversation. He merely nodded. It would all be over soon, and he could take his money and go, leaving this dreary corner of the world and spend his remaining years—rich ones they would be—in Paris: an appropriate setting, he felt, for a man of his taste and sensibility. He would be gone in a few weeks; the cable from New York folded in his breast pocket confirmed the urgency of his departure. He had little enough time, and less world.

They arrived at the International Communications Organization building on Huerfanos, where three military staff cars were parked at the curb. The uniformed drivers stood chatting and smoking with the armed guards at the building's entrance. The general and his companion stepped into a waiting elevator.

In the penthouse conference room on the twenty-seventh floor three men sat in leather chairs around a long oval rosewood table. They rose as Don Enrique and the general entered.

"Gentlemen," said Don Enrique, taking a seat at the head of the table, "we are ready to proceed, yes?" The others murmured assent.

"First let us consider if the conditions of ICO have been met." He turned to a slight, dapper man with closely cropped black hair and a thin mustache. Senor Saenz, would you please report on your findings."

Joaquin Saenz, the head of DINA, opened the file folder which lay before him and read in a monotone: "Since September twentieth the Magnometric oscillating alphagraph has been used on one hundred and four different subjects, ninety-one males and thirteen females. Information derived from these subjects as a result of their interrogation has resulted in almost fifteen hundred additional arrests, fourteen hundred and eighty-three to be exact. The names were derived from the computer printout during interrogation, and in no case was the subject aware that he or she was revealing information, because no names were solicited. Questions were programmed so that the subject thought of names, and these names were read off the scanner—"

John Fleming, ICO's president, interrupted, "And the names were considered sufficient evidence by DINA to warrant arrest?"

"Under the present state-of-siege law in this country," answered the director of secret police, "we do not need any more than that. Known association with communists is a crime. We don't have the complicated legal problems of your country, Senor Fleming. Our laws protect the innocent, not the guilty."

Fleming shook his head in agreement.

"Just tonight," Saenz continued, "we invaded two MIR cells and arrested a dozen dangerous subversives."

General Pinochet looked smugly at Don Enrique, a smile playing across his anthropoid features. The others nodded approval.

Saenz went on. "Of the one hundred four interrogated subjects, all but two showed no adverse effects."

"What happened to those two?" Fleming asked.

"They died," answered Saenz, closing the file folder. "The machine was programmed to shock severely if the verbal answer to a question differed from the answer on the readout screen."

"Didn't that happen frequently?" Fleming queried.

"Yes, but after the early days in September when the two subjects died, we reduced the intensity of current programmed for disjunctive responses. At any rate, the subjects died from heart attacks, and that is medically certified."

Don Enrique remembered the tests, the proving of all their efforts. The laboratory—gleaming, white, sanitary; the body strapped to the table, electrodes in place; and the familiar questions—family history, birthplace; answers coordinating with the flashes on the readout screen. Then the personal questions, the harmless lies: Have you ever had a lover? "No, I have been a faithful . . ." and on the screen a procession of *Maria*'s, *Juanito*'s, *Angelina*'s and *Jose*'s—current and remembered loves revealed themselves, bidden forth by the great force. No secrets were possible!

Then the technician, Walter, turning the dials to shock for disjunctive response, punishing the lies. And the question about lovers again. PAIN. The arching body, the shiver, the yell. Helpless struggles to free the arms, the legs. Eyes rolling in agony. Establish our power to punish if we choose . . . but no need really. The screen told all you wanted to know . . .

"Who was in the organization, in your cell?"—"No one. I never belonged . . ." And on the screen: *Antonio Sanchez Doctor Penaflor Raul Vergara Alberto Mendizabel . . .*

He told Walter to tune out the shock factor after the initial wave. Told him it was to establish dominance only. But the fool persisted, enjoying the power to hurt, loved the pain he could give the "dirty reds." After the two deaths, Oswaldo—gentle, patient Oswaldo—said he'd disconnect the shock circuit if Walter didn't stop, would refuse to repair or adjust the machine; and Don Enrique had to order Walter, fat Walter with his white coat and pistol strapped on, Walter the SS man who hated Oswaldo, who called him "Einstein."

"Why do you listen to him, *Oberst*? I know how to treat this scum on the table. Your brother is too soft!"

Guttural Hamburg language, the streets, the cheap bars, the

barracks—Don Enrique said no nevertheless. No high voltage, no more corpses. And Oswaldo agreed to stay away from the laboratory during tests, away from white-coated Walter—Oswaldo grumbling. He didn't understand the force for truth in the machine he had made. "Monstrous!" he called it.

Fleming cleared his throat, and brought Don Enrique out of his reverie. Everyone was looking at him. He begged pardon for his attention lapse, then lit a cigar and offered his case to the men at the table. Only General Pinochet accepted.

"Cuban, eh?"

Don Enrique smiled. "The unique benefit of Allende's relationship with Castro. From now on we'll have to suffer." The general didn't respond as a chuckle ran around the table.

"Senores Fleming and Osterholz, are you satisfied with the evidence?"

Hans Osterholz, ICO's director for Latin America, fingering a long scar which ran across his left cheek from the corner of his eye to his jaw, spoke with a German accent and chose his words deliberately. "The testing of the mechanism is very informing. We would, naturally, accept your word, Herr Saenz, that the interrogation was properly performed, but also, naturally, we would run many more tests, with simulated circumstances, and various circuitry refinements to date up properly the mechanism."

"But you are ready to accept it?" Don Enrique asked quickly.

Osterholz didn't answer but looked at John Fleming instead.

Don Enrique sensed that an unpleasant surprise was forthcoming when the German wouldn't commit himself. Why all the talk about further testing? Was it a setup for a hatchet job by Fleming?

Don Enrique didn't want to be a salesman, and sensed that he would sound defensive and not convincing. He decided not to say any more but instead to hold ICO to the terms of their agreement: fifty million dollars upon the satisfactory completion of testing. Half now and half when they took delivery within two weeks. He needed that money without delay, as the crinkling of the cablegram from New York had reminded him when he slipped his cigar case back into his jacket pocket. The money he had accumulated was enough to make him rich by any standard, but not enough when he left this country for good. Adequate, but that wasn't what he had planned for. Here in backward Chile he had stature, but over there? Hardly.

Now Saenz began to pitch; he didn't see Don Enrique's cautionary glance. "You must not only consider the effectiveness in large scale, but in the day-to-day questioning of those under suspicion of ordinary crimes. A prosecutor won't have to prove guilt in a murder case, for example, if the machine verifies that the suspect did commit the crime, whatever his overt alibi or denial. Every country in the world will want this, and ICO will reap all the profits."

John Fleming sat nodding his head in apparent agreement. In his custom-tailored suit of conservative gray and his horn-rimmed half-lens reading glasses, setting off his cherubically round face and neatly trimmed sandy hair, he looked like a Wall Street stockbroker. More like a middle echelon executive, Don Enrique thought, than the most powerful man in one of the largest multinational companies in the world.

"The tests sound fine, and no doubt there are many applications of the machine which have not even been explored yet," Fleming said, looking over his half-rims, first at Don Enrique and then at Saenz. But ICO has several factors to take into account before we conclude our arrangement . . ."

So he was going to equivocate after all, thought Don Enrique; the bastard was going to renege.

". . . not the least of which is that prior to receiving the information on the testing we have had no valid indicators that the machine actually worked as Don Enrique said it did.

"Moreover, this device is only a prototype: ICO has to redesign it with the newest circuitry available and absorb these as well as initial production costs. My board of directors and I feel that we cannot make other than nominal payments until we can 'lay off' the development and production costs in the sales contracts we negotiate."

"What does 'nominal' mean?" asked Don Enrique.

"It means ten percent of the money now and the rest when we cover our disbursal with advances from our sales contracts. That's the only way I can get the board of directors to agree. It's still a risk for us, but more limited."

Fleming resolutely reached for the jug of ice water which stood in the center of the table and filled his glass. Saenz toyed with the ends of his black mustache, and General Pinochet grunted and puffed hard on the Cuban cigar.

"It's not acceptable," said Don Enrique. "We had an arrangement concerning payment, and now you are changing it unilaterally. I am ready to turn the machine over to you, having developed and tested it according to our understanding. I expect you to keep your half of the bargain, in the terms of the unwritten agreement."

Don Enrique was furious, but tried not to let it show. He felt the pulsing of blood in his neck and struggled to keep his temper as he went on: "You don't expect me to let you take possession of the alphagraph without paying for it as you agreed, do you? 'Lay off' costs indeed! I cannot sit around and wait for you to do so. Moreover, why should I trust you in any way, since you have just proven that I . . . we . . ."—he indicated Saenz and Pinochet—"can only do so at our peril."

Fleming sipped at his water and then said, "You know, Don Enrique, that the contract is unenforceable . . ."

Don Enrique drew into his own thoughts while Fleming spoke. He saw his neatly coordinated plans going astray, his stepping stone becoming a desert island. ". . . arbitrate the situation . . ." he heard Fleming say, while he could see himself squelching the plans he had made for going to Europe. "What court could have jurisdiction over such an agreement . . . hopeless muddle . . . a breach of security . . . exposing us to publicity—"

"What are you talking about?" Don Enrique interrupted harshly. "There has been no breach of security!" His mind had been floating again, and now he pulled it back to earth. Fleming was getting to the reason, the real reason for abrogating the agreement and he wanted to hear it, but General Pinochet, taking the cigar out of his mouth with reluctance, interrupted.

"I am naturally most disappointed, gentlemen, because I came here to participate in a business transaction, not petty bickering." He turned the full front of his furrowed brows toward Fleming and narrowing his eyes until they were only slits, said, "There are many situations of risk, senor, in which large sums of money are advanced to show good faith and to support undertakings of mutual interest, for which there is no written contract. There are ways of enforcing agreements other than courts."

Don Enrique watched Fleming's face. To give the man credit,

he did not blanch or seem intimidated by the general's threat. Don Enrique suddenly felt safer than he had a minute before. The old cliché of honor among thieves. Pinochet was actually working for his protection money.

"What are you saying, General?" asked a shocked Osterholz, diverting the general's attention from Fleming, whose mouth seemed riveted shut by the jefe's stare.

"Our national interest will dictate what we do," Pinochet snapped at the German in a way that showed he was annoyed at the naivete of the question and that the asker was of no significance to him. He turned his eyes back to Fleming. "Your company's holdings are no less valuable to us than they were to our predecessor, but as an act of good faith were put back in your hands as soon as we took over. We kept *our* agreement, I point out. But of course . . ."

Fleming burst in, "You would expropriate our holdings once again?"

General Pinochet lit his cigar, taking his time, and smiled at the executive knowingly when he was done.

Fleming jumped to his feet, flushing rapidly. "You just listen here—"

"SIT DOWN," barked the general, and Don Enrique watched the changes in Fleming's face, as he first considered defiance, then apparently thought better of it and took his seat again.

Don Enrique felt he had lost control of the meeting to the anger of this confrontation between the two men. He felt suddenly tired, exhausted. He had done all he could do with the machine. It was ready. He wanted no anticlimax, just to take his money and enjoy the few physical and aesthetic pleasures of his remaining years.

"There are easier ways, senor, but of course anything is possible." Pinochet waited a moment, staring into the distance as though thinking, then continued. "If your organization wants to withdraw from its commitment, there is no obstacle to Don Enrique dealing directly with our Oriental friends, or even the Soviets or Americans . . ."

"The matter would be settled," Don Enrique said, trying to forestall any further confrontations or threats, "were ICO simply to keep its agreement now."

"We can't," said Fleming with a sigh, "and intimidation by

the general will make no difference." He addressed Pinochet now. "We poured so much money into backing you in September because we had our regular investment to protect . . . *and* we bought time for the testing of the machine. But now—"

"What about *now* is different from before?" Don Enrique asked, interrupting. He was perturbed at the turn of events and wanted to know whether Fleming was bluffing to cheapen the deal or if there *was* something throwing the whole thing out of kilter.

Osterholz, after getting Fleming's nod, answered: "The rumor of the alphagraph has gotten out of Chile with a few of the interrogation subjects, and we have certain information that a story is about to surface in the press—"

"Not here," said General Pinochet. "We tell them what to print!"

"But you can't do a thing in France, can you? Odette des Chavannes is hot on the trail of a story about torture in Chile, using the testimony of some of those whom your men interrogated and then were stupid enough to allow to leave the country," Fleming said.

"Who cares what a communist reporter says?" chortled the general, a look of disdain on his face.

"Nevertheless, whatever you think, General Pinochet, if she publishes a report implicating ICO in the torture of prisoners here and has any proof of our contractual support—verbal or otherwise—of the interrogation machine, the adverse publicity would be devastating," Fleming retorted.

"You could simply ignore any report and not dignify it with a response," said the general offhandedly, absorbed with the ash of his cigar again.

"Surely you have dealt with adverse publicity before," said Don Enrique. "I can't believe that ICO is frightened of one journalist!"

"Certainly not," Fleming snapped back, "but des Chavannes went to OMEGA!"

The silence around the table as Fleming mentioned the name of the elite counterintelligence organization was ominous, and Don Enrique sensed it, but he didn't know what the Greek letter meant. He turned to Joaquin Saenz at his right and asked. Saenz told him that it was the best intelligence agency in the world.

Don Enrique felt a knot in his stomach. It tightened, it squeezed; he felt suddenly helpless, old, trapped. The golden dream became a lead weight. If OMEGA investigated . . . even his patent registration on the alphagraph could be invalidated.

He tried not to let his anxiety show.

"How do you know what this journalist told OMEGA?" Don Enrique asked, trying to make the question sound innocuous.

Fleming smiled, seemingly amused by Don Enrique's innocence. "Look," he said impatiently, "this is getting us nowhere. We want the alphagraph and you want the money. Okay, but not if we risk losing the damned thing. So we're not advancing another cent until we can turn OMEGA and this lady reporter around."

The general, who had said nothing for a while, looked at Fleming and asked, "What did you have in mind?"

Fleming kept his eyes on the general; Don Enrique felt that the ICO president was trying to turn the conflict to his favor by creating a rapprochement between himself and the military chief. He couldn't afford to let that happen. Although Pinochet was unsubtle, he was dangerous, with an army behind him. He had the power to forestall everything and call the shots to his own advantage.

"If we knew everyone outside this room who had any damaging information, we could control the situation," Fleming said.

"With money?" asked the director of DINA.

"With silence!" Fleming shot back.

There was a cold, ominous hush in the room.

Don Enrique felt chilled, hated the man, yet admired the powerful audacity behind the innocent face.

"Who knows about it?" the general asked Don Enrique, leaving no doubt that he was ready to accept Fleming's suggestion. It was not a request; it was an order.

"Leboulier and Sepulvida," he said tiredly, naming the former defense minister and the army chief under Allende, "but I don't know where they are now."

"We do," said General Pinochet, his eyes glinting with pleasure.

"Director Saenz will see to them," he continued, looking at the secret police chief, who nodded acquiescence.

"Who else?" General Pinochet commanded.

"There's Eduardo Frei." At the name of the president before Allende, the general shook his head no. "And someone in New York," continued Don Enrique. He had always feared the man coming back to haunt him. Perhaps it was better this way.

"I won't touch an American citizen," said Saenz, "unless you can get him here."

"Never mind," Fleming said. "ICO will do it."

Osterholz asked Don Enrique to write down the name.

"And Frei?" the German asked.

General Pinochet stared at him, then looked directly at Fleming. "Untouchable," he said. "Anyone else?" the general then questioned grimly. Was it scruples, Don Enrique wondered—or a foregone understanding between the ex-president and the junta?

Don Enrique thought about the man he *hadn't* mentioned, the one who had sent the cable from New York. If Pinochet had scruples, shouldn't Don Enrique? He would never reveal the name of his old friend and deluded ally. That one would never betray. He'd had his chance years ago and had been silent. Besides, the man had too much to lose if he were implicated. It wasn't only loyalty, just a man protecting his own head. Don Enrique said no, shaking his head.

"What about the reporter and that secret agent?" asked Fleming.

"The reporter is insignificant," Saenz jumped in. "She has only rumor and hearsay to go on. To get anything else she'd have to come to Chile. Then I might worry about it, not before, and I advise you to do the same. Concerning the OMEGA man, that is absolutely out of bounds. I'm sorry, Mr. Fleming, but we're not big enough to take on OMEGA. Subterfuge, yes. But no termination."

"What if we do it ourselves?" asked Fleming. Osterholz murmured approval.

Saenz answered harshly, "I do not think you would be so desperate or foolish to underestimate OMEGA's power."

Fleming looked crestfallen, and Don Enrique was glad to see him rebuffed. He realized that Saenz had spoken to preempt the general's assent. Saenz wasn't going to let Pinochet's greed compromise DINA. A careful man, he preferred not to take risks beyond his means.

"Well, maybe we can wrap all this up before OMEGA gets too

close, and can get the damned machine out of here to a safe place," Fleming conceded.

"What about the money?" asked General Pinochet.

"As I said before," answered Fleming, "ten percent of it is here for you now, to show we're earnest. The rest when these 'contracts' are completed and ICO takes delivery of the alphagraph." Osterholz handed attaché cases to Pinochet, Saenz and Don Enrique.

General Pinochet stood up stiffly, and puffed out his barrel chest. "Agreed," he said. "But the work and delay isn't free. You can add a million each to the final payment for Director Saenz, Don Enrique, and me, for our time and trouble."

"B-b-but," stammered Fleming, "you can't do that," his face going red.

"I can, and I did!" said General Pinochet, and walked out of the room, followed by Joaquin Saenz.

Don Enrique gathered his papers and picked up the case Osterholz handed him, murmuring good-bye to Fleming, who sat looking uncomposed.

When he reached the lobby, General Pinochet and Saenz had already departed, but had left a car and driver at his disposal. He told the man to take him to his *pied-à-terre* on the Costanera, and sat back in the limousine's deep dark leather cushions, lost in thought. The sun was coming up over the eastern rim of the mountains cradling Santiago, and the military driver drove quickly through the gray and empty streets.

* * *

The randomness of chance: how absurd it all was, Don Enrique thought later that day as he sat in the waiting room of Joaquin Saenz' office. After a few hours of fitful sleep, he had called the DINA chief and asked to see him before returning to the south. How everything had shifted so suddenly . . . all by chance. "A throw of the dice will never abolish chance"— Mallarmé's line sauntered into his thoughts, but even the wisdom of his favorite poet was no comfort. Don Enrique could not allow for randomness. The events, in this case, had to be controlled because only one outcome would do. He wasn't about to let the years of work and risk become meaningless because there were some new combinations in the game.

He sat in the spartan anteroom folding and unfolding the cable he'd received, while a secretary typed furiously on an antiquated machine, and the murmur of voices came through the translucent glass door to the inner office.

Joaquin would help; he had been a good friend for many years. Although he was motivated by reasons that were far from idealistic, Joaquin was dependable, as long as his own benefit was at stake. As Don Enrique sat in the bare anteroom with its wooden chairs and the dull yellow electric fixtures which reminded him of the schoolrooms of his childhood, he wondered about Joaquin . . . in the light of what he had said about foreign nationals, Don Enrique might have to force the issue.

The door to the inner office opened and a portly, balding man came out followed by Joaquin Saenz, thin, elegant and meticulously groomed. As usual, thought Don Enrique. Even the lack of sleep didn't show.

"Que le vaya bien," said Saenz, as the stout man rotated his shape through the door into the corridor. "Saludos a su Senora."

The other man smiled, said nothing, and left.

"That is my best man," Saenz said, as he closed the door of his office after Don Enrique, "and to think that he's not even a Chilean—only an Argentine!"

When they had settled comfortably in their chairs and the formal courtesies of coffee were completed, Don Enrique got right to the point. "Joaquin, I was disturbed at last night's meeting, as I'm sure you were, but for reasons which went beyond what was mentioned."

Saenz smiled grimly and said, "I saw that you were upset, but of course, I know you well; to the others you must have seemed your usual unruffled self. Even the general remarked to me on the way out how well you behaved under pressure. But Fleming got to you, did he? Don't worry, amigo, we'll do what we have to and everything will go according to schedule."

"I don't like being the one who authorizes murder," said Don Enrique. "Not that my hands are so clean, but I am uncomfortable with that."

"Oiga! Leboulier and Sepulvida have been on our list for a long time," Saenz said, "and I think that General Pinochet was just waiting for the right moment, or the right excuse, so don't blame yourself. What ICO does in New York . . ." He shrugged. "It is already out of your hands. No use in worrying now. Personally, amigo mio, I wouldn't let *anyone* stand in the way of fifty million dollars if I was getting it, believe me, Enrique."

"No, it isn't that . . . there are two things . . . I . . ." Don Enrique hesitated, wondering whether he could confide in Joaquin without compromising himself further. He'd have to be cagey.

"You worry too much, viejo. Forget it; leave it to me. Just don't talk in your sleep!" He laughed sarcastically.

"It isn't a laughing matter, Joaquin," Don Enrique said. "That OMEGA man could endanger me, you, and all the money. What could he possibly know?"

"It's naive of you, my friend, to think that OMEGA, with access to the largest classified information source in the world can't discover almost anything they want to, providing the records exist. Then it becomes a question of simple research, and they have all the facilities and manpower needed, at the touch of a button. Even so, what are you afraid of?"

Don Enrique sighed. He chose his words carefully. "The machine has origins, shall we say a provenance, which would be better if not brought to light. The patent I hold and the right to transfer it would be in question."

Saenz toyed with a cigarette he held in his hand, then lit it. He leaned back in the swivel chair behind his desk, blew the smoke at the ceiling and said, "I think you don't realize how much ICO wants the alphagraph. Actually I believed Fleming . . . although perhaps I am being naive. In other words, you're saying that if the Americans could lay claim to the machine, then ICO will be wasting its money and time?"

"It's the Americans who concern me," Don Enrique said flatly.

"It is theirs, really?" Saenz continued. He looked incredulous. "Do you think Fleming knows that?"

"I'm sure he doesn't. It would be almost impossible for him to find out."

"I certainly won't tell him," said Saenz.

"But this OMEGA outfit might find it out, if they're as good as you say!"

"Considering the inaccessibility of the alphagraph, and the impediments I can create *legally*," Saenz said, "I think you can rest easy. Time is in our favor. If ICO does have a legal battle with the Americans, it won't be for a long time, and our money will be safe by then. At that point, Fleming will be clever enough to cover both his and our tracks, because ours implicate him. And then he'll work the deal with the Americans to ICO's advantage."

Don Enrique felt that the policeman was right. He could probably let the subject rest like that. OMEGA might be good, but he was just as clever. More so. And he'd taken great pains . . .

"What's the second matter?" Saenz interrupted his thoughts. For Joaquin, Don Enrique realized, the first was finished. It was only a problem if it became a problem. Dormant, it could remain so. Joaquin had a tidying mind, not a ruminative type like his visitor.

"Another American . . ." Don Enrique hesitated for a moment and then plunged in. He told Joaquin Saenz about the cable he'd received, but circumspectly. There was just so much the DINA chief needed to know—and no more.

"So what do you want, Enrique? You want us to kill him too?" asked Saenz, an impatient look on his face. "You know my feelings about touching non-Chileans!"

"No, I mean, not after what you said yesterday. But I think there might be a necessity for such drastic measures if someone were to get too close." He felt uncomfortable asking Joaquin for the favor but knew he had no other way, not outside of South America.

"I was saying that for Fleming especially," said the policeman, smiling blandly. "For you, I would take care of anything I could: you know that! Except for OMEGA. There I draw the line."

Don Enrique wanted to say that Joaquin would erase the line for money, but didn't.

"Not necessary," answered Don Enrique. "I just want you to get in his way, put him off, even threaten him or rough him up a little, but no killing. I don't want that. Okay? And ICO *must not* know!"

The policeman shrugged his shoulders. "Anything you say, my friend."

Saenz took a piece of notepaper from his desk drawer and unscrewed a gold fountain pen.

* * *

Joaquin would do what he could, Don Enrique thought, as he sat in a taxi on his way to the airport an hour later. If nothing else, his old friend would act because he wasn't assured of the financial outcome, and Don Enrique had counted on that: if Joaquin thought that his own stake would be in jeopardy, he would move. It cost him nothing, he had said, just a little finger exercise for his operatives in the United States.

If Joaquin was effective, then the only problem, the only possible source of information was the one who sent the message. But he was scared too. Or else why the cable? Don Enrique took it out of his pocket, read it once again, then ripped it in little pieces and threw it out the window of the taxi.

They were on the outskirts of Santiago now and Don Enrique looked out at the dismal scrubby growth in the flat fields as they approached the airport at Los Cerillos, where the plane was waiting to take him back to the south, to the green fertile temperate zone which had been his home, his self-imposed prison for more than enough years. So he'd called for death and intimidation: so what? He would rather not have done it, but he felt no remorse. It was only a matter of paying some money to get more money. People didn't count anymore. However many or few years were left to him, they would be lived where and how he pleased, free at last from care.

His mind was still whirling as the Lear jet taxied out onto the runway, got its clearance from the tower and gathered speed on the ground before flinging itself into the air.

Don Enrique was hardly conscious of the ground falling away below his porthole, though he was staring at it. He noticed that the mountains ringing the city still had snow on them even in November, springtime below the equator. He had never gotten used to that. Well, with luck, it wouldn't be much longer that he'd have to think about such nonsense.

He turned and watched the mountains recede as the small jet leveled off, straightened out of its turn and headed west toward the Pacific. There it would turn south and follow the coastal route. He usually enjoyed the flight, especially on a clear day like today, when he could see the mountains on one side and the sea on the other. But today he could hardly take any pleasure in the sight; he was too preoccupied.

To think that he had spent a third of his life working toward the day he could leave Chile, this all-too-pleasant end of the world where nothing ever happened that meant anything for him, and return to civil society—he would use the French identity so carefully established over the years—and live off his accumulated wealth in Paris. For him the world revolved around the city of light and he felt that his presence there would be accepted with the fewest questions.

He let his mind wander to the Tuileries, the Louvre, the bridges across the Seine, the cafes, the boulevards, the cultivated air of a city where it was an honor to be accomplished. Where he could read Mallarmé and listen to Debussy in the beautiful countryside of Cézanne and Monet, his favorite painters. To be able to wander in the streets, browse for books, live without the perpetual care about estate management, the infernal alphagraph and money. Yes, that was the place; this, outside the plane's porthole, held nothing more for him. He must become unfettered from the ghosts of the past.

*　*　*

The old man looked up from his book when Don Enrique walked into the library, putting his finger on the word his eyes had just abandoned.

"What do you read, Oswaldo?" Don Enrique asked in German.

"The Cabala," the old man answered in the same language, turning his attention back to the text in front of him. He moved his finger along the line of ciphers, and then stopped and looked up at Don Enrique, apparently surprised that he was still standing there.

"I find it hard to understand, that a scientific mind such as yours could find any meaning in that prattle."

The old man smiled tolerantly, as though at a child, and said, "It is just another way of trying to make order out of chaos, to impose upon the randomness of the visible and imagined world a coherent explanation. Like modern science, it is also a claimant for truth."

"Truth?" Don Enrique exclaimed sarcastically. "With all that nonsense about the hexameron and the golem?"

"There is more than one idea of truth, Enrique, in case you've forgotten. What happened in Santiago?"

As there was no need for Oswaldo to know all the details, Don Enrique said simply, "There's been a slight delay about the money, but it shouldn't affect our plans much."

The old man seemed satisfied by this answer and turned back to his open book.

"There'll be enough money?" he said as an afterthought, looking up again. "Enough for me to live on when I get there?"

Don Enrique had answered the question many times before but once again he had to placate Oswaldo: "More than enough for the rest of your life. But I still can't understand why you insist on Israel. You could live with me very nicely in France."

"No!" The answer was emphatic, as it had been before.

Don Enrique resolved to himself, as he had many times, that he would never ask again. But he always did. He knew he would miss Oswaldo, who had been like a brother. Indeed, as far as the rest of the world was concerned, he was his brother. Lately Oswaldo had been very peculiar, especially since the confrontation in the laboratory during the testing. He wanted nothing to do with the machine now, and he wouldn't even go over to the laboratory to look at it. He spent all his time reading books on mysticism, biblical archeology, and ancient history. Books Don Enrique ordered from the catalogues Oswaldo browsed in endlessly, sent in from England, France, Germany, Argentina, and in as many languages; just as he once had sent for scientific texts.

Oswaldo closed the book and stood up facing Don Enrique; he steadied himself with a cane, trembling slightly as he had for the last few years since the stroke. With his long white hair and shaggy brows he looked like an Old Testament prophet. He was only three years older than Don Enrique, but there seemed a twenty-year difference. He raised an arthritic hand, and, pointing a finger at Don Enrique, said, "Why? You want to know why? Because I have spent my life in the service of Moloch; I thought my contribution to cybernetics would advance medicine. But science has become perverted to the ends of power and domination. Monstrosity, abomination, and I want none of it. Even a Nobel prize would be a bad joke now. I am tired, I am old. All I ask for is to be allowed to live out my years in peace. I have no one left . . . they're all dead, and Europe to me is a graveyard filled with the painful memories of what might have been. The thought that I have created something to augment the monstrosities is unbearable. If I had the courage to take my own life, to destroy my golem, I would . . . would have done it years ago. But I didn't. I am powerless . . . unless I want to allow the past to be raked up . . . and for what? To punish you? God will do that. Whatever mankind could do would be insufficient, and I, certainly, will not be responsible for bringing any more pain into the world, even to one who deserves it. Justice? In this world, it's only a word in the dictionary!"

As he spoke his hand had stopped trembling on the cane and he drew himself up taller. Don Enrique felt as though he were facing judgment before the ancient god of the Hebrews.

"You could easily kill me now. I have served my purpose," Oswaldo continued, "but you do not choose to do so, and I am to be given a choice. Very well then, I have chosen. The Holy Land is not place—it is time, history. There is no *place* for me, as you think there is for you. Enrique, you delude yourself: there is no country for old men. Especially us. Persist in your vanity if you must. Become a boulevardier, and I sincerely hope it gives you pleasure. It will be small recompense for eternal damnation, where, no doubt, you and I will meet again. But for me, for the few years I may have left of a wasted life, there . . . in the promised land, maybe I could redeem some time from eternity."

He seemed to shrink as he turned his back and shuffled away, his hand trembling on the cane, his eyes fixed on a distant vision of Canaan.

Don Enrique stood in the library watching Oswaldo as he walked through the door into the corridor. Maybe Oswaldo was right. They were both damned. Don Enrique more so. He had made and would have to pay for his compact with Mephistopheles. Someday. But for now . . . What was it Oswaldo had said? "To impose upon the randomness of the visible and imagined world a coherent explanation." He liked that.

5

New York–Times Square

LOFTY PLUMP CLOUDS scudded across a clear sky and cold wind tasting of winter gusted from the north down the avenues of Manhattan. Central Park West and Broadway were lined with people behind police barriers from 77th Street to 34th Street, where the Macy's annual parade ended in front of the huge department store.

Parents huddled deeper into their coats with each gust, while children, the cold forgotten in their excitement, shrieked and giggled with delight as each gigantic caricature balloon floated into view, and oohed and aahed at the pageants rolling past.

"Look, Uncle Nick, the Cookie Monster!" shouted Larry, pounding his hands on Nick Burns' head.

Nick laughed and shifted the boy a bit on his shoulders to prevent Larry from slipping off.

"Dumb kid," Melissa said, snuggling deeper into her uncle's side. "Who cares about that baby junk?"

"Come on, Meli," Nick said, "stop picking on him. He's excited by the parade. You used to be the same way when you were his age."

Melissa, at thirteen, had no patience with "baby stuff," as she called it, and even less with nine-year-old Larry. She seemed bored by the entire parade and let Nick know it.

"I'm tired," she whined. "Let's go back to Grandma's."

"No, I won't go," cried Larry. "Why'd you come if you didn't like it?"

"I didn't know I wouldn't like it, you brat," Melissa snapped at him.

"Uncle Nick?" Larry begged.

"Meli, we're staying awhile," Nick said.

"Can I have a hot dog, then?" she asked, pointing to the vendor with the blue and orange umbrella on his push wagon, fifty feet away, at the corner of 44th Street.

"Me too," shrieked Larry, afraid he would be done out of something she got.

Nick reached into his pocket and pulled two dollar bills from his money clip, handed Melissa the money, and eased Larry down from his shoulder. It was a relief to have the little boy on his own feet, because Nick's shoulders were aching from the pressure.

"You stay here and mind the place, Nick. I'll go," said Carol, his sister, who had walked over with the kids from her apartment on the East Side to meet him.

Her long blonde hair blowing out over the collar of her sheepskin coat, Carol took Larry and Melissa by their hands, and edged them through the crowd toward the hot dog man.

As he turned to watch them, Burns noticed a black man with a short goatee, a blue stocking cap and short ski jacket who leaned against a doorway listening to a transistor radio. The peculiarity which caught Nick's eye and changed him from a doting uncle into an operative was that the man pulled the radio from his ear and spoke into it after Carol had passed.

Burns felt the adrenaline pouring in; his breathing became rapid. You're becoming a paranoic, he thought, the guy's probably New York Police tactical patrol. The place must be loaded with them. Always in crowds at mass gatherings. Burns turned to look at the parade and then back quickly, soon enough to see the black man avert his eyes. It's got to be, he thought. But he didn't know why he should be under surveillance on vacation. The Paris business still? Because he was a professional and used to the game, Nick wasn't upset, just angry that his family was in possible danger. No mission was yet defined, so who was tagging him and why? Those ICO security creeps? He knew he could confirm his suspicions by moving, but the kids and Carol . . . ? Couldn't expose them. What a business, he thought; not even a chance to be an uncle without intrigue.

Nick fished his pipe from his pocket and turned to a neighbor to ask for a light while he checked the tag.

The black man in the ski jacket was still in the doorway. Nick knew there were others: there had to be if a communication linkage was in use. But they could have been anywhere. Most likely one was in a building nearby, with high-powered binocs trained on him, and a floater in the street somewhere. That was a classic pattern for surveillance. If there were three on the street, then he'd worry. Three was for a kill. He had to check it out.

Larry was the first to reach him. "Up, Uncle Nick, pick me up." Mustard was on his face and the half-eaten frankfurter was squeezed in his hand.

"Okay, buddy, but don't drop that stuff on my head!" Nick laughed as he hoisted the boy onto his shoulders.

Melissa, mollified by the hot dog, seemed more enthusiastic than before, and stood watching the parade without complaining. Carol offered Nick a sip of her coffee.

"Change places with Meli, and stand next to me," he told her as she handed him the paper cup.

Carol did as he asked, shifting Melissa to her left and moving next to Nick.

"Carol," he said calmly, "I don't know why, but I'm being watched, maybe followed."

"Oh, come on, Nicky; the government work is getting to you, giving you cloak-and-dagger fantasies."

"I wish it were the case, Carol, but I think I spotted the ta . . ." he hesitated before using the trade jargon, and said instead, "the person watching me." She looked worried, he thought.

"No problem, Carol, but I have to separate from you and the kids. First of all, can you give me a key to your apartment without being obvious?"

"Yup," she said, and slipped her hand into her coat pocket. Then she put her hand in his pocket, and he heard the clink as her keys dropped in.

"Now this is what we'll do . . ."

A drum-and-bugle corps strutted past, making a deafening noise, so that Nick's leaning over talking in Carol's ear seemed quite natural.

Five minutes later Burns shifted his nephew down from his shoulders. "We're going now, kids. Time to go home."

A chorus of objections from both children, even though Melissa had wanted to leave only a few minutes earlier. Nick took each child by a mittened hand, and they began to edge through the crowd. As they got to the corner of Broadway and 43rd Street Nick looked back and checked the black man; he was moving along the street in their path, talking into his radio all the while.

When Nick, Carol, and the children turned the corner onto 43rd Street there were fewer people, and they were able to walk toward Eighth Avenue. Stopping for a second to retie Larry's scarf, which didn't really need it, Nick saw the tag ambling behind them about one hundred yards. He thought he spotted the floater too, a man in a heavy gray overcoat and Tyrolean hat on the other side of the street, strolling slowly in the same direction idly looking into the windows of closed shops. He wore a hearing aid. Nick knew better.

By the time they reached the corner of Eighth and 43rd, the gray overcoat had passed, turned downtown and was stalling there.

"Wait here a second, everybody," Nick told the kids and Carol and he stepped into the public telephone booth on the street corner.

Looking back, he saw the black man stop and talk into his radio. Nick completed his call and stepped back onto the street.

"Okay, kids, you go with Momma; I'll be at Grandma's a little later, in time for the turkey." He didn't want to leave them like this but knew he must. Nick hailed a cab and helped the kids and Carol into it. He gave the driver the address.

"Straight down Ninth Avenue and right into the building, please," he told the surly youth sitting at the wheel. "See ya later kids." He slammed the door and watched the cab ease out into traffic. Nick made a mental note of the license plate. He saw the gray overcoat getting into a taxi on the other corner, alone.

Good deal, he thought, now two are isolated. He waited, as though he would cross the street, while the gray coat passed in his taxi, and noted those plates as well. Then he turned back and stepped into the phone booth, dialed and recited both plate numbers into the mouthpiece.

"I'll need a pickup detail here right away," he said, watching the goatee window-shopping farther up the street. "Meet me at . . ."—he looked around—"Shelby's Coffee Shop." He gave the address. "I'll wear a red carnation!"

He hung up the phone. He was enraged to have to involve his family in operations. Also to have to give Carol some idea of his instant liaison with active musclemen was not Nick's idea of good cover. His jaw twitched with the anger as he stepped out of the phone booth and began walking back toward Broadway. He crossed the street for a better view of the goatee, and so that the tag would not have the opportunity to cross.

He hoped that the guy would stay where he was, thinking to get behind Nick when he passed. Fortunately the man didn't move, but remained in front of a closed menswear shop, apparently looking at the goods displayed.

When Nick got opposite the goateed man, he crossed the street quickly and walked up to the window behind him. Without a word Nick swung his doubled right fist into the black man's lower back where he knew he'd hit the kidneys.

The man screamed with the sudden pain. "Whad you doin', motherfucker?" he yelled and wheeled to the left, a switchblade gleaming in his right hand. But Nick was too quick for him, and with his raised left hand, struck him on the neck, just below his left ear.

The man fell to his knees, partly stunned with pain, dropping his blade. Nick kicked it away and watched it skitter down the sidewalk to the gutter.

"No chances, take no chances in street-fighting; if you can't completely disable, then *kill*," he heard his training instructor at Wheelock shouting in his head. He kicked hard, right in the stomach. The man screamed and writhed with pain.

In a split second, Nick was down on the ground: he twisted the black man's right arm behind him and with a knee on his back kept him face down. Nick hooked his free arm around the man's chin and pulled back, hissing fiercely in his ear, "Who, who are you working for, you SOB?"

"Don't know what you mean, man," the other sobbed, "you crazy honky!"

Nick twisted the arm and pulled back on the neck. "Tell me, or you're dead in ten seconds." Then he had a sudden moment of fear. Maybe it was a mistake! But no—the guy *was* following him. He increased the pressure.

"I don't know who, I swear," the man gasped, "lemme go."

He pulled back harder. "Where's the radio control?"

"Don't know." The man's eyes were ready to pop.

Nick tightened his grip. "You *do* know or you die."

The man's face was contorted with anguish. Veins stood out on his forehead and his eyes looked as though they would pop out of his head. "Room 1120, Allied Towers," he gasped, and seemed to pass out.

Nick stood up and brushed his clothes with his gloved hands. Some passersby had gathered in a circle.

"What happened, mister?" asked a short fat woman with a shopping bag.

Nick shook his head and snorted like a horse. "The guy tried to mug me, to take my radio." He leaned over, picked up the transistor set and put it in his overcoat pocket. "Somebody please go call a cop," he pleaded.

Two teenaged boys ran toward the corner. Nick took out a handkerchief and wiped his face and then remembered the knife.

"Keep your eye on him," he said to a burly man in a pea coat, and stepped to the curb to pick up the switchblade. As he bent to get the knife he heard someone cry, "Watch him!" and turned to see the goateed man struggling to his feet to begin a sprint. Nick stepped forward quickly and hit him once hard with the edge of his right hand just behind the ear; the man went down like a deadweight.

"Hey, not fair!" said someone behind him.

"Is this fair?" Nick held up the switchblade. "He tried to use it on me!"

At that moment two policemen arrived, out of breath from their half block's trot.

"What's going on?" asked the younger one, dark, with a drooping mustache. The other cop, an older, short man with gray hair and reddish cheeks where broken vessels showed like a road map, didn't say anything but simply stood, feet apart, rapping his nightstick against the palm of his hand.

"I can explain this, officer, but I don't need an audience," said Nick and showed the younger cop his identification.

"Holy shit," the cop muttered as he saw Nick's picture on a card emblazoned with the shield of OMEGA, describing him as Senior Officer, Grade 3. He whispered quickly to the older cop, who began to move toward the crowd.

"Okay, come on, show's over. Everybody go home," he chanted through his nose as he menaced his way toward the bystanders.

The younger cop nodded as he listened to Nick talk for a

minute. "Sure, we'll hold him," the cop said. "And if your people appear with the proper authorization, we'll release him to their custody."

"Ya gonna press charges?" asked the older cop, who had frightened the pedestrians away. He stood over the black man with club ready to flatten him.

"I'll explain later, Harry," said the mustached one. "We'll take him to the station house now." He pocketed the switchblade and the piece of paper on which Nick had written an official phone number and an outside clearance code.

"Okay, boogie woogie, on your feet," said Harry, poking the groaning man with his nightstick. "Next time you won't be so quick to mug someone. Jeez, this guy's really done in! Who was the other guy?" Harry asked his partner.

"I'll tell you later, buddy. Let's go."

Harry snapped the cuffs on the sullen "mugger" and they started for the station house on the West Side.

* * *

Disheveled and a little dirtied, Nick was drinking coffee at the Shelby Coffee House when the enforcement crew of three walked in. They took seats flanking him in the almost empty shop.

"What's yours, fellas?" asked the cliché platinum blond behind the counter, smiling as she chewed her gum.

They looked at Nick.

"That's all, honey, thanks," he said and put a dollar on the counter. He wanted to be nice to a stranger, a small compensation.

The four men walked out to Eighth Avenue. On the street Nick gave them the address, handed over the radio and told them what he wanted. They seemed to know their business. He watched them walk down the street and then stepped into the public telephone booth.

"Yes, sir," said the friendly but official voice at the other end. "We picked up the man as he left his taxi. Right on our doorstep. We had another car and driver waiting and rushed your wife and children home as soon as they got here."

Nick didn't correct him; he asked for a pickup on the goatee instead.

Next he called his mother to assure her he'd be there before dinner, not to worry, and he took a cab across town to Carol's apartment. He wanted to call Barnwell in private.

While Nick waited for Barnwell to call him back—the switchboard operator at the Washington Square town house said she'd get to the director quickly—he thought about the strange outline this situation was taking, and so soon. In less than a week since he had met Odette and heard the story of a weird machine, a story she had pieced together from people who had supposedly been subjected to it, they had both been followed, and the computer relay had filled his desk with printouts of information and reports from the files going back thirty years. In addition to the scientist who had invented the damned thing and whose disappearance had never been solved, there were other names, people he had never heard of, like Lee and Ben Winkler, Max Hartman; and some he had, such as Harry Raven, the guy Eric had been writing a book about for so long.

All of the information gave Nick a headache. He was no detective. Accustomed to assignments with a narrowly defined goal, determined by the director, he felt out of his depth with all this information. He couldn't piece it together, and all his mulling over it just gave him additional doubts about his ability to really direct operations should he ever get the opportunity.

When the phone finally rang he was feeling thoroughly disgusted and sorry that he had ever considered opening this can of worms, even if it was for Odette. He didn't know what to do with the squirmy mess.

After he told Barnwell about the incident at the parade, he raised the issue of his own befuddlement with a mass of information he couldn't begin to digest.

"I have problems with it myself, Nick, and there's no one on the inside who can help. I spoke to Sir Galahad"—the director's pet name for the reputedly amorous and ever-galloping Secretary of State—"and he wants us to give it priority. I'll have to cancel your home-leave and ask you to handle this."

"Oh shit, why me?" Nick blurted out, disgusted with himself for starting the whole thing, and annoyed with Barnwell for allowing him no rest.

"I don't really have to tell you, do I?" asked the director.

"But I'm out of my depth," Nick said. "I can't deal with history. Strictly a current events man!"

"That's why I want you to get in touch with your friend Eric Newman. I think he can help us. Didn't he do a book on the forties?"

Nick remembered Eric's *The Distorted Years*, which was hailed as brilliant by the critics. Nick had a signed copy, still unread, in his Paris apartment.

"How the hell can we pick his brain without his knowing what we're up to? Besides, he doesn't have clearance," Nick said, annoyed that Barnwell would bring nonprofessionals into the case, and Nick's close friend at that.

"Just let me take care of the details," Barnwell said calmly. "We often use consultants—and pay them well. Maybe that will ease your conscience a bit."

Nick had no answer for the director; he merely groaned.

"Call him," said Barnwell, "and try to set up an appointment for tomorrow . . . neutral territory. Make it afternoon, so we can meet in the morning and go over details. Maybe I'll have something on the characters you picked up today."

Barnwell rang off, but not before he had wished Nick a happy Thanksgiving in the most avuncular tone.

Nick looked at his watch. Just after one o'clock. He'd call Eric now and then get the hell out to Forest Hills, where he might have a brief respite from spooks in the present and ghosts in the past, among the warmth of God, mother, family, turkey, and apple pie. All the lovely homeliness he was asked to believe that his absurd job somehow strove to protect.

* * *

"Nicky, you old son of a gun. Where in hell are you?" Eric practically whooped with joy into the telephone. "What am I doing? Just lazing around. No, you didn't wake me. I had to get up to answer the phone anyway."

Nick sounded calm and relaxed. He had just come from the Macy's parade with his niece and nephew and said it was duller than usual. "Maybe I'm becoming an old fart," he chuckled. "It all seemed like a bad old comic book. But enough of that. How's everybody and everything?"

Eric rubbed his eyes hard. "Answered standing on one foot—okay! For details, see footnotes."

Nick's phone call had wakened him from an alcoholic sleep. He could hear the TV going in the living room and assumed

Lucy was watching it. According to the bedside clock it was 1:10 in the afternoon, but the sun was starting its wintry descent over the Hudson, slipping knife edges of light through the drawn venetian blinds. He must have been exhausted: who wouldn't be after a night of drinking wine and making love with ravenous Lucy. She couldn't get enough, and her complete abandon and open demands excited him; Eric had spent himself.

"Did I really wake you, old buddy? I'm sorry!" Nick's voice sounded unbelieving. Eric felt good to hear his friend's voice again.

"Nicky—Oh, man, am I glad to hear you. Maybe it's all a dream."

"What's the matter, Eric?" He sounded worried.

"Aah, it's too complicated to explain on the phone. Listen, hold on a sec, will you?"

He put the phone down, staggered to the bathroom and splashed cold water on his face.

"Lucy," he called, "got any coffee?"

"Right you are, sir," she said in her best fake British, and came into the bathroom and kissed him on the cheek.

"Bring me some in the bedroom, will ya please? I'm still on the phone. It's my old friend Nick Burns."

He walked back to the phone. "Okay, Nick, I'm awake. Almost. When did you get to town?"

Nick said he'd be in for the weekend, and then would be going on to Washington for briefing before a probable trip to Chile.

"Eric, I want to see you, naturally, just for the sake of it, but I also want to pick your brain on the Chilean situation. They'll give me the official views in D.C. but I want the academic scuttlebutt from you."

Eric felt flattered. "It's not really my specialty—I mean the politics. I could tell you something about the scene there, just what I've picked up in conversation with one of my colleagues and some visitors who passed through Columbia."

He said he wanted whatever Eric could give him, and they arranged to meet for lunch the next day.

* * *

Nick and Eric had met in college. By laws of randomness and chance, they both turned up in New Haven in the fall of 1955 and were assigned to share a suite of dormitory rooms. Eric, with his Brooklyn proletarian *cum* middle class background, was more wary of the laconic prep school patrician with his Brooks Brothers clothes than Nick was of Eric. By the end of a semester together they were close friends, each having learned something of another social and ethnic world, blended and smoothed out by the ambience of Yale.

Nick was very much at ease in the social atmosphere, Eric in the intellectual. With Eric's shaggy blond hair, chinos and work shirts, and ever-ready contentiousness, and Nick's crewcut and tennis sweaters, and acceptance of the system which paid his way, they complemented each other. After the first year they found an apartment off campus and roomed there together for the next three years. It was a great time in Eric's life; he and Nick grew to be like brothers.

Nick split his major between political theory and comparative literature and Eric between intellectual history and comparative literature. In the senior year Nick sat for the Foreign Service exams, following a family tradition, and Eric went on for a master's degree—returning to New York and Columbia University.

Nick was posted to Buenos Aires as Third Assistant Cultural Affairs Officer after a few months of training, and Eric won a Fulbright Fellowship, and packed off to Santiago, Chile the following spring, after one semester in the doldrums at Columbia. The year in Chile was a happy one for Eric. He exchanged a few visits with Nick and they explored the Magellan Strait and Patagonia on vacation. After Eric returned to the States, Nick met Phyllis, who was a co-worker at the American Embassy, and a year later they were married. They came up to New York for the wedding. Eric felt a sense of loss, not so much for his friend, as for the relatively careless days of their youth, for the "just us guys" camaraderie which had to be lost forever, or at best replaced with something else.

It was replaced, for Eric, by Elly, the proverbial Jewish girl from Brooklyn. Dark hair, olive-skinned, with beautiful full lips, she was the ideal resting place it seemed to Eric, especially with his head tucked into her large bosom. Soon they were married and Eric commuted from New York to New Haven twice a week to finish his doctorate while Elly worked as a secretary in an export company.

They lived in a tiny studio apartment in Greenwich Village,

and saw a lot of Nick and Phyll, who were sent back to Washington for additional training. Phyllis did film editing for USIA, and Nick was learning German language and history for an eventual transfer.

It occurred to Eric that Nick was being groomed for intelligence work and he said something one Saturday afternoon. The Newmans were visiting the Burnses in Virginia that weekend and staying at their apartment in Alexandria. With two salaries, Nick and Phyll could afford a guest room, and Eric and Elly were regular monthly visitors. "Like your period," Eric used to say—always good for a laugh.

When he broached the subject of intelligence work, Nick joked it off. Eric remembered getting into Nick's car after a hard game of doubles with two of Nick's Foreign Service colleagues and asking Nick if he was really training for the CIA. He laughed too hard, Eric thought, and looked quizzical under the brim of his floppy white tennis hat.

But when they were both seated in the old Plymouth, Nick hesitated a second before starting the engine. The cherry blossom smell drifted into the open windows. Eric felt that some great revelation was at hand. But Nick simply said, looking straight ahead. "No, that's not my game. Does it interest *you* as a career?"

"No," Eric answered, "you want Greenberg the spy, on the second floor. I only read spy novels for amusement; my big adventures take place in research libraries."

"Well, there's room for everyone." Eric could still remember Nick's answer, could taste the moment, its tension and unspoken understanding. There was trust and love between them, and he didn't ask anymore.

Maybe Nick was sounding him out, trying to recruit him. But it wasn't for Eric. Nick was his friend, and that was true whatever he did. They went home to the women and song.

That had been thirteen years ago. Tragedy hit Nick when Phyllis died giving birth—along with the baby—and he resolved never to make himself vulnerable to such pain again. Then he was posted to Frankfurt. Eric finished his Ph.D. and got a job at the State University at Stony Brook, and moved to Huntington, Long Island, halfway between the "devil and the deep blue," an hour's drive east to work and the same west to the city.

Nothing of moment happened for ten years. Eric wrote his first book and became a young academic hotshot; Nick did his work, was promoted to Press Liaison. Nick went to France after Germany; Eric and Elly stayed on Long Island and had two kids. The friends saw each other once in Europe, and Nick saw Eric and Elly—and after the breakup, just Eric—every time he was in New York, usually twice a year. But they kept in touch with monthly letters—"paper periods," they were. Nick traveled a lot, kept getting kicked upstairs, but they never lost touch.

After eight years of the State University and many job offers—Eric got a lot of response to his acerbic book and vituperative articles in the quarterlies—he was offered a job at Columbia, a *plum* as he saw it, and accepted. Then he simply drove west rather than east every day. Elly didn't like it. Comfortable in both her split-level in Huntington and her role as a suburban faculty wife, she found the social scene at Columbia trying, felt nonplussed by the "city sophisticates" (as she called them) and soon began to decline invitations to dinner and cocktail parties.

For Eric it was manna in the desert, and within a year he and his wife separated. He supposed he had been asking for it without saying so, but his nice Jewish girl wanted to remain a princess in her same split-level castle, and he had a taste for a wider domain.

* * *

"The coffee's good," Eric smacked his lips. "And now for breakfast." He reached over and slipped his hand into Lucy's robe. She stroked his stubby face.

"Want me to shave?"

"No, I like you this way, warm and smelling of sleep, my own gorilla," she said and Groucho Marxed her eyebrows as she slipped into bed.

He closed his eyes, and kept remembering the days of innocence and hope, when he and Nick shared their dreams. Despite the so-called accomplishments, it had been downhill since then, at least for Eric. A lost Eden. He knew he couldn't regain it, wanted something more, but damn him if he knew what it was!

"Eric, you're somewhere else!" said a narrow part of the wider domain from under the covers. Lost in his thoughts, he had stopped fondling her.

"It's unfair," Lucy continued. "You get me back into bed, make me all excited again and then fade away from me."

She was indignant, and, he supposed, she had a right to be. They were using each other—he at least had no illusions about that—but he couldn't expect Lucy to put up with the meanderings of his mind while he was committed to being attentive to her. She wasn't really satisfied with only the physical, and he knew he was a fool to think that she could be. He also knew, however, that with her, he couldn't give more. Phenomenal in bed and very caring, nevertheless she bored him.

He put his hands back to work.

"That's better," she said. "Oh . . . oh, so good . . . yes, right there, don't stop."

He didn't, and it wasn't until they had made love again that he was left alone with his thoughts.

Lucy went into the kitchen to prepare dinner. She had brought over a turkey the night before, had prepared and put it in the oven while Eric slept earlier, and now he heard her clanking pans and rummaging cabinets for utensils, humming, carrying on a conversation with Horace the cat, and thoroughly enjoying "playing house."

He stayed in bed for a while longer, feeling miserable and sorry for himself and her, responsible for her happiness. Dissatisfied with the very fabric of his life, he had thought an extra stitch or two might strengthen it. Now the thread had taken hold, and he was looking for another place to unravel. Just because she liked being with him and they had good sex—"how to" manuals could be based on their performance—that made everything okay by her. To her way of thinking, what else was there? If you made it in bed, more or less liked each other and got along, no further complication was necessary. No liberated woman, Lucy, her idea of the division of labor was I cook, you eat—as it is written. Maybe she was right!

But something was missing; Eric wanted more from living, and he didn't know what it was. The discontent all began to rise up like a chunk, a hairball he had gotten inside him from licking so hard at his wounds like a cat. He wished that he could see things as simply as Lucy; then life would be a lot easier. What else there was he didn't know, but he wanted whatever it was. His work interested him, his everyday life had its moments, but he wanted more: to be transported, carried away by an ineffable vision, to be taken out of himself and his kvetching by some transforming power . . . of love perhaps, or of some absorption which would lend its magic to his life.

The combination of Nick's call, the postcoital down, and the mindless joy Lucy took in both Eric and her turkey brought on the rising gorge, he thought, as he got up and made for the shower. Eric wanted to be ravished—the rest was ennui and the dead hand of the past.

6

New York

IT WAS COLD and gray with an occasional hint of sunlight and, Nick thought, a definite feeling of snow in the air as he crossed Washington Square Park and climbed the front stoop of a red brick nineteenth-century house on the north side of the park—one of a row used mostly by New York University. There were few passersby, as the university was closed for the long weekend. He rang the bell under the nameplate of polished brass reading Omega House. A casual observer would think that the building was part of the NYU complex. Indeed, the placard under the brass plate said International Scholars Exchange, and the entrance level office and reception area was just such an office. An inquiry, however, would be met with the response that this office was merely administrative, and that the executive offices of ISE were housed in a building opposite the United Nations.

Nick waited for the hidden closed circuit scanner to identify him, and was then admitted to the closed off entrance vestibule, where he identified himself to the receptionist seated behind bulletproof glass. Omega House was the nerve center of the operation housing the computer, satellite hookup, and the communications center. In appearance, it was no different from any high level administrative office: all office equipment, files and the communications center were housed in separate, and in this case, security-tight rooms at the ground floor and basement level, and the executive offices on the upper floors had the tasteful and subdued appearance of sitting rooms modified only by a table and a telephone in each one. This was Barnwell's style, and the institution bore his unmistakable stamp.

When Nick was ushered into the library, furnished in dark oak with authentic accoutrements of the Federal Period, four walls lined with books, the director was sitting at the long table in the center of the room studying a large map by the light of a heavy brass lamp with a pleated shade. Nick had never seen Barnwell at a desk with papers piled high. Indeed, if the director owned one, it was hidden away from view. Nor would a desk, cluttered with the impediments of a bureaucrat's life, have suited Barnwell: he always seemed the cultivated gentleman, with an air of civilized propriety in all things, a sense of noblesse oblige which enveloped him.

Barnwell motioned him to a chair and plunged right into the subject. "The man you intercepted is Rodney Howard, age thirty-five, a small-time hood who does odd jobs in the black underworld: bagman, driver, enforcer. Works mostly for the Harlem syndicate. He has a long record of arrests, no convictions. The other man intercepted at the entrance to the interagency motor pool is Edward Kopcik; he runs a radio and TV repair shop in Yorkville, no known criminal record. His customers include a number of diplomatic personnel and he is suspected as a wireman in various electronic infiltrations. His shop may be used as a message drop, but surveillance and transmission sweeps have been negative."

Nick couldn't see a pattern yet. "What about the control in the Allied Tower?" he asked.

The director picked up a typed sheet which lay on the table and read: "Interception team requested by Officer Burns proceeded as directed to room 1120, Allied Chemical Tower, and effected entry. The office was unfurnished and empty but showed signs of recent use. Subsequent inquiries revealed that the space is leased to Modern Communications Company, Guido Cappella, president. Cappella, a telephone electronics technician, formerly with the Bell System, was not at the home address listed with the management of the Allied Tower and his whereabouts are not known."

Nick thought a minute. "Do you know that it was Cappella who was in the office?"

Barnwell shook his head affirmatively. "Both Howard and Kopcik identified him as the one who hired them. We have an APB out for him with the tri-state police, but we won't know more until he's picked up."

"But these guys seem like small potatoes," Nick said. "What are they doing in this operation? Did they know they were getting involved with cointelpro's?"

"Apparently not," Barnwell answered. "They were hired by Cappella, and I would guess that he's a cutout, or else is directed by one. We'll have to find him before we can take this any further."

"So where does that leave us?"

Barnwell looked at Nick with his ice blue eyes. "We know that someone is interested enough in this ETT business Mademoiselle des Chavannes is researching to follow her and then you. It's important enough to tag you back in the States as well. They're not very good at it, though, so they're probably not opposition government. Or . . . they want to be visible for some reason as yet unknown. Meanwhile all we can do is try to trace them, watch you and des Chavannes for other tags in the hope of flushing them and finding the source, and, at the same time, continue our own operation."

"What's the operation?" Nick asked. He knew the director wouldn't tell him everything, but he was impatient.

"Twofold objective," answered Barnwell. "The first is to find out if this electronic thought translator is in use by the Chileans, and if so, how they came by it. Second, whether or not it had any connection with the prototype we were working on during the Second World War."

"The one that disappeared?" Nick was puzzled. "How could you prove a connection?"

"Only because of the people involved," the director said, "and that's where your friend Newman fits in. This Goldfeder, the scientist who was working on the project when he disappeared, ran with a crowd which included Ben Winkler, the left-wing writer, Harry Raven, the poet who committed suicide—"

"The guy Newman is writing about?" Nick interrupted. He was beginning to see why Barnwell wanted him to pick Eric's brain.

"The same," continued Barnwell, "and perhaps we could work out the linkages in the present if we knew more about them in the past; and the only man who can help us is Newman. He can save us months of work!"

"You're assuming that there are linkages with the present situation," Nick said. He felt that Barnwell was making an illogical leap or not telling him something.

"It's largely suppositional," the director admitted. "But all the monitoring of cointel reports that I've done over the years has given no indication of any project development anywhere of this nature. I don't know, for a fact, that there is any relationship to the ETT Goldfeder was working on, but it's all I have to go on."

"Even if it is, what relevance?" Nick asked.

"Because if it's the same or a related device, then it's ours!"

He stopped for a few seconds, poured some coffee for himself and Nick from an electric pot on the sideboard, and continued: "If it's ours, we want it. If it's not ours, we want to know whose it is, and how they got it. I think that here is where Newman comes in."

Nick was puzzled. The director's explanation had better be good before Nick would take it upon himself to blow cover, even to a friend, and to make use of him in an operation, no less.

"It's only a hunch," said Barnwell, "but I think there's a connection between the death of Harry Raven, the disappearance of Leon Goldfeder and the whole damned circle of writers and artists they frequented . . . but I can't figure it out!"

"But why do you have to?" Nick asked.

"Because somewhere in there is a cover-up. Winkler, for example, was doing some reporting for OSS during the war, and came up with some yarn about seeing this Raven alive in Argentina. It was discounted, naturally, as a fantasy induced by stress and strain. Or this Goldfeder, who was a mildly left social democrat, friendly with Winkler, a committed yet nonaffiliated communist at the time, and Raven, who was a rabid card-carrying party man. Yet all of them are friendly with Max Hartman, a book dealer who was a Nazi; FBI thought he was local control for a spy network but were never able to prove it."

"I'm not getting what you're driving at," said Nick. The details were giving him a headache, because they formed no meaning for him yet.

"Hartman was the one who reported that Goldfeder was missing, and that was the day after Raven committed suicide. At the same time, the laboratory had been sacked, all the blueprints and notes and the ETT prototype itself taken. Now where the hell did Hartman come to be intimate with a German Jew émigré scientist working for the American government, and how was Winkler tied in here? If we can work that out, we'll have a handle on the beginnings of all this business. Meanwhile, we'll try to find out what's going on down there in Chile."

"I'm really overwhelmed," said Nick, feeling out of his depth. "You're asking for a lot; for the first part you need a large team of detectives and researchers with long memories and plenty of time. For the second, you need an infiltration operation with a lot of manpower and equipment. Isn't it all something that Central Intelligence could handle?"

The director seemed to hesitate and then said, "The Secretary doesn't want the Company involved. There may be a security problem and he wants to play this all very close to the vest, confined to the White House, which means us—we're the vest pocket!" He chuckled at his own little joke. "Besides," Barnwell continued, "if the Agency starts running down all this information and trying to put it together, it'll take months. Too long. You're dealing with a large bureaucracy there. The lag time we can't afford."

"So what can Eric do for you that you haven't already done?"

"He can put together a picture which we can't, and quickly. He has the bona fides to go and talk to people, to interview where we can't, and without raising suspicions. In other words, perfect, airtight cover. My feeling is that if we can understand what happened in 1943, we're ahead of the game. Then the rest will fall into place."

Nick shook his head in disbelief. "It doesn't sound right!" he said.

"You just get Newman to put together some information for us, let him get to Hartman, Winkler, and some of the others I've noted and report to you, and we'll take it from there," Barnwell said with finality.

Nick couldn't think of how to approach Eric. "How do I explain to him what he's doing, and for whom? I can't use the USIA cover for authorization."

Barnwell wasn't going to be put off. "I'll leave the details to you, but you can sweeten it by offering him a consultant's fee, the standard per diem plus expenses. I'm sure he can use the money.

Meanwhile I'll issue a pro tem security clearance for him." He smiled at Nick with tightened lips, a gesture which said that discussion was ended.

"If he agrees," Nick asked, "where does he start?"

"With the Goldfeder–Raven connection and what the living —Hartman and Winkler—can tell us about the dead," the director answered, standing up.

Nick rose too. "Into history, then, with the quick and the dead," he said. It was as close to saying yes as he could allow himself.

Barnwell responded by extending his hand.

* * *

The noise on Bayard Street in Chinatown outside the restaurant where Eric sat with Nick later that day rose in a crescendo of horns and angry shouts and then subsided to an occasional honk. Tourists passing with schoolchildren on holiday had to jostle and squeeze between the storefronts and high stacks piled at the curb of the narrow sidewalk: baskets of vegetables with exotic names and crates of glistening fish whose eyes peered through crushed ice counterpointed the sprawling mounds of broken plastic garbage bags from yesterday's meals spilling into the gutters. Cars inched through the clogged roadway between double-parked delivery trucks, and sky and street combined in a conspiracy of dirty gray.

Because there was no English menu in the window offering choices from column A or B to the tourists, the restaurant was almost empty despite the crowds outside, except for a few Chinese truckmen gobbling from rice bowls held up to their mouths. Eric waved the empty teapot in the air to get the waiter's attention.

"Mortmain is an idea which appeals to ruminative types like you," Nick said, helping himself to some more of the bean sprout, bamboo shoot and sauteed shrimp dish he had ordered.

Eric had spent the last hour telling Nick what he had heard from his leftist friends about Chile, information Nick said he could never get from official sources. The waiter brought a new pot of tea, and Eric poured some more steaming oolong for each of them, then told him about the Raven manuscript. "Why can't you live with uncertainty, an unclosed circle?" Nick asked. "We all do!"

"Well how the hell can you write a biography or study history or anything that has to do with the past if you don't ruminate about it," Eric asked, "try to close the circle? If all events and lives are random, and there's no pattern, no effect on the future, then all the assumptions our entire civilization is based on are groundless, and we have no meaning."

"And thinking that you can really see a cumulative effect in the past is artificial," Nick said, putting down his chopsticks. "You do it by selective evidence to prove a hypothesis—not scientific at all.

"Completeness is always an illusion, a chimera," Eric retorted. "I can't even give you a complete version of what's happening now, at this table—but as a historian, I'm bound to try."

"Maybe France has rubbed off on me more than I think," Nick answered, "but I think that the attempt at closure is absurd, failed before you start because you can't *know* truth—only your version. The illusion is that you can set all things right, and return to Paradise. Somebody's theory of the detective story, isn't it? The closed circle again, the Garden of Eden."

"So there you are," Eric said, smiling. "Dig up the dead hand and kill it again."

"No mortmain here, Eric," he laughed, and continued, "unless we're eating it!"

"Could be; neither of us reads Chinese."

Nick leaned back in the booth, took a pipe from the pocket of his tweed jacket and filled it from a plastic packet of French tobacco. He lit a match and the pungent scent of the caporal enveloped them.

"What's eating me is that I have to ask you for some help, and don't quite know how," he said finally.

"You say, 'Eric, old bean, I need a favor,' that's how! A woman?"

"Is that your idea of my only helplessness?" he asked, smiling, then continued: "No, not directly, look . . ."

Nick mentioned a rumor of bizarre torture in Chile.

"Part of my work is gathering information, intelligence—" he went on.

"So it is Greenberg the spy, after all," Eric cut in.

"Hardly," Nick retorted. "It's mostly information to help

make policy decisions . . . and basically not much different from what you do. Gather, evaluate, and make recommendations."

"What a bullshit artist you are," Eric responded. "There isn't any comparison. I sit in libraries and research public information which no one has reintegrated yet, then write about it. You poke around in secrets, bribe officials and all that cloak-and-dagger stuff, don't you?"

"No, I don't. You write books and articles for publication. I write reports for a limited readership of policymakers. Period. I'm not James Bond, Eric. No one is."

"Every day," Eric laughed, "every day another illusion shot to hell. I *want* you to be James Bond. I *need* some vicarious experience."

"Then go read spy novels," Nick answered, "but first, do me this favor. Go see a Max Hartman, an old pal of your Raven, and ask him some questions about a scientist who disappeared, a guy named Goldfeder."

"How do you know about Hartman . . . and Goldfeder?" Eric didn't believe what he'd heard.

"Unimportant how I know." Nick's eyes turned hard, uninforming. "Question is, will you do it?"

"That's a fucking riot, the weirdest coincidence."

"Why?"

"Because I was going to see him anyway, about my book on Raven. And, coincidentally, this Goldfeder's name is in the notebook I told you about."

Nick looked startled. "Great, so you can kill two birds . . . and make some money too."

Nick explained that the government often asked academics to do research and paid a consultant's fee of one hundred and fifty dollars a day plus expenses.

"You know where to find him?" Nick asked.

"Of course, and I'm going to do it anyway," Eric said. "Forget the money."

"Don't be a schmuck, you schmuck," Nick came back. "You'll take it!"

He didn't have to twist Eric's arm too hard. Maybe a few days of that consulting and Eric could get a little ahead of himself financially, so Elly could stop bugging him about the kids needing this or that. He would stuff her mouth closed with a check. A pleasant vision danced before his eyes: Elly choking on dollar bills he was ramming into her greedy mouth.

"What are my liberal friends going to think?" Eric asked. "I'll be a regular Greenberg the spy."

"Nothing," Nick came back quickly. "They'll think nothing because you aren't going to tell them. This is strictly entre nous. You mustn't tell anyone, anyone at all, that you are helping me. Okay? Agreed?"

He said okay. "But why don't you do this yourself, Nicky?"

"Because you have a perfectly valid reason for asking such questions without raising any suspicions. I don't," Nick answered.

"About this Goldfeder? Why should I be asking anything about him?" Eric asked. What could he possibly find out from Hartman that the intelligence people didn't already know?

"Just ask Hartman to tell you about Goldfeder's disappearance. We want to compare versions. Goldfeder was a friend of your Raven, too, wasn't he?" Nick asked.

"More of an acquaintance," Eric answered. "But how the hell did you know that?" Eric didn't like the cat-and-mouse routine, not with Nick.

"Just happened across it in an old report," he answered.

Eric knew Nick was lying, but let it slide for the moment. "You can give me the questions you want answered," he said, "and I'll try to get what you want, but only on one condition!"

"What?"

"That you check out whatever is available in the secret files on Raven and a few other names I'll give you, and share the information with me, providing it doesn't violate security regulations. Most of it is probably declassified by now."

"Then you can get it yourself by writing directly. The new Freedom of Information Act is on your side," Nick said.

"But time isn't," Eric snapped. "That's your part of the bargain, if it's to be."

"It's a Hobson's choice," Nick protested, "but I'll do it." He signaled to the waiter for the check, then paid it, over Eric's feeble protestations.

"I'm going to give you a copy of this manuscript notebook I just came across; it's in the car," Eric said, as they walked out of the restaurant onto Bayard Street in the thin grayish afternoon sunlight, "and I'll check off some names he had written down. You can find out whatever there is for me, but I *don't* pay you as a consultant!"

Nick outlined precisely what he wanted from Hartman while they walked over to the parking lot where Eric had left his car. He usually kept it in the garage underneath Columbia's International Affairs Building where he had his office, but wanted Nick to see it, a 1965 Porsche he had picked up cheap and had rebuilt. Despite the strain on his finances, he wouldn't give it up; its cachet was linked with an image of himself as less than a drone, an impoverished grind.

"You want to drive it, Nick baby?" He did; missed the Maserati in Paris.

"This is how I pretend I don't have financial problems," Eric said as they got into the car and headed toward East River Drive. Something in him had always craved Nick's approval, because he was used to thinking of him as having style—what Eric felt he lacked. When Eric was in his dream machine, zipping around the city, there was an equalizer.

"You still drive like a maniac," Eric shouted above the roar of the engine as Nick urged the speedometer up to eighty on the Drive.

"But safely," he said. "Just wanted to see what she'd do. I believe you. Beautiful machine. Now I'll slow down."

Mostly because he didn't want to get a speeding ticket, Nick said, he eased over to the right and let the needle drop off to the legal limit. They passed 23rd Street, and the highway lifted up around the curve as upper Manhattan, the UN building, and the 59th Street Bridge came into sight. The river glinted in the faint sunshine and Eric was flooded with a sense of losses, regrets.

"I used to want all this; it was going to be mine when I grew up, and now mostly it seems . . . I don't know, not worth it, or let's say beyond . . . aghh, I can't put it into words. But I can't find what I want, not in marriage, not single, not even in history or biography, all others' lives. I want my own and don't know where I'll find it. Once in a while, driving like this, I get a half-sense, almost mystical, of the fullness, the whole . . . but I can't touch it, and it fades." He had to tell Nick that; he was the only one Eric could really open up to.

"I'm not sure I'm looking anymore," Nick said. "Maybe it

isn't finding anything that counts, but losing yourself, that out-going of yourself to another. I found it only once since Philly died, but ran from it, afraid to get hurt again."

"But you're satisfied with things the way they are?" Eric asked.

"In form but not in substance," Nick answered, staring at the gray roadway, but glancing sadly over at Eric. Nick the existentialist sounded like a theologian.

The Porsche cornered catlike around the left curve of the exit ramp at 42nd Street as Nick downshifted through two gears instead of braking. He double-clutched to mesh and match revs on the way down.

"Missed your vocation, Nick," Eric said as they waited for the light to change on First Avenue. "Le Mans needs you."

He had taken the Xerox copy of the Raven notebook out of a manila envelope and was checking off the names he wanted Nick to run through his computers.

"You too, from what I remember of your driving," he teased.

"Yeah, but what's it got over Columbia?" Eric responded.

"It's in France," Nick said, grinning.

Horns started to blow behind them. In New York City you can be blind and still drive. As soon as a traffic light hints that it's going to change color, someone will start that impatient tooting.

"Let's go, Sterling," Eric said.

Nick stopped at Third Avenue and 53rd Street, where he took a train to Forest Hills, and Eric continued across town and then through Central Park up to Morningside Heights and home.

Hartman was next, tomorrow, and Eric was putting money in the bank.

7

ERIC LEFT LUCY asleep and put a note on the refrigerator door saying he'd be back at midday. Horace was pesty, so he opened a can of cat food and dumped it on a paper plate before easing out the door. Upper Broadway was beginning to awaken, and some bleary-eyed students who hadn't gone home for the holiday stood next to him staring, half-stoned, into the morning, as he waited for the downtown bus. Eric stamped his feet in the bleak cold to warm them.

* * *

"What do you want with Hartman?" When the superintendent opened the door to her ground floor apartment, she kept the chain latched across the inside of the gray painted door. A smell of cooking cabbage sidled past her into the stark hallway of the small apartment house. Behind her, in the apartment, a fat man in an undershirt sat with his back to the door watching TV.

"I'm a book collector. I thought he might have something I was looking for."

"He know you?"

"I've spoken to him on the phone. When I tried to call this morning, the operator told me the number was disconnected so I thought I'd come over."

"It's disconnected, all right," she said. "If ya ask me, he's disconnected too, I mean up here." She pointed to her forehead. "Thirty-five years he lives in the building. Imagine that. Thirty-five years. And he always pays on time, never once does he miss it. I'm only here fifteen years, but the super before us said to me, 'Gertrude,' she says, 'Mr. Hartman is a little funny, keeps to himself, has a lot of foreign gents visiting him at all hours, but he'll never give you no trouble.' And he didn't. Never. Then last week he knocks on the door and says he's moving. Just like that.

Pays for the month in cash, like always and that same day the movers come and poof, he's gone."

"Where did he move?"

"Beats me, no forwarding address, no phone, nothing." She looked annoyed. Now that she had told the story, she started to close the door.

"Hold it, please! You have no idea at all where he went to?"

"Nah, but I hope it was big enough for all those books, even the movers were complaining. They must've worked for six hours. Filled a whole truck too with those boxes and boxes of books. Like a regular library his place was. The men was complaining, seeing as how we got no elevator here."

"Is his apartment rented already?"

"You interested?"

"Yes, well, I'd like to see it."

She looked at Eric sternly. "I don't rent to no troublemakers. This is a good, clean building. No undesirables."

He knew what that meant: no Hispanics, no blacks and in this Yorkville section, preferably Germans, and no Jews if she could help it.

"What's your name?"

"Newman, Eric Newman."

She looked at his blond hair. "Sprechen Sie Deutsch?"

"Yes, I do, my parents were German," he answered in German, half-truthfully. Viennese Jews who escaped Hitler, they were both dead now.

"What do you do?" She looked like she might have run a Gestapo substation once.

"I teach—a professor at Columbia University."

"Okay, I like that. Go up and look. Third floor front. The door's open, there's a woman looking at it now, but she's a foreigner. If you want it, I'll give it to you."

He had passed the test apparently, and she shut the door with no other word.

The hallway smelled as strongly of pine disinfectant as Mrs. Kleinmeister's apartment had of cabbage. Eric sprinted up the three flights, turned on the landing and saw the door to one of the two front apartments ajar. He knocked on the gray paint.

"Ah, please come in," a woman's voice with a French accent called out.

In the middle of the large front room stood a tall woman of about thirty-five. Dark brown shoulder-length hair framed a thin angular face. She pulled her glasses down from their perch atop her hair and looked hard at Eric with blue eyes; strange eyes, he thought, almost dark blue.

"Are you looking at this apartment for to rent it, perhaps?" she asked.

"No, I was looking for the man who used to live here. I didn't know he had moved."

"Oh well, it doesn't matter; it is too large for me anyway," she said. "You could have it if you want."

"I don't want, I just wanted to find Mr. Hartman."

"He is your friend?"

"No, he sold rare books and I thought he might have something I needed," Eric said.

He walked around touching the dusty shelves that lined the front room and the alcove on the side—it must have been a dining area—looking for something that would tell him where Hartman was. The woman walked toward the back of the flat, saying, "I wish this was a bit smaller and more modern, then I would take it."

Eric watched her finely shaped legs under the fitted navy skirt and the nicely rounded contours of her behind.

"Are you leaving now?" he asked.

"Yes, why?"

"Wait a second, I'll walk down with you."

He walked to the front window where the dead telephone stood on the sill. Under the phone was a mover's business card.

"Oh, here, this is great!"

"What is that?" said the woman in the next room, puzzled at his exclamation.

"The mover's name. Maybe they'll tell me where he went."

"Is he the only book dealer in this city?"

"No, but he may have the thing I want." He slipped the card into his jacket pocket.

"Oh, you *are* persistent, aren't you?" She smiled at him warmly, coming closer.

She had a stylish and self-assured manner he associated with French women. Her firm, well-fleshed body wsa dressed in a fitted blue skirt with a beige checked blouse and a loose belted safari jacket which matched the skirt. Her blouse was opened at the neck down to the third button, mid-cleavage, and was tapered to fit her waist. Eric had the feeling that the blouse would not button up so easily. Her large tan handbag matched her high-heeled shoes.

Walking down the stairs behind her in the trail of her fragrance, which suggested early spring hyacinths, he ventured, "I haven't had my coffee yet this morning, would you join me? There's a good bakery around the corner." He waited for the rebuff.

"Love to," she said. "I've heard of mad book collectors before, but I never have met one. Ah! Here is the concierge's key. Alors, you give it to her."

The landlady took the key through the crack in the chained door and hauled it back into the safety of the commercials and cabbage of her apartment. The hairy man in the undershirt hadn't moved away from the tube.

"Ya want the apartment? Either of you?"

"No," said the Frenchwoman, "merci, but it's too large for me."

Madam Sauerkraut frowned more deeply. "And you?"

"I don't know, I'll let you know if I want it."

"Okay," she snorted as she closed the door in his face.

Out in the sunshine Eric's companion said, "Did you tell her you were apartment hunting?"

"Well, sort of. I wanted to find Hartman but I thought it was easier not to go into the whole story with her."

"Eh bien, a deceiver of the innocent!" Her very deep blue eyes glinted in the strong Saturday sunlight, and a mischievous smile crossed her face. "Perhaps this bakery is not real either?"

"Oh no, it is," he protested, so seriously that he didn't realize he was being teased until she began to laugh, the humor, with Eric as its butt, breaking all through her face and eyes in a sudden eruption.

"In fact, they have the best croissants and brioches in town, and excellent coffee."

"Wonderful! Which way, corrupter of the innocent?"

"You've really got me wrong," he protested again. She began to laugh again and the sparkle broke through her face.

Instantly infatuated. An experience he had never had before, and it embarrassed him.

"We'll go to Mrs. Krim's, here on Third Avenue and 81st Street. This way. I'm Eric Newman, by the way," he said, hoping he wasn't blushing.

"Odette," she said, holding out her hand. "Odette des Chavannes."

"Related to Puvis des Chavannes?"

"Oui, in fact my grandfather's brother—'great uncle' I think you call it in English."

"Wait a second!" Eric was startled. "The journalist?"

She smiled acknowledgment with her eyes. What a coincidence this was, Eric thought. He had read her articles for years—often in *La Nouvelle Observateur*, *L'Express* or *Le Monde* and occasionally in *The New Republic*. And thought of her as the world's best interviewer.

At Mrs. Krim's he ordered croissants, but Odette wanted a bagel.

"When in New York, do as . . ."

"Romans do."

She was a good listener, and Eric liked to make her smile. He told her about his biography of Raven and about the difficulties of writing it.

"The academic writers are always so . . ."—she searched for a word—"bound up, constrained to make each word perfect and documented. They—you—should take a lesson from us. There's nothing like having to meet a deadline to make you write. 'Go with what you've got' is what *we* say. You'll never know everything."

She told him that she was in New York for a story, and *L'Express* had also offered her a New York correspondent's post. Part of her considering it had to do with looking over the apartment possibilities. "But it is so *cher*, dear, here to live."

"Paris isn't cheap either," he said.

"Yes, but there is value for the money. That apartment we looked at has no . . . charm, only space. Not for me. I like atmosphere. Just to live in a box anywhere isn't enough."

"Where do you live in Paris?"

"On a little street, near the Eiffel Tower, by the Champs de Mars . . . and you?"

"Near Columbia, where I teach, but I may move." He explained that his job depended on finishing the book.

"You Americans, always moving. In France we have a place for a long time: we don't change every two years."

"Here we move, get married, divorce, get another job, move, marry again, divorce, change jobs, and so on. A regular routine."

"Now you are teasing me," she laughed. He loved the sound of it, and saw himself in Paris with her, laughing forever. Maybe he could teach at the Sorbonne? "Finish the friggin' book," Drake's voice echoed in his mind.

"Okay, okay," Eric answered him, exasperated, aloud.

"Okay, okay, what?" she asked, puzzled at his outburst, and embarrassing him.

"I'm sorry, I was answering the voice of conscience, of my boss at the University . . . of doom, you might say," he said.

She shrugged her shoulders. "A long time ago I learned that there is more wisdom in insecurity. Otherwise one grows stale and ceases to try to exceed onself . . . and for a creative person, that's death. There are plenty of jobs for bright people, and no one with talent starves."

"I wish I could feel that way, but I'm afraid to let that umbilical cord get cut," Eric said, resisting French pith and aphorism with the pseudopsychology his generation was famous for.

"You're not alone," she responded, "and look at the dependence that attitude has produced around the world—full of clients, for welfare, for everything. Entire nations become that way, losing a sense of initiative, having their lives smothered in that deceptive womb."

Her eyes glittered with fervor as she spoke, and Eric knew that here was not only a beautiful body, but a fine, independent mind. But he had already known that from having read her articles all these years.

"Look," she continued, "I wasn't telling you the . . . truth before."

"About what?" He was surprised by her statement.

"About looking for an apartment. I'm not. I'm looking for Hartman too!"

He was really surprised. "But why, and why the business of

apartment hunting and all that? Are you really Odette des Chavannes?" Eric was a bit annoyed because he didn't like being manipulated, for any reason.

"That I am. Do you want to see my credentials?" She began to open her handbag, but he waved her gesture away.

"I wanted to be sure you were who you said before I told you," she continued, "because . . . well, let's say that I'm following up on a story which may be unacceptable to some powerful people, and they might want to prevent me . . ."

It sounded overly cautious, somewhat paranoiac to him, but he let it go. Anyone could look for a book dealer, and here was a way of getting to know this woman better, he thought. Why not?

He called the waitress and ordered two more coffees, stalling for time. Odette lit a cigarette after refusing one of his.

"If I can find Hartman today, I want to see him," Eric said, "but I do have some questions to ask him in private, so if I can locate him, I get to see him alone, first. Is that a deal?"

She agreed, and he took the card he had found and went to the telephone booth at the rear of Mrs. Krim's.

It took ten minutes of being shunted from one extension to another to get the right person on the line but finally a Mr. Ten Hagen said, "You know, Dr. Newman, we don't give out information on our clients except to authorized agencies, such as police, insurance investigators and the like."

"I know, Mr. Hagen."

"Ten Hagen," he said.

"I'm sorry, Mr. Ten Hagen,"—Eric imagined him correcting people fifty times a day—"but it's strictly a business, not a personal matter. I'm a researcher. Mr. Hartman has some information I need for a book, and I simply want to locate him. Your company moved him, so short of a police investigation, which I can't authorize, or a private detective, which I can't afford, only you can help."

"Well," said Mr. Ten Hagen, softening, "let me call you back."

Eric gave him the number, told the waitress he expected a call and went back to look at Odette and dream of climbing Everest on the Eiffel Tower.

Fifteen minutes later Ten Hagen called back. "We checked

you out," he said with a touch of pride. "You're *bona fide* all right."

Eric was glad to know it, he said. "How did you do that?"

"Oh, we have our own security service. They do a good job."

Comforted that his validation as a legitimate person was readily available, even to a moving company, Eric asked for the address.

"It's in Brooklyn. 527 Henry Street. That's in Brooklyn Heights."

Eric thanked Mr. Ten Hagen and said that if he should move he'd use Ten Hagen's confidential company and hung up.

Information had no number for Hartman. They had installed a phone but said it was unlisted. Eric would have to go see him.

On the subway ride to Brooklyn, Odette told him that Hartman was a link to someone from years ago, who might be connected to her story on torture in Chile.

"He knows a lot of people," Eric explained over the clattering roar of the Lexington Avenue subway they took to Brooklyn. "Rare book dealers are often like that—moles themselves, but everyone who collects seeks them out, and they have extensive contacts."

She nodded but didn't answer in the noise of the rushing train.

What a coincidence he thought, that he had met her like this. Maybe he would go to Paris come summer vacation, visit Nick and see this beautiful animal in her natural habitat. Another one of those people who seemed to get out and seize the world, while Eric sat like a mole and fed off bushels of details in other people's lives, other souls' musings, and other countries' doings. He meant to ask her if she had ever met Nick Burns in Paris, but forgot to because they had come to the station, and he was growing excited with the assignment he had to carry out, for himself, and *mutatis mutandis,* for his country. He felt like a secret patriot.

The sycamore trees lining the streets of Brooklyn Heights were already bare of leaves and the mottled bark looked tired and defeated. The old turn of the century brownstones were mostly well cared for because the neighborhood's face was being lifted by the younger professional and *New York* magazine types who were buying, remodeling or renting houses and apartments. It was a cutting edge; a landmark area where the people were taking a stand against encroaching slumward pressures.

527 looked like most of the other houses on Henry Street, except that the ground floor had been turned into a garage. The stoop was removed and the hallway was at ground level. In front of the driveway a telephone company van idled, the driver inside writing on a clipboard.

Eric rang the bell marked M. Hartman. No answer. He rang again. Waited. Odette was patient, saying nothing. A short, fat woman came in from the street with a grocery bag.

"Can I help you young folks?" she asked.

She didn't look much older than Eric, but he didn't need to enlighten her, and said only that he was looking for Mr. Hartman and would like to knock on his door in case the bell down here wasn't working properly. Would she let them in to go up and check?

"You don't look like muggers to me, but I really shouldn't . . . I suppose there's no harm," she decided after some hesitation. She took out her key, declining Eric's offer to hold her package, fumbled the lock open, and let them into the hallway.

"He's up on the third floor," and she walked to the rear of the ground floor, opened her apartment door, and disappeared.

They climbed the carpeted stair lit by small bulbs in wall fixtures which had been converted to electric from gaslight jets and reached the third floor.

MAX HARTMAN—RARE BOOKS AND MANUSCRIPTS was printed on an index card held to the paneled oak door by a bright green thumbtack. There was no buzzer. A knock moved the door in an inch.

"Mr. Hartman," Eric called, pushing on the handle, "Mr. Hartman, are you here?"

No answer. He stood there for a few seconds and called the name again. "Wait here," he told Odette, and walked into the apartment. A radio was playing classical music in the room to his left. Maybe Hartman didn't hear because the music was very loud.

"Mr. Hartman?" Eric walked into the room. Books and papers were strewn everywhere. On the floor were dishevelled heaps of papers, and all the books had been pulled off the shelves and thrown on the floor.

In the middle of the unlit room, Hartman sat in a desk chair facing Eric across a small table, staring. In the center of his forehead was an oozing red crater, and where the back of his head should have been, it wasn't! Spattered blood, bone, and grayish slime covered the back of the chair where his head rested.

Eric had never seen a man with his brains blown out. His body went cold and he started trembling. Was the killer hiding in the closet to kill him and Odette too? The vomit started up in his throat. He swallowed it and then he screamed and bolted out of the room into the hall. Odette had run in when Eric screamed, and he almost knocked her over. "He's been murdered," Eric yelled, "let's get out of here." He grabbed her arm and yanked her after him down the stairs, stumbling. Eric was terrified that the killer was up there and coming after them.

When they got to the street the phone company truck was still there. He would know how to get the police. These trucks had shortwave radios, Eric thought.

He pounded on the door. The driver turned his attention from his clipboard and looked at them. It was the President!

"My God, this is crazy."

The President stared at Eric, his face fixed in one expression. The driver was wearing one of those lifelike rubber masks which pull over the head.

"Open up and stop fucking around! We need help! There's been a murder!" Eric yelled.

The driver turned his masked face away and suddenly accelerated out of the parking space onto the street and sped away.

Eric began to run in the same direction, and Odette hurried after him toward a phone booth on the corner. He dived into it and dialed 911.

"New York City Emergency Unit," a woman's voice answered. "Hold on please." Just then he noticed a police car rounding the corner onto Henry Street, shoved the phone at Odette and ran into the roadway toward the car.

"Help! Police!"

They stopped.

"There's been a murder," Eric shouted into the window at a young blond cop with a mustache.

"What? Where?" he asked.

His partner, a beefy older cop, had jumped out of the opposite door meanwhile.

"Hartman's head is blown off and the President drove away in a telephone truck."

"Oh man, another loony—the President of the U.S. of A?" said the beefy cop. "C'mere." He walked around the car and took Eric's arm in a vise grip, steering him to the curb. The blond cop doubled-parked and got out also.

Odette came over.

"You with him, lady?" the young cop asked her.

"Yes."

"And you saw the victim?" he questioned.

"No, she didn't," Eric butted in, "but she was with me . . . and I went in . . . and he was smiling . . ." He couldn't get the words out. His mouth moved, but nothing came.

"Calm down, buddy," said the young cop. "Billy, let his arm go."

"Officer, I'm not crazy." They couldn't understand the urgency!

"Okay, sure, fella."

"Where did this happen?"

"Just up the block, I'll show you."

"And you think the President did it?"

"Yes . . . no . . . I mean . . . a mask on the telephone guy . . . the truck drove away."

"All right, relax. You just show us where, and then we'll have a nice talk," said the blond mustache. "Can you take me to the body now?"

"Of course I can. Right there in the middle of the block, number 257, I mean 527."

"Billy, bring the car."

"Man," said the beefy one, "lotsa nuts on this beat!"

Eric saw the mustache unsnap the guard on his holster as they walked toward Hartman's house. Odette looked calm and subdued but Eric's heart was pounding so loudly that he thought everyone could hear it.

* * *

It wasn't until late afternoon that the police let them go. At the station house they had to repeat the story four different times: to the officers who had gone into the apartment, guns drawn, to verify the cause of their fear; to the precinct captain; and to two teams of detectives. The detectives checked Eric's account of how he had gotten the address from the moving company—he was sure Mr. Ten Hagen would never give out such information again, even after a security check—called the French consulate to check on Odette, and finally let Eric make a phone call.

He called Lucy at his apartment because he thought she'd be waiting and didn't want her to worry, but there was no answer. She must have given up on him and gone out.

Then he remembered that he was temporarily a government secret agent, but he couldn't tell the cops that. He called Nick at his folks' house.

"Hartman's what?" When Eric started to tell Nick the story, he cut him off, saying the phone wasn't such a good idea, and asked just where Eric was.

Nick arrived in half an hour and walked into the lounge area of the detective squad room where Odette and Eric sat waiting.

"Nick!" she cried, leaping to her feet and running to embrace him. It was Eric's second great shock for the day.

"You two know each other?" he asked, gawking like an idiot. "This is crazy!"

"For years," Odette said, "from Paris."

"That's what I do there, Eric. Press Liaison," Nick said, as if he didn't know. Eric thought Nick was telling him to play mum.

"But you two?" It was Odette's turn to be incredulous.

"For years," Eric mimicked, only conscious that he was doing so as it came out: "from college!"

She blushed. Not the slightest dishevelment or strain had shown on her all through the day, which had been a real ordeal for Eric, and not a hair out of place on that cool, professional head in the face of a brutal murder, the endless questions from the police—who seemed to imply that Eric and Odette had killed him—but now, standing in the grungy Brooklyn station house, between Nick and Eric, a vivid rose flush covered her cheeks and forehead, like an embarrassed schoolgirl.

"How did you get here, and involved in this?" Nick asked her, sounding a little annoyed.

"I'll explain later," she said, "after we leave this awful place. Are you here to help or to continue the questioning?"

Nick didn't answer her, but excused himself and made for the door. As he opened it, he beckoned to Eric and said in an undertone, "Not a word about your doing any of this for me. As far as she's concerned, it's all your initiative. Got it?"

"Yeah boss," Eric answered in a tone he didn't think Nick liked. Did he think that Eric was so stupid that he had to tell him? Eric had seen enough spy movies to know better.

Whatever Nick did or said while he was out of the room, it was effective, and ten minutes later the three left the station house. Eric felt washed out.

Nick drove them back to the city; he had his parents' Mercedes, and the luxury of being driven home after the ordeal was welcome indeed.

"Isn't that wild with the guy in the phone company van. In a mask? Weird sense of humor," Eric said, yawning in the backseat. He noticed an exchange of looks between Nick and Odette, but couldn't make out why . . . and he had no reason to ask, so let it go.

He dropped her off first, on Central Park West and 68th Street. "Au revoir, Eric," she said, getting out of the car, and as though to anticipate his next question, she tore off a page from her notebook and wrote a number. "Call me tomorrow when you've rested."

He didn't want rest, he wanted her, but there was no choice.

No sooner had she entered the building where she was staying —in a friend's apartment, she said—than Nick began to ply him with questions: how he had met her, just what she had said; he wanted all the details.

"She wanted to see Hartman about Goldfeder too?" He didn't believe it. "How could she find out about him?" he wondered aloud.

Eric certainly didn't know. But then, he couldn't figure out what Nick wanted the information for either, and he was too exhausted to ask.

"What a way to earn a living," Eric said as Nick drew the car up in front of the apartment house on 113th Street.

"You wanted adventure and excitement, pal," Nick retorted.

"So soon and so much?"

"Just think of the fringe benefits," he quipped, then copied Odette's number and drove away.

* * *

Eric couldn't believe the mess in the apartment. He thought that Lucy must have had a fit of anger because he had stayed away so long. What with Hartman's brains blown out and the cops and all that, he had forgotten Lucy after his first attempt to call. The place looked like Hartman's without the body. Books and papers strewn everywhere in the living room. The cushions were off the couch and everything had been pulled out of the storage cabinets. The bedroom was worse: each drawer had been emptied and the bedding was all off the bed.

Then he heard some banging from the bathroom. Horace? He opened the door. The smell of shit was awful. Horace leapt out, but lying gagged in the bathtub trussed up like a steer for branding, Lucy had been kicking her feet against the wall to get attention. The smell came from her!

After Eric untied her and helped her out of the tub, she hugged him hard, clutching him as though to crush his breath away. He had to hold it anyway.

"Oh God, Eric, I was so frightened; I thought you'd come home by noon. I couldn't move in there and was worried they'd come back."

He stood there not knowing what to say. It was almost seven o'clock.

"What happened? Who did this?" was all he could manage in his stammering mouth.

"Two men. I had just gotten up—about ten o'clock. Saw your note and was making some breakfast, thinking you would be home or call, and the stereo was playing loud. I turned around and they were there. They must have had a key."

"What kind of men were they?"

"One minute, Eric—let me clean myself." He closed the bathroom door and went into the living room, cleared away some stuff, threw the cushions onto the couch and sat down.

"Would you get me a glass of wine and put on some water for coffee?" she asked, when she came in, showered and wearing his bathrobe.

She knocked the red wine down in one gulp, lit a cigarette, and said, "They were Latinos. Spoke English but with an accent . . . I don't know."

"Did they hurt you?"

"No, not at all. They tied me up right away. The phone rang and they wouldn't let me answer. I heard it ringing later but I didn't know when—after they had gone."

"It must have been me," Eric interrupted. "I called to say I'd had to go to Brooklyn."

"Well, anyway," she went on, ignoring his attempt to excuse the absence, "they were polite. They asked me where you kept the manuscript. I thought they meant for your book, and I told them it was at your office. They said I was not being truthful, they knew there was a copy. And they started to go through everything, pulling all the books and papers off the shelves, as you see.

" 'If you tell us where it is, you'll save a lot of trouble,' one of them said. I told him that as far as I knew your book's manuscript was at your office. They said no, they meant the Raven manuscript, the notebook. I didn't know what you had done with it, and said so. They asked me about a copy, a Xerox, and I said I didn't know. So they put me in the bathtub, gagged me and then did what you see. I guess they didn't find it—or did they?"

Eric wouldn't know if the spare copy was missing until he cleaned up but he knew the original was safe. He withdrew the notebook from his jacket pocket.

"I have it with me. I took it home from the office yesterday to put away in a safe place."

"So you're carrying around that manuscript that someone is ready to kill for? You're mad!"

"No! I brought it home from the office to put in a safe deposit box on Monday morning."

"What time is it?"

"Almost eight."

"My God! I was in that tub for ten hours. Should we call the police?"

"I guess so; I don't know. What else did they take?"

"It's hard to tell—we'll have to clean up first." She shuddered at the thought.

"No, first some coffee."

He made the brew and they sat and drank it among the debris. He felt sorry for her. Really lousy. What started as a sidetrack was turning into a road to hell, and he was afraid now that someone innocent might get hurt because of him. Eric wanted to drop the whole thing. If Columbia would let him go, okay, he'd get a job elsewhere and just teach and live; let the ghost of Harry Raven go fuck itself, and not his life.

"Police?" she asked.

Eric called the local precinct and then called Nick, who made him promise to get the safe deposit box on Monday. "And keep your mouth shut about it. No more copies either; just take notes from the original, at the bank only."

"Seems too cautious to me, Nick."

"You really are a dunce, Eric," he said angrily. "You have living proof that someone is after that material, is willing to take criminal action to get it, even the copies, and you wonder about too much caution! You want to wind up like Hartman?"

"Okay, okay, I'll put it away in the bank." Sacrilege aside, Eric would have burned the goddamned thing if he could have overcome scholarly inhibition.

For the second time in one day, New York's Finest came to the rescue: the police seemed to be more suspicious of the victims than of the looters, especially when Eric told them that nothing seemed to be missing.

Lucy remembered that both men wore gloves, and the patrolmen made it clear that since there was no robbery involved, "just assault," except for some photocopies "of no market value," the case would probably end with the report they made.

One cop did them a favor and explained, "There ain't even no fingerprints, so whatta we got to go on? Two guys tied ya up and messed up the place. You sure they wasn't lookin' for more than papers?" He looked knowingly at his partner to make it clear to Eric and Lucy that they were suspected as kingpins of a multi-million dollar international drug conspiracy, and then left, telling the couple that the detective division would call to follow up the initial report.

Eric looked at the mess again and let out a disheartened groan. Lucy, slightly more composed than she had seemed before the police arrived, went into the kitchen and returned with the bottle of wine and two glasses. She sat down next to him on the partly reassembled couch, where he slouched with his feet up on the coffee table.

"I didn't have such a great day either," he groaned, wondering just how much he could tell her. He knew he'd have to leave Odette out.

When they finished cleaning up, the looters' purpose was confirmed. The Xerox copy of the Raven manuscript was gone, but there were some unexpected benefits: a lot of stuff went into the incinerator, and the apartment looked orderly for the first time in months. Lucy seemed particularly pleased.

"That ought to last a few days," Lucy said.

"Only if I'm not here," Eric answered. "C'mon, let's go out to eat."

The detectives hadn't called yet.

They ate empanadas and drank cheap wine at a local Chilean restaurant, open late for the Columbia crowd on Saturday night. As he told her about Hartman, Eric felt sorry for and protective of Lucy, yet he wanted to be angry with her so that he could run after Odette with a clear conscience. But Lucy ate the food and looked at him so lovingly that he felt guilty—confused. How could he do this? He must be mad to eschew such love and devotion. Suddenly he wanted her. Usually Eric went along for the ride, a willing victim of Lucy's high level of lust.

"For dessert I want you," he told her as the waiter cleared the table. She flushed with pleasure.

"I haven't heard you say that in ages," she said, reaching out and running her fingers through his hair. "Let's go; I'm twitching already."

Eric could never accuse Lucy of being coy. Their energetic lovemaking flooded the night, engulfing them with need, and in the midst of it all, Eric wondered where all the complications were going to land him, and why bother when life could be so simple, so easy.

8

BARNWELL STOOD at the window, staring out at the rainsoaked streets and Washington Square Park, deserted that morning except for a woman walking a poodle. Nick watched his back and waited for an answer. He had asked that Newman be dropped as "consultant." The idea that Eric and Odette might have been killed if they had gotten to Brooklyn half an hour earlier infuriated him. Now could Barnwell use a private citizen in that way? Nick was paid to take risks, and he was aware of them. But Eric? He was a pawn in this game, and almost a sacrificial one at that. Barnwell, it seemed, had a passion for the game but no compassion for the pieces he moved around at will.

Barnwell turned to face him. "Explain to me again how Odette des Chavannes came to be looking for Hartman," he said, not answering Nick's request.

Nick reiterated what Odette had told him when he went back to see her after leaving Eric at his apartment.

"All from having Goldfeder's name?" the director asked.

"Yes." Nick had just told Barnwell that he had thrown the name as a sop to her investigative hunger, and she had run down the information in old newspaper accounts of the scientist's disappearance.

"Which I understand to mean," Nick went on, "that anyone with some rudimentary knowledge of research could come up with the same data; it's wide open."

"It was your error, despite what you said about her being ready to trade information," Barnwell said, judgmental as God and not to be swerved.

"It's public domain data, sir," Nick protested.

"There's no point in belaboring it now," Barnwell continued, ignoring his protest. "The question is whether she's discreet and if we can continue to use her."

"In addition to Eric—that's crazy! They're both amateurs and up against professionals—"

"Who *aren't* after them," the director cut in, "and moreover, they are both professionals at research, better than we've got. No, I think that as long as we run some kind of defense for each of them, they'll lead us to where we want to go more quickly than we can get there ourselves."

There was no point arguing, Nick knew. The director would authorize baby-sitters for both Eric and Odette, and that gave Nick some relief, however small.

"What now for Newman?" Nick asked.

"He's got to press Ben Winkler about Goldfeder's disappearance. You can show Newman these." He handed Nick two old-fashioned sepia tone picture postcards mailed from Argentina. Each one had an innocuous message of the having-a-wonderful-time-wish-you-were-here variety. No signature.

"Any meaning I should know?"

"I doubt it, but it's a carrot for Newman we found among Hartman's things . . . show him this too," he handed Nick a folder stamped *Eyes Only*. "Oh yes, and as far as the names in this manuscript are concerned,"—Nick had given it to Barnwell the day he saw Eric, before going back to Forest Hills—"tell him they're in the computer, you'll get the printout tomorrow, in Washington."

"Washington?" The bastard loved surprises.

"In the Secretary's office at two o'clock. I want you to be present at a meeting he's set up."

Barnwell wouldn't tell him with whom the meeting was, and Nick knew better than to ask. He left the director watching the Sunday rain, and went into an adjacent office to telephone his sacrificial lambs.

* * *

Odette stood in front of Picasso's "Guernica" on the second floor of the Museum of Modern Art. Seeing the painting was like a pilgrimage for her whenever she was in New York, and today it seemed to have a special significance. For her there was an analogy between the civil war in Spain and what had just happened in Chile: the fascists inside were helped by the fascists outside to massacre an innocent population. She wasn't so naive as to attribute all good to the left and all bad to the right; she knew that the intellectuals had wanted another Cuba. They were blind too . . . but she was still sympathetic to their dreams of justice, if not the maneuvers toward it.

All Europe understood what had happened there, just as they had seen it in Spain in 1936. But here, in the States, they were oblivious to the consequences of fascism, willfully, as long as it stayed abroad. She walked to one side, then the other of the enormous canvas, the horror of the mutilated forms impressing itself deeper on her consciousness than ever before.

When Nick telephoned earlier, she was on her way out the door and told him to meet her at MOMA in front of the "Guernica." What better way to spend a rainy Sunday afternoon in New York than trying to alter the warped values of an American diplomat—and she had a question or two to ask him about Eric, who seemed so nice but was probably a spy like his friend.

She was being too harsh. Eric's fright when he saw that murdered man was real, he was not acting. Probably not an agent. But the two men, what an unlikely duo of friends. Something wasn't right, and she was going to find out.

"Getting worked up about the imperialist warmongers of Wall Street increasing their swollen profits at the expense of the suffering masses?" Nick asked, alongside her.

She hadn't seen him come in and stand there. She turned to look at her handsome companion, looking casual and debonair as usual, in a turtleneck sweater and tweed jacket, smiling at her with a faint touch of irony around the eyes.

"How could you tell, you servant of the exploiters?"

"By the set of your mouth and the anger on your face. I've been watching you for a few minutes," Nick said, taking her arm and walking into the next room.

"Then you really are a spy, as I always knew," she laughed and squeezed his hand. She *was* happy in his company, despite the pain of the past.

"I want to spy on the Motherwell they just bought," Nick said. He had a catalogue in his hand and had evidently looked at it before coming upstairs.

"Frivolous," Odette said, "like you, mon cher." She saw her chance for the edification of his social conscience going by the boards. A French shrug of the shoulders said that she recognized the futility of further discussion with an ineducable such as he, and she relented, walking with him toward the next gallery.

"This Eric, he works for your government too?" she asked as they ambled past the Jackson Pollock painting she hated. A middle-aged bearded man stood looking at it, belching aloud.

Nick turned to her as though he didn't believe the question. "Not at all. He's strictly an academician. But that's a good idea. Thanks. I'll ask him to drop all his other interests and bore himself to death with journalists who ask silly questions. Why do you want to know?"

She knew he would lie even if it were so; he used sarcasm to intimidate.

"Because there is something lovely, naif . . . something very soft and gentle about him. I like that in a man," Odette answered, realizing that she hadn't intended to say anything about her response to Eric at all. There had been no advance by him, nothing to indicate that he had any interest at all. And here she was telling his friend, her former lover, about her attraction. Could she trust Nick? Emotionally, she decided, but not politically. "I'm sorry I said that," she continued. "I don't mean to hurt your feelings."

He looked surprised. "Couldn't happen to a nicer guy!" Nick said.

Odette caught the ambiguity of the words and then decided not to push for clarification. She liked the uncertainty of the words; it was something special about English, and she let the answer hang in the air.

After Motherwell and Pollock, Gottlieb, Rothko, Louis and the other abstract expressionists Nick was so fond of, she needed a cup of coffee, and they found a table near the window in the garden level cafe.

"Are you staying on this story?" Nick asked as he sat down with the two steaming mugs of black coffee.

"Of course I am. How else can I succeed in proving to the world how conniving and deceitful your government is?" Odette answered, sipping her coffee and taking a box of Gitanes from her bag. Nick refused one, as usual.

"In this case you're wrong," he answered. "If that device exists at all, *we* didn't put it there, and I want to know who did."

"I knew you were a spy," she said, smiling.

"No," he didn't smile this time or joke, "I have to tell the press the truth, that's my job, and I have to know what's true first."

"Even though I don't believe a word you say, Nicholas," Odette said, leaning across the table and giving him a kiss on the cheek, "you're a marvelous liar, and so forgiven in recognition of your fine art!"

"We can help each other," he said. "Both looking for the same thing, so why don't we cooperate?"

"To what extent?"

"Exchanging information, noncompromising, of course."

Odette pulled her glasses down from their perch atop her hair to rest on the bridge of her nose, and looked out at the soaked garden with the Rodin statue of Balzac. Then she swung her head toward Nick, and looked at him hard. "If I had *his* magnitude as a person, as a writer, I would tell you to go to hell," she said to Nick, wondering why she didn't do it anyway, "but since I haven't a hope, okay." She smiled, but sadly, at this betrayal, at the political gaucherie of her acceptance: expedience trumped the ideal once again.

"Don't fret," Nick said, placing his hand over hers on the table, "you'll get your story this way."

"Certainement, by selling out," Odette retorted, already regretting her agreement.

Nick looked thoughtful and then said, "Wasn't it one of your left sages who said that 'freedom is the recognition of necessity'?"

"Engels," she answered, "but he meant it in a different context."

"Well, it applies here," Nick answered, "for both of us."

He took her to dinner at the Palm restaurant, and by agreement, talked of nothing but other people. She learned a lot about Eric.

* * *

Eric and Nick were sitting in Eric's office at Columbia. Nick had come up on Monday as planned when he'd called the previous morning.

Eric looked up from the documents he was examining. "Oh, almost forgot," he said to Nick and handed him a key. "Spare to the safe deposit I rented." He wrote the box number and address on an index card and shoved it across the desk.

"What about these papers?" Nick asked.

"He sounds like a nut!" Eric blurted. "Out of his tree. Are you sure they're his?"

"I know so little about this stuff, you wouldn't believe it. You wanted some material? Here it begins!" Nick said.

Eric could hardly believe the documents Nick had brought. Ben Winkler's letters to Rockefeller when he headed the Inter-American Affairs Committee during World War II sounded like the controlled ravings of a paranoid. Phrases stuck in his mind—he couldn't copy them, only look. Nick said there was clearance because the stuff was so dated, but could not get copy authorization. Eric skimmed the file ". . . connection between the mind-reading machine and the death of a great literary figure. A personal interview is . . ."

Winkler had also written that he had information about a spy ring he had uncovered, which he was reluctant to include in a letter: "A personal interview is . . . I will come to Washington . . ." Old Ben had wanted to rub elbows with power and authority, it seemed, but his very pink background gave the big boys an excuse to ignore him.

"This is a shitload of nonsense," was the expert opinion.

"Is that all the brilliant young scholar, biographer of great poets, consultant to his government, can say?" Nick asked.

"And you're a friend?" Eric asked. "How could you possibly know that I needed more leads to make my life miserable? I have too much information already. If I start chasing Winkler down, I'm really sunk."

"You're chasing already," Nick shot back. "Don't bullshit me, and this is for money, not love. You don't *have* to do it!"

"Yeah, but Raven, not Ben Winkler. So he was a nut, saw connections between his friend's death—and I presume that is what he's referring to—and a mind-reading machine. What kind of science fiction crap is that? And spy rings? Oh, man!"

Eric realized that he might have hurt Nick's feelings, mocking when Nick thought he was helping.

"I thought it might help, but I guess not," Nick muttered, slouching more than usual in his chair. "How could you follow this up if you wanted to? Would you ask Winkler?"

"Not at first," Eric answered. "I'd need a more solid base for questions, so I'd look at his papers—journals, letters, stuff like that. Actually, I've seen some already, mostly letters he wrote to Raven."

"Where are Winkler's papers?"

"He gave all his papers to Penn, his alma mater. Look, Nick, it's interesting, but I may not follow it up—I'm halfway up the creek already—any more diversions and I'll be high and dry."

"Don't you want to know how Rockefeller responded?"

"I can't stop you from telling me—out with it, man."

"He agreed to see Winkler . . . in October of 1943 and apparently heard him out. Afterward Rockefeller wrote or dictated a memorandum of his conversation, I've got it." He produced a several-page Xerox copy bearing the letterhead of the Inter-American Affairs Committee.

Eric glanced at it. Three pages of single space typing.

"Take it with you."

"Isn't this secret stuff?"

"Nope. It's in the National Archives. Public record, not classified."

"Good research for an amateur," Eric teased him.

"Maybe I want your job," Nick answered, polishing his pipe on his aquiline nose and taking out his packet of tobacco. "I need some adventure in my life."

It was exciting, Eric had to admit. Despite the nightmare scare of finding Hartman, and the business with Lucy being roughed up and the apartment ransacked, he was exhilarated, but fearful.

"Look, Nick," he said, "I'll go down to Philadelphia this afternoon to look at Winkler's stuff, but I don't want to get killed because I get in someone's way. What if I had been home when those creeps came in? What would I have done?"

"In the first place," Nick answered, "you wouldn't resist. Give them what they ask for. Your safety's not worth the paper. Secondly, it won't happen again. So don't worry."

"How can you say that I shouldn't worry? I've stepped into the middle of something I don't understand. Why me?"

"You wanted adventure and excitement," Nick teased, "and anyway, knowing you, following this out is what you'd do even if I hadn't asked you to. Besides, you've plenty of insurance."

"Only about twenty-five thousand dollars from the University, and if anything happens, that's not much for my kids' future."

"Eric, that's a simpy, middle-aged excuse. I don't buy it, not from you!" Nick said vehemently. "And if it sets your mind at ease, the big Uncle covers you while you do this consulting. If you're beaned, next of kin will get two hundred fifty thousand dollars."

"That's comforting—to be factored by ten. Now I know my worth."

Nick looked annoyed with the sarcasm, Eric rushed to reassure him. "I'm not being sarcastic just to needle you, Nick. I'm concerned about my kids if I'm gone."

"Eric, you are quite simply full of shit. Face it. You were never a devoted father and you haven't changed. I'm not putting you down, just observing that you become a family man when it's convenient—as an excuse. You don't have to do this for me, or for the government, if you don't want to. But I'm your friend, whichever way you go, and I don't like when you bullshit yourself and think that it'll work on me . . . and I don't have to be polite with you. Come off it."

Nick had always been able to get to Eric's sensitive spot. He knew Eric's routine too well. Eric backed off a bit: "Maybe I'm the wrong one for adventure and excitement. That's your department." He could see himself wriggling, uncomfortably, but there *was* a fear in him, and he was doing his best to say so without saying so. Eric was kvetching and knew it; so did Nick.

"Wait a minute, my dear friend," Nick retorted quickly. "I don't spend my days piecing together the mystery of another man's life; I don't find clues, missing manuscripts, discover corpses, track down people and information, etcetera." He snorted. "You're the sleuth, not me. If you think living in Paris is more exciting than New York, or that spending days arranging for the Women's Glee Club of Purdue University to perform in some lycée, or fending off hungry journalists who need sensational copy to justify their big expense accounts is exciting and adventurous—you're mad!"

Eric felt a little intimidated by his vehemence and looked down, toying with a pencil.

"I suppose, Nick, that somewhere deep inside I'm not happy with things as they are, but afraid of what's different. I can lose myself in the work, but sometimes wonder for what; I don't even know if I want the rewards I'm supposed to want."

Nick looked grave. "Seems to me," he said, "that you've become a lonely hunter . . . and aren't we all, deep down. You're just closer to it. I bet you can work through it. Just bag this last quarry, and then who knows? Maybe you'll take up another sport, and stop collecting trophies. I think you're just depressed: why not? You're under pressure to produce, you're torn by a dilemma, and then add the horror of the other day with Hartman. The uncertainty now—that's what the real world is like outside these walls." He continued, "Oh yeah, I forgot the economics of alimony and child support. Man, you've got a weight to carry."

"Then we are full circle," Eric said, "the mortmain again."

* * *

When Nick had left Eric at Columbia shortly after eleven o'clock on Monday morning, he caught a cab for LaGuardia Airport, the noon shuttle for Washington, and with half an hour to spare arrived at the State Department. A container of weak coffee tasting of cardboard and a leaden corn muffin he had brown-bagged onto the plane served as lunch. Whatever he had said to Eric about the disadvantages of France, he missed the small touches already: the crusty bread and rich aromatic coffee; the joie de vivre in small things you didn't find elsewhere.

Barnwell was waiting for him when he got to the Secretary's office. "I'm afraid I brought you down here for nothing," he said, "but I couldn't reach you in time. We were going to meet with Leboulier, the former defense minister in Chile, but he was killed this morning—just about two hours ago, in fact. A bomb in his car up near the DuPont Circle."

Nick waited for the director to continue; he couldn't make a connection yet.

Barnwell looked at him with his ice blue eyes. "And I suppose you saw this morning's paper, and you noticed that General Sepulvida was assassinated in Buenos Aires?"

On the plane Nick had read the report in the *Times* of the machine gun attack on Allende's former chief of staff in Buenos Aires. He had assumed it was part of the mop-up the junta would carry out now to consolidate its power by eliminating any viable alternative leaders in the opposition. The former ambassador, Leboulier, was probably on their list, Nick commented.

"Normally, that would be my assumption too," Barnwell said, "but I think there's something more: Leboulier already had one meeting with the Secretary, and was prepared to testify before a Senate investigations committee. He wanted the Secretary to guarantee Sepulvida's safety if he brought him up here to testify also."

"Testify about what?" Nick was still puzzled.

"About the use of an alphagraph for the interrogation and torture of prisoners in Chile!"

Before Nick could say anything, the receptionist told them to go into the inner office.

The Secretary of State, a short squat man with glasses perched on a small hooked nose reminded Nick of an owl. The Galahad image Barnwell used didn't apply physically, but Nick knew that it was to the amorous, rather than the political reputation that the director alluded. Politically he was a keen and deadly predator, with sharp eyes and a long reach. He seated them across the huge desk and wasted no time opening the subject.

"When Director Barnwell contacted me concerning the use of this ETT by our Chilean friends, I was surprised at the coincidence, because I had learned that Armando Leboulier was preparing to testify to a Senate committee. I felt that his testimony could prove a great embarrassment to our administration and I asked him to see me first, hoping to bring some influence to bear on him, that he might not give the political enemies of our president—who dominate the committee—any more ammunition than they think they have already. Leboulier was to see me today at one o'clock, and I had suggested that Director Barnwell join us at two. The rest you know."

Nick noticed that the Secretary gestured with his hands as he spoke, but clasped them together in front of him as soon as he stopped, fingers interlocked, as though the gesture would restrain him from going on.

"The investigation will take its normal course," the Secretary continued, his hands moving, conducting the orchestration of lives at his disposal, "under the jurisdiction of the local and federal authorities, but lacking further information from Leboulier, and assuming that Sepulvida could have confirmed or amplified that information, I want OMEGA to deal with the problem." He reclasped his hands.

The director looked at Nick and then spoke: "Mr. Secretary, what precisely do you want us to do?"

The owlish man kept his hands together and said, "Investigate, confirm, search and destroy!"

Nick was surprised at the Secretary's mandate, spoken with such a quiet finality. "Isn't such an operation, strictly speaking, the province of Central Intelligence?" he asked.

The Secretary stared at him, eyes hard and unblinking for a moment, then replied, "Mr. Burns, I am told you are OMEGA's best. You are here at your director's request and enjoy, I assume, his complete confidence. I am breaching no faith, therefore, if I tell you that CIA has some very close ties with the Chilean military government, and I could not guarantee the security of any such operation I might authorize through them. Those aware of *this* operation are confined to this room, at the moment. If it succeeds, your government will be grateful; if it fails, it will not. In either case, we will deny any responsibility, and no one will be wiser for it. For our own reasons, we are excluding any other agency from access to the information. It must remain that way."

He stood, walked around the desk and extended his hand to Barnwell and then to Nick. "Gentlemen—thank you," was all he said. They were dismissed.

Barnwell didn't speak until they were out of the building and in the staff car carrying them to the airport. "You heard the man," he said. "Any comment?"

"A needle in a haystack," Nick said. The battle lines were fuzzy. "I don't like working against our own," he told Barnwell.

"It's an order," Barnwell grumbled, "and I didn't give it. You were there too. We don't have a choice." He didn't seem particularly pleased by the turn of events. OMEGA was being handed an enormous job, bypassing the Agency. And they wouldn't be happy . . . might even get in the way. It meant a lot of juggling. Tricky, uncomfortable. Only success would be acceptable, but how to begin, and with what approach?

"I'm convinced," Barnwell said, as they got out of the car and walked into the airport terminal after a virtual silence of fifteen minutes in the taxi, "I'm convinced that what we've started with Newman will get us to that proverbial needle faster than by any other means. Let's see what he gets at. Meanwhile, we'll try to find out what's behind the assassinations."

" 'We,' I suppose means me?" Nick asked, sitting down on an irritatingly bright blue plastic bench. Someone's idea of waiting room "friendliness." But Nick had more than blue plastic seats to be annoyed with. Barnwell had just destroyed all vestiges of home-leave.

"But . . . in Chile," Nick said as they filed toward the boarding gate at the flight call. "Who helps there, without complications we don't want? Or am I a solitaire without support?"

"Our friends at Defense," Barnwell muttered, stepping onto the boarding ladder, "and maybe a bit of assistance from 'The Company'—baby-sitters, and so on—but we'll have to keep them at arm's length. You heard the man."

9

Philadelphia

"WHAT A FLURRY of interest there has been in Mr. Winkler's papers lately!" said the white-haired librarian at the University of Pennsylvania's Book and Manuscript Room as she took the file boxes back over the desk to return to the storage area. When Eric handed her the Xerox request forms, she took off her tortoiseshell glasses and let them hang from the ribbon around her neck.

"But you're the only one who wanted copies made. I do hope this is the beginning of a Winkler revival! He is such a nice man. He deserves better than the neglect he has gotten."

Eric asked if she knew who the other visitors were.

"Oh, I'm afraid I can't say, other than Mr. Winkler himself who dropped in for a chat last week. We keep all the names of researchers in our record book, the one you signed before—that is, when they request materials—but the records are confidential. I'm sure you understand." Eric kicked himself for not thinking of looking at the book when he had signed in earlier in the afternoon.

She lifted the glasses from the bodice of her green wool dress and put them on to look at him with the firm eyes of a guardian of the treasure house.

"No, I don't understand," he said in a loud voice. "What's the difference who examines the manuscript and if we know who the others are? Why the secretiveness? We're not in commercial competition."

The noise was sufficient to draw the attention of three others using the room. One, a bearded graduate student type in blue denim workshirt and chino pants, put his finger to his hairy mouth and said "shush."

"Okay," Eric said irritably, "your rules are silly but they're yours. Can you please put a rush on the material I requested?"

"We'll try, young man," she said primly; "you're not the only one to request material."

He didn't want to stand there arguing because it was almost six o'clock and he wanted to walk to the Thirtieth Street station to catch the 6:45 Metroliner.

Eric looked back through the glass doors to the reading room while waiting for the elevator in the hall and saw the bearded grad student standing and talking to the librarian. What a ball-buster she must be in her quiet way: he was showing her some identification, she was shaking her head emphatically, no! Then, apparently swayed by his blandishments, she was grudgingly reaching for something under the counter. Most librarians he had worked with were very helpful and cooperative. Some, however, acted as if you were intruding upon *their* private collections. This one kept shaking her head in disapproval as she handed the grad student a large book. The elevator came, and Eric stepped into it with relief to be out of there.

It was already dark and the streets were cold. He thought about a taxi for a minute but then decided against it. Waiting around the cavernous station would be depressing and this way he'd use up the time with some head-clearing exercise. Walking south on Walnut Street with his collar turned up and hands thrust deeply into his pockets, the thin leather envelope briefcase pressed to his side under his arm, Eric thought about Winkler. The sly old leftist was a real character. He *was* working for the government before and during the Second World War, as a *secret agent*! Eric didn't want to believe it, but there it had been in the files in black and white.

The letter from the file, indexed as a memorandum addressed to William Donovan, head of OSS during the war, was drafted on 14 April 1942:

Dr. Goldfeder is convinced that the theft of a copy of his plans for the mind device is related to his recent visit from my friend, Harry Raven. I cannot see any connection whatsoever between the two events, because these two men have been casual acquaintances—as mutual friends of mine—for at least seven years. They met on a number of occasions at social gatherings at my apartment, but their interests . . .

The letter went on to detail a recent meeting Goldfeder had mentioned to Winkler. Apparently Goldfeder had gone to lunch at the Columbia Faculty Club and quite by chance met Raven, who was the guest of some other faculty member. The three sat together and talked. Afterward Raven pressed Goldfeder to show him his laboratory because he thought "science was the poetry of the twentieth century." Goldfeder said that Raven was curious about everything and rather knowledgeable about science and technology for a poet. A week later some superseded blueprints the scientist was using for reference disappeared.

Winkler concluded the report saying that he thought Goldfeder was overworked, and that under pressure to complete his work, he was succumbing to the *post hoc, ergo propter hoc* fallacy.

Eric was musing while he walked to the station and the cold was beginning to bother him. He quickened his pace along Walnut Street, nearing the University's large hockey arena which loomed on the skyline.

Winkler himself had been delusional about Raven too, probably because of the emotional shock when Raven stole away with Lee. Then Harry killed himself and a day later another friend, Leon Goldfeder, disappeared. It blew Winkler's mind. He mourned in the journals for a long time for both.

A year after the letter to Donovan, however, there had been another letter—also a carbon copy; Winkler wanted posterity insurance:

> . . . in Buenos Aires while on my recent mission, passing the German Embassy, in a taxi one day I noticed a familiar looking man entering a staff car. He was a German officer who looked like Harry Raven! I stopped the taxi and called his name. The man looked at me briefly, stepped into his car and was driven away. Traffic conditions precluded a chase.
>
> I'm convinced that the attack on me several days later by a group of hooligans on the street at whose hands I would have died had not the police answered in time were related to my encounter with this officer . . .

Eric had copied out some passages but they seemed absurd. When he got the Xerox copies in the mail he'd be able to examine the wording more closely, but he thought Winkler was off base. Popular with the Latin American intellectuals because of his Spanish Civil War role and his antifascist speeches over the Argentine radio in 1943 during his lecture tour—a group of fascist goons had tried to do in the Jew. The way Eric saw it, Winkler puffed himself up too much. Fanciful cloaks and daggers!

Winkler emerging from the past to say that he saw a ghost? Enough, already! All Eric wanted right then was to forget all the Raven business for the moment and think of the evening ahead.

He had turned off Walnut onto the cross street, with two more blocks to the station and two more hours to Odette.

"Hey man, hold on!"

A large, new Pontiac made a U-turn in the roadway and pulled up in front of him.

The passenger's door opened and a tall thin man with a pencil-line mustache stepped out. He wore a heavy shearling coat.

"What are you doing here?" he asked with a Spanish accent, and then, before Eric could answer, continued, "Where are you going?"

Eric's face felt frozen and a shiver ran through him. He'd lived in New York most of his life and had never been mugged, and here in Philadelphia, brotherly love notwithstanding, he was about to get it.

The thought crossed Eric's mind that maybe he wasn't a mugger but some kind of cop. "I'm from New York, on my way home," he said, trying to control the tremor in his voice.

"Oh yeah? Listen, che, we don't like your kind around here. You got to pay your dues in this place."

"I don't have much money," Eric said, and he really didn't. He was fairly certain the guy didn't take checks. "And my watch is a cheap Timex."

The man took his hands out of his pockets. In the left hand he held a gun pointed at Eric's chest. His heart started to go triple time.

"What's in that briefcase?" the mugger asked as he grabbed the leather envelope from under Eric's arm.

"Only some paper, notes."

"Bank notes, man? Give me your wallet, and watch it. Take your hand out slowly or you're dead."

Eric reached into his breast pocket inside the overcoat and the mugger kept his eye on the movement in the side glare of the headlight. Eric was still reaching for the wallet, trembling, when the driver blew the horn sharply several times.

"Oye, cuidado por allí!" he shouted through the open door at the man with the gun, pointing his hand through the driver's window toward the street behind Eric. The mustache rose in a sneer and a gold tooth glinted.

"Mierda!" he hissed and leapt for the car, still holding the briefcase. Screeching tires and burning rubber, the big Pontiac made a U-turn and sped away.

Eric turned around, still trembling to see two men running toward him fast. He started to run toward the station, but they were faster. "Stop!" He heard the shout right behind him. He thought his heart would stop from fear. Then his arms were grabbed and panic clouded his eyes, but it was only the bearded graduate student from the library, and another man also wearing the perennial uniform blue jeans and army fatigue jacket.

"Are you all right?" the bearded one panted.

"Yes sir," Eric answered, relief flooding through him. He was still shaking. "Thanks to you and your friend. What luck! I thought you were another set of muggers!"

"Did they hurt you, professor?"

"No, but the guy had a gun, and he might have gotten nasty when he saw how little I have in my wallet."

"So they didn't get anything?"

"Only my briefcase, with the notes I took this afternoon, that's all that was in it—nothing else of value, except the case itself." The shivering had subsided. Eric realized that one of the copies of the Raven manuscript was in the briefcase. Why hadn't he listened to Nick? Shit, shit, shit! He defaced his own pigheadedness. "I'm lucky," Eric went on, drained, still catching his breath, "really lucky you guys came along."

"Yeah," said the bearded one. "I guess you are. We were on our way to a restaurant near the station and just turned the corner when we saw those guys and figured something was fishy."

"But you could have gotten hurt, if those clowns had started shooting."

The other student wiped his perspiring face on the sleeve of his fatigue jacket and said, "We didn't think about it. Maybe we've all got dumb luck today. Jack here just started to run and I kept him company."

"By the way," said the bearded one, "my name's Jack Harris. This guy's Bill Rosenbloom."

"Eric Newman's mine."

They shook hands all around.

"Would you recognize those characters if you saw them again?" Jack asked.

"The guy who held the gun, probably. Thin, Hispanic, well-dressed, mustache. The driver, probably not. I didn't see him. I heard an Argentine accent though, or maybe Chilean. Why, do you think I ought to report it to the police?"

"It wouldn't do any good," said Jack, "and besides, do you want to come back to Philadelphia for identification, and a possible trial? With only your word as evidence . . . well, it's not likely that anything would come of it. Besides, they'll never catch the guy; they won't even look. Forget it!" He offered Eric a Camel.

"It is my lucky day," Eric said. "My brand, and I'm empty."

Jack had a healthy, open smile and looked as though he was enjoying his paternalistic role of the moment.

"How did you know I was a professor?" Eric asked, inhaling deeply, feeling the flush of the first good taste of tobacco after tension—always the same pleasure.

He looked stumped. Then he said, "Oh, I just assumed you weren't a student, and, uh, I overheard the librarian address you that way. Are you?"

"Yes, at Columbia. I'm at the Institute for Inter-Cultural Studies."

"Anything you can't replace in the briefcase?" Bill asked.

"No, it was just a copy of a manuscript I'm working on and some notes to play with till I get the Xerox copies in the mail." He kicked himself again for not following Nick's advice to leave the Raven manuscript *and* the copies at the bank.

"I'm glad for you that it wasn't worse," said Bill. "You know this isn't the safest city in the world."

They began walking toward the station. Eric looked at the watch he'd almost lost. He still had eleven minutes to catch the Metroliner.

"I've got to hurry, fellas. Since I'm alive yet, thanks to you, there's no reason to worry the lady who's waiting."

They hurried with him to the station, came inside the gloomy mausoleumlike building and waited until he was safely aboard.

"I owe you guys a drink."

They laughed. "Next time you're in Philly, look us up at the Grad House."

"Will do," Eric said as the doors closed. Nice guys.

* * *

It amazed Eric to be able to place a telephone call from a moving train: the up-to-date plastic luxury of the Metroliner wasn't quite up to the standards of opulence set by the Orient Express in movies and books, but he was, after all, on his way to foreign intrigue—with Odette . . . and he was on a mission. Only a trench coat was lacking.

"Eric, I'm so glad you called; where are you?"

He said he was traveling toward her at a hundred miles an hour on the Metroliner and was calling from a public phone on the train.

"Oh, you Americans; what a silly idea! Why put a telephone on a train, except to prevent you from enjoying the ride?"

"The only thing I'm enjoying about this ride is that when it ends I'll see you," he answered.

"You are a flatterer," she laughed, musical, enchanting, "and it will get you everywhere. But why are you on the train?"

He told her he'd been in Philadelphia all day and was mugged a few minutes before boarding.

"Oh, you poor man. You're not hurt?"

"Not at all; only wrung out by the scare."

"Eh bien, then instead of meeting me at a restaurant, you'll come here to the apartment and have a wash, or a shower if you wish, and a nice long drink so you can relax. After that, we'll go out. Is that convenient?"

He said it was fine, wrote down the address and returned to his seat, buying a double scotch on the way.

The darkened factories and railroad sidings flicked past in the black, moonless evening. The industrial wasteland of this rail corridor gave him little diversion and he just sat and thought, trying to sort out some coherence, some pattern in the situation.

It was all too complex; after all, he was merely a cultural historian trying to write an academic biography of a dead poet. Suddenly, a missing notebook materialized and everything became different. All of the people close to him were pushing and pulling in different directions. It seemed that his job, his personal life, his safety, and even his mental stability were on the line. Discovering a murder, having his apartment ransacked, being mugged. Now, to top it off, he had an uncomfortable sense of someone following him. Eric couldn't define the last part, but found himself looking over his shoulder and feeling his flesh crawl at odd moments with the sense that he was being watched.

He sipped the scotch and looked out the window. Then Eric stood up and took his coat down from the luggage rack and pretended to look in the pocket for something. He folded the coat again, put it on the seat beside him and sat down again. A minute later he finished the drink with a gulp, picked up the coat and walked through the coach to the next one, then into the next one and sat down in the vacant seat. The car was half-empty. Eric looked around. No one followed him. Relief.

Could that sense of being watched be only guilt? Wasn't he using the Raven manuscript to forestall mature acceptance of the limits of reality? He supposed this applied to all academic researchers who drag out publishing projects over the years: one stays "in school" that way, a perpetual youth. As long as the "important book" remains an unrealized potential you never have to take the risk of failure.

And to live at his fingertips, as he'd always wanted to, he would have to stop stalling and start risking. When his marriage ended, he convinced himself that he was taking a big risk, giving up the comfort and security of a nice split-level life in the suburbs. After Eric had moved into the city, he felt like an existential hero in his shabby furnished apartment. Right at the edge, looking into the abyss. Mostly, it was the chasm of self-pity which yawned away beneath him into infinite depths. It was too vast and too deep for him at the time, however, and he had been scared underneath the bravado. So he drew out his research: it was a safe grip. A ledge to stand on.

Eric mulled over the past few years spent clinging to safety, uncommitted, as the Metroliner ran through the flat industrial wastelands of Jersey and the factories became more numerous and taller. The train wasn't far from New York and the conductor announced their approach on the intercom, giving the outside temperature and the exact number of minutes until the train would arrive. Not content to be a train, the Metroliner had to ape the airlines.

Land of illusions, Eric thought, fostered in plastic parentage. A train was a plane, a plane was a living room, a living room was an "environment" replete with airplane seats, church pews or hammocks and ship's fittings . . . with stereotapes to simulate the atmosphere of whatever you wanted.

He stopped himself, recognizing the old technique. Deliver the carping criticism of the world, regret the past, qualify the present, and however true it might be, however real the outrage, you could avoid the real confrontation with yourself. You could transform your rage, parlay it into wit and devastation of the surfaces, and sidestep the depths.

Just then, as the train "touched down" in Penn Station, he felt a pang of longing and emptiness as he stepped toward the street above. He thought of Mike starting prep school and Nina primping in the mirror or practicing on the piano and spending hours on the phone. Often when he tried to call the kids of an evening, he couldn't get through.

This loneliness descended on him sometimes in the midst of doing something completely unrelated to his former domestic life; it was the irrevocability of the situation. Having had a marriage he couldn't or wouldn't live with, Eric left it. But not without pain, because after all, that's not what nice middle-class Jewish boys did. Part of the package, leaving Elly and her endless demand for well-regulated ordinariness, included leaving the children who were the bases of her demand, because she could see no other way to give them "stability," and, Eric supposed, neither could he. All of his protest to the contrary, at present, he couldn't even define one version of an acceptable life for himself. Everything seemed to be a form of playing hooky.

10

New York

THE REASON for his present truancy was staying in an apartment on Central Park West. The building was new, modern, with large glass areas, offset in its harshness by thick maroon carpeting in the hallways, Barcelona chairs, and a Nevelson sculpture inside the lobby. The uniformed doorman announced Eric, then showed him to the elevator, where the operator took him to the twenty-sixth floor.

Odette opened the door of the apartment and held out both her hands in greeting, "It's good to see you, but you look worn out, mon ami!"

"I don't feel that way anymore," Eric said, "now that I see you."

"You are a terrible flatterer, Eric . . . and I love it." She laughed with that bell sound, high, clear and resonant. It wasn't an American laugh. Not that Eric knew what an American laugh was, but he knew that this was not it.

"But come in; we can't stay in the doorway all evening," she said, taking his arm, and showing him into the apartment. It was furnished in expensive modern taste: a large brown leather couch, oatmeal-colored carpeting, a glass coffee table, and two steel-framed "S" chairs made up the living room furniture. A large abstract triptych hung on one wall; the other two were floor-to-ceiling glass facing east and south and commanding a panoramic view of the city. Eric could see the Queensborough Bridge, the East River, the Empire State Building and all of lower Manhattan stretching away like an electric arrow into the night. Below, the dark mass of Central Park, paths lit so the muggers could see the lovers they lived off.

"Quite a place," he said. "It really is beautiful."

She smiled at him, and as he was recovering said, "Yes. Pierre has very good taste, but it isn't his journalist's salary that permits him to live this way. He is a member of our working aristocracy and has a family fortune to amuse himself with."

"Where is he now?"

"Back in Paris on vacation. He is the New York correspondent for *Le Figaro*."

Eric walked over to the painting on the wall. The three panels were done in acrylic earth tones with precisely edged swaths of dark and light browns which flowed across the inches of empty wall space which separated the clear lucite box frames. A dynamic force was generated through the painting and out into the room, charging the atmosphere.

"Who did this?" he asked.

"It is by a Washington artist, a friend of Pierre. Interesting, n'est-ce pas?"

She came and stood next to Eric as he admired the painting and he could smell her perfume.

"But do come sit down, Eric, and let me give you a drink. What will you have?"

"Scotch," he said, then changed his mind. "No, make that a dry vermouth with some lemon if you have it; I already had some scotch on the train; any more and I'll be sleepy."

"I like a man who knows his limits," she said as she walked out of the room into a corridor that he assumed led to a kitchen.

In a minute she was back in the room. Eric had closed his eyes while she was gone and didn't hear her return. At the sound of the drinks being placed on the glass coffee table, he opened his eyes.

"Salut," Odette toasted as they lifted the glasses and touched them together.

"To new friends," he answered, and she smiled with her blue, her very dark blue eyes.

"Seeing you with your eyes closed when I came back into the room convinced me of what I knew when you first walked in," she said.

"What's that?"

"There is no point in going out to a restaurant. You're too tired after your trip. I will make us some dinner here."

"No, no," Eric objected, hoping she would brush aside his

protest, because her suggestion thrilled him, "I'm not tired at all."

"Well then," she answered, looking mischievous, "I am, and prefer to stay here."

"You win then, but you mustn't fuss."

"How would you like a large omelette, salade, and cold white wine?"

"Perfect."

"Bien. Then I go to the kitchen and you can go shower and freshen up if you wish."

Without waiting for an answer she got up, extended her hand and led him down the corridor past a steel and formica kitchen to a gleaming white tiled bathroom. Next to the bathroom a doorway led to a bedroom, which seemed empty of furniture, except for a large platform bed.

"In the cabinet under the sink you'll find towels, and there is shaving soap and a razor, if you want one, in the medicine cabinet."

The shower felt delicious and renewing, and Eric took her hint and shaved. He felt much better when he emerged from the steamy room. Odette had changed her black dress for a pair of blue jeans, the very tight French style which showed her rear end to perfection, and a checked blue gingham blouse. She had put a record on the stereo and the sound of Bach filled the apartment.

"What are we listening to?" he asked.

"The Bach Partita Number 6 in E minor. Glenn Gould playing."

"I like him," Eric said. "He's very good, at least to my taste, and I really don't know much about the technical aspects."

"He is superb," Odette said, "although I hate to admit that about an English musician."

Eric objected that Gould was Canadian.

"La même chose," she responded. "To me, the English colonials have all of the faults and few of the virtues of their mother country."

The classic French Anglophobia: they were hard put to acknowledge that the high water marks of civilization could be found anywhere but in France. But Bach, of course, not even the French could deny.

Odette stood with her head tilted sideways, her brown hair falling to one side, her eyes of deepest blue, limpid as the clear flow of the music.

"This is the opening toccata," she said, "my favorite movement. When it is complete I make the omelette, while you sit and listen to the rest. Notice that Gould sings along—écoutes! Lovely, no?"

He objected when the toccata was over and she started to go. He just wanted to watch her while she wasn't aware of it. "I'll help you."

"Eric," she said with a smile that spoke of amused determination, "I am a liberated woman, as I have to be—but not a feminist. I don't believe in men in the kitchen, at least not while I'm there. Go sit. I'll only be a moment."

"Orders are orders are orders," he said, and sat on the leather couch letting the stream of Bach glisten past his mind.

Odette also glistened in Eric's mind while he rested in Arcadia. He would have been content, he thought, to just be in her presence that evening without touching her. But there was something evanescent about her; she had appeared in his life without warning, like a sprite, like a water nymph, and that evening he felt like Mallarmé's faun when he awakens and thinks he has only dreamed the delight of nymphs: "Ces nymphes, je les veux perpetuer."

Eric wanted to make her endure, not disappear again. After the omelette, a watercress salad, the Sancerre wine, crackling cold, and the coffee, he felt expansive and slightly drunk. He told Odette that she was the most beautiful woman he had ever seen, and that he had dreamed of her since they had met.

"No more dreams, mon cher," she said, getting up from her chair and standing beside him. "I am very real, and here for you right now."

Then she bent over and kissed him on the lips, her fragrant hair hanging over his face as he lifted his satyr's eyes and head toward her. Eric was sure that his pointy ears gave him away. He stood and embraced her, unable to say a word.

* * *

He woke up the next morning around nine and found himself alone in the bed. A note was taped to the bathroom mirror saying that Odette would be back by 9:30, please wait. So he shaved and dressed and brewed some coffee. Odette returned as he was drinking the first cup.

"Look, croissants!" She was bubbling with enthusiasm. "I found a small French bakery not far from here."

"No bagels?" he asked.

"Not today. How do you say?—I paid my dues already," she answered.

They breakfasted by the windows overlooking the city, and she asked him more questions about his work. Eric told her as much as he could about the Raven notebook, the Winkler complication, and the problem he was going to have finishing the book.

His ambivalence must have been pretty clear because when he had finished, she asked, "Why are you torturing yourself with this project? It is a big world and there is so much to do, to investigate, to write about. Surely you could turn your talents to something else, if, as you say, this present work is not letting you live?"

"I have too much riding on this, too much time, effort and money invested. I can't let it go now," Eric responded quickly.

"Even if it kills you!"

"It won't."

She smiled; wistfully, it seemed to him.

* * *

Nick was peeved about the whole thing: starting with his ruined vacation, continuing with the way he had to instrumentalize Eric, and now with the burgeoning intimacy between his best friend and his former lover.

"Where are you, Eric?" Nick asked, annoyance in his voice, when he heard Eric on the telephone. It was almost eleven in the morning, and the day was wasting. Must have been a long night, Nick thought. He knew very well where Eric was from the babysitters, and about the Philadelphia incident too. Nick wondered why he had asked. To test? To make Eric a bit uncomfortable? To force his best friend to lie? The cat-and-mouse game so close to home made life obscene. And Eric evaded him.

"Can we meet tomorrow? I need to go through the stuff you gave me, and I'm swamped with classes and papers till then. I need time . . . to get my act together."

Indeed! Nick thought, miffed. He said he'd be at Eric's office at 3:00 the next afternoon, then went down the carpeted corridor to Barnwell's office. The director motioned Nick to a chair, shuffled some papers on the long library table in front of him and plunged right in. "The police found Hartman's killer last night, and he ties in with our problem," he said, smiling behind his ice blue eyes.

"Who is he?" Nick asked. He wished Barnwell would be more direct. It was always move and countermove. "How tied in?" he added, playing the game, the only way with Barnwell.

"Guido Cappella, the radio monitor man who set up the tag on you last Thursday, and the controlling verb is 'was.' He was found dead."

No emotion in the man's voice. Chess game. The opposition lost a pawn.

"Where?"

"In Brooklyn, over near the docks—Bush Terminal. He was found in a telephone company van, garroted. A .32 caliber automatic with silencer and a clip of dumdums was found in the truck. Hartman's murder weapon. Cappella had been dead for more than forty-eight hours."

"So he did the job and then was killed?" The style of killing and the double cross had overtones of syndicate work, but Nick couldn't make sense of it. Not yet. He pushed the idea aside.

"In any case," Barnwell continued, "the police have nothing to go on, no prints they can trace except Cappella's. And by the way, they found the mask, so Newman was not hysterical after all."

"And, concerning Newman," he went on—Nick feared he was going to get a report on Eric's evening with Odette, but the director spared him that, at least—"the Pennsylvania turnpike police picked up the alert from Philadelphia and spotted the car Newman's muggers used. They did nothing, as instructed, except observe the drivers—they resembled what Newman told our fieldmen—and traced the registration. The car belongs to the Undersecretary for Economic Development at the Chilean Embassy in Washington. That's cover for the head of their security force."

Nick let out a whistle. "So now you're convinced of what you only suspected." There was a hush-up going on, and without realizing it, Eric held compromising information. No proof, but it added up that way.

Barnwell pulled at his mustache and made a note on the yellow pad in front of him. "Now, as to this notebook Newman got hold of," Barnwell said, "It *is* an unusual document, and it is no great surprise that a man of Newman's perspicacity would be curious about it, to say the least. Harry Raven had dimensions beyond the usual for a literary man. He seemed to have some wires into the highest levels of our government."

Nick didn't understand. "Do you mean he was working for us, like Winkler?"

"No, it doesn't appear to be the case. But he seemed to know at least two cabinet officials, someone in the War Office and a State Department official."

"That doesn't prove anything except that Raven knew some government people," Nick said, deciding to play devil's advocate. Barnwell was one of the few upper echelon types who valued the adversary relationship, who really believed that truth emerged from the clash of ideas. Nick liked this in the director and decided to accommodate him.

"He was, after all, a well-known poet and a sort of enfant terrible, even for radical bohemia," Nick went on. "Why shouldn't he know some government types? He probably met them at cocktail parties!" Nick said, throwing the ball into Barnwell's court.

And the director slammed it back: "But these were all officials who had access to secret information. Notably, they shared a knowledge of the magnometric oscillating alphagraph, what we've been calling the ETT."

"Why don't you ask them?"

"They're all dead and gone!"

"And you're suggesting that this Raven character was spying?"

"Perhaps," Barnwell answered, "but for whom? The Soviets? The man was a very prominent fellow traveler . . . and the supposition . . ." Barnwell trailed off in mid-thought. "There's something that doesn't fit properly," he said after what seemed to Nick like a long delay.

"I'll say!" Nick responded. "It all seems like a long stretch of the imagination. Maybe Raven did have . . . let's say 'social' relationships with these people. Why should that imply that he was a spy? Moreover, the Russians had plenty of moles inside the system, and wouldn't use a high profile type. The old NKVD was too smart for that! In any case, it's absurd; there's no evidence. Can you verify anything other than the names in the book?"

"We're trying," said the director. "But *we* always start from scratch. Newman has all the links in his head; *his* work is to make the connections. The research staff is looking into various records for any confirmation, but they're not up to your friend's standard. That's why we need to keep him in the game!"

Nick doubted the line of development. "It's a wild goose chase. You know, come to think of it, maybe Raven had compromised and was blackmailing some of the people you're alluding to, and they were powerful enough to have him eliminated."

The director stared ahead and then looked directly at Nick, boring in with his cold blue eyes. "Raven's suicide may have been just that," he said quietly.

Terminations were part of the business, but all this seemed really farfetched. Nick couldn't see what bearing the speculations Barnwell was testing on him had to do with the mission. The whole situation was growing very complex, and he wished it were as simple as the Secretary had suggested. Search and destroy. If the administrators who gave the operational orders only knew . . .

"I'm meeting Eric this afternoon, and I'll raise that possibility of Raven's being a Russian spy," Nick said. "It's just likely to laugh him right out of this operation!"

The director wasn't pleased with Nick's remark. "Then don't say that to him, under any circumstances. I want to *keep* him in the field, so to speak."

"You realize that doing so is inimical to his own interests?" asked Nick.

"I beg to differ with you," Barnwell answered, studying his hands. "We are promoting his interests while assuring our own. A rather ideal relationship, I think!"

Nick knew that there was to be no argument from the almost lilting tone in Barnwell's voice and the professorial smile with which he made his point.

"I still don't see how we promote his interests by leading him down the primrose path. He's riding point and drawing fire; he's a sitting duck, a decoy, call it what you wish,"—Nick fumbled for words, recognizing his own clichés—" and I don't see what he will get from it. His own work will be delayed, and he'll get hurt. At the least he'll lose his job."

"The situation is unusual, I'll warrant you," Barnwell said, "but you can't possibly see the whole picture from your vantage point. Were you an ordinary officer, however competent, no explanation would be proffered, nor asked for. You are more than that. As far as I'm concerned, you're the best in OMEGA, and I intend to recommend you for my position when I retire in the near future."

Nick flushed with surprise and embarrassment. Here he was, criticizing the director's operational planning, and the man was telling him that he was the handpicked successor. Maybe this is soft soap, Nick thought, to co-opt him in a situation he found repugnant.

"I'm certainly flattered by what you say, but you realize that the effect of your words is to embarrass me for being critical," Nick said, after a pause to let the dust settle, "and to worry me, now that you've shown me the glittering prize I won't get unless I'm a good boy and do as I'm told."

"I am aware of that," said Barnwell, "and felt I had to take that risk, because you're essential to this operation and *must* understand. On preliminary examination," the director continued with the matter at hand, having made his point, "the manuscript Newman has links together names, all of whom were in some way involved in the planning and development of the magnometric oscillating alphagraph, or the ETT as we've been calling it."

"But what were the names doing in a poet's notebook?" asked Nick.

Barnwell shrugged. "It could be coincidence, but we don't know—yet! And frankly, we won't unless Newman finds out for us."

"I can't believe that," Nick said, shaking his head, "with all the expertise at our disposal."

"It's odd, I know," said the director, "but we can't, or at least not unless we have someone with all Newman's knowledge of the subject, training as a researcher, ingenuity, and focus; and we don't, so he's the one. We have no choice."

"This means that Winkler wasn't off the wall," said Nick.

"Yes, but he was an amateur with a fertile imagination," interrupted Barnwell. "It's premature to press him. He wants the past buried now, and might just clam up . . ." He trailed off in mid-sentence.

"In any case," Barnwell continued, "Newman must be encouraged to follow this through. The Buenos Aires connection is where he should start. If he's as clever as I think, he'll pick up on a tease I supplied. He'll need to follow it up in Argentina. Take him to Buenos Aires!"

Always the little surprises, Nick thought. "I don't see why he should accept," he said. "He has a job he's committed to and he can't just up and—"

"You'll convince him," Barnwell snapped. "With a cash offer —tax free. His consultant's fee, all transportation etcetera, as standard, plus a twenty-five thousand payment when he's completed the research."

"But he'll lose his job; he won't go," said Nick. It was ridiculous.

"Then you'll double the offer. Even if he loses his job, that's more than two years' pay for him, and he can write his book or do what he chooses while he looks for another job. I don't think he's so pure that he'll refuse."

"What if he does?" Nick asked.

"He won't. He's too curious and too creative to pass up the opportunity for exploring every dimension of the subject in depth."

Nick got up to leave.

When he got to the door, he turned to say something, but decided against it when he saw that Barnwell was lost in his own thoughts, staring straight ahead.

The director, Nick thought, has a passion for the game, like a chess master, but no compassion for the pieces he moves around, so many chunks of wood or ivory.

* * *

Love and postcards turned everything topsy-turvy for Eric. Looking through the material Nick had left with him, his mind wandered between all the strange and frightening happenings of the last few days and the wild magic he felt inside—the floating sensation of knowing that he was in love again, caught up in a whirlwind with the woman of his dreams. He had spent a second night with Odette and now could think of nothing but her, the softness of her voice, the quiet sexuality she radiated.

It saved him trouble that Lucy told him she was through. She had thought she would be a nice surprise, waiting at his place to gobble him up, down, and sideways, when he got home from Philadelphia. When he didn't show up she worried, then cried, she said, and then gave up. As he walked into the reception area of the office the next day, she said, "Did you get my note, old reliable?" with heavy sarcasm.

"What note?"

"The one I left in your apartment when I got up this morning, you two-timing son-of-a-bitch," she hissed, threw his keys at him and turned her back, walking away, dramatic, hurt.

Eric had no answer, and felt that he didn't want to explain. It was easier this way; he couldn't be tied to Lucy's gritty earth, not after he had wandered in Paradise.

Love absorbed him, and he rehearsed the endless permutations of the future while he sat at his desk absentmindedly flipping through the most recent material retrieved by Nick's minions. He glanced at the postcards.

Nothing important. Eric had seen many cards Raven sent to friends from abroad, and he recognized the handwriting and innocuous messages immediately. He turned past the cards and went on to the "Memorandum of Conversation" Rockefeller wrote up after he saw Winkler—and then it hit him.

The cards! He flipped back to them. Unsigned, one sent from Buenos Aires to Hartman in October of 1943, the other in April of 1944. Couldn't be! Raven was dead in July 1943. Eric looked at the postmarks carefully. No question of the dates.

Maybe they were from someone else with a similar handwriting. He'd have to check it with some expert in graphology. Probably in the Archeology Department there'd be someone. Just to satisfy his own curiosity he compared the cards to the writing in the Xerox copy of the manuscript in his desk drawer, then with some letters on Raven's on file. Eric was sure. He needed expert opinion, but as far as he could tell they were written by the same person.

Maybe . . . he really had been alive, and there was some crazy mistake in dates. Then he thought of Winkler, his report. A sane man that one. There was much more here than a routine fantasy.

But Raven was dead! There were witnesses who saw him go overboard. It couldn't be. He got out the news clips. Right! The captain of the ship, the steward, and one crew member all saw him go over the side. After that the search teams found bits and pieces the sharks left over. But here were the cards in his handwriting, written later. How was it possible?

Eric was pacing around, trying to make things fit, when Nick walked in. He didn't give him a chance to sit down.

"Come on, we can talk in the car on the way downtown," Eric said, grabbing his coat before Nick could remove his. Nick didn't object, although he was certainly surprised by Eric's animation as they took the elevator down to the garage and eased the Porsche up the ramp. It was only a matter of ten or fifteen minutes down the West Side Highway and they were at the Customs House. By then Eric had explained to Nick what he was doing. Nick didn't say much while Eric babbled on about his "discovery."

The Customs House Library is rarely used. The librarian therefore, with little to do, was very accommodating. Within five minutes Nick and Eric were looking at the manifest of the SS *Libertador* when it cleared pratique and docked on 15 July, 1943. The names and national origin of all crew were listed. Two Eric knew already. It was the third witness whose name he needed.

"What about if there was an accident, a man overboard on that trip?" he asked the librarian. "Where's the record?"

They were directed to the Coast Guard Records Center, a few blocks away. The inquest would have been under their jurisdiction.

Nick tagged along while Eric found the record of the hearing. The third witness, like the other two, was an Argentine national, a ship's engineer named Manuel Becari.

"I don't get it," Nick said. "What's so unusual that the crew of an Argentine vessel should be Argentine nationals?"

"Nothing," Eric answered. "Except that two of the three names are listed in Raven's notebook, with their addresses, and he was supposedly never in Argentina. But the names were entered months before his death. I wouldn't have made anything of it if I hadn't seen those postcards you showed me, the ones you found at Hartman's. They were in Raven's handwriting, and dated *after* the suicide."

Nick smiled. "What a mind you have, Sherlock."

"Yes, Watson," Eric said, "but now starts the difficulty in following this." As he was saying it, he realized that Nick could get what was needed through his sources. Let the government grinds do it, and at their expense of time and money.

Eric wanted the Argentine manifest of the crew and passengers for the day the *Libertador* sailed on that fatal journey, and the current addresses of the captain, steward, and chief engineer, if they were still alive and residents of the country. They ducked into the Seaman's Cove, a pub across from the Coast Guard Office, and he called his office from the telephone booth at the back while Eric stood at the bar for a much needed scotch.

Nick came back and ordered the same. "If it's to be had, it'll be on my desk in the morning," he said. "I'll call you when it comes in."

"What desk? I thought you weren't working, just nosing around."

He didn't answer the question.

"Eric, how would you like to go to Buenos Aires yourself and run this down?" he said after taking an appreciative sip from his glass. The offices in the surrounding neighborhood hadn't let out for the day and they were alone in the pub, except for the bartender.

"I'd love it if I only had a rich uncle and didn't have a job to worry about. But why do you tempt me into a fantasy I can't fulfill?—it's cruel and makes me want another drink." Eric called the barman and reordered.

"You *have* a rich uncle," Nick said and then laid out the details of what he was offering.

"Jesus. It must be pretty important to Uncle to have these dribs and drabs of foolishness!" Eric said.

"Look, you jerk," Nick said in his most affectionate tone, "you're crazy if you do it, and you're even crazier if you don't."

"DON'T???" Eric practically shouted.

"Sssh."

"Don't?" he repeated. "How could I not? But it's going to raise some hackles, lotsa flak."

Nick said that he was going to Chile anyway on an inspection tour for USIA and would route himself through Buenos Aires so that whatever Eric might find would be of use to him right there.

It occurred to Eric that Odette was on her way to Chile also, and he wondered aloud if she was a Greenberg too.

Nick shook his head, regretfully Eric thought, and said no: on his honor, it was just a coincidence.

"Man, wouldn't it be great if she could route herself through Buenos Aires too?" The idea of it excited Eric. "What a great time the three of us could have!" He felt like a kid. Something was renewing in him, an enthusiasm he had lost, he thought, years ago.

"Bubbeleh," he said—Eric knew where Nick picked up these Yiddish endearments; it was part of his Yale heritage, from the sacrosanct precincts of their rooms—"it isn't a vacation. It's work, and possibly dangerous, I want you to know. You're not an ostrich. Someone is suppressing information by dumping the people who have it, and I want you to be aware of that."

"That's what the big insurance policy is for! No?"

"Yes . . . You're incorrigible, Eric . . . yes!"

Eric had to leave. "Come, Watson!" he said. "The game is afoot!" and they scurried through the just starting rain to the parking lot. He couldn't wait to see Odette. They had a rain check on dinner out and a lot to talk about.

PART TWO

11

Buenos Aires

A CITY OUTSIDE of time, out of Eric's dreams of growing up: sophisticated and vigorous, Buenos Aires is a living anachronism. In love with its own past, with the myth that it once coped, the city is a monument of the frozen forms of time. In the busy downtown streets; among the elegant apartments and town houses in the Barrio Norte; along the tough resilient waterfront of La Boca; in the hundreds of statue-saturated parks and plazas; in the cafes on every corner; in the 1930s style nightclubs where thin men with pencil mustaches and slick black hair still dance pliant, elegant women across the polished floors: you hear tango.

This is the rhythm of Buenos Aires, a song of longing and frustration. Nothing is consummated in the tango, one is left crumpled, like an old piece of newspaper blown across empty concrete spaces by the wind of autumn which comes up from the southern pampas and howls through the streets.

And it was always like autumn in Buenos Aires for Eric. He saw this city as a faded queen looking over her shoulder, in love with the past which might have been and longing for a future of sentimental death.

It was late evening when Eric, Odette and Nick finally got into town and the sleepy night clerk at the Hotel Francia showed them to their rooms on the eighth floor facing the plaza with its traffic circle and converging boulevards. Odette had insisted on her own room—"for the sake of appearance"—and Eric didn't want to push his luck.

He wasn't tired yet, and his room was hot. Despite his autumnal orientation, it was summer, so he turned on the air conditioner and went out for a beer. He wanted to be alone after twelve hours of airplane togetherness. Soon the room would be comfortable for sleeping, and he knew that there were a few cafes two blocks away near the Avenida Alvear, just the thing for easing into the spirit of the place. He took the elevator downstairs and walked, avoiding the little park by going around it, mostly out of New York habit, because Buenos Aires is one of the safer cities in the world, even at night. Public safety for the law-abiding is one of the fringe benefits of an authoritarian government. Paramilitary police with Sten guns roam the city in pairs, and can be found on every other corner, with ready-made woe for anyone who looks suspicious or out of place, and instant clink for someone stopped without proper identity papers.

The cafe was fairly well crowded, but he found a table on the pavement three rows back from the prized streetside tables, and ordered a Pilsner from the waiter. Since leaving the hotel, he had the uncomfortable feeling of being followed once again, that same desire to scratch the back of his neck he had had on the train from Philadelphia a few weeks ago.

Maybe it was guilt for acting against the conventional wisdom.

"I'll take it as sick leave," Eric had said to Drake last Thursday. "I have a lot of time coming to me."

"That's for physical illness. Yours is mental," he shouted in his office.

"Well, I'm doing it anyway. There's just one week of classes left and then the final." The semester ended the second week of December. "And I'll leave a final with Lucy for the survey course, the seminar has only the papers. I'll do it all as soon as I get back, so their grades should be in right after New Year. I don't think that's so bad."

"I do," Drake had said angrily, "and this won't stand you in good stead with me." He was furious at not controlling his subordinate more than anything else, Eric realized, because colleagues who had important and not so important conferences to attend did the same thing all the time, and Drake knew it. Screw it, Eric thought. It was his life, not Drake's.

Winkler had pleaded ignorance to the questions Eric asked him on the phone. He didn't remember what he had written in his own journals, he'd have to go look sometime. Eric didn't want to stall around with him.

"You're wasting your time, Eric—past is only prologue," Winkler said.

To what? Eric wondered as he put down the phone.

Then Elly had done her usual number: "Rather than keeping your promise to involve yourself more with the kids, you keep breaking it, increasing your trips, distancing yourself," his ex-wife had said when Eric called her to say he was going to Argentina. "This isn't what I want for my children—a long-distance father, a telephone voice. You're just like a child yourself—needing heroics, playing roles, hoping to die in the service of some grand cause. Oh God, it's all so stupid," she had said, and hung up.

Accustomed to evaluating everyone else's judgment and acting only after long pondering, Eric was out of character. He knew the impulse had felt right, but it went against almost thirty-seven years of conditioning. He was pleased with himself, but still anxious. Perhaps he was projecting his anxiety and peopling the streets with personifications of his fears . . .

The beer had arrived and stood on the marble-topped table, begging his attention. He lifted the glass and took a long swallow.

And then Eric saw him again. An ordinary-looking man with a round flushed face and horn-rimmed glasses, the thick-framed kind that went out of fashion ten years ago. He was wearing a dark brown suit, and looked like thousands of other Argentine businessmen. He had seen the man at the taxi line at the airport, and later noticed him at the hotel bar, and now as he eased his bulk behind a table at the other end of the cafe. Had he been following Eric—or all of them? Why should he? Anyone could come into Buenos Aires, register in a hotel and go out for a drink on a hot night. But why the same time, same hotel, and same cafe as Eric?

He finished the beer, ordered another, and asked the waiter for a packet of Particulares, a pungent black tobacco cigarette whose smell he associated with Buenos Aires.

By then it was one o'clock and time for bed; finally the tiredness, the beer, or both had begun to get to him, so he paid the bill and ambled back toward the Plaza Francia. Half a block away Eric turned to look for round-face, but the man wasn't at the table, or behind him, so he chalked up one for projection, and kept going toward the hotel.

Crossing Avenida Alvear, he suddenly heard the whine of a car accelerating rapidly in low gear. Turning in the direction of the sound, he saw a black Peugeot without headlights coming at him fast. He was paralyzed. Then the headlights flashed on, blinding him. It would be only seconds before it hit him, but Eric stood rooted to the spot, not knowing how to go, and not able to go anyway.

Suddenly he was gripped by the arm and pulled back to the curb so hard that he flew onto the sidewalk. At that instant the Peugeot screamed past, and sped on down the wide dark street and was gone. The lifesaver and Eric picked themselves up from the sidewalk.

"Milliones de gracias," Eric said as he brushed the dirt off his sleeves. It was the man in brown. He adjusted his glasses.

"No hay de que." He continued in good, accented English, "You must be careful, senor. You are a stranger here, I can tell by your American accent, and perhaps are not aware that in Buenos Aires the drivers are madmen. The machismo, a national disease, but knowing that won't help you when you are dead."

Eric thanked him again, and they continued across Alvear. He looked very carefully in both directions this time.

"I believe we are staying at the same hotel," brown suit said; "I noticed you leaving before." At the park he said, "We can go through, I always do. It's safe."

Eric wondered nervously if he was going to be jumped in the park—but nothing happened.

They reached the lobby of the hotel and Senor Montilla, who had introduced himself as a sporting goods salesman from Rosario, rode the elevator as far as the fifth floor, where his room was, and bade Eric goodnight and a pleasant stay. "Just be careful crossing streets," he said as he got off the elevator.

* * *

"I'm going over to the Reuters office today," Odette said at breakfast the next morning, "to see if I can run down some more Chilean exiles who'll talk to me."

"Why Reuters?" Eric asked.

"I have contacts there; that's the quickest way into the action for me," she answered.

"Whom do you know there?" Nick asked.

"Hal Osborne."

"So do I."

"I don't," Eric said, "so I can't contribute to this morning's session of 'Small World,' brought to you by the folks—"

"Shut up, Eric," Nick demanded. "He did this all the time at college. I can't take it first thing in the morning."

But the spirit of Buenos Aires was in Eric and he wanted to tango out into the street on this gorgeous day—mindful of crazy drivers naturally. He poured a second cup of the aromatic strong coffee.

"I'm going to try to see Becari, if I can reach him," Eric said, sipping.

Nick had gotten the address for Eric, along with the steward's. The captain, Novaes, was dead, lost at sea when the ship went down near the end of the war. Eric wanted to see Becari first, because he wasn't in the notebook—he was Eric's find.

Odette took out her compact and glossed her lips. "Can I be of any help to you too, Eric?" she asked.

Too? Nick avoided Eric's eyes. Had he lied, Eric wondered, about her working for *them?* He let it go without comment, and answered her:

"You could check out some names for me; I'll run them down later in the library if you don't get there, but maybe your sources . . ."

She reached down into her handbag and produced a note pad where Eric wrote the names he wanted her to look up, and she left for downtown with Nick, who said he'd find her all the exiles she needed from the list of applicants for asylum in the United States.

Eric took a bus in another direction, toward the waterfront section called La Boca. An early morning call to the yard got the foreman, who said his boss would be in later on.

At YATES BECARI, the sun was already bright and fiercely hot. There was a slight breeze. A yardman said that el dueño was "Por allá," pointing down a gangway leading to the floating docks. "Derecho al final, preguntales por él." It was a long walk to the end of the dock. In parallel finger slips lay millions of dollars worth of large sailing craft, most of them tended by professional crews, who were busy sanding, scraping, varnishing, and rigging, or just sitting and watching the very limited world go by. Near the end were the smaller boats, racing craft with no auxiliary engines, some of them getting ready to cast off. Becari, a rigger pointed out, was kneeling near a red boat fitting a turnbuckle to the forestay.

He stood up when Eric asked to speak to him—a huge man, at least a head taller than Eric's six feet, perhaps sixty-five years old, rugged-looking, with a close trimmed salt-and-pepper beard, leonine features and a full head of curly hair.

When Eric introduced himself and said that he wanted to interview Becari for a book, he looked surprised.

"Me? What could I have to say worth putting in a book? Come, I'm finished with this. We'll sit down over here."

At the end of the dock there was a large locked box fastened down and painted green. He opened the lid, put his tools inside, and then sat down on top, gesturing for Eric to do likewise.

"My book is about an American poet named Harry Raven who committed suicide by jumping off the *Libertador*. You were a witness at the Coast Guard inquest in New York. Do you remember?"

Becari looked at Eric long and hard, with suspicion in his eyes. "Like it was yesterday," he said, "but why is this important? Will it bring him back to life?"

In a sense it would, Eric said, if he could finish the book and tell people all about Raven's life. His death was part of it.

Becari listened intently. He seemed like a simple man, but there was a wariness, almost a crafty look behind his bearlike demeanor.

"Was this Raven important . . . a master?"

Eric told Becari briefly about Raven's literary career, and he listened intently, then said, "I tell you, Senor, that was my first experience with a man overboard, and I was amazed at the way that the boat crews were organized." He had been on deck after his watch, just before turning in, when he heard the captain trying to prevent the leap. Then the search for the body, the submarine, and the giving up. Eric knew all that from the newspaper accounts and the depositions taken by the Coast Guard. But here was an actual witness. What else did he know?

"And you held the searchlight on Raven in the water?"

"Claro, but we were steaming ahead pretty fast, maybe twelve, fifteen knots, and the body fell astern very quick."

"Did he struggle, or go right under?"

"That's the funny part: neither one. He just floated face down, like a corpse in white."

Eric felt as though his heart had stopped, and a numbness spread over his face and hands. "Are you sure?" he asked, incredulous.

"As I know I'm sitting here! I heard the captain in a struggle, but when he handed me the searchlight, I saw a dead man in the water!"

"That doesn't make sense," Erick said quickly, his voice high with tension.

"Who said that anything made sense!" Becari countered. "I'm just telling you what I saw, I don't try to make sense of things, I just try to live."

"But you didn't say that at the inquest, that the man was dead."

Becari shrugged his shoulders. "I couldn't be sure that he *was* dead, but it looked like that. Before the inquest, Captain Novaes called me in and asked me what I was going to say. I told him that—you're not from the police?"

Eric reassured him.

"And he told me that I should only talk about how I heard the commotion and heard the man fall. I was young, afraid of the captain, so I did as I was told." He fell silent, as though he had moved back in time and was fearful of the captain all over again.

"Why did you fear him?" Eric asked, after a moment of silence.

"I was young, impressionable, and he seemed very powerful," Becari answered. "I was afraid of ending up overboard myself. Look—Novaes was a real Nazi. When we were in Buenos Aires, the German Embassy used to send a staff car to pick him up. Who knows what he was carrying for them? We used to get mysterious arrivals, people and goods, in the middle of the night, and sometimes launches would come alongside when we were out at sea. There were all sorts of rumors among the crew. Of course I was down in the engine room most of the time, or sleeping when I wasn't on watch."

"What did you do on the ship?" Eric wanted to ask more about the suicide but held off a bit, wanting the man's confidence first.

"I was an engineer, tended the engines, worked down in the engine room. You know, like the hero of your American play, *The Hairy Ape*." He laughed, shaking all over at his joke against himself. "I'm sure you can see the resemblance," he continued. "Maybe I was his model."

"There's no resemblance at all, Senor Becari."

"Oh, I'm disappointed." He continued to chuckle to himself.

"I just wanted to live, needed to be left alone. What good would it have done to say that little bit of my observation? I could have been wrong. Who would be helped—the suicide? He made a decision to die, I made a decision to live. It was one of many choices I had to make in my life, a decision to live," he repeated, "a decision: to act, to live or to die."

"Surely, one doesn't *make* a decision to *die*. It seems to me that this is made for us, either biologically or by external circumstances."

His eyes looked distant for a moment, as though he were reaching back into the past for a memory which was difficult to grasp. "Ah, my young friend, I don't agree with you. It is possible, if one has the will, to overcome most situations, even those of seemingly absolute . . . with little hope, I mean." He rubbed his beard with his huge toughened hand, then took out two cigars from his jacket pocket. He lit his and his guest's, leaned forward, put his hand on Eric's forearm, and looked into his eyes. Eric felt a deep sense of Becari's power, his experience.

"Look, I was torpedoed off the coast here, during the war. The ship went down and most of the lives were lost. I survived. Just me and a few others. The rest of the crew drowned. But I *had* to live, I needed to live, and I did. I made it to shore from several miles out. I made it. I forced it. The others didn't because they didn't want to. They didn't want to live, and I'll tell you, what's more, they didn't want me to live. I didn't let *them* prevent me, because I had the will."

"I'm not sure I understand why you think the others didn't want you to live," Eric said.

His eyes grew fierce. "They could have made it," he said. "Most could swim, but it was easier to drown, easier to die. To live, for me, is to fight, to struggle, to say no to disaster, to make it meaningless. The only thing that had meaning to me, there in the water, four miles off the coast, was that I, I, I wanted to live. So I began to swim, slowly, toward the shore, and you know, the others tried to stop me. 'Wait here with us, Manolito,' they said. 'Hang on to this crate, or this hatch cover,' some said. Helpless, like infants, waiting for someone to rescue them, or divine providence to save them. Not me. I swam, slowly, slowly. Some of them tried to stop me. One man actually left the timber he was holding on to and tried to hurt me. He grabbed me and pulled me under. Fool!" He stopped and relit the cigar.

"Fool," he continued. "He let go of his life support in order to prevent me from trying to live. He wanted to strangle me."

"What did you do?"

He looked around. "You can't write this in a book; you promise?"

Eric promised.

"I killed him," the huge man whispered. "I had to. He wanted to die and take me with him. I wanted to live. It was a matter of clear choice there. I had no other options."

Eric didn't answer but looked away from his eyes, his burning eyes, in silence, wondering if he himself could ever do such a thing.

"Then I had the plank he had given up, and I put it under my chest, like a surfboard, and paddled to shore. The wood let me float and rest when I was tired, and I made it. Most of the others could have done that too, except for the ones who were actually killed by the torpedo, or trapped in the ship. But only a few did survive, and they had the same experience with the others as I did."

He stood up and looked toward the River Plate and said nothing for a few moments.

He puffed his cigar abstractedly and continued, "But I tell you, because I'm no longer afraid. I have lived as I wanted to, and fear is dead. I tell you. And as to this Raven, I'm not imagining that business about the body floating. When the rescue crews lowered the lifeboats, the steward—Ordoñez was his name, like the bullfighter—stood with me by the rail and remarked that it was a waste of time. I remember how he shrugged his shoulders and walked away."

"Did you ever mention it again?" Eric asked.

"No, we hardly saw each other on the ship, our duties didn't overlap, and the few times we did, there was no reason to talk about that. I really wasn't interested either. But if you want, you could probably turn him up."

"Where?" Eric thought it best to play ignorant.

"Here! He was a porteño. I didn't keep in touch with him, but I think he's still in Buenos Aires because I saw him once, bumped into him on the Calle Florida a few years ago. We said hello and a few words, nothing more. All we have in common is that he was one of the survivors too, but he did mention that he was living here. Up near the Congreso, I think. You can check it in the phone book," he said.

Someone came down the dock looking for the boss, a yard hand to say he was wanted on the telephone in the office.

Walking along the dock toward the shore, Becari commented on some of the more beautiful yachts. He seemed in no hurry to get to the telephone.

"I don't know why I told you all those details, Professor Newman, after all these years, but I suppose I always wanted to say it to someone and never had the chance. Besides, if you quote me in your book, I'll deny that I said anything. You understand why?"

Eric nodded his head, disappointed that Becari was removing attribution, the mark of authenticity from the story. "But you don't have Novaes to fear anymore. He's dead."

"I should know," he said, turning toward Eric and stopping. He lowered his voice: "Professor, Novaes was the one who tried to drown me, the one I killed!"

A shiver ran through Eric despite the sun and heat. The air had grown very still.

"So what do you fear?" Eric asked. Becari looked as if he could still take on the world and win.

"Ghosts!" he answered. "Don't mention me to Ordoñez," he said abruptly, then waved his hand, and was gone into the office. Eric walked through the dusty yard toward the street, thinking about the ghost of Harry Raven in a white dinner jacket, floating face down in the wake of a fast-moving ship.

12

THE FORMER STEWARD had been easy enough to find. Nick's listing was confirmed by the Buenos Aires telephone directory: Eduardo Ordoñez, H. Yrigoyen 2240. The same as in Raven's notebook! Eric called Ordoñez and said he was doing a book on survivors of shipwrecks and asked for an interview. Ordoñez was cautious. "Where did you get my name?" he had asked, suspiciously. From the Maritime Records Bureau, Eric told him.

After vacillating on the telephone, he asked Eric to come to his apartment a little later that morning.

"How can you expect me to remember clearly events which took place thirty-one years ago?" asked Ordoñez. "All I know is that I helped the man up on deck because the captain asked me to. This man had been drinking steadily and was a nuisance for the entire trip. On this night, the captain summoned me to the man's cabin and said that the man needed some fresh air. We helped him up to the first-class afterdeck and then I left him with Captain Novaes. That's all I remember."

"That's fine, Senor Ordoñez," Eric said, "but are there any other details you remember? What time was it, what was said, and so on?"

"I told you, it's too long ago for those details."

"Ten minutes ago you told me about the shipwreck and how you survived, in great detail." Eric took out a packet of Particulares and offered them. Ordoñez took one and lit it. This man looked so frail compared to Becari. Eric couldn't see him as a survivor at all.

"Look, Senor Newman, there is a difference between an experience of terror, swimming several miles through surf in shark-infested waters to save your own life after a torpedo hits your boat and scares you mindless to begin with, there is a difference between that and helping a drunken passenger to the deck for some air. I'm sure you agree."

Ordoñez got up and walked from his living room to the adjoining kitchen. He was a tall man, with gray hair slicked back, Argentine fashion. He was about sixty years old, Eric guessed, but looked younger, and apparently lived alone. "Will you have some coffee?" he called in. A minute later, Eric heard the kettle whistle and the clatter of preparations.

Ordoñez came back into the living room with a small battered aluminum espresso pot, two small cups, and some lumps of sugar on a plate.

"You know," he said, sipping at his cup after he stirred in four lumps of sugar, "I thought you really wanted to know about the shipwreck, but you seem far more interested in this writer Raven. I have told you all I know about that. Now if you want to know more about the torpedoing I lived through . . ." He paused, watching Eric's face closely.

"I'm really more interested in why your address appeared in the notebook belonging to the dead poet!" Eric said forcefully, to surprise him.

His face registered no response, but Eric noticed that his left hand trembled slightly when he put down the coffee cup.

"That is absurd," he said, staring at the wall behind the couch where Eric sat, "because . . . I didn't live here then. I moved after the war. Anyway, what has this dead writer to do with the shipwreck I experienced?" He seemed thoroughly confused.

"I'm not really writing about shipwrecks," Eric admitted, "I'm doing a biography of Harry Raven, and I thought you might know something about his death. I mean the circumstances. I'm sorry to upset you."

"No, no!" Ordoñez objected. "I'm not upset, only puzzled why *I* should be of interest to you."

"I told you!" The man was exasperating. "I want to clarify details for this biography, and your name and address match the address in the writer's notebook."

The telephone rang. A conversation about going somewhere on the weekend with Alfredo not being able to get tickets yet.

When he got off the phone, Eric said, "Thank you for the time: there's nothing to be gained by pursuing this. I'm not trying to pry into your life; I just want details of the man's death to clarify my book where I describe it. Eyewitness accounts."

"You understand my hesitation, senor?"

Although he didn't, Eric tried to look understanding.

"In this country," Ordoñez continued, "life is not easy for those of us with . . . *tendencies!*"

Eric nodded sympathetically.

Ordoñez picked up his coffee cup and seemed to relax a bit. "You asked me before what he looked like that day. All I remember," Ordoñez said, still seated, "is that he was wearing a white dinner jacket. A short, heavyset man, balding, in a white dinner jacket, and very drunk, practically unconscious.

"He had stayed in his cabin throughout most of the trip; I brought him his meals there. I had the impression that he was incurably ill, with his wheelchair and all. You know we were on the run from Buenos Aires to New York, and I think he was hardly out of his cabin for the entire two weeks, except to go ashore once. Maybe it was in Havana, who knows?"

Eric was confused now. Raven had *boarded* in Havana! Wheelchair? He was about to ask when Ordoñez continued.

"I think you misunderstand, senor. I have seen it happen before: a person who is incurably ill goes on a long sea voyage, for relaxation and health, to get away from it all. Out there he becomes depressed, knowing that he will never be better. At home with family, friends, everyday business, he forgets about his ailments. At sea, the hopelessness is brought closer to him, despair sets in, and the temptation to end it all is very strong. All around you is the answer. Too much to drink one night—and it happens!"

Eric had enough. He thanked Ordoñez for his philosophical interpretation and eased out the door, assuring him that if the book was published he would send a copy, and not give Ordoñez' name as a source. He seemed satisfied.

It was only noon, but Eric felt a strong urge for a drink. The cafe on the corner was open and he walked directly to the bar. "Whiskey, por favor."

"Nacional o importado?" asked the barman.

"Nacional." He felt cheap today.

Not that he gave a damn that Ordoñez was an old queer trying to protect his reputation; Eric certainly wasn't going to betray that tawdry little secret. What bothered him was that Ordoñez was using the story for some other reason. He relied on Eric's naivete to protect himself, but Ordoñez was a barefaced liar: Harry Raven had been tall and thin, with a full head of long flaxen hair, and he had never been sick, other than a cold, in his life.

Eric's next stop was the Biblioteca Nacional. He wasn't far from a subway station, and in his momentary economical frame of mind, he took the train downtown to the big public library. Odette was there too, deep into some files. He said hello and let her be. Within a few minutes he knew what he wanted to. The census for 1940 listed Eduardo Ordoñez as the sole resident of apartment 15 at Calle H. Yrigoyen 2240. The telephone directory published two years earlier confirmed the information.

Meanwhile Odette had been checking some other names and addresses fom Raven's notebook. Sitting there under the stained-glass windows of the huge rotunda in the main reading room as she showed Eric what she had discovered, retracing the steps, he grew more and more depressed and exhilarated at the same time. The stack assistants had kept her supplied with bound copies of old newspapers and the large ledger books of official records, and with each new bit of information that she dragged out, a clearer picture emerged. Eric didn't like it at all. Although the list was brief, the Buenos Aires names and addresses in Raven's notebook were a Who's Who of Argentine Nazis during the World War II years!

"Let's have something to eat and go back to the Reuters office," she suggested.

In Argentina good steak is ubiquitous and very cheap, so they opted for a local sawdust-floored restaurant and ate well, gorged in local color.

* * *

"Where the hell did you dig this up, and is the source reliable? That's what I'd ask one of my own men if he came to me with this kind of stuff," Hal Osborne asked, removing his glasses for an unnecessary polishing, and staring at Eric with penetrating eyes that seemed out of focus.

Nick was with him when Odette and Eric arrived. Osborne was everyone's source, an information broker. In his office at the Reuters bureau in the La Prensa building on Sarmiento it seemed as though the news business was a sideline, his hobby-horse the major concern. Odette had said that he was the big "Hitler-is-alive-and-well-in-Argentina" buff and thought he'd be able to help.

"The background stuff comes from newspapers, public records and so on. The source of the names is Harry Raven's notebook. I don't know if Nick mentioned to you that I was writing his biography." Eric explained briefly about the notebook and his need to settle the anomalies before he could write the book, satisfied that he had done his homework.

Osborne nodded. "Nick mentioned something about it. I always found that stuff, his poetry, too complicated; had to read it in college. Anyway, this is dynamite!"

"Except here I am, stuck with it. I don't have the ignition caps. I don't know what to do with all this now. These wheels were listed in Raven's notebook. Maybe he was a buff like you." That had occurred to Eric on the spur of the moment, but Osborne didn't buy it. Eric regretted calling him a buff: investigative reporter would have been more appropriate.

"You know what to do as well as I do!" Osborne snapped. "The question is, do you want to?"

"You're giving me too much credit," Eric said. "I don't know."

Osborne rolled his eyes toward heaven and then looked at Eric, this time with his glasses on, hard and focused. "You find out if any of these people are still around, and you go to see them on some sort of pretext, and you ask about Raven at some point in the conversation. Surely you've done that in interviewing for the book?"

Eric had done just that today, but wasn't comfortable with cover stories; they always seemed transparent to him. He felt guilty and too ready to confess.

"But why should they want to reveal themselves, talk to me?" he asked.

"I'm assuming that these weren't war criminals, just Argentine Axis sympathizers," Osborne answered, "and that went for a very large majority here during the war. Let's see the list."

Eric passed it across the littered desk.

Alberto Castelli Bravo
Hector Villacampos

Ricardo Montenegro
Klaus Immerman

"Forget about Montenegro," Osborne said, after a minute. "He died a few years ago. Castelli Bravo used to be the editor of *El Pampero*, a right-wing rag the Nazis backed with lots of dough. He's still around. Retired. Probably a lot of background information there because he had plenty of contacts; if he'll talk."

"What about the others?"

"Villacampos you can forget about too."

"Dead?"

"Insane. He's been in an asylum since the late forties, and besides, he was never important, just rich. The Nazis played on his delusions of power and used him for his money. Must've given them millions. Story is that he did it all to spite his wife, Alicia. She was an ardent communist. You know—one of those matches decided by family. She turned him off and no wonder. I heard he was as queer as a three-dollar bill. He got his revenge by making it big with the world masters. Now he's a fucking lunatic."

Eric would see the wife. He knew about her before this: she had been Winkler's sometime lover after Lee ran away, and later too, he thought.

"Immerman I don't know much about. Import-export business. My guess is that he was their chief courier. Had the setup, the credentials . . . don't know much more."

He paused, then reached for the office phone, glancing first at Nick. "If anybody knows, this guy will."

"Who's that?" Nick asked.

He dialed the number. "Chaim Zak, the Israeli guy . . . you know him," Osborne said, covering the mouthpiece with his hand. "Buenos tardes. Senor Zak, por favor."

He held his hand over the mouthpiece. "This guy will have it or no one will."

"Who is it?" Eric asked.

"He's the first secretary of the Israeli Embassy here, but he's into all this stuff. The guy got Eichmann!"

He broke off when the voice spoke on the other end. It was a loud aggressive voice and Eric could hear it from where he sat. "Herschel, vas machts du . . ." it said in Yiddish.

"Do they let you speak Yiddish in that joint, Chaim? I thought it was a no-no."

Eric couldn't hear the reply, but Osborne laughed—a professional laugh, the information seeker's icebreaker—he'd probably cultivated it for years as a reporter and editor, a valued tool of the trade.

"Listen, bubbeleh, I've got a guy with me, a professor from Columbia. . . . No, the university. He's trying to run down some information, the kind you specialize in . . . yeah, that's it—a tourist: ten days in Israel including free entrance to the kibbutz woman of your choice. Can you see him? Tomorrow at ten?" Osborne looked over at Eric for confirmation. "Okay, Chaim, we're on. Name is Newman, Eric Newman. Guess who's here with me—Nick Burns, remember?"

He handed Nick the phone and they spoke. Nick told Zak he'd come with Eric in the morning, and then left them. He had an appointment at the Embassy, something official, and would see them tomorrow.

Osborne accompanied Eric and Odette to a cafe on Florida and ogled passing women while exchanging gossip about colleagues with Odette. "At least I'm never bored," he responded to her teasing about his wandering eyes. "That's the main thing!"

"For me, you're the 'main thing,'" Odette said later, after Osborne left "to follow his heart," as he put it. "I like Hal a great deal, but his overt womanizing appalls me."

"*So* judgmental," Eric said, exaggerating the words so that she would know he was half kidding. "I wonder how you judge me?" he continued. "After all, my track record isn't so terrific."

She looked at him, puzzled. "I don't know what you mean by 'track record.'"

"I mean my history, specifically my relationships with women. You must judge that unkindly too, as you do with Hal," he said.

"No, I don't," she jumped in quickly, "because he and his wife have this 'open marriage' agreement, which I find repulsive to begin with, and he uses it simply to promote his own indiscriminate lechery. I like him very much as a working professional, and find him very helpful, but . . . he should not be married, then he could do as he chose."

She really looked zealous as she said this, and Eric realized that it was a sensitive area, some hurt concealed perhaps; he didn't know, but sensed he should be careful.

"You're very traditional for a liberated woman."

"I've learned the hard way," Odette answered, reaching for her Gitanes. "If I should ever marry—and at this age I doubt it—there will be no 'open marriage.' If my husband wants another woman, it will be solely his responsibility, not mine. I will not sanction it. And if I found out, I would kill him, and maybe her too."

"I'm glad you warned me," Eric said, laughing, finding a cigarette to cover his nervousness in the face of her passion.

"I'm sorry," she said, laughing too. "It is only hypothetical, of course, and I don't think I could hurt anyone, at least not for passion, but I get carried away. I have not been ready for marriage, except once, because it *is* a sacrament for me, and I have preferred to be sacrilegious in my life. But if I were ever to marry, I would treat it sacramentally."

"Then you *must* judge me poorly," Eric repeated. He needed an answer from her.

She thought for a minute, sipping her dry vermouth slowly. "No, I don't," she said finally. "I think that you are the sort of man who would be extremely loyal if you were in the right relationship to a woman. Evidently that isn't what you had in your marriage, and perhaps you will always be looking for that. On the other hand, maybe you will find what I think you want."

"What *you* think I want?"

"Yes, that is the only standard I can judge by," she answered.

Later, in her room, *she* seemed to be what Eric thought he really wanted, only he was afraid to say so, like a child who believes that you can jinx something by mentioning it. His own belief in magic surprised him, that residue of childhood.

* * *

"Today I'm a working woman: interviews," Odette said when she woke Eric early. "We'll have coffee out. Bien, mon chou?"

She rang Nick's room. He was out already. A message in Eric's mailbox said he'd meet him at the Israeli Embassy at ten o'clock.

Calle Florida still smelled damp from its morning hosing, and the heat of the day hung back for a while. The cafes had their tables out already, at eight, and they saw Osborne seated at one, talking to three other men. He rose to greet Eric and Odette.

"We don't want to distract you from your colleagues," Odette said, kissing him on the cheek.

"Nah—I see those guys all day," he answered. "Just shoptalk."

They moved to a table out front. The sun was hot but felt good on Eric's pale face.

"Seems like we've done this before," Osborne said, as the waiter arrived with the coffee. It was the same cafe where they had had drinks the night before.

"It's pleasant here," Odette remarked, and indeed it was. Calle Florida, permanently closed to traffic, is an ambler's paradise of shops, galleries, restaurants, and cafes, but there are also many offices including that of *La Nacion*, the stolid, moderate daily newspaper with the largest circulation in Argentina. The commercial presence on the street tempers the touristy quality, and if only Eric had been in the mood for the world, it would have been a wonderful place to sit and watch it go by.

But he wasn't. When he had stopped to read the lead stories in that morning's *La Nacion*, posted on the ground floor window of the office, a police story caught his eye, because a familiar name jumped out at him:

SHOOTS VISITOR, DIES OF HEART ATTACK

Acting on an anonymous phone call, police went to the apartment of Eduardo Ordoñez in Calle H. Yrigoyen and discovered the bodies of Senor Ordoñez, the inhabitant of the apartment, and Heriberto Montilla, a businessman from Rosario. Senor Montilla had been shot to death with a pistol found in the hand of Senor Ordoñez, who had apparently died of natural causes.

According to police sources there were no signs of forced entry to the apartment, and one highly placed official speculated that the two men had quarreled and Ordoñez had shot Montilla fatally, after which Ordoñez suffered a massive coronary occlusion and died instantly himself.

Autopsies are being conducted to determine the precise times and causes of both deaths. . . .

The story jumped to an inside page after that and Eric couldn't finish it. He bought the paper at a kiosk, as though it mattered now. He had wanted to confront Ordoñez again with his lies about Raven. Now another link would be missing, forever. And the guy from Rosario. That was too much; he was the one who saved Eric's life two nights before, the man from the hotel!

"What's eating you?" Osborne asked when he noticed Eric was toying with his coffee and roll and keeping silent. Eric showed him the paper.

"Just consider yourself lucky that the old bugger didn't shoot you," he said. "Count your blessings ands drink your coffee."

Odette looked at Hal sharply. "That's insensitive, Hal. It was important to Eric and his book to see this man again. Think of when you were out on the street as a reporter, in the days when you were idealistic and thought you had some talent,"—he winced but didn't say anything in response to her barb—"and a witness, or a source disappeared, or how do you say in American—'dried up.'"

Hal waited for her to finish and then answered, quiet but tough. The hard core journalist took over the kibbitzer. "I'm aware of the difficulties, Odette, but you should know that you don't get anywhere in this business without developing an elephant hide! What the hell can Eric do now that the guy's dead? Nothing. It's too bad, and I'm sorry for the guy and for Eric, but if he sits around and broods over it, he won't get his story from the other possible sources, especially if they're tied in with this guy Ordoñez and take the incident as a warning to go to ground."

It was Osborne's professionalism speaking, and deep down Eric knew that he was right. Odette seemed confused and said, "I really don't know what you're talking about, because I think you are confusing sound practice with emotional response, and that's why I think you are callous. It's no wonder you have trouble with women."

Osborne knew he was being needled and laughed, "Too old to change, m'love, and besides, I do all right.

"Furthermore," he continued, "I'm not sure that Eric needs *your* protection from the real world. He's a big boy. Don't be such a mother hen."

"Hal," she said, *"you're* overbearing and intimidating, but that doesn't always mean that you're right. I'll do things my own way." She didn't say anything more, but finished her coffee and then found her cigarettes in her cavernous handbag, and sat smoking and watching the passersby.

"What about the police? Won't they want to see anyone who last saw this Ordoñez alive?" Eric asked.

"With due respect to my distinguished French colleague," Osborne said in an ironic tone, "don't be such a naive shithead, my friend."

"For once, Hal's right," Odette cut in. "The Argentine police will only waste your time and involve you in endless red tape. They may even hold you in custody as a material witness. If they want to see you, they'll contact you; otherwise, leave them alone."

"But it's a normal thing to do!" Eric objected.

"Maybe, only maybe, in the U.S. of A.," Hal interjected. "Not here."

He went to his office. Odette stayed a moment and then went to interview an exile leader from Chile. Eric decided to walk the ten blocks or so to the Israelis.

* * *

"Sorry to inconvenience you with these security measures," Chaim Zak said, shifting his large frame in the desk chair, "but it's quite necessary here." Nick had preceded Eric, and lounged on a chair, looking tired.

Eric had just expressed surprise at the steel shuttered windows to Zak's office, and had been even more surprised at the thorough body search he had to go through in the antechamber of the Embassy, where one man searched him while two others watched —dark-skinned Israeli security police who looked like they could break you in half with one hand and enjoy it. Eric had to leave all his personal possessions in an envelope at the entrance, including watch, wallet, and briefcase. They allowed him to carry in some loose paper, and the Xerox copy of the Raven manuscript.

"Unfortunately we are plagued here by lunatics, and they are encouraged and supported by Arab propaganda and lots of money. Every day there's another bomb scare, attempted kidnappings, and every morning the cleaning staff scrubs off the anti-Semitic slogans that have been painted on the outside walls the night before. It's not pleasant, but it's the real world for us. The embassy here is like a smaller version of Israel, and the precautions are those we live with every day."

Eric was beginning to feel that he came from a very protected environment.

"Let's get down to business," Nick said; "I have to get back to my office."

Zak, who looked and spoke more like a linebacker for the Dallas Cowboys than a diplomat, listened carefully as Eric explained the basic situation.

"No one we are looking for ourselves," he said when Eric had finished his summation and showed Zak the list. "Even when we find a big one, we have problems. When we do find someone of the stature of Eichmann again, it will be a great coup for us, a great blow to the Arabs, and a great confusion to American Jewish liberals who will debate endlessly in the press about justice . . . because," he added in a bitter tone, "they never had to live as we do," pointing to the steel shutters, "on the edge of survival."

Zak took them through the hall of the old mansion to a small elevator, then down to a subbasement, a large square room about thirty feet in dimension, covered floor to ceiling by shelves and file cabinets. An armed guard sat at the door, and admitted them, looking at Zak quizzically. Inside, an attendant looked up from the newspapers he was clipping and filing, and rose.

"This is where we keep the records of Nazi criminal activity during and since the Holocaust, exclusively in Latin America," Zak said, dropping his huge frame into a chair and gesturing for Nick and Eric to do the same. "Our records cover the continent. Some of this material is top, top secret," he continued, "and I'm afraid that I can't show it to you. The very fact that you're here is already a violation, but if Nick Burns vouches for you it's okay by me. Look, this is the deal: we open our resources to you, and you help us out by being open to us if you come across anything you think we should know, however minute it may seem to you. That is your part of the bargain."

Nick had the devil's advocate habit from years of dealing with journalists and said to Zak, "But you said you aren't interested in 'revenge,' in ferreting out every crypto-Nazi for a public burning. So why do you bother with all these miniscule bits of information?"

Zak stood, stretched his giant form and smiled. "I don't mean we wouldn't be interested in some spectacular arrest and certainly if we could find Borman, we would do for him what we did for Eichmann. Same broadcast; equal time. But our business is political: we use this information to get what we want as a state. The information we have about somebody who is now in a position of power is more valuable to us than throwing the guy in jail to rot. This way we can often accomplish our political ends more quickly. As a diplomat, a few cracked skulls bleeding onto swastikas do me no good. Our power comes from information we can use to our advantage."

"A born sophist you are, Chaim," Nick chided him. "Why don't you just say *blackmail?*"

"Because it's an ugly word for my delicate constitution," Zak answered. "Have I made myself clear to you Professor Newman?"

Eric said he understood the quid pro quo.

Zak then showed him the way the material was organized; it was based on documents captured by the Allies, he said, at the end of the war. A master plan for the division of Latin America into specific control groups under the hegemony of the Third Reich accompanied by a detailed map was the basis of the indexing system. Keyed to this were the master lists of the German commandants for each sector and the staff at his disposal. Included were the names of all operatives. If they were German nationals, rank and document numbers were included. If they were citizens of the country in that sector, their carnet de identidad numbers as well as the numbers on any false documents for aliases were included.

It was a masterpiece of German thoroughness. From the sector lists, the Israelis had drawn up a list, alphabetized on index cards and cross-indexed in several ways: name and aliases, actual country and sector in the Reich schematic, rank and function, and participation in known espionage operations. This was simply a reference library, and Eric felt quite at home.

Not so for Nick. "I'd get lost here," he said. "I would spend years reading every file."

"The best way to use this material," said Zak, "is when you have a specific name or detail you want to run down."

Nick said he didn't, and left with Zak, who had to sign out all of his visitors. He instructed the attendant to cooperate with Eric, and then said to Eric, "Call me on the interoffice phone when you're ready to leave, and I'll come down and sign you out. No notes, please!"

Eric was left alone with the underground mine of evil stretching out miles of paper around him.

The task was relatively simple, a straightforward research cross-checking. He ran through the names from Raven's notebook and came up with essentially what Osborne had told him the day before.

There was one peculiarity which struck him, however, in the Immerman file. According to the record, Immerman had been a double agent, suspected of selling copies of plans for something called a magnometric oscillating alphagraph to the OSS, documents received from Oberst Krähe of the Abwehr (German military intelligence). This betrayal, or at least the suspicion for it, had cost him his life. The curious thing was that Immerman died (was "terminated" in the language of the dossier) on 15 July 1943. The same day that Harry Raven committed suicide.

There was a cross-reference to Project Xeno mentioned in Raven's notebook but the file was not available at the moment, the attendant said disinterestedly, and waited until Eric handed him materials he had been using and signed the log indicating the time borrowed and the time returned for each item in use.

"May I use the phone?" Eric asked him. The man turned his mousy face and said, "It's only for inside calls."

"I want to call Mr. Zak, that's all."

"Extension 451," he said, walking toward the file drawers with the folders in his pale hands. Zak came down at once.

Eric told him that there seemed to be a focus of these people around Project Xeno, but that the file was not available.

He shrugged. "That I can't help you with; it may be upstairs with the political section. This is a bureaucracy, which means that even a signature or an initialing of a document could meet with countless delays and postponements. Updating a file sometimes takes weeks."

Zak was bluff and hearty, and Eric was convinced he was lying.

13

Buenos Aires

OUTSIDE ON THE street, the heat hit Eric like a red brick. He walked to a cafe two blocks from the Embassy and used the pay phone. The bar was dark and cool and he ordered a draught beer when he bought the telephone fichas from the barman.

Castelli Bravo was away for the day; call tomorrow, Eric was told. Disappointed, he called the house of the doyenne of the Argentine literary world.

Certainly! He should come over immediately, said Alicia Villacampos. She would be happy to meet with him and tell him what she could. Any friend of Ben Winkler's, and so on.

The house was only a few blocks from where he was, and he walked through the elegant streets of the Barrio Norte, acclimated now to the warmth, enjoying the buzzing of life, the little groups in sidewalk cafes, the housemaids lined up at the local bakers for the luncheon bread: the long thin flautas clasped in one hand as they emerged from the shop. But for the language, he could have been in France, so imitated here, so deferred to culturally that it had almost obliterated traces of Hispanic America. "When a good porteño dies he goes to Paris"—Eric remembered the cynical saying as he rang the bell at the art nouveau gate of the large mansion set back from the street behind tall garden walls. A maid came out and admitted him when he gave her his name.

The senora stood waiting in the entrance foyer.

Alicia Villacampos had been known as a beauty in her day, and even in her seventies retained an air of elegance, and a brilliant pair of eyes, almost black in color, with wide irises and long lashes. But time had done its ravaging and her aristocratic hands were gnarled with arthritis; her body looked wasted and emaciated.

"Professor Newman, how good of you to come," she said when the maid showed Eric in, as though he were doing her a service.

She hobbled at his side into a large drawing room with French doors open onto a manicured garden. The room itself was like a nineteenth century salon: mauve velvet couches, silk curtains and a concert size ebony piano. Freshly cut flowers were in vases everywhere. Alicia Villacampos guided Eric directly through the garden doors to a shaded veranda.

She picked up a small bell in her twisted hand, rang for the maid, and said something to her in a low tone. The maid left, to return a minute later with a decanter of whiskey, a bowl of ice and two crystal glasses; she poured two healthy measures over ice, offered one to Eric and raised her own.

"Now go on, please," the senora said, after swallowing a large mouthful in one gulp, smiling with pleasure.

Eric decided not to dissemble with her but asked directly about Winkler and Raven. That seemed the line to follow with this candid woman.

She put down her glass, smiled sadly and said, "I have lived a rich life, Professor Newman. Although to look at me now you wouldn't think so, I was once very beautiful and sought after by many men. But of all the men, Benjamin Winkler was the finest, the most passionate and the most interesting I have ever known."

She stopped talking and finished her whiskey in one swallow, then stared at the polished terrazzo floor. Lifting her beautiful eyes she said, "But in the spring of 1944, when he was still obsessed with that *maricon* worm Harry Raven, who had to prove himself a man by running off with Benjamin's wife, that spring, Benjamin was beside himself. He was, how do you say, *fixated* on Raven. Even when he was beaten up by the fascists, I nursed him back to health, right here in this house, and in his delirium after the attack he kept saying, 'Raven in the street,' 'Raven in the car,' 'Raven watching them beat me,' 'Raven the Nazi!' Benjamin would scream and have nightmares, and when I would come to his room to calm him down he was in absolute terror, saying, 'Raven this, Raven that,' 'Raven here, there, everywhere.' It's lucky Benjamin was nursed here. If he had been in a hospital they would have locked him up in the mental ward!"

"Did any of it sound real to you, as though he were not hallucinating?" Eric asked her.

"He said several times that the attack on him was only a pretext. He said that they were looking for a notebook but that it was in the safe at the American Embassy. It all sounded like a cloak-and-dagger fantasy, but he told me that calmly, several times, and then would become silent when I asked him to elaborate. I think there was some truth there, but it really didn't concern me."

Eric pressed her on the notebook. "Did he ever say which notebook?"

"No," she answered. "Only that it was safe and that he would know what to do with it later. Benjamin was a wonderful man, but his experience ruined him. I didn't see him again for almost five years, and by then he had lost his zest for life."

She rose and rang for the maid. "I'm afraid you must excuse me, Professor Newman. I hope I have helped you, but now I must rest or I won't be fit company for my evening guests."

The maid appeared on the porch to show him out. Eric thanked the senora, who bade him come back or write to ask questions." I hate the telephone. It has destroyed the art of letter writing and conversation."

As he said good-bye to her she said, "Good luck with your biography, and I do hope you can show the world what a despicable vermin Harry Raven really was."

Eric walked slowly under the heavy shade of the plane trees toward the corner, where he thought he might find a taxi. It was almost two o'clock and he wanted to be back in the center to meet the others for lunch.

On the shady, quiet street, half a block from the Villacampos mansion, a black Peugeot pulled up alongside him and the driver tapped his horn lightly. Eric turned to look and the front seat passenger got out, walked up to him, and stuck a gun into his stomach. Eric's body went rigid with fear, and he began to tremble and sweat simultaneously. He was being abducted, kidnapped—God! How did he ever get into this, it was sheer madness, a bad dream.

The man motioned toward the car with his head and prodded Eric with the gun. Then the back door of the sedan swung open and he realized that there was a third man in the rear.

They weren't going to do this to him! He had to get away . . .
or wake up. He couldn't just let himself be taken off to slaughter.
He pulled away from the car, away from the door to death, and
the gunman, instead of shooting him, raised the gun and hit Eric
on the side of the face, knocking him to the ground. The pain
ricocheted through his head, and he thought the gunman would
now kill him. A trembling started and Eric cowered, braced for
the shot he was sure would come next. But the gunman grabbed
Eric's arm and started dragging him to the car instead.

He could feel a violent nausea; he was going to die; he knew
it. What the hell had he done? Asked some questions? It was
Nick's fault, stupid Nick and his spy games. Eric shouldn't have
come here. Odette. To never see her again. Oh God! He screamed
and the gunman let go. Eric scrambled up and started running.
Let him shoot, he thought. At least he could die trying to escape
and not like a trapped animal. Then he saw two men were
running toward the car from across the street. Eric's would-be
captor turned toward them and raised his pistol. One of the
running men dropped to a crouch, held both hands out in front
of him. Eric saw a puff of smoke and looking back, saw his
assailant scream and fall, dropping his gun. He heard the sound
of the shot afterward, echoing in the quiet street, and the burnt
smell of cordite hung heavy in the still air.

In the car someone shouted "Vaya!" and the engine roared.
Eric stopped, frozen in the place by fear. His legs were lead. The
man who had stopped him was writhing on the ground, his gun
lying where he had dropped it a few feet away.

As the Peugeot started to pull away from the curb, a black and
yellow taxi screeched to a stop in front of it, blocking the street
diagonally, and a delivery van lumbered up at the rear. What
had been a placid residential street was now filled with running
men and the roaring of the Peugeot, gears grating as the driver
tried to back away from the taxi.

The rubber screeched and a volley of shots boomed out from
the delivery van. Suddenly a sheet of flame enveloped the
Peugeot, and the running men stopped. Two men from the delivery van reached the flaming black sedan quickly enough to
pull the driver and passenger out and drag them, half-dead and
scorched, to the sidewalk.

Eric felt dizzy and nauseated, and staggered, leaning back against a stone wall behind him and sank to the ground where he sat, sobbing like a baby. He didn't know what had happened, only that he was alive and three other men were dead or almost dead because of him. Maybe he would be dead in a second when these other characters got to him; but he couldn't move. It was easier to be killed. All he could think about was that he had gotten caught in the battle between urban guerilla terrorists and the street police. Another executive to kidnap and ransom . . . or murder if no one paid. Who would pay for his life?

Suddenly, he was pulled to his feet roughly and someone said, "Ven conmigo. Estes seguro. Somos amigos."

Eric didn't believe the man but was too weak to resist, and was led to the taxi and helped in.

"El centro, donde el quiere ir," the man said to the driver, and to Eric, "No tengas miedo," as the taxi reversed and made a U-turn in the street.

He could already hear the sound of sirens as he fell back in the seat and stared out the window like a zombie.

* * *

"Salauds!, filthy animals," Odette said when Eric arrived at the cafe on Florida and told her why he had been delayed. The cab, as promised, had dropped him half a block away, and wouldn't take any money, although he kept the meter on all the way, for appearances Eric supposed—or hack inspectors. At least he got a free ride for his trouble.

Nick had had something to do at the American Embassy and wasn't there yet, so Eric ordered a double whiskey and a sandwich and told Odette about the files that Zak let him use, and what Senora Villacampos had said. He was exhausted and bedraggled but not really damaged. His face hurt where he'd been hit, but that was all.

She sat listening quietly, smoking one Gitane after another while he talked, her anger and annoyance showing clearly on her face. "Either they thought you were someone else, or someone is after you for other reasons." She toyed with another Gitane, and then decided against it. "Are you sure you're not a spy?" A smile flickered in her eyes. Then she said, "Maybe it was a jealous lover," and then, more menacingly, "Or husband?"

"You're getting to be an unhealthy influence," Osborne said, as he sat down and beckoned the waiter. "I sure hope you don't plan to pay *me* a formal visit."

"What the hell are you talking about, Hal?" Eric asked, in no mood to be needled.

"Castelli Bravo is dead. The call came in to the office as I was leaving. That's why I'm late. I stayed for the detailed report."

He looked at their faces, which must have registered the shock and amazement he wanted, and then he said, "The police found him in the park—hands tied, bullet in the neck—gangster style rub-out. Someone saw a black Peugeot sedan leaving the scene in a hurry, found the body and called the cops."

Eric gasped. Probably the same characters that attacked him, he realized. If not for that unexplained rescue squad, he'd be a second corpse in the park. The waiter came with Osborne's order.

Then Eric told him what had happened. Osborne just shook his head from side to side.

"I'm not letting him out of my sight," Odette said.

"Lot of help you'd be." Osborne began to laugh and choked on his drink, coughing red wine onto his shirt front.

"Good for you!" she said joyfully. "It proves that there is justice in the world, you male chauvinist!"

"The only place you'll find justice is in the dictionary," Osborne said, laughing too, but at himself.

"Seriously though," he continued, "what if the police come up with the fact that you had some contact with each of these men just before their deaths?" He paused. "You sure you're not a hit man?"

Everyone, Eric thought, suspected him of being something else. He didn't even know what he was anymore! Osborne had been talking, and Eric tuned back in.

". . . they're going to pick you up for questioning. And that is not to be desired, as I told you already, because they play rough, often for no particular reason, but to show machismo. Is there any way they would know you visited the old sailor, Ordoñez?"

"I don't see why, unless he wrote it down. I doubt that." Eric gestured to the waiter and asked for coffee. Then an idea struck him as he remembered being served coffee by the steward. "Hal, can you get to a source who'll give you some details on this double death?" Eric asked.

"I think so, why?"

Eric told him, and Osborne got up and went to the public phone inside the cafe.

"I got so wrapped up in my own little adventure that I forgot to ask if you had any luck today," Eric asked Odette when Osborne got up.

"I thought you'd never ask," she answered with a trace of sarcasm. Reaching into her voluminous handbag, she brought out a small tape recorder. She placed it on the table between them and without a word switched it on:

A man's voice said:

"I was so frightened when they arrested me, not so much of being shot, but of being tortured. We were transported somewhere, I'm not sure exactly but I think it was in the south, because the weather got colder as we traveled in this closed-up troop truck—a full day. But when they took me in finally to the interrogation, where I expected to see branding irons and fingernail pullers, there was only a room that looked like a medical examining room and a man in a white coat.

"They made me lie down on a table and strapped my arms and legs down and attached electrodes to my head, arms and chest. Then they placed a large lens, something like an X-ray camera, above my head, and asked me a lot of questions about people I knew, what they did, where they were, and so on. Most of the questions were simple, and seemed harmless. I lied a few times about specific details, but mostly there wasn't any necessity."

"But you were never hurt by the fascists?" (Odette's voice)

"No. Only once did I feel any pain, and that was after they asked me the same question three times and I lied each time. The second and third time I lied, I felt the most severe electric shock. It ran through my entire body, like being kicked by twenty people at the same time."

"What happened then?" (Odette)

"They took me back to a cell. The next morning I was transferred back to a truck and driven with other prisoners back to Santiago. I stayed in Tres Alamos prison for almost two months, and then they let me go, as a gesture of amnesty. Unlike the godless left, the junta illustrates its Christianity."

"Maybe your wife bribed some juntista." (Odette again) "She's from one of the richest families in Chile."

"I don't know, but I'll tell you, it would have been better if they had killed me. Nobody talks to me now; I am a pariah among the exiles because they think I betrayed the movement, gave away the entire group."

(A pause and some sobs)

"Within the week after my interrogation, everyone in the movement at the School of Journalism—I taught there—was arrested or disappeared, the secret meeting room was raided and sacked, and everything we had worked for was wrecked. But I did not give them a single name or address!"

"Maybe someone else did." (Odette)

"I was the only one of us detained. My wife told me that on the telephone when I got to Buenos Aires two weeks ago. Even she has stopped talking to me."

(Again sobbing)

"I beg your pardon for this emotional demonstration."

Odette turned the machine off.

"Well, what do you think, Professor Newman?" she asked, smiling.

Eric said that he thought the man had been under a great strain.

"I would feel guilty too, if I had caused the demise of thirty people. They may have given him one slap in the face and a promise he'd be released if cooperative, and he told them everything. On the other hand . . ." she trailed off, looking bemused.

Eric wasn't up to making any judgments. "But that's just the kind of information you wanted!" he said, surprised that she should be so skeptical.

"You're right. It's just like the report in Paris," she answered, lighting another cigarette, "but it still sounds incredible. Perhaps all those who betrayed their compañeros—and so far I have spoken only to people who were detained at the same time— perhaps they fabricated this hocus-pocus to hide their treason. I don't know." She shrugged her shoulders and looked dejected.

He didn't know what to make of her unwillingness to accept the very confirmation she had been seeking. He supposed that she had her own high standards of verification; that was what made her the superior journalist she was. Why should he think less of her need to verify than his own?

"The plot thickens," he said to Odette, intentionally inane.

"I don't know what you mean," she said with annoyance, and then added, "No, don't explain. Je suis fatiguée. Let's do something entertaining tonight, and stop chasing ghosts, getting attacked, and precipitating death. It's time for a little rest!"

It was the second time he had heard Odette really annoyed, and firm in her needs. The first was when she spoke about marriage the night before. He liked the way she knew her own mind and made demands clearly, rather than whining, pouting, or being a sexual Machiavellian. "What would you like to do?" Eric asked.

"There's a recital at the Teatro Municipal I'd like to go to. Dietrich Fischer-Dieskau, whom I will forgive for being German because he is doing Debussy and Fauré. Also some Schubert for the diehards. Would you like to go? I can get press passes."

Eric wasn't overly fond of art songs but felt like being agreeable, so he said yes. "Just you and me, though," he requested.

Just then Osborne returned. "Got it," he said, sitting down and sipping at the diluted Campari in his glass. "The gun was found in Ordoñez' right hand. What's the point?"

Eric had thought that would be the answer. "The man was left-handed! I saw him pour coffee, and write, and wipe his eyeglasses. Would he fire a pistol with his right hand? What about Montilla?"

Osborne lowered his voice. "He was a Chilean undercover cop —secret police."

"But how . . . why—" Odette started to ask.

"You think it was a double wipeout, staged to look like the murder of an intruder by a man with a weak heart, and a collapse?" Osborne asked, interrupting her.

"Eric, you have the mind of a writer of romans policiers, and I thought you were a scholar," Odette blurted out.

"I'd call it a comic-book mind," said Osborne.

"That's what Nick always told me when we were in college," Eric retorted.

Osborne looked serious. "But it's worth looking into. Not your mind, but the case," he said.

"It sure is, especially since this Ordoñez was a Nazi agent during the war!"

Hal looked at Eric with wide eyes. "You sure?"

"Checked the records of your buddy Zak!" Eric said, and almost immediately regretted revealing it. "This may give you some material for your witch-hunt, Hal, but it's nothing to me," Eric added, trying to back out of his blunder.

Odette said, "It all sounds absurd!" She was impatient to leave. "Well, sleep on it, Hal, if you have the time," she dug at him. He remained seated at the cafe, deep in his own mysteries, as they walked away down the crowded Florida mall; Eric was dirty, dragging his feet and needing a shower and change of clothes badly.

* * *

Annoyed to his fingertips that he was getting nowhere while risking his friend's neck, Nick Burns sat in Chaim Zak's office bitching about the situation. He needed the secure ear and trained mind of a fellow intelligence officer, but had to keep away from the CIA people. Zak was the only one he could use for feedback.

Nick had just finished saying that he knew the Buenos Aires police could solve the Sepulvida assassination if they wanted to. Such gangland-style rub-outs—machine gunning cars and drivers in broad daylight—don't happen in a vacuum. The underworld has those who know, and you can too if you want to—*for a price*. Nick wanted to glue it together, to see the relationship of these fragments.

"But the Argentines knew that good relations with their Chilean neighbors—the sympathy of one military regime for another—demanded that they publicly lament and then quietly forget the incident, assurances to the world notwithstanding," Zak said. "If the hit men were locals, they would talk—if the police would only find them."

Nick retorted, "But if they were a team brought in from outside, forget it; they're gone."

Zak quickly responded that he was sure they were outsiders. The job had the stamp of the international class: they used Uzis, the Israeli submachine guns, just as the Leboulier killers had used plastic explosives with the radio controlled detonator. No local hoods would do that. Not that they couldn't. It just didn't happen,

"I want a lead," Nick lamented, "just one fucking link to show where the control came from, prove that the killings were not random. And now Montilla, our double in DINA bought the ticket too." When Nick learned that Montilla had been assigned by Santiago to tag Eric, even harass him, he thought they'd get a break. But now only a dead end. He felt helpless.

Chaim Zak heard Nick out, leaning back in his swivel chair, his eyes intent on his American colleague. "The problem with you Americans," he said when Nick finished, "is that you are 'hung up,' as you say, on the legal, on the semblances of legality. What else could one expect from a nation of lawyers? Governments made up of lawyers write laws and then manipulate them so everything seems legal. Governments of soldiers make wars, inside and outside—"

"And what about governments of refugees, of survivors? Like yours," Nick interrupted.

Zak leaned forward in his chair, his eyes flaring. "They survive . . . by any means," he said quietly. "I don't work through the police," Zak continued. "I only use my own people, and we usually get results. The world doesn't love us for our methods, but we're alive against incredible odds."

Nick sighed and put his hands up in frustration. "Every one of us has his instructors in reality, their version; so what's yours for me?" he asked, his usual slouch when seated growing deeper.

"Take your people off Newman and Odette," Zak said firmly. "If we make a pickup, I'll handle it here . . . no police. And you'll get your results. The Gestapo weren't a total waste!"

Leave it to the Jews to salvage something from every disaster, Nick thought, five thousand years' worth . . .

An hour later when he first saw the bruises on Eric's face, Nick had to pretend he didn't know about the abduction attempt.

They sat in Nick's room at the hotel, Nick undoing his shoes, and Eric, dressed, on his way out for the evening.

"I'm scared shitless, Nick. Forget all that business about 'excitement and adventure.' I can't handle this feeling of being watched wherever I go. Sometimes I think I'm going bananas. And then something like this afternoon happens. It was the same car as the other night!"

Eric hadn't told him about that before, or about Montilla saving him.

The whole thing wouldn't be worth a damn if he didn't keep Eric going—and his friend wanted to quit, not that Nick could blame him. Nick searched his mind for a way out of the dilemma.

"And if you do go home now?" Nick asked. "You think that you can leave all this alone and just write the book as you would have? No sir. Every bit of experience changes the way we see, and you can't let it go now." He needed him now, and hated himself for putting his friend's life on the line, for following Barnwell's suggestion. He could have said Eric wasn't willing, but the decision had been made. It was ancient history as far as Nick was concerned, and you couldn't change it. The larger purpose superseded both of them, especially now that Odette was pulling some of the fragments together. *Eric had to stay in!*

"What did you find out at the Israeli Embassy today?" Nick asked, hoping he could steer Eric away from his fear.

"Nothing I could make real sense of. Look, I'm not being diverted, Nick. I liked the idea of doing this sleuthing, but it doesn't mean enough to me to get dumped by some creeps. I don't want to talk about it now, because I'm going out to try to enjoy myself like a normal human being—whatever that is. I'll talk to you in the morning—maybe I'll feel different then."

Nick sat with his shoe in his hand, looking down at the worn carpet. He didn't have Eric's options, so there was nothing for it. Perhaps he should get out for a while too. He picked up the phone to call Osborne. An evening's pub crawl with the newsman might be just the thing. Then he put down the phone. He shouldn't expose the Reuters chief too much, even though as a visiting press liaison officer Nick had built-in cover, even for socializing. But caution swayed him. There was always the Embassy cocktail party; and the little blond number, that cute assistant in cultural affairs, had asked him if he'd be there.

He put his shoe back on and went into the bathroom to wash his face. Not so innocent a diversion, but safe.

The long evening was just beginning in Buenos Aires when Nick left the hotel. He decided to walk a bit before going to the cocktail party; maybe the mood of the city would seize him too, take him away for a few hours from the staggering complexity of what was happening: he had never before been on a mission like this one. Sure, the Secretary had defined the goals. It was easy for *him* to sit in his office and do so. For Nick the pieces weren't even beginning to fall into place. He wouldn't know much more until Eric got his act together, if he ever did. Yet Barnwell, not a replaceable political commodity like the Secretary, wanted more than a demolition job. He wanted to know the whys—to redeem history from time and ferret out the hidden rats. OMEGA needed it all in a tidy, proven package.

Nick walked through the busy streets in the waning daylight. The housewives, maids, and people returning from work were lining up at the bakeries to buy their loaves for the evening; couples were sitting in the open cafes at small marble tables, sipping drinks and laughing, and through the open doors of shops or large casement windows of apartments, he heard radios. Everywhere the tango: modern, jazz versions, classic. Songs of frustrated passion, and always the litany of regret.

The city and its rhythms got to him. He remembered the early days of his career, and long walks with Phyllis, the plazas, the parks, the feeling of being in love and the world being his, and hers, for the taking. No longer: except for the days in Paris, the first year when he felt so vulnerable, so open to a woman who could fill the gap in his life . . . and then the decision, the decision that he would not involve another human being in the demimonde of his career. He had thought himself stoical, resigned, but now he saw that he had made his life a constant replication of limited experiences, like Gabrielle. Someone who would do for a while. Avoiding the possibility for real closeness to another, he refused to take that risk. It kept him the way he was: no growth without risk. He was some fine friend to advise Eric!

Yet Eric seemed ready, and Nick thought that this whole episode, this willingness to move out of the academic, was a sign. Even, he admitted painfully to himself, the man's pursuit of Odette showed that he was ripe for change, but Eric didn't see it. And here Nick was, Eric's closest friend, pushing him to risk, not feelings, but his life. The paradox of it all: Eric wouldn't grow without a commitment to change; but a continued commitment to the mode of change Nick had made available to him might result in his demise.

By force of habit, Nick stopped at a shop window, looked in it and then behind him for tags, didn't see any, then crossed the street and took a taxi in the opposite direction. How like Paris this city was, he mused, as he sat back after giving the driver the address where the reception was being held; and how ironic that he should be forced to return here. He had never wanted to, never wanted to be reminded of the salad days, the happy days. Worst of all, he couldn't even be alone in his misery, but had to face the second great loss daily in the presence of Odette . . . He watched the town houses flit past, the roofs of the apartment dwellings covered with greening copper, their shapes so like the houses in Paris. Nick wanted to get this mission over, go back to Paris, to Gabrielle or her successor, to be comfortable once again without the agony of regrets. He would call her in the small hours, it would be morning in France by then. He had opted for no complications in his emotional life, and he wanted to reassure himself that the easygoing, undemanding lover was still there, softly waiting for his return. But how could he call if he went home with the girl from the Embassy as he hoped, even planned to? Maybe he'd throw a sop to his conscience by not staying the night. All he needed was the diversion of some drinks, some amiable chitchat, a good supper and hopefully a woman to bed with. Nick had chosen this way of life and knew he would live it until it killed him—as the odds said it must . . .

The taxi man, giving up on conversation, tuned in his radio, and the cab was filled with a woman's voice, singing an old-fashioned tango, a rhythmic institution of loss.

14

Buenos Aires

ERIC WAS SINGING in the shower the next morning, mauling one of the Schubert lieder Fischer-Dieskau had sung. He had heard it before, and so was more familiar with it than with the works by Debussy and Fauré. Eric stood there in the shower singing— "Eine Krähe folgt mir . . . la dee dum dum deedle deedle dee"— and began to laugh to himself about turning Schubert into a Yiddish chant, when it suddenly hit him. He jumped out of the shower, and ran into the hallway in his robe, dripping, and knocked at Odette's door.

"Quick, where's the telephone directory?" he shouted at her sleepy face. She found it under the telephone. Eric started to turn the pages, but was so nervous he couldn't find anything; his hand was trembling and his eyes wouldn't focus.

"What are you looking for? You are acting like a lunatic," Odette asked, alarmed.

"That's me, inspired by the moon! It must be full. Find the number of the Israeli Embassy. I get great ideas in the showers!"

"Please go get a towel. You're dripping all over everything." She mumbled some French he couldn't catch.

"Dial the number," he shouted from the bathroom, and returned wrapped in a towel.

She handed him the phone as it connected. Eric asked for extension 451. The phone rang and rang, and he grew more and more anxious.

"Maybe he went on vacation," he said.

"Who? What are you saying? A total madman, and in my room," Odette said, threw up her hands, and went into the shower.

The operator cut in. "I'm sorry, sir, he's not in. It's only eight o'clock and he usually doesn't come in until late on Thursday—Wait a minute, he's coming down the hall now. Senor Zak, telephone for you."

"Zak, this is Newman, Nick Burns' friend . . . Yes. I realized there was something I forgot to look up yesterday. Could I possibly come over this morning?"

Zak hesitated and said it was highly unusual, they didn't keep public hours like libraries. But he finally relented and asked when Eric could get there.

"Within the hour, just as long as it takes me to get there from here."

"Whoopee!" Eric danced across the room, grabbing Odette who had just returned from the bathroom, and waltzing her around. She laughed, and he kissed her.

"What is it, chien fou?"

"I'm not Chinese," he said, "but I do know some German and it occurred to me in the shower that 'Krähe' is the equivalent for crow, or raven!"

"So what? Why so ecstatic?" She seemed unimpressed. "Anyway, 'die Rabe' is the right word for raven in German. Ugh, what an ugly language," she continued.

"Okay, but those files I went through yesterday. One mentioned Oberst Krähe. Colonel Krähe is a link to Immerman, and it is just vaguely possible that there's some relationship between—"

"Harry Raven, the dead American writer, and Oberst Krähe of German Military Intelligence?" Odette interrupted. "Ridiculous! A famous poet in the Abwehr? You really, *really* are a complete madman! Why didn't you tell me before we went to bed together?" She held up her hands in mock supplication.

"Maybe it is a wild idea," Eric said, coming down off his cloud a bit, "but I've got to check it out. Raven was educated in Heidelberg, you know. There *could* be a connection!"

"I'm coming with you," she said. "You're in enough trouble already. Madmen need their keepers."

"Not all of them are as lucky as I am, to have such a beauty for a keeper." He kissed her again, then went to his room and got dressed.

They had a quick coffee at the cafe downstairs, a mandatory

ritual. Eric smoked his first, much needed cigarette, and then they took a taxi to the Israeli Embassy. It was close enough to walk but Odette feared that Eric would fall into a manhole.

"Or maybe the dogcatcher will grab me," he added.

Zak was in his office, and they were shown in after the security guards searched them. It amused Odette, but irritated Eric to lose the time. He wanted to get to the files quickly.

When Zak saw Odette he became very effusive, switching from linebacker who could rip one's jaw off with his thumb, to urbane, polished diplomat and man of the world.

"Ah, Mademoiselle des Chavannes," he said in flawless Parisian French, "I do hope you're not here to interview me. I left my armor at home today." He laughed at his own joke, and Odette smiled. She wasn't going to get caught by the provocation.

"No, I just came along with Eric, taking advantage of the opportunity to meet you, so that when you are Ambassador of Israel to France, I will be one step ahead of all the other interviewers."

Zak turned to Eric, still smiling, but with a searching look in his eyes. "So, you have come across something that I should know?" he said, looking at Eric intently, the diplomat turned interrogator. The Israeli's ability to change roles abruptly and convincingly perturbed Eric. Could he trust a guy like that?

"No, not yet. I just want to check out something I forgot. Something that might give me an overview . . ." Eric hesitated, never able to lie convincingly under pressure. Zak sensed it.

"All right," Zak said with a knowing smile. "But don't forget, we have a deal. If there's anything you think would be helpful to me . . . One hand washes the other. You'll pardon the cliché, but my English is faulty."

It wasn't faulty at all, Eric thought. It was as fluent and idiomatic as his chameleon role changes. The two men went down to the subbasement while Odette remained in the anteroom to Zak's office, under the watchful eye of his secretary. Eric had wanted her to accompany him, but Zak insisted not.

"It is enough of a security breach that she knows of these files," he said in the elevator, "or that you and Osborne do: I may live to regret that too. But I can't go beyond that, not for the moment. When I go back upstairs I must make it clear to her that what she has seen or heard is 'deep background' only. Not for publication."

Another role, Eric thought: the serious bureaucrat protecting state secrets from journalists—but Zak hadn't mentioned Nick as a security breach. Eric stored the omission for later use.

The mouse-man brought the master list Eric asked for and he looked up Krähe. Same for Rabe, die Rabe, von Rabe, and those articles before Krähe. Nothing! He was very disappointed, sure as he had been that he had hit on something. Evidently not. The list was useless. Chalk it all up to a crazy hunch. He went over to the gray attendant to ask him to call Zak. Eric wanted to leave, cut his losses.

The attendant was speaking to someone on the telephone in Hebrew, and stopped to look at Eric questioningly. He covered the mouthpiece.

"I want to go; would you please call Zak?" Eric said in Spanish.

He put the phone down, but as he did, Eric remembered something else.

"No, wait," he said as the mouse-man began to dial the phone. "First I want to see the big map, the one I saw yesterday."

He brought it. With their impeccable logic, the Nazis had divided South America into five regions. Argentina and Brazil remained pretty much as they were, except that the latter had been expanded westward to incorporate Bolivia and Peru, up to the eastern side of the Andes. Ecuador, Colombia and Venezuela were incorporated as Neuspanien; the Guianas formed one; Chile ran from Tierra del Fuego to just south of Guyaquil, Ecuador. Chile incorporated all of western Peru and everything east of Africa, the northernmost city of the real Chile—the territory reached far inland, a third of the way across the continent. A corridor to the sea, the one Bolivia has always wanted and fought for in the war of the Pacific back in the 1880s, was arbitrarily drawn in from northern Argentina to the Pacific coast at Antofagasta.

It was a brilliant reorganization of territory, if you ignored people, language, ethnic groups, traditions and so on. The master race had little use for such niceties.

What interested Eric most was that this *Luftverkehrsnetz der*

Vereinigten Staaten Sud-Amerikas Hauptlinien gave so much territory and importance to the western corridor between the Andes and the sea; while the United States, with its emphasis on eastern America, reinforced by the trade patterns of the European nations, paid the greatest attention to Argentina and Brazil.

If the Argentine–Brazil fixation affected North American and European thinking, he reasoned, wouldn't it have influenced the Israelis? Could they have left something out? Or been less than attentive to Chile in their indexing.

He asked the attendant if there was a separate Chile file which the master catalogue had used as source. The man dug out another folder.

"All that is important here has been incorporated into the master lists when we reorganized this material several years ago. What is in here is irrelevant to our interests," he said as he begrudgingly handed Eric the folder. Like librarians everywhere, he had come to 'own' the material in his collection, and resented anyone questioning the thoroughness of cataloguing. But years of adventuring among collections had taught Eric to be skeptical.

He opened the file and looked through various technical documents until he found the agent list—and then felt like Archimedes! If mouse-man hadn't been watching so closely, Eric would have shouted "Eureka!" but the attendant sat across the room, his eyes glued to Eric's face. He had to be serious, undemonstrative, as expected of a researcher, a professor!

There *was* an entry under "Krähe, Heinrich"! The hunch was right. Dummy, he thought, why didn't you think of it yesterday?

"Are there any case files on individuals not in the master list?" Eric asked the attendant, who now sat munching on some cheese and crackers, as though to fulfill Eric's expectations of him in even exchange.

"There are some, but likewise of no importance. Either the names were listed elsewhere, or else the person was of little consequence to our purposes and was selectively weeded out," he said. "You will waste your time. Those files are very thin."

Eric asked him for the file on "Krähe, Heinrich," nevertheless. Annoyed, he went to a cabinet in a far corner and withdrew a manila folder, which he first recorded in his log, then handed over.

Eric read it in complete amazement, wondering if this whole thing was a crazy dream.

Recruited for the Abwehr by Canaris himself in 1930 when a graduate student at Heidelberg, Harry Raven (aka Heinrich Krähe) was an agent in place at the start of World War II. His control was Max Hartman. He did become important enough to merit promotion to Oberst, however, when he delivered plans for something called the magnometric oscillating alphagraph to Argentina in April of 1943.

God! That was the mind-reading machine both Nick and Odette wanted!

Then Krähe returned to Germany and took up a position as administrative assistant to Admiral Canaris. He was back to Argentina six months later, attached to the administrative staff of the German Embassy. In 1944 the record stopped.

Included in the file were clippings from several newspapers—the *New York Times, Die Neue Deutsche Zeitung,* and *El Pampero*—on the suicide of Harry Raven! So it was faked! Becari, the engineer, had seen someone else go over . . . and Ordonez knew it! Was he killed to shut him up?

Eric was a bit ahead of himself when he closed the file. He did know for a fact that Harry Raven was a German agent prior to and during the Second World War! According to this document, he was alive *after* the "suicide." That explained the postcards to Hartman! And then, what happened in 1944? Did he just disappear?

Of course, this proved that Ben Winkler was probably right when he wrote that he saw Raven in Buenos Aires, but how in God's name could Eric prove all this, and what did it do to his book? It was beyond insanity now. The book he had labored over was a mythical structure now exploded, blown to bits. He'd have to start all over.

Eric handed the file back to the attendant and then played a long shot. He asked if there were other files not keyed to the master catalogue or the sectors of the original ordnance map of the continent. The mouse brushed the crumbs of cheese off his desk into the wastebasket, and said that he'd check. He picked up the phone, dialed, and then spoke in Hebrew.

"It's okay," he said, and handed Eric the phone. Chaim Zak

asked, "What happened to you down there, Professor Newman? You've been down there almost two hours!"

Eric said he was a slow reader.

"By the way," Zak added, clearly amused at the transparent lie, "Miss des Chavannes had to go back to her office—a charming woman. But I find that because of a cancellation, I'm free for lunch. If you are, perhaps you and she would join me as my guests. Then you can tell me all of the interesting things you culled from our files."

Eric said he'd be happy to if Odette was free, and if not, would join him anyway.

"Good," Zak said, "I'll call her, and if it is all right, I'll arrange to pick her up in the staff car when you ascend from the lower depths. And I hope that's soon, because I'm getting hungry."

A few minutes later Eric had a short list in his hands, but he was disappointed. There was no entry under Krähe. Only one familiar name: Immerman, Klaus. The double agent who had been "terminated," in the bizarre euphemism of the spying profession. Maybe there was more of interest here? He asked the attendant for the file folder on Immerman. It was a small but continuing record of a man presumed dead!

This Klaus Immerman, a German-born Argentine citizen, had left for Chile in 1944, acquired Chilean citizenship a few years later, and had not been heard from since. Eric asked the mouseman for the first Immerman file. One glance told him what he wanted to know: there was no similarity in the physical descriptions of the two men; but the numbers of their carnets de identidad, their Argentine identity cards, were the same! Could the death recorded be a mistake? Or was Raven still alive in 1944, perhaps even now, living under another identity? Churning with ideas, Eric returned the file to the surprised clerk within a minute of his having received it, and asked to call Zak. He was finished and needed to get out of there and test his hypothesis.

* * *

Lunch was almost over before Zak introduced the subject of Eric's discoveries. The Israeli had taken his guests to La Cabana, very atmospheric with high beams and similar prices, in the Calle Entre Rios, only a few blocks from the street where Ordoñez had lived. When they had first sat down, Eric said he had been in this district only the other day, and felt a sharp pain in his shin as Odette kicked him under the table.

"Sight-seeing," he continued.

"Ah yes, the Congreso is an interesting building," Zak said, looking bemused. "There's also a municipal office around here with fascinating decorations: mosaic tiles cover the outer walls . . ."

By the time the coffee came, they were all on a first name basis, and Odette and her new friend Chaim had concluded an interesting interchange on France's position vis-à-vis Israel and the Arabs. It was good, intelligent talk, and Eric enjoyed listening.

Zak now sipped his espresso and said: "So, the moment has arrived. What is to tell? You can speak freely in front of Odette. I trust her."

Eric told him what he had found.

"But Immerman was killed because he was a double agent, so what makes you think it is the same man?"

"The carnet numbers were identical," Eric answered.

Zak shrugged. "So what! They used an old name on the rolls. Probably the first Immerman, if he was in fact eliminated, was killed without the Argentine government knowing. Then his ID was used with a changed picture and thumbprint for some other bastard to get away. It happens all the time. Good idea, Eric, but it doesn't hold up."

Eric wasn't to be put off, because he thought Zak was just testing his ingenuity.

"Okay, then let's say someone else used it. Could it be some other big Nazi? What if . . . could it have been this Krähe?" Eric asked.

Odette listened, without saying anything. Eric had noticed this was a method of hers previously. She waited until the end and then killed with one blow.

"We don't act on 'ifs,' " Zak said firmly. "If my grandmother had wheels, she'd be a wagon"—the Yiddish cynicism slipped out. "Tell me more about this Krähe/Raven," he continued, "not as a poet, but as a Nazi spy—although, my friend, I must admit that however fascinating the idea is to play with, it is as farfetched as could be imagined, and you could probably never prove it."

"If he's still alive, I could," Eric retorted.

"But he committed suicide you told me. There were witnesses, dozens of crew members searched the water."

"Only three witnesses," Eric answered, "but two were Nazi agents." He told Zak what Becari, the engineer, had said. Zak brushed the story aside.

"Okay, let's leave that alone. It's not enough to build a case on," he said. "Tell me of Krähe."

When Eric finished Zak said: "I'm sorry to disappoint you, Eric, but an educated guess based on years in this business is that this Krähe was himself eliminated, and probably here in Buenos Aires, if he was attached to the German Embassy."

"But why would they do that?" asked Odette, suddenly becoming animated.

"Because," Zak answered, "after the generals' plot failed—you remember the attempt on Hitler's life on July 20th, 1944—about seven thousand people were arrested, and almost five thousand of them were executed, including Admiral Canaris and half of the Abwehr. Anyone who was recruited by, and served under Canaris directly, was certain to be eliminated. It was a purge of unbelievable extent.

"If the man was a Canaris partisan, even far away here in Argentina, and there was in any way a hint of his sympathy with the plot, he could be in an unmarked grave anywhere on this continent, and probably is."

Eric felt crestfallen and looked it, because Zak said:

"I'm sorry to shoot your hypothesis full of holes. Maybe I'm wrong, but I think you're wasting effort."

"Could it be that this Immerman is someone you're looking for?" Odette asked him.

Zak looked surprised. "Sure, it *could* be. Borman, Kessler, Meyer, Schultz . . . but we won't go running on any wild supposition. Eric has given me some valuable insight, and I think we have to rework our files. Their organization is not all we thought. The very idea that an agent reported terminated reappears, with the same papers, is a mystery itself worth looking into, but if it is *only* Immerman, we're not interested. He was a small fish."

Eric thought of the body of Harry Raven floating face downward behind the ocean liner and said, "Maybe Immerman could enlighten me!"

Odette and Zak both looked at him as if he were mad.

"I mean," he continued, "if this is actually the man to whom Raven/Krähe delivered plans for some top secret device, then—"

Odette interrupted: "You are totally and hopelessly insane. What makes you think that he'd talk to you, let alone admit that he was an ex-Nazi agent? Why should your appearance, thirty years after the fact, be an incentive for him to speak freely? How naive you are!"

"She's right," Zak added, "and these are dangerous people. They are protecting themselves from history. At the same time, some still nurture the dream, the nightmare delusion of a return to power. Their money has been behind many of the right-wing putsche."

Odette made a disgusted face at the last word.

"Pardon," Zak hastened to add. "I mean, coups d'état here in Latin America, and you think you're going to go with a tape recorder and say 'Excuse me, sir, but I'm writing a book and need your help.'" He laughed bitterly. "Fat chance! What is it you really want? To die in an alley?"

Zak called for the check, paid it, and went to use the telephone. While waiting for him to return, Eric was absorbed with the last question. To die in an alley, was that risk worth it? Odette smoked a cigarette contemplatively, and sat still, staring ahead.

"I still think I want to know the truth," Eric broke his silence when Zak got back from the telephone.

Zak looked at him strangely. "'What is the truth?' said jesting Pilate,'" he quoted, "'and would not stay for an answer'— and you'll pardon the association, Eric!"

He rose and left a generous tip on the table. Eric thanked him for the lunch, and for the use of the files.

"Both courtesy of the government of Israel," he said affably. "The lunch is goodwill, the files opportunistic *on my part.* Whatever you do, please remember that you have privileged information, and its keeping is a matter of personal trust."

"Au revoir, mademoiselle," he said to Odette outside the restaurant. "Keep an eye on this wild-eyed romantic. We'll all meet again someday."

"No doubt in Paris when you are Ambassador, Chaim, and then I'll buy *you* lunch," Odette added, ringing her bell laugh.

Zak smiled with all his diplomatic charm.

"May your wish come true."

He conferred with his waiting chauffeur briefly, then turned to Eric and Odette again: "I have had a change in plans and am not going downtown. Would you mind taking a taxi?" he asked, and without waiting for an answer hailed one from the curb.

The cab pulled away rapidly into the traffic and eased into a bumper-to-bumper crawl.

"Can you take a more indirect route?" Odette said to the driver, "and get us out of this?"

The driver didn't answer, just nodded his head sullenly and swung into a side street, then took a series of one-way back streets. Odette took out her compact and began to powder her nose and put on lipstick. It was clear that she didn't want to talk, so Eric kept quiet and just watched the passing streets. He noticed that Odette was using her compact mirror to look out of the rear window.

Suddenly she said, "Oh my God! Sit still and don't say anything," gesturing with her head to the left.

A brown sedan had pulled up alongside on the left, and the front seat passenger held a gun pointed at their taxi driver. A familiar face . . . Eric searched his memory. *It was the guy with the mustache who had mugged him in Philadelphia!*

"Pull over to the curb and let your passengers out," he said to the cab driver, quietly but menacingly. A glint of gold tooth. Eric felt his body go cold with fear, but Odette seemed unruffled.

"Do as he says," she ordered.

The cab swung to the right and the other car did likewise, blocking any escape. Eric started to get out, trembling at the idea that those creeps had been after him all along, and he never knew!

"That was the guy in Phila—" he started. Odette put her hand on his arm. What graduate students could save them here?

"Ssh—not now," and then said quietly: "Don't get into the other car, just walk back the way we came from."

When they were both on the sidewalk, Odette began to walk rapidly back along the one-way street, tugging Eric. The brown car couldn't follow. There were some passersby, but they didn't seem to notice anything unusual.

"Hey, you two, stop!" the man called after them.

"Look for a bank," Odette said, "and ignore him. And *don't* look back," she hissed, yanking Eric's arm hard as he tried to turn.

"Won't he shoot?" Eric asked, breathless from the tension.

"Not in this crowd," she answered, hitching her bag higher in front of her and fumbling her hand inside without looking.

There was a lot of hooting of horns by now, as the traffic backed up behind the taxi and its interceptor. Eric and Odette kept walking rapidly, looking for all the world like any couple rushing back to work.

There was the sound of running feet behind them and Eric's trembling began again. Odette had taken her hand out of her bag and now held it against her stomach, letting the bag swing back to her side. Underneath her swelling breasts she held a very ugly-looking snub-nosed pistol. He gasped.

"Are you cra—"

The running steps stopped and a familiar voice called:

"It's all right. You can stop now!"

They both turned hesitatingly around to see Chaim Zak, flushed but smiling. He took them, one by each arm and said, "It's all over. We have them now and I'm sure they will tell us some interesting things back at the Embassy."

He explained that his driver had noticed that they were being watched on the way to the restaurant, and as soon as he was able to confirm this he radioed for assistance. Zak let them take a taxi and then followed the pursuers, a few car lengths behind. When the gunmen made their move, so did he; and by the time Eric and Odette had walked twenty feet, Zak and his men had surrounded the other car and disarmed them.

He put the relieved couple into his car and told the driver to take them wherever they wanted to go. Then he got into another car, a Cadillac limousine with diplomatic plates. In the rear, on the two jump seats, sat two sullen, tough-looking men, their hands handcuffed over the seat backs. Behind them sat the two barrel-chested security men who had checked Eric in at the Embassy. They didn't look like they were on their way to a tea party. Zak waved good-bye as his car left the curbside. The taxi and the car the would-be assailants had used were gone, Eric noticed, and he sat back on the leather upholstery and sighed in relief. "Why a bank?" he asked Odette, when they were once again moving.

"Because there are always armed guards there, and it's less likely that these characters would come in with drawn weapons."

"What about that thing you carry: would you really use it?"

"If I had to," she said matter-of-factly.

Hypothesis piled on hypothesis in Eric's mind as he lounged on his bed at the hotel later that afternoon. Zak hadn't been encouraging. But if he wasn't onto something, why was he being bothered, almost abducted, ransacked, nearly run down? If Raven hadn't died that night thirty years ago and had reappeared in Buenos Aires later on, where was he now? Crushed, as Zak said, by the paranoiac hand of the dying Third Reich? Eric knew that his only link was Immerman—if he still existed; and the trail was clearly marked to Chile, despite what the Israeli had said about ex-Nazis. He'd go—the contract with his own curiosity had to be fulfilled. And if he couldn't trace this Immerman, he'd drop it, go back to New York, and finish the book. Not that he knew how to anymore, because the information he had now couldn't be used.

He had pledged that it was deep background only, not for publication—and of course, *nothing was changed*, despite all the data he had uncovered. But he'd come this far . . . Eric sat up on the bed, reached for the phone and asked for Nick's room; there had been no answer earlier.

"You know what happened today?" Eric asked his friend when he answered, launching into his latest escapade.

Nick said, "Come down here."

"You quitting?" Nick asked as he let Eric in. He dropped into an armchair and slouched low.

"What if they had gotten me, us, into their car? I don't want to be found dumped by the roadside in the park!"

"But they didn't get you, did they?" Nick asked. Someone *was* looking after you—"

"Like a helpless dependent," Eric interrupted. "I don't like it."

"An alive dependent, not a dead superhero," Nick retorted. "Look, are you in or out? I have to know. Not that I'd blame you. I don't want you to stop, but I'd understand, and no hard feelings."

"You asshole," Eric said. "You know me better than that. Of course I'm in, but I'm really worried I'll get creamed by some of these creeps chasing me, the ones who get past the defense."

Nick looked surprised.

"What defense?" he asked, eyes wide and innocent. "It's coincidence that you were with Zak. He's closely guarded, to your benefit today!"

Eric resented the bad acting. "Play your stupid Greenberg games, Nick! I have eyes. It's *too much* of a coincidence that everytime I get into trouble, there's someone there to cover me before I get mauled. But what happens when the defense isn't there? I'll be a quarterback when the line has been broken through and the big beef is coming at him with horns out. I don't know which way to go, because not only do I not know the shape or size or direction of the field, but I don't even know the name of the game!"

"It's not football!" Nick said, grinning.

"Brilliant, clever diplomat, my friend, the critic of metaphor! What the fuck is it then?" Eric asked, chafing.

"Hounds and hares?" Nick asked, still smiling.

"Hide the Raven," Eric retorted.

"Is that really a game?" Nick asked.

"Yeah," Eric said, seriously mocking: "A street game from Brooklyn. See what you missed growing up privileged? Poor rich guy!" His annoyance faded with the jibe.

"I'll make up for it and buy you a drink," Nick said, taking Eric's arm in hand, "to show what a democrat I am," and led him out the door to the elevator.

Odette was almost ready to follow her story to Chile, she had told Nick, but wanted some more time in Buenos Aires. "A weekend alone with you," she'd whispered to Eric, and they had booked a Monday flight. Nick would precede them tomorrow morning, still keeping up the pretense of a junket, an inspection tour. For whom, Eric wondered? He felt that so much depended on himself, on what he could cull from his research, because he knew now that they each wanted the same story. Only the point of view changed.

When Nick had said good-bye and gone upstairs to pack, Eric and Odette dined at a local restaurant and in unspoken agreement, somewhat flushed with wine, went straight to bed. Eric already felt sentimental; leaving Buenos Aires drew them both closer to the end. Though it hadn't been peaceful here, he knew that Santiago was the target area, the war zone, and this was their last respite before everything went skittering under fire.

He was afraid that this newfound intimacy with Odette wouldn't survive. Did she feel strongly about him? Did she love? He thought so; she had said so, yet the cynic in his marrow hinted that Odette was after a story, and once it was done, so was he. Eric didn't want to believe that, yet couldn't a woman use a man the way men traditionally and unfairly used women? Discard when empty.

These thoughts gave a hunger to his lovemaking, a desperate holding on. Grasping, squeezing, plying his tongue into every hidden turning of her body, every entrance, as though he could guard her, possess her completely by omitting nothing, permitting no closed doors. Odette responded with delirious excitement, as though her need to hold on to the moment matched his own. Her body moved in rhythm with his, stroke for counterstroke, meeting the inward thrust of his penis with a forward motion of her hips, complementing and adding to the collective energy. She contracted her inner muscles around him strongly, and he felt as though her hands held him from inside, grasping, pulling, kneading his penis with a strength that seemed beyond her, taking him, giving herself.

Her lips covered his face and arms with kisses as he hovered over her, one hand under her buttocks, the other gently massaging her large erect nipple between his thumb and forefinger.

She was moaning now, moaning endearments in rapid French he hardly understood. He felt her breath get shorter, panting, and then with a gasped "a . . a . . a . . aiey" shuddering through her body and charging the space with electricity, she began to come: uncontrolled, wild spasms shook her body, and with each one she drove her pelvis hard up into him, as if trying to pull his swollen penis deeper and deeper into the pulsing spasmic ecstasy which rumbled through her center. He tried to thrust deeper but she put her hands on the small of his back, saying "No, hold still," and she took up all of the movement, making it her own. A second wave of orgasm engulfed her body as she drove hard onto him, and in the abandonment of the endearments, the whispers of love, the cries of joy, she sank her teeth into his shoulder, biting and sucking.

The combination of the pain where her teeth held his flesh and the intense pleasure of her vagina rhythmically massaging and holding his penis down to its hilt, absorbing him completely, was too much for him. Eric couldn't hold back any longer, didn't want to: there was nothing to prove. He let go, started to come, and unable to keep still began to thrust hard into Odette. She moved her hands down to his buttocks and pulled him into her with each plunge he made. It seemed as though his entire body were pouring out, draining from his ears to his toes into the sucking, whirling vortex of her body.

She let go of his shoulder with her teeth and moved her lips to his ear, licking deep with her tongue, sucking on the lobes. He exploded uncontrollably and poured out of himself in waves; it seemed that a river, a swollen torrent burst the dam restraining it and raged in the splendor of its own energy.

There was nothing left to say or do. Odette reached over to the night table, switched the light off and the radio on, and they fell back together, her back to him like spoons in a soft drawer, and they slept, the sweet smell of their sex-joined bodies filling the air, his hand across her hip.

Later—he didn't know how long—Eric was wakened, drawn back over the margins of sleep. The radio was still soft with perpetual tango, but Odette had turned in his arms, their sex no longer joined. He had been pulled back into consciousness by stifled sobs. He leaned up on his elbow.

In the light filtering in from the street, he saw that there were tears in her eyes.

"Why are you crying?" he asked, brushing away the wetness on her cheeks.

She shook her head and bit her lower lip.

"I want this never to end," she said, "but things being what they are, I fear . . . I know, it must."

"How can we say now what will happen?" he asked, trying not to voice his own fears by denying hers.

"I've been here before," she answered, looking away, and would say no more about it.

Eric simply couldn't, didn't want to allow himself to accept the possibility that this affair could be so intense, yet short-lived. It was only two weeks old, after all. He needed something more, a permanent institution. And next to him, staring into the beyond with watery eyes, her black hair caressing his face, was *the woman*, the woman he wanted that more to be with. Yet after this journey was over, there would be no paradise regained, he feared. The ring might be closed as far as the book was concerned, but as far as his life went, it would be open and bent out of shape with a three-thousand-mile gap.

Eric felt Odette's warm face in helpless silence. Only the radio made a sound: the tango . . . the tango . . . the tango had it right after all.

PART THREE

15

Chile (the border)

THERE WAS SNOW on the tops of the mountains and it looked like an overnight snowfall had made the Uspallata pass impassable. Don Enrique looked down from the porthole of the Lear jet at the enormous mountains separating his adopted country from Argentina and wondered how San Martin, the liberator, had ever made it across with mules and foot soldiers and cannon. Crossing the Andes was no small feat. What zeal there must have been in that man's soul, what a need to throw off the colonial weight of Spain, what a drive against oppression he had mobilized within himself and others. Heroism was dead, and most causes that were worth fighting and dying for as well. There was only the self and its survival on accepted terms. A solipsism of self-validation.

The aristocrat leaned back in his seat. He had no idealism left; it was a romantic sentiment, tenuously held on to by a few fools, perhaps a few patriots or old dreamers like Oswaldo who still acted in the name of abstractions like freedom. No, there was no more worthwhile ideal than his own liberation. He had hidden, run, avoided, and risked enough—for most of his lifetime, certainly the last half of it, and now it had to stop.

He didn't like killing, but it had to be. It had been imperative to get to those people before Newman did. Castelli Bravo, that old flannel mouth, that was easy. Don Enrique knew that the Argentine would respond to his phone call. Just a brief meeting in the park, he told him . . . and the thugs he had hired took care of the rest. They didn't even know who Don Enrique was. A telephone call, some money in an envelope at a post office box, and that was that. They messed up the part with Newman and got caught. No matter. He couldn't be implicated. The cutout was effective. He had hoped that when they picked Newman up and beat him he'd stop. It hadn't worked with Winkler though! Well, Don Enrique would see. Newman was the least of his problems now that the sources were silenced.

The professor was good, Don Enrique had to admit to himself. He got to Ordoñez first, but the man hadn't said anything, he swore to Don Enrique afterward. He swore, and was still swearing as the poison in the coffee took him suddenly. He remembered the look of surprise on Ordoñez' face. If only that DINA man hadn't come in, damn him. The drug would have dissipated in Ordoñez' blood and it would look like a heart attack, but as soon as Don Enrique heard the man letting himself in when Ordoñez didn't answer the bell, he had taken out the silenced pistol. When he recognized the squat fellow Joaquin Saenz had described as his best agent, Don Enrique had to shoot; he mustn't be identified. No way out.

He realized that Joaquin was trying to gain an edge now that he had seen those Xeroxed pages, trying to find out what it was that the aristocrat was hiding, why he wanted to keep the professor at arm's length. And he didn't trust Joaquin; no, he couldn't trust anybody. Given the opportunity they'd all betray unless their lives depended on you. Like Oswaldo . . . like Winkler . . . if they stood to lose, you'd win. There were no heroes, only winners and losers. Foxes, scavengers, and carrion. For practical purposes, there were no lions.

The moon was already out, shining brightly behind the plane, lighting the frozen wastes atop the mountains below. Ahead he saw the glow of the sun, orange heat sinking into the deep black sea. A luftmensch, five miles up in the air between night and day: no one would have missed him.

* * *

"I can't help it if your men are incompetent," said Don Enrique to the chief of DINA, the following day. "They mess up a simple job of pushing somebody around a bit, and you're angry with me?" He sensed that the best way to deal with Joaquin was to take the offensive position, then ease off a bit. "But our major problems are over, aren't they?" he went on.

"Only halfway," conceded Saenz grumpily. The secretary knocked and came in with coffee.

The two men had just returned to Saenz's office after another meeting with Fleming, Osterholz, and General Pinochet at the

ICO building in downtown Santiago. Fleming had been satisfied that the "impediments" to concluding the deal had been removed, and offered to proceed as planned. To show good faith, he signed three draft orders in their presence, authorizing the transfer of funds to three numbered accounts in the Banque Euro-Suisse of Geneva. The general looked at his number carefully and then the sum:

"I see that you have carried out our demands as we have done so for you," he had said to Fleming, referring to the additional half million dollars indicated on his balance sheet. "Are you satisfied, gentlemen?" he had asked Don Enrique and Saenz. They agreed that they were.

"But I'm not completely at ease with this just yet," Fleming had said, his cherubic features drawn and worried looking. "There's still the question of OMEGA, and of course that French journalist. She's in Buenos Aires now,"—Saenz looked from under his eyebrows at Don Enrique who looked away quickly— "and she has been seen with the man from OMEGA. What are we going to do about that?"

General Pinochet smirked, then he spoke: "I think you worry too much, Senor. There will always be reporters snooping around for stories, and as for spies, they are as thick as flies around here. Nothing to be done. Just get on with it."

"Yes," Saenz cut in, "the conditions have been met, the rest is simple."

Fleming hadn't seen it that way.

He wanted to be able to operate in a vacuum.

"If it will ease your mind," Saenz said, "we will deport the journalist should she arrive here, if she even looks like she's going to make trouble; that is very easy to do. You have nothing to fear from her."

"And the OMEGA man?" Fleming had pressed.

"I told you at our last meeting," Saenz had come back firmly, "he's untouchable, off limits, and that's final."

Saenz was not going to alienate the Americans, nor would General Pinochet permit it. The deal with ICO was small compared to what the military men would reap if the junta stayed in power long enough, and they needed to keep their allies in Washington if they planned to be around for any length of time. In fact, if they had to, they would cooperate with the Americans and betray both ICO *and* Don Enrique. Saenz was sure Don Enrique understood that; although he also sensed that underneath his tough veneer, Fleming was just like the baby his round face suggested, and understood nothing. Safety in a playpen.

General Pinochet grunted and said, "If you take delivery of the machine as soon as possible, it will be gone, and in your hands before anyone gets close. That is if you want it. If not, I don't want to waste my time on this any longer, and will cancel our agreement immediately. Then you can stop worrying, and we can sell the alpha wave magnetron to the highest bidder. I'm sure we'll have no trouble." He folded his hands across his ample stomach and sat back, an apelike grin broad on his face.

Fleming gave in. "We'll take delivery within the week. I'll make the transportation arrangements today."

* * *

When his secretary had poured the coffee for the two old friends and closed the door behind her, Joaquin Saenz continued with the idea he had withheld:

"What I didn't say at the meeting, Enrique, is that the journalist and the professor booked for a flight here on Monday. The spy is already in Santiago. He came in on this morning's flight."

Don Enrique felt his blood pressure shoot up. He forced himself to hold back his temper. His own men hadn't succeeded in their second attempt to frighten off Newman. The police had them now, but there was no way any connection could be made between those thugs and Don Enrique. But DINA men were pros. Yet they slipped too. He regretted that he had to kill Joaquin's agent, the fat Argentine, but he couldn't afford to allow DINA any of the information that the old Ordoñez might have been persuaded to give Newman repeated to anyone else. Once he had made the decision to kill Ordoñez, the rest followed. The decision was made before he had left Chile, he knew, or else he wouldn't have taken along the poison and the silenced pistol. But that was all beside the point now. They were insignificant; vermin who crawled in his path.

"After my first man met with an unfortunate and curious death," the police chief was saying, "I assigned two others, who were picked up when they attempted to seize Newman and the woman off the street. They may be convinced to admit that they worked for DINA by some very severe methods—I don't know who has them. If it was the police . . . But they have vanished!"

"Hoist with his own petard," mumbled Don Enrique in English.

"What's that?" asked Saenz.

"Nothing, nothing, just thinking aloud," the aristocrat said. "But like it or not, Joaquin," he continued, "you have only the incompetence of your own staff to blame—"

"NO!" Saenz raised his voice, "I have *you* to blame for involving *me* in a situation which isn't my concern."

"Six million dollars *is* your concern, however!"

"It certainly is," retorted Saenz, "and what I'm telling you now is that I'll allow no further interference from you with regard to this Newman. If you had asked me to get rid of him, it would have been much easier than this foolish business of threatening. I can't waste any more effort on him. No more! Either I stop him completely, very easy for me now that he is here in Chile, or we just forget him and go ahead as planned."

"Hold off," said Don Enrique. He was intrigued by Newman getting closer, and wanted to play him, like a fish on the line, until he'd wriggle off the hook himself and return to tell the others of his great adventure—some kind of fish myth. Otherwise, if the angler set the hook firmly enough, he would just haul Newman in himself for the kill. The idea amused Don Enrique.

"Okay, my friend, I'll hold off, as you say. But I tell you now, that it is now within my power to act when I choose to, and in the interests of security, I will do so, at my own discretion. The matter is out of your hands," Saenz said angrily.

Don Enrique knew he had to leave it at that. There was no reason Joaquin would act against Newman now unless he felt compromised, and Don Enrique didn't see how that could happen. He'd sit back and watch. There was no harm. The machine would be gone before the professor even got close, and then Don Enrique could decide what to do. Once he had the money, he might even enjoy meeting this biographer of dead poets.

He got up to leave Joaquin's office.

"If I were in your position," he said to the thin, elegant official, sitting with a worried look behind a desk which dwarfed his slight form, "I'd be far more concerned about that secret agent. The professor and the journalist could be deported for looking cross-eyed at a policeman, but they aren't professional hunters. He is!"

"I am concerned, amigo, but I am in a very difficult position," said Joaquin Saenz, "because I may have to act and suffer the consequences personally, unlike . . ." He paused, thoughtfully, then continued. "You can be sure that if anything happens or goes wrong, I will be held responsible. They won't come after Fleming or you."

Saenz stood up, walked his old friend to the door, where they shook hands and bade each other effusive farewells in conventional Chilean fashion, as though the lives in question were no more than the minor chitchat of a normal social visit.

* * *

New York

The brief message Nick Burns sent had been waiting on the director's desk when he arrived at the Washington Square town house Friday morning. He had called Buenos Aires and spoken to Chaim Zak. The Israelis had spared all niceties in their interrogation of the agents they had picked off Newman's and des Chavannes' back. When Newman had identified one of them as the mugger from Philadelphia, Burns asked that Zak's interrogation team turn up the heat.

As a result the Israelis had in their hands the confessed assassins of Armando Leboulier. "Keep them on ice," Barnwell had said to Zak and had phoned the Secretary of State immediately.

"Those lousy bastards!" the Secretary screamed into the telephone. Barnwell held the receiver away from his ear until the tirade died. "I won't have it," the Secretary said. "If they have to clean up, bury their skeletons, they're not going to do it here, under our noses. We've got enough problems with the whole damned human rights crowd and don't need this shit—and Leboulier was here for asylum. It's bad for our image. They'll pay, those lice, let me tell you; they'll pay! Stay where I can reach you," and he hung up without waiting for an answer.

The Secretary called back fifteen minutes later.

"You told me that the ETT was originally ours?"

Barnwell explained the history briefly. He made plain that it was hypothetical, the assumption that this *was* the same machine.

"Change the battle order then. We want it back!" insisted the Secretary.

"But we don't have the facilities for that kind of operation down there," Barnwell objected, although this was what he wanted from the outset. He knew how to play the Secretary: opposition would confirm the man in his own decision.

"You just get me a date certain from your man, and I'll authorize Defense to send in whatever he needs. He can run the show. All I want is results. I'm sending you exact details of location by courier this afternoon," the Secretary said.

"Where did they come from?" The director was curious to know how the Secretary had obtained in such a short time what it had taken OMEGA three weeks to learn—with assistance.

"From the very top!"

After the Secretary hung up, Barnwell sat quietly composing the cable he would send to Nick Burns.

* * *

Santiago

General Pinochet had been very surprised Friday when he was told that the President of the United States was on the telephone. He straightened out the creases in his military tunic where it bunched up under his protruding stomach, breathed deeply, and with a broad smile on his face lifted the receiver from the hook.

"Mr. President!" he said, beaming, but before he could go on, the voice at the other end crackling over seven thousand miles cut him off in mid-speech, very rudely, thought the general.

"We have clear evidence that the assassination of a former high official of the Chilean government, a brutal murder which took place here in Washington just two weeks ago was the work of agents of your government who are now in our protective custody. They will be brought to trial with all the attendant publicity speedily, and I'm sure you're aware of the effect that will have on any further appropriations . . ."

The President went on to detail the conditions under which

the men would be released into Chilean custody without any additional fanfare.

The Chilean boiled with rage. He wanted to kill, maim. The *fools*, but he needed the Americans more than he needed the money from ICO, more than he needed Fleming, or Saenz, and certainly more than he needed that damned pansy, Enrique Cuervo, with his airs of a snooty haciendista. He called his secretary for a file and gave the President the information he demanded. Only then did the American executive assure him of continued good faith between the two great republics.

The Chilean put down the phone furiously, the smile on his face transformed into a threatening scowl.

"Get me Director Saenz," he shouted into the intercom. "I want him here immediately."

By the time Saenz arrived fifteen minutes later, the general had worked out a plan. It had a military simplicity:

"We can't redeem your blunders, Director," he said, after he had given Saenz only part of the story—that his assassins were in the hands of the American authorities and that the general was under pressure—"so you will immobilize the American agent. Take care of it personally, and you will send for the French journalist—is she here? And give her the information that a certain machine has been developed," continued General Pinochet, "by our friend Don Enrique as a purely private venture, sponsored by our predecessors and funded by ICO."

"But Mi Generale!" Saenz objected. "They will implicate you and all of us if the publicity comes out."

General Pinochet shook his head in disagreement.

"Fleming is not so stupid that he would lose the entire ICO operation in Chile over a few million dollars. He and Cuervo will share responsibility, and we will be clean. Allende will be the villain, then Leboulier's death, and no doubt Sepulvida's, will seem more justified."

Saenz thought the plan was absurd but dared not say so. He feared General Pinochet's wrath.

"And to guarantee *your* success," the general continued, a cunning look in his eye, "I will hold the money you were given as security! Give me the notice of deposit Fleming gave you for the Swiss bank!"

Stunned by the turn of events, Joaquin Saenz removed from

his inner tunic pocket a long wallet, took out the letter, the piece of paper which gave him more money than he had ever dreamed of having in his life, and handed it over. He was not an emotional man, but at the moment he had to fight the lump in his throat and tears in his eyes.

"This will be returned to you when your assignment is completed satisfactorily," General Pinochet said, taking the folded paper from Saenz. He dismissed the DINA director with a curt wave of his hand.

After Saenz left the office, General Pinochet told his secretary to reach the Chilean Embassy in Switzerland. When the call was placed ten minutes later, the general spoke to his ambassador, instructing him to withdraw all the funds from the Banque Euro-Suisse de Genève from two accounts whose numbers he was transmitting by telex, and to deposit them in a different account the general had established recently in another bank.

When Joaquin Saenz was finished with the task at hand, General Pinochet knew that he had no further use for him. Someone else would run DINA.

* * *

Joaquin Saenz returned to his office in a state of partial shock. Pinochet's subtlety was like a rifle butt. He thought he could detect what the junta chief had in mind and realized that if he wanted to outsmart him he'd have to be as a fox to a lion: he would double back on his own tracks and overcome the more powerful beast by indirection, by thinking one or two or three steps ahead of him, all the while staying out of range of his crushing jaws. First he had to do what he had wanted to avoid: get rid of the OMEGA man. That would slow down the game. It must be clear, however, if there was any investigation, that the order came from General Pinochet. He turned to his typewriter and composed a memorandum. There would be enough time to warn Enrique afterward.

The slight, elegant secret police chief told his secretary that he wasn't in to anyone, and as he typed, his mind raced through alternatives open to him.

16

Santiago

NICK BURNS had just returned to his room after a tedious evening which began with a duty cocktail party at the Instituto Chileno-Norteamericano to celebrate the opening of the American Artfilm Festival. Nothing he saw screened had the slightest hint of political or social commentary. As a result the "festival" was a boring series of experimental scratching, blotching, and artsy-craftsy montage. Nick had, however, established his cover for being in Santiago—inspection junkets were perquisites of USIA officers at his level.

He had expressed some very strong opinions on the way cultural programs should be administered, and in general, the way USIA did it was not satisfactory. He thought that the best possible propaganda the United States could have was the simple unvarnished truth: the differences of opinion in the press, the dissent from the left and right, the freedom of expression in all aspects of public life and utterance, without censorship. These customs, habits, rights, said more for the meaning of liberty and democracy than any censored puffery. An emasculated film festival, art show, poetry reading, or dramatic presentation was just so much hot air, convincing nobody but those already partial to the States. Anything else was shortsighted, naive.

After two hours of hearing about how wonderful the film festival was from the Ford Foundation sponsors and Embassy people, who seemed oblivious to his criticism, Nick excused himself.

So did Donna Harcourt, the assistant cultural affairs officer, an attractive blond who had Bryn Mawr written all over her. She had been assigned to chaperon the visiting fireman, and was taking her assignment very seriously on her home territory.

"Come up to my place for a nightcap," she had said as they

drove down the Costanera toward the center of town in her white Corvette. "My escape hatch," she called it.

"I'd love to, but I have some work to do before I go to sleep, and need the time," Nick said, and then, because she seemed so disappointed, added: "But I'll take a raincheck!"

"How about lunch tomorrow?" she asked quickly, glancing over at him in the darkness. "I'll make it at my place. You must be tired of restaurants and official dinners."

She was silent, driving quickly but carefully, waiting for an answer.

"What's tomorrow?" he asked. He tended to lose track of the days when he wasn't anchored by the everyday realities of routine.

"Saturday, thank God," she answered.

"I was planning to drive down to the coast." Nick started to excuse himself. "I wanted to see Valparaiso and Viña del Mar. Thought I'd make it a business trip. See what they're doing at the American Institute there." He was supposed to be on an inspection tour.

He also had a meeting with an operative set up for three in the afternoon at the Cafe Florian in Viña, but he really did want to see the beautiful coast again. It had been years since he had been there.

"If you don't mind company," Donna offered, "I'd love to drive down there with you. We can stop for lunch at a favorite restaurant of mine. Not the home cooking I promised, but the freshest seafood you've tasted in years, and a spectacular view."

"Okay," Nick laughed, "you're on; I like persistent people." He knew that he could easily excuse himself for an hour in the afternoon, and the girl was pleasant company.

"I'll pick you up at nine," she said as she let him out in front of the Hotel Sheraton Carrera.

Nick walked into the lobby and picked up his key at the front desk. Though there were newer hotels in Santiago, the Carrera had a cachet about it that he liked, something like the Waldorf-Astoria in New York. Moreover, the side entrance which he walked out of was convenient—diagonally across the street from the American Embassy on Agustinas.

Nick spoke to the Marine guard at the Embassy entrance and took the elevator to the sixth floor. There another Marine looked at his credentials, spoke to someone on the interoffice phone and waited with him until a security man came to the front desk to escort him to the cipher and code room, where all the overseas cables and radio transmissions were coded and sent, or received and decoded.

He expected a response to the lengthy message he had sent from Buenos Aires yesterday. The director had some homework to do.

The cable had been there for about an hour, the cipher clerk said, but had not been decoded because a key hadn't been cued, as Nick had requested.

A thin, sparrowlike man in a crumpled white shirt, the clerk coughed from the cigarette he had just lit from the butt of the preceding one, asked if Nick wanted the cable decoded.

"No," said Nick, "I'll do it myself. Let me have book four, series seventy-three, of the retrograde inversion double digits."

He took the large loose-leaf binder and sat down at a table in the opposite corner of the room, turned to the code he wanted, and began to decipher. The clerk looked over at him resentfully a few times, but said nothing. Nick read and reread the cable which gave the precise location he needed. It included a surprise "Prompt action mandatory. Retrieve mechanism. No Company involvement. Confirm date. Priority over data research."

He coded his brief reply: "Proceeding as requested, target 12th."

The twelfth was Wednesday, and didn't give Nick much time; he still needed to coordinate the assault team. Monday's meeting was already set up. Close, but he could do it. Haste would blow it. Barnwell hadn't said "immediate" and Nick wanted final data from Eric, although he didn't need it anymore. But he had to prevent any blunder by his two friends. The mission had priority.

He returned the code book to the sullen clerk, dropped the cable decode and his draft response into the shredder, started it and waited until the off light flickered, and left the room after handing the cipher over for transmission. There were still five minutes left till curfew, but the streets were already deserted as Nick entered the side door of the hotel and made his way up the service stairs to his room.

Craft-sense told him that something was wrong when he entered the room; there was a smell of someone else, as he opened the door, a hint of a strange cologne; man smell. Cautiously he slipped into the room, leaving the door ajar behind him in case he should want to bolt out suddenly. He eased open the closet door: nothing. The bathroom was empty too. He thought he saw the long draperies move ever so slightly. Stepping across the carpeted room silently, he pulled the curtain back swiftly, prepared to kick hard, but no one was there.

Nick looked through his personal effects. There was nothing among them which would identify him as anything but a USIA cultural affairs officer, but he wanted to see if anything was missing. Everything was in place. He looked in the lamps, telephones, and behind the pictures for "bugs": everything was in order.

The smell lingered in his mind as he went to the window, after shutting the light and double-locking the door, and drew the draperies aside. The plaza was deserted. No car, no bus, no pedestrian moved through the streets. A large open truck filled with soldiers rattled past the Moneda, its bleared facade lit up by the half moon, and a small blue van opposite the hotel, the kind used by the secret police, sat waiting. Waiting, Nick thought, until it was late enough to catch suspects at home in bed.

The streets were dead with enforced silence and Nick closed his eyes and drifted into uneasy sleep.

* * *

"The coast road or the mountain road?" asked Donna Saturday morning as she maneuvered the white Corvette convertible through the truck-clogged streets in the warehouse district. There was no direct access to either road leading west from Santiago and a slow moving line of vehicles, trucks and private cars, stopped and started and finally moved along at a steady pace near Los Cerrillos, the local airport.

Donna matched the car in a white blouse and loose cotton skirt with a red bandana tied around her dark blond hair.

Nick looked around for tags but couldn't spot any. The awareness that someone had been in his room had set him on guard.

He hadn't answered her question. She sensed his tension and suggested they stop for coffee.

"The mountain road, I think, if the drive isn't a big hassle," answered Nick finally. He had only been to the coast once, years ago with Eric, and as junior officer and poor student they traveled by bus along the flatter southerly route.

"No hassle," said Donna, swinging the powerful car off the road shoulder where she had parked while they breakfasted among the truck drivers at a roadside restaurant. She cut into the traffic now, through the five forward speeds, accelerating rapidly and authoritatively.

"In fact, I prefer it this way," she said, veering to the left at an intersection. Arrows in both directions read Valparaiso. "Most of the trucks and buses go the other way, so this'll be less crowded, and it's so much more beautiful."

"This is quite a car," said Nick, feeling rather jazzy in this sporty car with a young, good-looking woman, and at the same time at odds with his instinct for inconspicuousness while on a mission. The Maserati in Paris was his "toy" too, he realized, but there he used it to enhance his cover role: swinging bachelor diplomat. He wondered about Donna's high styling too. It seemed out of place here.

The road ran straight and flat past the airport and as there was little traffic, she opened up the throttle. The powerful engine responded instantly and the speedometer needle hovered at the eighty MPH line. Nick was a little sorry he hadn't suggested the more conventional road.

"Won't you get a ticket for speeding?" he asked, hoping she'd take the hint.

"Not with CD plates, and if they should stop me, they'll let it go. The cops are very nice to American diplomats now. I understand that before the junta came in, they'd give you a ticket for sneezing. The mood was very anti-American."

He watched the scenery in silence. After a few kilometers, Donna slowed down to the legal speed as the road began to wind into the foothills of the coastal mountain range. The landscape reminded Nick of northern Spain: mountains covered with low scrubby growth and the valleys below crisscrossed with dried-out stream beds. The arable land was cut up into small homesteads centered around brownish adobe houses, ill-kempt and mostly in disrepair. The contrast between his and Donna's elegantly conveyed and dressed Saturday outing and the lives of squalor and poverty he saw in those brown huts depressed him.

But the scenery, taken in total, was magnificent. The road curved up and up, and the Limoges china blue of the cloudless sky, the warm sun and cool wind on his face made him feel young and lucky. In contrast with the misery in those houses, he felt more than usually privileged. He didn't like the thought.

After about an hour of climbing upward, Donna negotiating each curve with great skill, maneuvering her gearbox like a professional, they reached a sort of summit: a lookout point with an area for the cars to pull off the road.

"Great view from here," Donna said as she nosed the car into the parking area. "It's the only place on this entire road where there's a safety rail. Would you believe it?"

They stood and looked over the landscape, Nick taking the opportunity to light a pipe, she a cigarette. Another car, a blue Mercury sedan, pulled in and then left without stopping. The mountains stretched away in all directions. There summer greenery sharply contrasted in the morning sun to the baked clay color of the bare spots.

Nick felt the sense of exhilaration he missed from day to day. His life had been too filled with work lately, until he knew nothing else, thought about nothing else. The tasks, the manipulations, the operations overshadowed everything, consuming all of his life like an insatiable monster. There was little real joy left, but at least he could still feel enough to know what he lacked.

Donna stood opposite, her eyes searching his face for a sign, a word, perhaps, but he kept his thoughts to himself. "I feel good right now," he said. "I'm glad you invited me to invite you to join me—so you could drive."

She laughed. "Do you want to drive? Be my guest!" and handed him the keys.

Nick hadn't driven such a responsive machine in years. His own expensive car was better appointed inside, but not as lively. He liked the way the Corvette hugged the ground, the solid centering of the wide tracking wheelbase around the curves.

After five minutes at the wheel, already accustomed to the car, he felt like he owned the road.

Passing was a pleasure in this car. When he came to the first vehicle in front of them, a green delivery truck with MUEBLES PAR TODOS, ARTURO PRATS 74 Valparaiso painted on the rear doors, he simply down-shifted from fifth to fourth gear, touched the accelerator lightly, and the Corvette shot past, its eight cylinders thrusting the car forward like a rocket. He felt the torque pressing him back into the bucket seat. "This is a bad road to pass on," he said, turning for a second to Donna, wanting to share with her his feeling of control and yet his doubts.

"That's because there are no shoulders, no room to maneuver in a tight situation, but that adds to the excitement, I think. The imminence of danger adds something to life," she said philosophically.

"That shows the difference in our ages, Donna. I like to play it safe. I've become an autoroute man: straight ahead, no curves, strict speed limits." Except when he drove someone else's car, he thought.

"But something inside you doesn't like that," she said, smiling knowingly. "I can tell by the way you drive. All I have to do is put a man behind the wheel of this car, and I know whether I want to know him better."

"Do I pass the test?" Nick asked.

"Definitely."

They had started the downhill run and he shifted down to third gear to hold the car back. In front of them the blue Mercury sedan they had seen in the lookout car park was cruising in the middle of the road. Nick blew his horn.

The Mercury increased its speed but stayed in the middle.

"Crazy SOB," Nick muttered.

Then the sedan slowed again and moved to the right, but Nick couldn't pass because a bus was laboring up in the oncoming lane. No sooner did the bus pass than the Mercury was back in the center. Nick leaned on the horn, but the driver was either crazy or deaf, and the sedan was slowing down.

Nick decided that he would simply cool it. Just slow down and let this clown play his games until the road leveled out so that he could pass safely. Maybe there would be a shoulder once they got off the mountain. He eased off the accelerator and let the car coast. The speedometer dropped to thirty-five. He would hold the car there until that idiot was far away. He wished there were another place to stop for a while, but they were going down a ridge now. The road was straight, with a sheer drop of hundreds of feet on either side.

He looked in the rearview mirror. The furniture truck was coming up fast in the left lane. It was going to pass! But how? The Mercury was still in the center. Suddenly the Mercury pulled over to the right and increased its speed. Nick did too, watching the needle climb to fifty-five, sixty-five . . . the tachometer hovering at twenty-five hundred RPMs as he shifted up through the gears.

The blue sedan was fifty yards ahead, and Nick thought he could get through with a burst of speed, but suddenly, the green truck was alongside, and the Mercury was slowing down.

The truck edged to the right and then back to the left again. Then he knew. "Oh God, how stupid of me!" These guys were not simply crazy Chilean drivers. The trucks didn't use this road! He should have realized he was set up; they were going to force him off the road, and the newspapers tomorrow would report a tragic accident which killed two American diplomats . . . and nobody would be the wiser.

He had been so happy to relax, and enjoy this day in the company of this bright girl, the drive in this lively car, that he had violated the primary rule of any operative, and had let his guard down. He realized that the blue sedan had pulled into the lookout point right after they did, lingered for a moment, and had driven off without stopping because they were tagging him. He was in a box pattern; not for surveillance this time, but for killing!

Now they had him sandwiched, classic. And he was as good as dead, and furious with himself for not keeping alert and for getting Donna into this. She sat there next to him, a concerned look on her face. He wondered if she knew what was going on.

Maybe he could break through in the fifty-yard gap! Nick started to accelerate, but MUEBBLES PARA TODOS was faster than it looked and kept pace with him. The needle climbed to seventy-five. The blue Mercury was forty, twenty-five, then only fifteen feet ahead—and in the right lane; the truck alongside Nick, keeping pace. In a minute it would sideswipe him, he knew it!

"Hit the brake hard!" shouted Donna, as the truck suddenly swerved to its right for the bang over into oblivion.

He did, and felt the safety belt dig into his lap and shoulder as the brakes gripped and the Corvette slowed dramatically, tires screeching in complaint, and rubber burning.

The truck driver wasn't quick enough to realize what his intended victim had done and went barreling past; nor was the driver of the Mercury prepared, and he slowed too quickly. With so much momentum on this downhill straightaway the truck couldn't slow down enough, and when he hit his brake, he swerved hard into the left rear quarter of the Mercury. There was a crunching sound and a screech as the sedan went out of control, spun wildly to the left, and launched itself off the road into the air, where it seemed to hang for a moment and then flipped forward, end-over-end into the valley five hundred feet below.

Nick had stopped the Corvette by now, and they watched the truck careen off the road ahead of them into a boulder-studded field on the right and stop with a jolt, a clear sound of breaking glass and smashing metal—and then silence. Nick eased the car forward slowly to the place where the truck had gone off the road. The ground leveled out here, and there was a narrow shoulder on which he parked the Corvette and cut the engine.

Except for insects buzzing, there was no sound at all, no other cars, just the silence of the mountains.

"Close!" he said and let his breath out in a rush.

"Lucky I had those disc brakes replaced recently," Donna said, wiping the perspiration from her forehead with a handkerchief she had taken out of her handbag. "Here," she said, handing him the handkerchief, "you're dripping wet. Sorry I screamed at you, but that was our only chance!"

Nick knew she was right.

He walked to the other side of the road, looked down at the blue Mercury, upside down in the valley, its wheels spinning slowly in the air, crushed and broken like a huge beetle someone has stepped on and tossed on its back. Flames were licking their way back from the engine, and he expected to hear an explosion any second.

"No point in going down there," he said to Donna.

"You wait with the car and catch your breath," she replied. "I want to check out the truck."

Nick objected, but when she smiled, insisting, there was a determination in her eyes. She began to walk, calling "Don't worry, I'm all right!" over her shoulder.

He got into the car and sat watching her walk gracefully toward the truck in the middle of the mountain meadow, white skirt billowing in the breeze, her handbag slung over her shoulder, looking for all the world like an advertisement for some fancy perfume.

His heart pounded, and the taste of death in his mouth seemed to fade. The consciousness of being alive yet, of having survived by skill—or more likely by luck—reasserted itself, and he was oddly exhilarated. It was Donna's victory, after all. She had sized up the situation coolly and made the right judgment. He would probably have tried to pass the blue sedan, and would now be flipped over, burning in the bottom of the gorge below.

Donna came back to the car quickly after inspecting the truck. "Let's get out of here," she said. "I'll drive. You relax."

Another mile and the road flattened out onto the coastal plain and they began to hit more traffic where other roads merged with the mountain road. They rode in silence until Donna exclaimed, "That's it!" and pulled the car into a gasoline station. As the attendant filled the tank, she walked around the car, looking in the trunk and under the hood casually. Then she drove away from the pump to a corner of the station where the air hose for tire inflation was. She checked and inflated the rear tires, feeling under the fenders with her fingers as she worked. Then she bent down and looked under the car. "Got it!" she exclaimed, and then to Nick, "No don't get out, just sit there."

Donna got back into the car and slipped into traffic. On the console between them she placed a small gray metal box with a magnet on one side. He saw that it was a homing device.

"What's that?" asked Nick. She looked at him unbelievingly.

"You don't know?"

He shook his head innocently.

"It's a homing device. Somebody put it on the chassis. They must have had a hard time because the body and fenders are fiberglass on this baby." She laughed.

"The truck had a two-way radio," she explained. "There must have been a tracker in the sedan too; that's how they found us. They probably did it when we stopped for coffee!"

"Who was the driver?"

"Not *how?*"

"Okay; how?"

"Very dead. Right through the windshield, throat cut."

Nick shuddered.

She continued: "He was a cop, DINA, the secret police! Oh my God!" Donna held up a wallet she fished from her handbag. "That was Joaquin Saenz—the chief!"

Nick examined identifying documents in a folded wallet she handed him. The name meant nothing to him. But the long leather case smelled from cologne—the scent which had hung in his room last night! "I see, or rather, I don't, but in any case, it wasn't clever to take this trophy," he said. "Let's get rid of it. Could get us hung!"

She looked abashed. "Righto. Dumb of me. I'm sorry."

Donna pulled into the next gasoline station and asked the attendant if she could use the baño.

"En la casita detras de la camioneta." He pointed a greasy hand toward the fuel truck parked near the office, its motor idling. Chileans use the diminutive for everything, Nick remembered.

Donna thanked the man and walked to the bathroom.

"That's that," she said as she got back into the car a few minutes later and guided the powerful machine back into the coastal traffic.

"An empty wallet followed some burned documents down the tube and," she laughed mirthlessly "they're going to have a lot of fun tracking that oil truck to Concepcion." The city was five hundred kilometers to the south. She had slipped the homing device under the tanker's fender.

"You may be a bit wet behind the ears, but you do have a good sense of humor," said Nick, laughing despite himself. Then he turned it off and became very serious. "Now, who are you?"

She smiled, sweet and Bryn Mawr once again. "I thought I'd wait until three this afternoon at the Cafe Florian to introduce myself. But circumstance being what it is . . ."

Nick's jaw fell. "You're the fieldman? Not possible!"

"Another sexist! Mr. Burns, I know what I'm doing, believe me."

Nick shook his head from side to side unbelievingly.

"Who assigned you?"

"The station chief," Donna answered.

"Did he brief you?"

"No, he said he didn't know what the mission was, but that you would brief me, and then I would report to him. Oh and there's another—a local man, who'll supply muscle, which I'm sure you think I lack." She glared at him, frowning.

"Donna, I'm sure you're a very capable young lady . . . woman," he corrected himself, "but this is a dangerous operation. I'd rather have veteran operatives. I'm sure you're good but this is paramilitary, and I'm certain you haven't experienced that before."

Donna looked very disappointed. "How will I ever get the experience if I don't have it, and I'll never get a mission which takes me away from my desk until I'm experienced. It's the famous catch."

Nick liked her persistence. "Look, I'll think about it; that's all I can promise. Not out front on the firing line, but maybe I can use you. If not—that's it, and nothing further."

Brightening a bit, she said, "Okay, fair enough. But I thought the station was in charge."

"No, I am. They don't know my mission: that's true."

"Isn't that unusual? It *is* their bailiwick. It slaps the Company face to bring in a solitaire."

Nick shrugged. "I didn't make that decision. My orders come from elsewhere."

"You're OMEGA, aren't you?" She shuddered involuntarily as his superior authority became clear.

"Does that frighten you?" Nick asked.

"Yeah . . . yeah. It's like having the Grand Inquisitor or his deputy sitting by your side, waiting for the wrong move to send you to the stake."

"It's nice to be well thought of," Nick said, smiling at her. She was really up front, and he liked her for that. "If I'm so scary," he teased, "what are you doing here, now?"

"First of all, I am taking you to lunch. Second, I'm spending time with a good-looking man who *seems* to like my company. Third of all, I'm doing my job, on my way to a meeting with my boss—I think."

They had reached the outskirts of Valparaiso, and rounding a curve in the road, there suddenly was the Pacific, glowing a bright green in the late morning sunshine.

Traffic was backed up for a quarter mile ahead. Standing up and looking over the other cars, Nick could see that the road was blocked and that soldiers were checking papers.

"You think that's for us?" Donna asked.

"I doubt it. It's one of the power games authoritarian governments often play to remind the populace constantly who's in charge. I call it negative reinforcement. Big Brother is always watching, so keep your nose clean."

"Well, there's only one way to find out," said Donna, swinging the wheel to the left and passing all the waiting cars. The soldiers made them stop, but after seeing the CD plates on the car and looking perfunctorily at their diplomatic passports, waved them on through.

* * *

Valparaiso: terraced hills and white houses sprawled lazily in the bright sun, surrounded the wide bay like a lover. The road wound down through the ramshackle upper city, the poorer residential district to the lower city, the port and business district, with its winding streets, narrow alleyways and cobblestones.

They parked the Corvette in a garage and ambled around the old city, stopped at the American Institute, introduced themselves and were shown around, to make the trip a legitimate expense for Accounting, and then drove north to Viña del Mar, the sister city to Valparaiso, stopping only when they had passed through the elegant resort and were on the road leading up the coast. Nick kept checking for tags. He didn't pick up anything at all, and with each moment in the clear, he felt himself relaxing more. But he wouldn't let the guard down again.

The coast north of Viña reminded Nick of northern California: small, crescent-shaped beaches sandwiched between large rocks against which the waves broke in plumes of spray, sparkling in the light, sudden cliffs were where the water leaped to spend itself trying to climb the land, and the endless din of the gulls and pelicans fishing from the rocks.

"Is this far enough from the madding crowd?" Donna asked, as she stepped out of the car.

Nick was enchanted by the scene. The tension in his body and the worries of the past two weeks seemed to flow out of him to be carried away by the endless ocean. He knew that it was illusory; after all, someone was trying to kill him, but for the moment he could be content. If he had to die in Chile, this would be the spot he chose, so let them come.

He felt drawn to this attractive, fearless girl, or woman—he corrected his thoughts—who stood next to him, her white skirt billowing, her long blond hair, the bandana removed, blowing back behind her in the onshore breeze. Was she truly brave or was it the bravura, the bright armor of her youth? He didn't know, and for the moment, didn't care. Only the moment counted; he felt fully alive and happy. This woman was really vibrant, alive to him, and he wanted more than just another tumble. Without thinking he reached out his arm and put it around her waist. She didn't resist but moved closer, as though she sensed that the moment was important to him. Her sensitivity made him feel toward her what he could only call love . . . and suddenly a memory of Paris eight years ago came barging into his mind and he felt remorse for the promise of life and love he had let slip away with Odette. The demands of reality had been unrelenting and had consumed his youth.

He turned toward the road: "I'm getting hungry," he said.

Donna, facing him now, put her hand up and touched his cheek, and kissed him gently on the other. Her gesture felt spontaneous, graceful and beautiful.

"You're a nice man, Nicholas Burns," she said quietly.

"How do you know?"

"I know. A woman knows!"

They drove to a restaurant about a mile further north and sat on the terrace in the sunlight and breeze, enjoying the sea and sky, the dry white Cousiño wine, locos—abalone—and the house specialty, Chupe de mariscos—a stew of seafood taken that morning from the waters at their feet.

All through lunch he kept the car in sight; not to be vigilant now had too high a price. Somebody wanted his head. Nevertheless, Nick was almost sorry when the coffee came: the half-idyll was coming to an end. Donna looked at her watch.

"Got a half hour to get you to Viña."

"I'm not going!"

"But why?"

"I think I'm being set up. Don't know why or how, but I don't want Company people on this mission. I'll choose my own."

"Pearl will be furious." She seemed worried about the CIA station chief's reaction.

"That's his problem. I'm running this my own way." Nick was firm and she didn't press the point.

"What about the man at the Cafe Florian: do you just leave him sitting there? He'll only call Pearl and they'll go bananas looking for us," Donna said.

"What's his name?"

"Luis Vergara: recognition is by sight; he knows me and has seen you. He works as a driver for the Embassy."

Nick filed the name.

"Let's have some more coffee," suggested Nick.

At three o'clock he went to the telephone, called the Cafe Florian and asked for Vergara, told the man the meeting was canceled, and his services would not be needed.

"What now?" asked Donna when he returned to the table.

He sat down, saying nothing, and then decided to risk it: "I'll brief you on the mission."

Her face almost glowed, he thought. He knew he was taking a chance on her inexperience and her subordination to the station chief, but his instincts told him that she was good for the job . . . and for him. The thought that she was an Odette substitute, or another Phyllis, and that he secretly yearned for the kind of attachment he eschewed, even marriage, entered his mind, but he thrust it aside. Such thoughts would make him sloppy. No reversals for him.

* * *

Half an hour later they left the restaurant and continued to drive northward along the coast. They would take a northern road back to Santiago. At one lookout point Donna stopped the car.

"Will a stationary sunset do as well as riding off into one? I wouldn't have asked before," she asked, "but now that you won't think I'm trying to bribe my way into a field mission, I can tell you that I have a summer house, rented of course, in Concon, and it's on a cliff, facing the water. Maybe we can go there, have a swim, and watch the sunset. There's plenty of time to get back to Santiago; the curfew's not until two on Saturday."

She took his smile for yes, and drove straight to the house about ten kilometers up the coastal road. Nick adjusted the right rearview mirror so he could watch the road without turning his head, and by the time they reached the turnoff to the house, he was sure that no one was following.

Half an hour later they were lying on the empty beach, Nick

wearing a pair of swim trunks Donna kept at the house for unprepared guests, and she in a bronze bikini the color of her sunbathed skin.

Climbing the steep path up to the house after their brief swim —the water was icy cold—Nick put his arm around her once again. This time she responded with full kiss, her lips parted, her tongue searching his mouth.

Two hours later, tired and happy, Nick was stretched on the living room rug, Donna beside him, gently fondling the hair on his chest with her fingers. He watched her lithe body, zoned into bronze and white by the orange sun reaching through the large plate glass windows facing the sea as she rolled away from him, got up and went into the kitchen. He heard the clink of ice and then she came back into the room with two martinis in frosty cold stem glasses on a tray.

"To drink to the setting sun," she said, "and our own way of riding off into it." As the sun dropped into the blackening Pacific, and an orange and purple band spread across the sky, Donna began to fondle him again. He felt himself stiffening, and flushed with pleasure, moved his lips down her body to her soft bronze open thighs. Her purrs of delight excited him once again.

* * *

They left for Santiago the next day at noon, a pleasant and unadventurous drive this time along the major road, and spent the evening at Donna's place, listening to classical music and making love.

Nick knew it had to end, that the world of Monday would dawn, with its betrayals and deaths for little pieces of paper, with its move, countermove, and counter-countermove in the service of an inchoate ideal that he yet vaguely held for truth. But he wanted to extend this interlude as long as possible.

17

Santiago

THE ONLY WAY Eric could characterize the atmosphere was sullen: he told Odette that he used to think of Chileans as an essentially placid and cheerful people, but now there was a mournfulness, a hangdog expression on most faces. Also he guessed, and in fact knew from what others had told him, there wasn't much money around. Everybody was scuffling to make ends meet. But there were plenty of soldiers roaming about, battle ready: tanks and troop carriers rolled through traffic alongside the taxi Eric and Odette took from the airport.

Downtown Santiago was a mess. The Moneda, the thick walled government palace in the center of the city, had been partially gutted by the Air Force's Hunter–Hawker jets which had strafed and bombed it. Tanks and fire had done the rest. The windows were boarded up and the facade was black with soot. Soldiers on foot moved in cautious pairs around the building. All the buildings around the Plaza de la Constitution were pockmarked with bullet holes and many of the windows were boarded up, because everything, including window glass was in short supply since the golpe de estado.

But the natural setting hadn't changed, nor had the faded modernism of the 1930s.

Because Odette had never been in Santiago, Eric asked the taxi driver to take a long detour past the hotel so he could show her the touristic outlines of the city. They drove up the Alameda to the Plaza Colon past the two universities, the Santa Lucia Park— a steep hill in the city center where office workers stroll at midday and lovers roll at midnight—and then back along the wide drive of the Costanera next to the dry Mapocho riverbed, plane trees shading the walks. Across the river, the San Cristobal hill with the huge statue of Christ, arms raised, blessing the city below, cable cars creaking to the top, and the Parque Forestal—"Santiago's Tuileries," she called it—near the Museum of Fine Arts, and finally, the crowded commercial market district near the railroad station.

The day was bright and clear, with snow on the mountaintops cradling the city. Odette liked it all—"It's like going back in time thirty years," she said, "a simplicity I love." The driver said that since the generals took over it was much better—"The people didn't like the communists."

Eric squeezed Odette's arm, so she wouldn't argue. They could wait for trouble, not invite it.

She had her own list of contacts, and as soon as they checked into the rooms Nick had reserved for them at the Sheraton Carrera, she went to the French Embassy and Eric went to the Hall of Records.

He explained to the official in charge that he was doing some research on immigration to Chile after World War II, and was sent to the Immigration Files, where he had to leave his passport at the front desk. Eric didn't realize that the research into as simple a thing as immigration records could be so complex, but it was made so by Chilean notions of organization: there was no centralized record system of all the people who had applied for citizenship or for permanent resident status. Because residency was a requirement, the application for resident working visa and permanent status had to be made in the province where the person lived at the time of application. After the residency requirement was fulfilled, the papers were filed in the county seat and handwritten duplicates were sent to Santiago. But these duplicates, including all the documents and affidavits, as well as certification that those who vouched for the applicant were themselves citizens in good standing—all of these documents, called *tramites* and *certificados de antecedentes* were then filed according to the province from which they had originated, not in a central alphabetical system!

This meant that there were twenty-four separate provincial files to check, and the task seemed hopeless. How could he know where someone had settled?

Eric started, naturally, with Santiago, and found five Immermans there, but none fit the bill; the first names, or the country of origin and the carnet number differed from what he wanted.

Same thing for Valparaiso. He was disgusted already: the light was dim, the files dusty with age, and the heat in the unventilated top floor of an old office building was suffocating.

Then he had a brainstorm: from his travels in Chile when he was an exchange student at the University, Eric remembered that a lot of Germans had settled in the forest regions in the south, a temperate zone dotted with lakes, because the topography was congenial to them, and the woods and arable land appealed to them in a familiar way.

There were only six provinces in this district. Maybe he could find his man here.

In Valdivia, perhaps? The capital of the province of the same name was a German immigrant town. Eric remembered its clean cobbled streets, the river which snaked through the town, the busy quay with barges and small commercial vessels, strollers, shoppers, and sailors. It was more central European in looks than anyplace else in Chile.

And he was right in his hunch because there, in 1944 Klaus Immerman had applied for permanent residence status, and was granted citizenship in 1950. There was no home address, only a casilla number.

Armed patrols were everywhere as Eric, excited by the chase, hurried through the ill-kempt streets to the public library, to look through old telephone books. Until 1950, there was a telephone listing for Klaus Immerman in Valdivia but the subsequent years showed nothing. The name Krähe drew a complete blank too. At a dead end, annoyed and frustrated, he walked back to the hotel. The jostling crowds seemed subdued, but otherwise nothing seemed to have changed their lives, except for the ever-present soldiers, sweaty in their battle garb, an undifferentiated anger at everyone on their faces.

* * *

Monday afternoon Nick had a chance to speak to Odette alone. He insisted that they talk in the street. They strolled in the Parque Forestal, "Santiago's Tuileries," near the Fine Arts Museum. She told him what she had learned from the French writer imprisoned at Tres Alamos. Another victim of the ETT. Mind blown—lucid in patches, the horror of the ultimate violation, the rape of the mind!

Nick had arranged for two of the Defense Intelligence security staff supplied by the military attaché to hover at a discreet distance, a third was covering Eric. When Nick stopped to light his pipe, he picked up his baby-sitter feeding the pigeons not too far away.

"What do you want?" she asked, "and why were the Israelis being so open with their classified files?"

"They probably have the same problem we do. You need a creative mind to make the connections. The technicians and bureaucrats can't cut it, no matter how bright they are. It's a different mind-set. That's probably why British Intelligence was so good during the second war, even though their operational branch was amateurish: they tapped into the best academic and creative minds in the country, took them right out of the universities, and those people solved problems, broke codes, everything imaginable."

"You're trying to tell me something, aren't you?" she asked. "Ecoutez, what an imbecile I am! You put Eric to work for you, didn't you? And you have been manipulating both of us like a puppeteer!" She seemed quite angry, glaring at him. He was taken aback by the anger but knew that he had helped them in their purposes as well.

"Perhaps I was a bit of a puppet master, but only insofar as you both were responsive to the strings. You wanted a story. Eric wanted to solve some anomalies in a manuscript so that he could finish a book, and I—I needed facts. We've all got what we want now, or almost. Eric is close to a solution of his mystery; you have a good story to sell; and both of you have helped me. Thanks." He thought for a moment and decided on a protective lie. "I'm leaving tomorrow for the States," he told her, "but I assume you are staying, still looking for the source. And Eric will probably lead you to it. So who is using whom, after all?"

"The head of DINA asked me to call," Odette said, "Left a message at the Embassy, but died in an accident on the weekend. Perhaps I might have gotten something there. But one cannot merely go about asking questions here. They're afraid, and so am I, for them and for me. I need Eric to navigate this secret chart!"

Then Odette turned and looked up at him. "You're right, mon cher, I am as much a user of others as you are. I wanted this story and did what I had to do to get it, and of course, it isn't over yet. I can't pretend an offended innocence with you. I'm a professional like you. For me the assignment is all that counts. Two opportunists." She smiled at him sadly, and looking down at her dark blue eyes, he felt once again the pain of having lost her so many years ago. It was the same decision she had just admitted to without realizing it! He was a professional, and the job had become his life. There was no escape. Even from the lies he'd have to use with both of them—and had already.

"We live in a world of users," he said. "You and I have to play by those rules. Otherwise we fail, and should have chosen different ways to go. But Eric—" He paused and she cut in.

"Eric is a naif, and is being used by everyone. I feel sorry for him," Odette said. "He's such a lovely man."

Nick looked down, stopped and dragged the toe of his shoe in the dirt. "You *know* he's my closest and oldest friend . . . and there's something ironic about you taking up with him . . . for convenience. It hurts a little."

She seemed offended and walked ahead a bit.

"What started as a convenience has become real to me, Nick," she said, stopping and looking back at him. They looked at each other for a long minute, and in Nick's mind, eternity passed . . . was gone.

He lit the Gitane she took out of her bag.

"You know there's someone following us?" she asked.

"He's mine; it's okay," Nick assured her. "Go back to what you were talking about. Do you love him?"

"I think so, but it's so impossible. And I think he is infatuated with me too."

Nick grimaced. "So whatever happens, Eric gets hurt. What a crazy fucking game. At least you and I are paid to play, but he isn't. What does he get but emptiness?" He took her arm and began to walk back toward the center of town.

"Perhaps," she said, "he gets a unique book . . . and maybe much more."

Nick stopped, stared at her, shifted on his feet. "Come on, I have work to do. The sooner I get this over with and life goes back to normal, the better I'll feel."

He had wanted just then to tell her about Donna, about how

it felt to be loved again, and to fly on your feelings, but he thought she knew it for herself; besides, it was unprofessional.

* * *

"So what do you do now?" Nick asked when Eric explained the impasse later that afternoon. Nick and Odette had been sitting in the hotel lobby waiting for Eric to return.

"Either I stop here, give up the wild-goose chase, or I go to Valdivia to look up this Immerman," Eric answered.

"Can't you check the telephone directory for Valdivia first?" Nick asked. "That's a long trip to look up a name. What if he's long dead?"

"Then there'll be relatives, a widow. Who knows, something to go on? Anyway I checked the current directory and there's no listing. I need the public records in Valdivia anyway."

Eric sat there and looked at both of them, his two friends, one old, one new. One he'd have forever, or the duration at least, the other would be parted from him soon. He had made his decision. There was nothing for it but to go. That was it. What could he lose? He announced it.

Nick surprised them both by saying that he wasn't continuing the journey.

"But why? I thought you wanted—" Eric broke off as Nick gave him a warning look. He had forgotten that Odette wasn't aware of the deal Nick had made with him.

"No, I just had to get together all the information I could," Nick answered, "and with your help, both of you, I've done it. Now I leave it to minds better than mine to decide what to make of it all, and how to act on what they've got. I'll stay here a day or two longer, write up my report, and then go back to Paris. I've been away long enough," he said, seeming glad that his job was over.

Eric knew he couldn't stop until he put the matter to rest, now that he had come so far. Nick went with him to the LAN Chile office to buy tickets for the flight south.

After they left the airline office, Nick stopped on the street, and said, "I think the heat will be off you now, but I want you to know that you'll be looked after; I mean I've got people watching out for you until you get back to the States. So don't think you're becoming paranoid. They're on our team. Just be careful."

237

"I don't want bodyguards," Eric objected, "I can take care—"

Nick interrupted, brushing aside objections: "No, you can't, buddy, and as long as you're being paid by us, you'll do it our way. It's for your own good. Besides," he kidded, "the Uncle doesn't want to pay the big insurance numbers."

Eric swallowed the lump in his throat along with his objections and kept quiet.

"You must think I'm crazy to carry this so far," he said.

"On the contrary, I admire your persistence and patience. You're a super investigator . . . in the wrong profession, maybe!" Nick responded. "Look," he continued, "if you do run into any difficulty down in Valdivia, or just in case, I'm going to give you someone to call for help. I'll write out the information and give it to you before you leave in the morning."

Eric was puzzled by Nick's dropping out of the chase at this point and told him. "I have to do this my own way," he replied.

* * *

At the airport the next morning Eric bristled when they were bumped from the overbooked flight, but Odette said, "There is no reason to become upset, mon cher. We'll have some breakfast in the restaurant, read the newspapers, relax, and before long it will be time for the next flight."

Eric didn't see how three hours would evaporate. He hated waiting, because he had a secret fear of planes, and hanging around terminals just increased the anxiety.

Nick, accompanied by Donna Harcourt, had taken them to the airport but didn't wait. "I'll see you when you get back to Santiago. By that time maybe my work here will be done, and if I can get the damned report written and recommendations made, I'll be able to get back to Paris."

While Odette went with Donna to buy some magazines on the other side of the waiting room, Eric asked him about Donna. He shrugged and grinned sheepishly. Following her with his eyes, Nick said, "She's the palliative that the doctor ordered, but not a steady regimen. I sometimes wish I had your courage to really love, Eric, but when it comes to that, I'm a coward."

"You want your life the way it is," Eric answered. "It agrees with you. Mine doesn't."

"I envy you your courage to love, Eric," Nick repeated.

Eric felt sad for both of them. "But it ends when I go back to

New York, and Odette to Paris. What then? 'Everything is figured out—except how he himself is to live a life?'—Hegel."

"Fuck Hegel," Nick answered angrily. "If you want it, man, you'll find a way. Meanwhile just don't blow it by getting hurt. If these people are ex-Nazis, you could get hurt badly. Somebody's trying to bust your head—those incidents in Buenos Aires." He seemed worried and tired all over again.

"Don't you worry," Eric told him. "They must have thought I was someone else—Greenberg the spy, maybe." Nick handed Eric an envelope. "Open this when you complete your research in the records, not before. Okay?" he said, forced a laugh, shook hands, kissed Odette's cheek—she had just returned laden with newspapers and magazines—and left the terminal abruptly. Donna looked good on Nick's arm, Eric remarked to Odette, but she merely nodded, absorbed in thought somewhere else.

* * *

From the airport, Nick hurried Donna back to the Embassy and, after checking for new cables, went to the fifth floor for his final briefing. He had gotten the station chief off his back by making him feel like part of the operation, asking him late yesterday for complete surveillance on Newman and "the Frenchwoman" on their trip south because their safety was vital to the operation. The deskman smiled when Nick double-checked. "That's been done already." He winked at Nick, in a just-us-boys-know-the-score way, and though the gesture annoyed Nick, he smiled back. He knew how it felt to be circumvented in an operation, and felt a bit sorry for the guy.

The meeting on the sixth floor took only an hour. The military attaché had gotten the word from the Director of OMEGA and was taking no chances that he would be faulted for noncompliance. The team he had assembled consisted of three handpicked men: a demolitions expert, a communication man, and a pilot. With Nick and Donna, they went over the scale maps of the estancia, the layout of the house, the guard schedule, the control room for the electric circuits and the household routine. From the way the details were in order and the information presented, Burns knew that the operation was completely professional. He still wasn't sure he had done the right thing in letting Donna take part. She sat through the briefing without saying a word. Nick went round the table afterward, asking each one in turn whether everything was clear, and answered all questions. They were flying south that evening on a U.S. military transport which made a regular weekly run with the supplies for the NASA tracking station near Valdivia and other military installations further south. From there, a transport helicopter and a Green Beret assault team was ready, waiting.

Everything was closely timed, even getting Eric and Odette bumped from the early flight had its purpose. If he was shoving them into the lion's mouth, he wanted to be there to pull them out before they were devoured. A diversionary tactic; he didn't like using them, but there was no other way. Eric couldn't be delayed any other way and Nick needed the time.

He *was* becoming a puppeteer, Odette was right; the choice had been his, the cast of the die his own. When Eric had told him just how he was going to proceed, Nick knew the timing had to be perfect.

18

Valdivia

As THE TWIN engine Astrojet banked and turned to begin its approach to Pichoy, Valdivia's airport, Eric showed Odette the estuary, the deep water bay off the Pacific, and the Port of Corral. Ten miles inland to the northeast, he could see the town of Valdivia, hugging the riverbank, looking from the air like a spired and gabled fantasy illustration from a children's book.

Later, Odette thought it beautiful from the ground as well. They were standing on the balcony of their adjoining rooms at the hotel Pedro de Valdivia, looking over the winding river, where the rowing team of the Universidad Austral was practicing. Large willow trees grew on the banks, and the shells scooted by on the west side, while the fishing boats and trading craft lined the stone quay on the east side.

The quayside was crowded with people shopping at the stalls for fish and vegetables, strolling, talking in small groups, and just idling, just as Eric had remembered the place: a benign anachronism. The sounds of their voices drifted up to their balcony.

"But it's so European," she said delighted with the ambience, "like some of the towns in Brittany."

Eric said he thought it was more like Germany, some of the river towns on tributaries to the Rhine.

"I prefer to think that nothing beautiful can be German," she said.

But the town did have a Germanic ambience. Many restaurants and shops had German names, the streets had a swept Northern European orderliness, and fair-haired, blue-eyed people were everywhere. Here Eric didn't look foreign.

"But most of the Germans came here in the mid-nineteenth century," he said, "people who also fled persecution in 1848."

"A boche is a boche is a boche," she said with a wink.

"Open-minded, aren't you?"

"No," she said, "that's an American luxury . . . and an illusion. Your country has never been occupied, so it is easy for you to maintain such ideals. Europeans are not so fortunate, and more realistic."

Being bumped from the early flight had cost him most of the working day and it was now almost five in the afternoon. But he thought that the Municipal Offices might still be open, asked the desk clerk where to find them, and walked the two blocks through the busy streets.

The clerk at the Records Office seemed pleased to have something to do, and brought the Immerman file. It was identical to the record in Santiago and told Eric nothing he didn't already know.

"Have you a tax roll for real estate?" he asked.

The clerk brought it: nothing there for Immerman.

Death records?

"If the man moved out of the province, we wouldn't have anything," the clerk said, looking pointedly at the clock on the wall. There were fifteen minutes until closing. The death records also told Eric nothing about his man.

Voter registration?

Immerman had registered to vote in 1951, the first year his new citizenship would have permitted the franchise. His place of residence was given as Pucon, a small town on Lake Villarrica, 300 kilometres to the east, the clerk said. There was no address given, only a casilla number.

"What about the actual record of his annual voting?" Eric asked.

"That would be at the board of elections in Pucon, if the person still lives there," the clerk answered, looking at the clock once more, and growing visibly less patient in his answers.

"Then I'll have to go there to look it up," Eric said.

The clerk agreed. "Senor, there are only five minutes until closing now. Please come back tomorrow."

"Would it be possible to stay just a few extra minutes?" Eric pleaded.

The clerk raised his right hand and pointing upwards with the index finger, shook it back and forth, palms toward Eric, a classic Chilean mannerism that Eric had come to detest in his student days, saying, "Eso no se hace, Senor"—that isn't done . . . "Unless you are from the government."

He looked at Eric questioningly, as if he would welcome an official reason for extending his hours, something justified by superior authority. Eric knew he had to plead with this martinet. He couldn't waste another day.

"I'm not an official, just a writer doing research, on a tight schedule." The clerk looked at Eric incredulously, as though a writer didn't do what he was doing, only policemen.

"In that case, I'm sorry, but the office closes—"

"Wait a second. What does this mean?" There was a notation on the bottom of the voting application. Printed in small letters was "cdnl/15 enero 1952" and an illegible signature.

"That means that the person has changed his name legally: cambio de nombre legal."

"Is there a record here of that?"

"Yes but I'm afraid . . ."

There were three minutes yet to go, and Eric said so. "The office is still open." The statement, factually precise, left the martinet no choice, and he went for another register. A rather small ledger book. "Not many people change names here; usually foreigners who want to have a Chilean name. But that's less and less common these days," he explained, as he handed Eric the ledger. "Please hurry!"

It took Eric very little time to find what he was looking for: in 1952, entered in the bound ledger as a separate entity and cross-indexed nowhere—so that anyone who did not know the year in which a magistrate decreed a name change couldn't find it without looking through each year's records—this was Chilean logic at work. In the year 1952 it was recorded that Klaus Immerman had requested and been granted, "for the purposes of normalizing his everyday functions and business relationships as a Chilean citizen," a change of name to Enrique Cuervo de la Ventaja; his permanent address was given as Estancia La Ultima Nidal, Pucon.

Eric had just finished copying this into his notebook when the clerk pulled the ledger away none too gently, closed it with a snap, and put it away. The clock stood at precisely 6:00 P.M.

Eric thanked him. He smiled faintly and said, "The office is closed."

Eric walked out in a daze, his head throbbing with the mixed happiness and fear that was always his reaction when he made a creative discovery. This was the end, almost, of his quest. He went into the first cafe, right up to the bar, and asked for a double pisco. The clear brandy burned his throat as he knocked it back in one gulp, but it brought him out of his daze.

There was no doubt that he had his man: Enrique Cuervo was about as close as you could get in Spanish to Harry (Henry) Raven, alias Heinrich Krähe, who came to Chile as a phony Klaus Immerman. The last part he couldn't figure out, but the play with the names told him one thing: Raven wanted to be found someday, if in fact this was Raven, and had left a barely legible trail, which Eric had discovered.

The absurdity of it all! He underlined who he was, even with the name of the ranch. Ultima Nidal, meant "the Final Nest" for the Cuervo, the crow, the Krähe, the Raven.

Then Eric remembered Nick's envelope in his pocket and his caveat that morning. Eric *had* completed his research: he *had* found Raven! He tore the flap open and read:

If you are going to the Estancia Ultima Nidal in Pucon, we are all vindicated; you found what you wanted through your own genius for research; I through an unexpected windfall. The credit is yours. Please go on to Pucon Wednesday morning, if at all. After that, I can't guarantee you'll find what you want. If you are going elsewhere, it's all been coincidence. Good luck. I'll see you when you return. Destroy this after reading. N.

Eric did the dutiful and tore the paper into little bits and flushed them in the bowl of the men's room. How the hell did Nick know? All along? Was Eric being led between the primroses unaware? Weak with confusion and suddenly wobbly with pisco, he dragged his feet unsteadily back to the hotel.

* * *

"But he may refuse to see you, in which case you will still not achieve your goal. Let me try," Odette said, sipping a pisco sour in the bar of the Hotel Pedro de Valdivia.

Eric felt as though she were picking up his ball to run with it, and he refused to allow her to call.

"You are really an imbecile, Eric! You are jealous that the man might agree to see me and perhaps, only perhaps, not you. What is important here? That we, or rather you, see him, or that we play games of vanity?"

Though he denied it, he was a little jealous. This woman was too shrewd. Always a step ahead of him.

"What reason could you have to see him?" Eric hoped she couldn't find one.

"Eh bien,"—She hesitated and he thought he had won this point—"I will say that I am doing a story for *L'Express* on Chile after the coup d'état, and wanted to interview some of the landowners." He lost the point.

"What if he says no?" Eric childishly hoped she was refused.

"Then *you* will think of some ingenious way. You are a strange man, Eric. I think you are actually a bit peeved, like a child, that this man might agree to see me before he would see you, but I'm just depending on my reputation and accreditation as a journalist. If he is the highly cultured man you think he is, despite his strange life, he has probably seen my name in print, and the recognition factor might work. Your name is unknown to him. And even if it were known, why should he want to see anyone who wishes to rip off his mask? What will you tell him on the phone?"

She was flushed, angry in her challenge, and Eric had to admit that Odette was right. He told her to call.

* * *

Don Enrique had thought himself beyond such emotion, but he was saddened by Joaquin's death and mourned his friend. Sitting in his study, he opened a notebook and began to write. It was all coming apart, he feared, slipping out of his control.

When the funeral service had ended that morning, Don Enrique had found Fleming standing next to him at the Recolleta Cemetery where Joaquin Saenz had just been buried with full military honors.

"It's been done already. The money has been transferred, and an ICO crew will be there soon to take delivery of the machine," Fleming whispered to him.

"Not until I have official confirmation from the bank of your deposit, my dear sir," said Don Enrique, irritated. The funeral had upset him more than he thought it would, and he had resented the crassness of the communications executive who evidently had little sense of propriety and was ready to discuss business at any time.

"The cable from Switzerland will be in your hands tomorrow," Fleming had reassured him. Don Enrique made a mental note to call the Swiss bank when the cable did arrive to make sure that the deposit had been made and that *they* had sent the cable, not one of Fleming's stooges. He murmured an acknowledgment and turned away from the spectacled cherub.

"Wait," Fleming had said with a boyish happiness—what an insensitive fool the man was! "OMEGA is gone!"

Don Enrique had turned and raised a querulous eyebrow.

"Well, almost. The man booked a flight out to New York for this afternoon. After he leaves our worries are over."

Don Enrique had assented once again and continued to walk away. General Pinochet had told Don Enrique the same thing an hour earlier but had added something else:

"You must delay delivery to ICO, even after they fulfill the agreement. I'll trust you to think of some excuse!"

"For how long, Mi Generale?"

Pinochet had scowled at him and then smiled, a dangerous crafty smile. "Until I tell you it is all right to deliver. Not before!" he had said, then added, "It won't be too long, just wait for my word, no one else's."

Don Enrique had known that there was no alternative but to obey. Fleming had the money, but the general held the power, the control of life and death. One word from that ape and Don Enrique would rot the rest of his life away in prison, if he lived long enough to rot!

Fleming had caught up with him again just as he reached the cemetery gate. "Do you have the facilities for a helicopter to land?" he had asked.

"Yes," Don Enrique had answered with annoyance in his voice. The man's childlike persistence irked him. "Right on the roof of the building which houses the machine. It was built for that especially."

"GOOD, good," beamed the willful executive, "I think that's the better way to go. Less jiggling around, and lots faster."

"Confirmation first, remember," replied Don Enrique, realizing that he had the power of delay, or at least the rationale right there. His limited options were clear. He had pulled away from Fleming abruptly and into the waiting limousine.

Fleming had stood at the cemetery gate, puzzled by the aristocrat's aloof snubbing of his enthusiastic good cheer.

* * *

After recording the incident and reminiscing about his dead friend, Don Enrique closed his notebook. He was still stunned.

Pinochet had to be behind this, he thought, staring at the sunset. One thing Don Enrique knew for certain: Joaquin would not have been on the road to the coast unless it had been mandatory. He had hated to drive anywhere, had an almost irrational fear of traffic, and would invariably lay on a police helicopter or single engine plane to take him anywhere outside of the capital.

He thought of his friend and protector dead. Alone now. Oh, it was true, he had had some misgivings about Joaquin's trustworthiness if his own interests were threatened, but who wasn't like that? Opportunism was for the victors of this world, he thought; idealism for the victims. Joaquin had been the only person in Chile Don Enrique had felt close to, and even then he hadn't told his friend much. Only what the intelligence officer had needed to know, many years ago, and dribs and drabs of the same lies ever since. Well, at least there was no further breach in the wall. Whatever Joaquin had surmised of the truth had died with him. Yet there was still that professor, that snooper in the ruins of history with no Joaquin to put him off. No matter; he saw no threat in Newman. He could be handled when and if the time came.

Once again in his life, Don Enrique felt alone, responsible for his life, survival by any means. Aside from his paid retainers there was nobody, nobody he could talk to, nobody he could trust. Except old Oswaldo, his brother in the wilderness. And now the stubborn old fool, a victim of his own reluctant idealism, would have little or nothing to do with his keeper, benefactor. If not for him, the old man would have become a bar of soap or a pile of ashes. He had saved him. They would have used him up and sent him out to slaughter. But now Oswaldo sat all day and read his mystical books, a voiceless prophet of doom in the wilderness, and Don Enrique had nothing and nobody. All the more reason to conclude this business as rapidly as possible, and get out. He didn't trust the general's delay. But what to do?

Don Enrique opened the notebook once again and began to write, self-absorbed. The maid knocked on the door to announce a phone call. He hadn't even heard the ring.

*　*　*

Nick Burns walked into the waiting room at Pudahuel, Santiago's international airport. He carried only hand luggage as usual, the kind of bag you could shove under a seat, or stow in the onboard locker. Years of country hopping had taught him that this was the easiest way to save time at Customs and Immigration. By now the mannerisms of his life had congealed from the amorphous, intellectualized convictions of his youth to habits he no longer thought about.

He went through the normal procedure of check-in at the Braniff counter for his flight to New York.

He didn't know who was watching—at a crowded airport it's hard to pick up tags if they don't hang in too close—but he hoped they were there to verify his departure.

As soon as the flight was called to board, Nick dutifully filed out to the plane, across the tarmac with the other passengers. When he reached the boarding ramp, he returned the stewardess' plastic smiles, walked toward the rear of the 747, and stepped into the first lavatory on the right.

Everything was there, as the Defense Intelligence chief had arranged. Five minutes later, Captain William Pierce straightened his peaked cap on his head, made sure the documents in the uniform pocket were in order, and opened the locked door.

Outside waited a man who resembled Nick Burns. He acknowledged the captain's presence with a nod, hesitated while the flight officer picked up the standard black flight case containing a change of shirt, underwear and a toilet kit, which had been placed next to Nick Burns' hand luggage on the rear locker shelf, and stepped into the lavatory, where he proceeded to strip his own garments and dress himself in the clothing Nick Burns had left behind.

Captain Pierce walked to the aircraft's center galley, stepped onto the single passenger elevator which dropped to the galley storage area, and stepped through the open companionway to the cavernous baggage area. A baggage truck with a string of empty flat bed carriers coupled to it had just unloaded, and waited while the airline officer stepped aboard and sat next to the driver for the/ride across the field to the baggage loading bay for the next pickup. The captain walked through the special and almost empty customs and immigration area reserved for flight crews alongside a Lufthansa contingent just off its inbound plane, stepped into a Braniff station wagon waiting at the exit, its special driver alert and keeping constant watch, and was driven away from the airport rapidly. No one seemed to notice.

The station wagon covered the two miles between the international airport and the U.S. military base very rapidly, was hastened through the gated entrance by the armed guard, and dropped the airline officer at the entrance to the low concrete administration building. Once inside, Nick Burns removed the visored cap which had been giving him a headache because it was a shade too tight and had been pulled down hard to cover as much of his features as possible, and stepped into the commander's office, where his technical assault crew was assembled for the flight south. After a change into battle fatigues and a flight coverall, he sat puffing on the pipe he had remembered to take from his civilian suit pocket at the last moment in the lavatory of the 747, and briefed the team once more on the plan of attack.

19

Estancia Ultima Nidal—Pucon

THE LEAN silver-haired aristocrat who greeted them at the door of the stucco, tiled-roof mansion was not what Eric had imagined. From pictures he had seen, Raven had been somewhat heavier in build, with a fleshy nose and a rounded hairline.

Don Enrique had aquiline features and a pronounced widow's peak. Although his hair was silver white, he didn't seem to have lost much of it, certainly not enough to create this appearance. Eric was a little disappointed. Plastic surgery? He didn't know how to tell.

"I am delighted to see you, Madame et Monsieur des Chavannes," Don Enrique said in impeccable French, showing them into a large cool room, sparely furnished in the Spanish mission-style, with dark floors of highly polished wide-cut planks and two comfortable-looking couches facing each other across a coffee table.

Scattered on the table were a dozen or so current magazines in several languages. The walls were stark white, and hung with canvases by European twentieth-century masters: Miró, Picasso, Modigliani, Ernst. In a corner on a pedestal stood a small construction by Giacometti. Calculating rapidly, Eric totaled at least a half million dollars worth of art in this room alone. It didn't make sense.

A maid brought in a tray of pisco sours. Eric decided not to correct the impression that he was M. des Chavannes until he was sure he could do so with impunity. On the train he had sulked over Odette's ploy, not happy about riding her coattails, but it had worked. They were here, invited to lunch, and he could observe the quarry without resistance. All for a minor deception.

"I have read your interviews with Willy Brandt, Giscard

d'Estaing, Aldo Moro, Henry Kissinger in *L'Express*, Madame,"
Don Enrique said to Odette, "and although I am certainly flattered to be sought after by so distinguished a journalist as yourself; frankly, I am surprised to be among such company. I, a mere
landowner in an unimportant country."

Odette explained that she was in Latin America on another
assignment and had thought up this one so that she could get
to see Don Enrique's beautiful country.

At this point, a stooped elderly man whom Don Enrique introduced as his brother Oswaldo entered the room. He mumbled
a greeting Eric could hardly understand and took a seat. "He
doesn't hear very well," said Don Enrique. "Please don't mind
him."

The maid came in to say that lunch was ready, and Don Enrique seated his guests at a country table in the dining room.
Except for the native Indian rug on one wall, and a sideboard
covered with silver serving pieces, the room was monastic in its
simplicity. Like the living room, a large veranda ran the length
of the room and was reached by glass doors, which were now
open, to allow the cool breeze to circulate.

During the elaborate lunch of sauteed fresh trout ("from the
lake this morning") and superb filet steaks ("from Argentina
yesterday") served with local white and red wines of chateau
quality, Don Enrique spoke at length of the political system, of
Allende's mistakes, and of the abuses under the present government.

"Mind you," he said, "I do not approve of these abuses, nor do
most of my peers, the landed gentry of this country; but even less
do I approve legions of unwashed illiterates who propose to take
over in the name of a different ideology and turn this country
into a communist boy scout camp."

The older brother mumbled something, and Don Enrique said
curtly, "That's ridiculous, Oswaldo."

"What did he say?" Odette asked.

"I said,"—Oswaldo spoke French too, it appeared, with a
guttural accent—"I said, that every government thinks it has a
premium on truth, but only God knows truth. The rest is the
dominion of arrogance . . ." He trailed off and turned his attention to the food.

"My brother," said Don Enrique, "has taken up religion lately and is becoming an unbearable fanatic. He even wants to make a pilgrimage to the Holy Land."

Oswaldo looked up from his fish, nodded and smiled before turning back.

"I hope he goes soon," our host continued. "He's becoming a dreadful bore." He laughed, cajoling his guests to side with his point of view.

"But he may be right," Eric said in Spanish, speaking for the first time since they had arrived.

Don Enrique looked at him shrewdly. "The gift of unknowing is man's blessing and curse." He stopped. "Do I detect an American accent?" he asked. Eric felt like an ass for such an easy giveaway and merely nodded, trying not to look sheepish. Should he tell the truth? But there was no oportunity as Don Enrique smoothly glosssed over any embarrassment.

"I'll be happy to practice my English," he said flawlessly, with a trace of British pronunciation.

"So then you support the military junta in their takeover of the government," Odette said, looking thoughtful, and trying to change the subject.

Don Enrique thought for a moment, then said in English, "Madame, you're too shrewd a person to ask such a naive question. I could not answer negatively for the public record, even if I wanted to, but I don't want to. Let me put it this way: as a youth I was a political idealist; I no longer am. It is a comforting feeling for a young man or woman to know that one can and will die for, kill for, and make any sacrifice for an ideology. That is the privilege and misspent passion of youth. 'To the barricades' is the cri de guerre of those who can afford to squander the lives of others, and in that mass hysteria which reinforces such passion is the essential human cowardice."

"Then revolutions are the acts of cowards? Is that what you are saying?" Odette asked, her eyes glittering. Eric could see that she loved this conflict, this thrust and parry.

"Ha haaa—" laughed Don Enrique. "You can't snare me with that generalization, because then you could call what the junta did a revolution, and place me in opposition to them. No. What I mean is that courage lies in defining the limits of a system, in challenging those limits publicly or privately as necessity dictates, even in rebelling against them—actively, if one must. But throwing your life into the meat-and-bone grinder of history as a gesture, is a waste of life and effort. Men who rule are concerned with getting and keeping power, and for them all ideology is a mask, or a masque—in the sense of charade—to convince the unwary that they have something to die for. The French Revolution, two world wars—all elaborate theater the masses die for, elevating History, Destiny, and so on to the status of God. What better proof of human folly could there be?"

"Then Rousseau, Marx, Nietzsche, Plato—"

He cut in before she could finish.

"Madmen," he said, his eyes passionate with the argument. "Madmen all. Who else would sit around and dream up systems, theories of the state? These are drams of glory,"—he laughed at his own pun, and continued the metaphor—"and a sometimes heady draught too, enough to keep their makers drunk for a lifetime. But such madness is the province of poets, artists. As long as they do not throw me onto the barricades in the service of their ideals, that's fine."

He paused, looked at each of them as though to allow time for a rejoinder, but nobody spoke. Eric knew this had to be Raven! The language, the metaphor, the brilliance of argument. Even the phrases sounded like the 'dead' poet.

"They, at least," Don Enrique continued, "have no power. That is left to a second breed of men, even more mad, who scheme and manipulate and eventually get power to apply those same systems. When they fully believe in the system they are implementing, these men are extraordinarily dangerous. Then you get a Robespierre, a Mussolini, a Stalin, a Hitler, a Savanarola. Witness the nightmares perpetrated in the name of ideology!"

Odette continued to ply him with questions all through the meal. Eric said hardly anything at all, feeling in league with Don Enrique's silent brother who said nothing, but smiled to himself. At least the old man had found God, thought Eric. He himself said nothing, and had nothing—no belief in anything but his own piddling in the graveyard of history, tearing up the stones in search of ghosts or worms. He tried, turned his mind to the contemplation of holiness, of beatitude, and all he could think of was "Thou preparest a table before me in the presence of mine enemies."

Whose enemy? It was inconceivable to Eric that he was the enemy of this eloquent, civilized man who sat facing him, enchanting with the urbanity of his language and the originality of his ideas.

Just after the maid had brought in a dessert of fresh fruit and cheeses, she returned to give Don Enrique a message. There was a phone call. He excused himself and left the room. Eric heard him talking on a telephone, indistinguishably, and took the opportunity to stand up and walk over to the open veranda doors. A dirt road led from the house to a long low building about three hundred yards away. From Eric's vantage point it looked as though the windows were barred, but it was hard to tell because a stand of poplars was in the way. Probably servants' quarters, Eric thought.

Then he noticed a pair of sentries in khaki patrolling the grounds around the low building, and saw another man also in khaki fatigues holding a submachine gun walking toward a grassy knoll shaded by a tree where he sat down, facing the open door where Eric stood. Were they under guard? It seemed unlikely! What reason could their host have for suspecting them? And of what? Odette's questions had been very professional, and her identity was clearly established, as well as the reason for her being here.

Eric was shaken from his speculations by Don Enrique's return. He looked pleased, as though the phone call had brought good news.

"If I have answered all of your questions, Madame des Chavannes," he said, "perhaps you would like to see the rest of the house. It's quite interesting." He stood at the doorway of the dining room smiling, the gracious host, accommodating and deferential; yet everyone understood that it was not merely a suggestion, but an order. He called the maid and instructed her to show Odette around. Oswaldo bowed and shuffled from the room.

"We'll have coffee when the tour is over," Don Enrique said, and turned to Eric. "Monsieur will find my study very interesting."

Odette followed the maid out of the room, catching Eric's eye briefly with a glance that said, be careful. She looked worried.

Don Enrique then showed Eric back into the sitting room on

the other side of the house, where he was once again struck by the fortune in great master paintings assembled, wondering were they real or expert copies. If they were real, a fortune hung on the walls. How could this be a poor poet in disguise? Eric had made a mistake. So had Nick. It *was* a wild-goose chase.

* * *

The study was reached through a door he hadn't noticed before, on the far side of the living room.

A large rectangular library table stood in the center of the room with a chair drawn up to either side. An Oriental rug covered most of the floor and a low couch was framed by the French doors open to the veranda, which Eric assumed ran completely around the house. Every inch of wall space was covered with shelving of dark wood and filled with books, from floor to ceiling. A quick estimate of the approximately thirty-foot-square space yielded five thousand volumes at least.

A tray with coffee steaming in a silver pot and a brandy decanter stood on the table with two cups and two glasses.

Don Enrique poured two cups of coffee, put some brandy into each snifter, turned to him and said:

"I understand, Mr. Newman, that you have been making not so discreet enquiries about me." He spoke in flat, unaccented American English and his face was dead set in a frozen, mirthless smile.

Eric felt his heart thump, hard. He was speechless, caught by complete surprise.

He knew he was taking a chance here in the hinterlands with nothing between him and sudden death, but decided not to be intimidated. "I have no reason to be discreet. Until a short time ago I thought I was writing the biography of a dead man. Now I'm not so sure."

Perhaps Don Enrique didn't expect that answer, because he suddenly stopped smiling—for a split second Eric thought his host was going to scream because his mouth opened wide—and then he began to laugh; loud, long and uncontrollable laughter from the depths of his body.

"That's very funny," he said, drying his eyes. "Writing a book! And I thought you were an assassin."

"An assassin?" Now it was Eric's turn to laugh at the clumsy transparency of his lie. But he answered straightforwardly,

"Why? Why me? I'm a university professor, a researcher, an academic writer, a failed poet, but not a hired killer. I hardly look the part."

"They never do," he said. "They never do. Look at what happened to Trotsky in Mexico, and so many others."

"Well, I'm not a killer, and you're not Trotsky."

Why that, of all the absurd ideas he could confront Eric with —an assassin? Maybe Don Enrique was a complete megalomaniac who saw himself as the center of the universe?

"What is it you want of me then, Mr. Newman?" Don Enrique asked. He had assumed once more the gracious role of dueño de la casa, and as he was asking the question, offered him a cigar from a large chest sitting on his desk.

"If I have one thing against the junta—and this I'll tell Madame des Chavannes—it is that I can no longer get my good Cuban cigars. These, I'm afraid, are from Brazil, but I assure you, the very best quality."

He was fencing, stalling. Eric decided to be direct as he took a cigar from the box, clipped the end with the gold device his host handed him, and lit it with the wodden match proffered.

"I am writing the biography of Harry Raven, an American writer, a poet who died in 1943." Eric hesitated, and studied Don Enrique's face. It was noncommittal. "And," Eric continued, "everything points to the conclusion that he didn't die at all, but that the death was staged, and that you, Don Enrique, are in fact Harry Raven."

Don Enrique stood and paced the room, and then returned to sit facing Eric across the big table, and spoke slowly, and Eric thought, sadly. "When I learned that two acquaintances of mine in Buenos Aires had died mysteriously after seeing you, and that Max Hartman had been murdered in New York, I simply assumed that you were the link to all, and that I was your target. Now you tell me that it isn't so, and I am not sure that I believe you, but I can see no harm in telling you the truth. It makes no difference now."

He stood again and paced, trailing clouds of rapidly puffed cigar smoke. Eric ceased to exist for the moment, as Don Enrique muttered unintelligibly to himself. If he had had a wooden leg, it could have been Ahab: that's how Eric saw him—larger than life, a doomed figure on the afterdeck, completely engrossed in his own needs. He stopped and faced Eric just as abruptly as he had started to pace, his face going through some elaborate transformation: he looked young and vulnerable, then old and wizened, his eyes seemed to darken and become sensual, smirking, lewd. And then, as abruptly, were distant once again. The aloof, urbanely polished Don Enrique was back before him.

"What do you want of me, Professor Newman? Do you want to interview me for your book? The *ultimate* source?" he asked, a sardonic and menacing tone in his voice.

"Yes," Eric answered. "I think you are Harry Raven, and what I want is the truth! I know about the changes of names, the disappearance—I mean the suicide, that must have been faked. I know that the great poet, the rival to Eliot and Frost for the laureate's crown in his own country, decided to give it all up, to forsake the legacy, his rightful place in history to steal some secret plans. I know that Harry Raven was involved in the disappearance of a scientist who worked on these secret plans for the American government, and I've traveled to the end of the earth to find him. To know why, to understand why a genius, a great artist steps over the line which separates the height of creation from the depth of destruction, the thin line between creativity and madness. I want to know why. I have hunted you so that I might write truth, not unwitting fiction."

Don Enrique's eyes were ice blue steel, so cold they burned into Eric, and he finally could not bear it. He averted his face.

"It makes no difference now," Don Enrique repeated, laughing without humor, chilling, menacing. "Who will care what *you* know?

"The TRUTH you say . . . how enormously funny that is!" He laughed again, and the intimation of a great capacity for evil resounded in Eric's ears. "The *truth* is that there is a distortion in your mind as to the meaning of truth," Don Enrique continued, his eyes burning, his voice intense. "You think that once you have the facts you can work it all out inductively, and that you can reach a general conclusion about the simplistic idea you call 'reality.' As though one could make sense of a man's life by adducing details, as though the mind of a man were perceivable at all, let alone from a ragbag of details, castoffs, the jetsam with which I choose to lighten my ballast, the flotsam you spy out in my wreckage after I founder. But what is the essence of me, the indefinable combination of elements which makes a creator, an artist? A poet whom the world reads and curses?"

"Curses?" Eric asked, incredulously. "Why do you think the world curses a genius who sees into the soul and reports it? They adulate him; they reward him as his talent, honesty, and vision deserve."

"Rubbish," he answered, a faint smile turning the corners of his grim lips. "Only if he comforts them in their desolation, and tells them that somehow it is all right, all redeemed; that to see it is redeeming, if only they look with him, through his eyes 'honestly,' and then return to the fat comfort of sloshing around in their own guts, avoiding or evading what they have been shown forevermore. What they want is cheap moral object lessons to purge discomfort. Laxatives for constipated minds! Oh, yes. Committees award prizes, reward the geniuses with money, alluring them, trying to buy them off, suborning, corrupting, subverting the artist so that his vision of horror is made more tolerable, since he too likes the comforts they spend their lives killing each other and themselves to get.

"And I did not want to be dealt with that way. I beheld a universe of monsters, feeding on each other, ripping out their own flesh, the flesh of others, and consuming the hot smoking gobbets, and dignifying the act, the obscenity of their existence by creating systems, elaborate rationalizations they called truth. TRUTH . . . with names like capitalism, socialism, fascism, magically to transform rapacity into terms which are acceptable. Where they elaborate superstitious fantasies into religious systems, converting their desire to destroy, to rape, to consume, into a fairy tale of goodness. Compensating with CARE packages: hospitals, social services, pennies thrown to unknowing beggars who can't even see their own degradation.

"And what do they do to those who see, those who see the real truth and name it and depict it? Do you know, my fine scholar?"

Eric sat there dumbly. His host didn't want an answer, he wanted to talk, and Eric had not come so far to argue. He had traveled the world to rediscover Harry Raven, and if this, in fact, was the man he sought, Eric wanted merely to listen, to record later what he had heard, and to bring to light in a book all the fascination and horror he was experiencing.

Don Enrique was shouting now, an orator, an attorney for the defense, making his final summation before a court of one.

"*They* destroy the vision, they co-opt it; and failing that, they destroy the seer—if not with the insidious kindness of 'success' and its rewards, then with death. In the so-called democracies where the sentimental and false ideas of law and justice are paid lip service, the visionary is destroyed with indifference and the sort of financial penury which forces him to be like every other working man: dimmed by labor, tired until dumb. He becomes part of the unleavened mass and is stuck, never to escape until dead. Why do you think so many artists kill themselves?"

He stopped pacing and stood before Eric, looking down, tense with emotion, caught up in the power of his own words, convinced, unshakable—

"I chose—*chose*, did you hear? I chose not to grow old shouting into the vacuum of America. So I made my own rules, abandoning all *their* rationalizations, *their* illiterate fumblings in the dark. I saw the chance for my own power, my own silence as I chose to make it, my own world. I seized the opportunity as presented to me, and let them all go to hell or stay where they were; it was the same thing."

He sat down, faced Eric, his eyes slowly losing their frightening intensity, and reached for the cigar box.

"So you *are* Harry Raven," Eric said. Ludicrously, it was all he could say, overcome by the intensity of his host's passion, a passion such as Eric had never felt personally in his entire life, for anything or anybody, even himself. What he saw before him was the ultimate form of narcissism, naked, raw, intoxicated with itself.

"The ghost of him," he replied. "Enrique Cuervo de la Ventaja sits before you."

Eric lit a cigarette. "In the interests of my limited, and possibly misguided notions of 'truth,' " he added to humor his host, "will you tell me some facts about Raven?"

"Only to repay your devotion to a phantom I once knew," he answered, "and only to show you how false is the truth. If you write *The Life of Harry Raven*, it might be well received, even I should enjoy reading it for its insight into the mind of a man I once knew, half a lifetime ago. But he *died*, ended on that night at sea thirty years ago, and there your book must end. The truth will never be accepted. You *must* perpetuate the myth all are happy to believe, or else suffer the professional consequences, a risk your career would not sustain. Because you cannot prove anything. They'll think you mad and drum you out."

Eric had to lie and say he agreed. There was no choice but to do so, because Don Enrique would not go on otherwise. Eric gave his word, and his host continued.

"While America and most of Europe floundered in the aftermath of the Great Depression," he said, "I thought that *some* Germans had the right idea. I became convinced that National Socialism was the answer to the world's economic and social problems when I was a graduate student at the University of Heidelberg in 1930. I joined the Nazi party and was recruited into the Abwehr, German Military Intelligence, within the year. At their instruction I then joined the Communist party, was publicly tossed out of the Nazi party to validate my unreliability and sent back to the United States as an Abwehr agent. I had become a German citizen by secret executive fiat, and had no qualms about being a spy."

"Didn't you feel like a traitor?" Eric asked. "Was your conscience troublesome?"

"No, because it was for my adopted country," he said. "And I thought that they were serving a higher purpose—the universalist dream of a united world. I really believed it. Besides, we weren't at war. And I was 'in place' only to report on the Communists—and, if possible, be subtly disruptive to *them*, not to America."

"What about Hitler? How did he suit you?"

"I thought he was a man of great charisma, who became utterly mad in the process of getting and keeping his power. And of course, I never held with his racist hogwash, his anti-Semitism, his death camps."

"Yet you worked for his cause," Eric accused him, "carried out the directives of his handpicked monsters and became one by association yourself."

"I saw through that rather soon, but by then was too deeply involved. Especially after the war in Spain. That was a fiasco, a waste, butchery, by all. If I had left, they would have killed me, or let the FBI catch me, or revealed me to the Reds. As good as dead, anyway. So I did as I was told. Afterward, I couldn't stay in the United States, couldn't go back to Germany, and I was afraid to do anything but continue. So I 'died' and started over. I believed in the ideals, but they vanished in corrupt hands—"

"And you still do? You still are committed to the ideology of a master race?" Eric interrupted.

"No. The idea of superior beings, yes. But so was Plato. No, there is no such possibility, not now. The only ideology I hold to today is my own! Money and personal gratification. We are past all political faiths; only charlatans and fools hold them any longer. The charlatans trick the fools and stay in power. The fools are incapable of knowing that they are fools. All that counts today is the international flow of capital in transnational corporate conglomerates. These governments, Chile, the United States, Russia, France—they are all theater. Masquerades to keep markets open, resources available, and to maintain the necessary continuity of waste, so that the expendable is spent and so that power becomes increasingly concentrated in the hands of the corporate directors. They are the new governors of the world, and control its life and death."

He thought for a minute, and Eric sat waiting, wondering if the man before him was prophetic or mad—or both. He had magnitude certainly, but it was disordered.

"These dreams—of a Salvador Allende, or of the junta itself to take the present examples—are naive," Don Enrique continued. "If Allende's regime had been conducive to the furthering of the multinational conglomerate plan, he'd still be in power. That's why Castro, Tito, and a few other leftists are in. Because they cooperate. They'd be overthrown tomorrow if they didn't."

Eric thought he understood now: Don Enrique—Raven, whoever this creature was—had a paranoiac delusion about the world: conspiratorial, idolatrous of power, yet suspicious and disbelieving of the same things he professed only moments ago.

"What is it you want? How does your life now fit into these schemes of the world?" Eric asked. The man seemed like a disembodied intellect. A person had been lost somewhere inside this abstraction.

"Look over here," Don Enrique said, getting up from the chair. He led Eric to the bookshelves. On one, taking up perhaps three feet of space were all the books he had written as Harry

Raven, another fifteen feet of shelves were filled with large black notebooks, such as artists use to sketch in.

"These contain what I have written in the past thirty years. I think that most of it is better than anything I ever published. To answer your question of what I want: to go live where people converse intelligently with each other, and to look at fine works of art and write in my notebooks."

He lit another cigar.

"But you could have done all that forty years ago," Eric said.

"That was different. Then I believed in something. When I stopped believing, it was too late to go back. I became another man. I even changed my features under the knife and no longer looked the same. Now I only believe in my esthetic pleasure, for whatever years remain to me, and after that the ultimate darkness. That is my only redemption, now that I've served the devil, marking time. I have been a Patagonian Faust."

"You did want to be found though," Eric said. "Your trail was easy to follow once I saw the pattern, and then the names. Why did you play with words so? Raven, Krähe, Cuervo . . ."

"And when I get to France, I will become Corbeau. It amuses me, that's why, and that's *all* I want to do, amuse myself. I knew that when someone as clever as you came along, he would find me, and I would tell him my story. Mr. Newman, *you* have given me great pleasure, because I have kept all this closed up inside of me for the past thirty years and more, and now I feel relieved. Only one other person has ever known—"

"Ben Winkler!" Eric interrupted, the flash coming into his head. The secret Ben had confined to his notebooks—almost—or maybe the missing pages?

"Yes, dear old Ben, knew. He, like you, figured it out and followed me to Chile. I thought that the beating in Argentina would be enough to warn him off, but he was persistent. He found me in Valdivia right after the war."

Why didn't Winkler make it public, why did he keep Raven's secret? Eric wondered.

Don Enrique must have read Eric's mind. "He warned me you would find me too. Sent me a cable!" he shouted. "But I welcomed it. Yes, I wanted it, I see it now!"

He turned around and faced Eric squarely. "Ben would never have given away the secret, because his own life depended on it.

If I was found and brought to trial, he too would face the firing squad. He helped me get into Goldfeder's laboratory to steal the plans for the alphagraph. You know about that incredible machine?" Eric nodded yes and Don Enrique went on. "And when our scientists saw that the project needed the genius of its inventor, Ben set up Goldfeder for the abduction. His hands are covered with blood, metaphorically."

"But why would a dedicated Marxist help the Nazis?"

Don Enrique smiled the sardonic smile again. "Because," he said, "the fool was deluded by his own adopted ideology, and I used the method of the judo throw. I simply let his own weight carry him along. He thought he was serving Mother Russia in its great antifascist cause, that I worked for the Russians, and that America would use the machine for more wicked purposes than the loyal sons of Marx ever might imagine. I fed his delusion, and he acted of his free will. Treason nevertheless. He *must* be silent."

Eric thought of Winkler's stories about Raven's zealotry in Spain, the international cause.

"So it had nothing to do with Lee?" he asked. "Her love for you?"

Don Enrique twisted his thin lips in a frown. "I did feel *something* for her once, but briefly. I realized that love would turn me into putty, and that was what I didn't want. I had to be strong."

"What happened to Goldfeder?" Eric asked. "Was he killed, dispensed with when he had served his purpose?"

"Leon? You might *want* to think he would be so treated, but he hasn't been," said Don Enrique. "For an enlightened man, Professor Newman, your mind is filled with clichés of thought! Leon has made the great invention work, and someday he will be remembered for giving mankind the ultimate source of truth, not the puny version you pursue. At present he is quite well, even contented."

"Where is he, then?" Eric demanded.

"You met him at lunch. My 'brother' Oswaldo. In his own way he is happy. He has been as dedicated to his own work as one could possibly be, and is that form of vanity any less than my own? When we leave here he will have his dream fulfilled and I mine."

"But a prisoner . . . for thirty years? How can you justify that?"

Eric was flabbergasted. Don Enrique saw no moral connection. He lived out the role of the Nietzschean ubermensch, and was beyond remorse, centered in himself.

"I do not justify, ever. I don't have to. If your small-minded set of values needs that kind of cheapness, you can imagine what Leon would be if not for me. A piece of soap in some ghetto museum. I saved him to do his life's work—his art, his creation of the greatest power for civilization the world has ever known."

Eric would have liked to argue, but it was pointless, as though each of them spoke separate tongues.

Don Enrique stepped toward the door and indicated that Eric should do likewise. "Come," he said, glancing at a gold pocket watch. "It's getting late, and I have much to do. We must find Mademoiselle and complete the interview she requested. Despite the naive ruse of you as her husband," he laughed snidely, "I hold no grudge!"

With his hand on the knob he turned and said: "No matter what you may think, Professor Newman, you will *never* tell the story I told you just now, because you have no proof, and no one will believe you. They'll laugh you off the university campus as a fabulist. *That's* my guarantee: the proof of my contentions is in the same small-mindedness of your colleagues who search for 'truth.' Say what you want to, because no one will believe you, and furthermore, I don't care. There is a statute of limitations for prosecution, and besides, I was never a war criminal, so no one is interested, not even the United States government. Too much dirt will come out in the wash. I was just a pawn in a game so large that I have only begun to grasp it myself. You are a pawn, too.

"Harry Raven died in 1943, and that's where your biography will end. And I hope—I know—it will be a good book, although to some extent fiction. But then again so is all life—an illusion we create and then believe in."

Eric's mind was racing through the endless possibilities and combinations of questions he would have liked to ask and didn't, but it was clear his interview was over.

20

Estancia Ultima Nidal

ERIC BELIEVED Don Enrique was insane—the man was convinced that his acts had no consequences. In his cocoonlike existence there at the end of the world, he thought all was obliterated when he didn't see it any longer.

As they passed into the living room, the telephone buzzed once: the intercom. Don Enrique answered. He spoke in low tones, monosyllables. Eric pretended to be polite and feigned interest in a Miró canvas, but he sensed something was wrong. He waited, tense, nervous. When Don Enrique put the phone down, he glared at Eric, then stepped quickly onto the veranda and whistled. A guard in khaki came running. Don Enrique turned to Eric angrily: "Your companion has created some difficulty for all of us. I should have known better than to leave her alone. She's too curious for anyone's good. Kindly accompany me."

The guard nudged Eric with his submachine gun, and Don Enrique led the way through the house past the study to a large room at the back. There was no furniture of any kind but the wall was covered with paintings, like an art gallery.

He led to a door at the end of the gallery. "When Madame saw this door, she asked, and was told it was off limits," Don Enrique said. "After being shown the house she was to have joined us— but disappeared, evidently through this door. Most unfortunate for everyone, her morbid curiosity! Now she has found what we were at pains to conceal, and has caused unnecessary trouble. You will both have to stay here now longer than I had intended. It is *mine* to show should I choose to, not *hers* to discover!"

Through the door, a flight of stairs descended to a tunnel lit by bare bulbs every twenty feet or so. Don Enrique led the way and Eric followed, the guard behind him, his gun nuzzling Eric's back like an overfriendly large dog. Eric stumbled several times, his legs leaden, not working! From the turns he realized they were headed towards the low buildings he had seen from the dining room window. At the end of the passageway was a steel door which was opened by a guard after he had inspected them through a peephole.

Still below ground level, they entered a windowless area resembling a hospital. A number of small rooms led off a central corridor, each room with only a bed and a chair in it. There were no windows but the place seemed cool and well-ventilated through the many air ducts. All the doors closed from the passage inward, and Eric noticed that each one had a sliding bolt, worked from the outside only. It was rather like a prison. Here, Eric thought, alarmed, he and Odette would be incarcerated till death. The hunter was caught—

Don Enrique opened a closed door at the end of the corridor, and they entered a large room with a table in the center and what looked like old-fashioned X-ray equipment suspended over it. At the foot of the table was a computer terminal and a read-out screen.

"This is what I might have shown you voluntarily, because I knew that you were only interested in the 'ghost' we discussed. But your lady friend wants a sensational story, and the moment does not suit my convenience. Her impulsive behavior, trespassing where she ought not be, has ruined the opportunity *you* had—as women so often do—and now I'm afraid I must detain you both."

He wore a faint smile, but his eyes were dead and cold, and Eric stood gaping: Odette was lying on the table, her hands and feet strapped, electrodes attached to her temples and forehead, and to her arms and legs just above the elbows and knees.

"Odette, are you all right?" Eric shouted, lunging toward her. A short stocky man in a white laboratory coat who had been standing at the control panel dove at him, grabbing him before he could reach her, and pinned him back, saying something in very guttural German to Don Enrique.

"Madame has not been harmed," said Don Enrique to Eric, "but she can be electrocuted instantly if you try anything funny, and Walter here will not hesitate to do it. Consider yourself warned."

"May I speak to her? *Please*," Eric begged. He felt helpless, like a dreamer in a nightmare who wants to wake up but can't.

Don Enrique nodded, and the stocky man let Eric go.

"I'm all right mon cher," Odette said, but she didn't look it. She had a bruise on her cheekbone, and there was dried blood in her nostrils. Her blouse had been ripped down to the waist and her bra cut open in front where the electrodes were placed.

"Cette bête là," she said in rapid French under her breath, her eyes rolling to indicate Walter, now behind him, "je veux le tuer." Then in English: "It will be all right soon; just take care of yourself."

Don Enrique had been talking to Walter while the guard watched Eric and Odette, his eager finger tapping the trigger nervously.

Don Enrique stepped up and took Eric's arm, none too gently.

"Stand over here with me and watch this. I am sure it will interest a man of your intelligence."

He guided Eric to the foot of the table. "Proceed, Walter," he said.

"What is your name?" the short man in the lab coat asked Odette in Spanish, adjusting some dials on a control panel to the right of the table.

"Odette des Chavannes," she answered. On the screen at the foot of the table the words *Odette des Chavannes* appeared.

"What is the name of the man who came here with you?" Walter asked her.

"Eric Newman." The name also appeared on the screen.

Don Enrique stood there, smugly, his hands folded in front of him. Eric didn't know what the point of this was, but he was uninterested in whatever game they were playing at Odette's expense and wished they would stop. He wanted to stop *them*, at that moment, and would have killed them if he could.

"This man is your husband?"

"Yes." On the screen it read: *No   He is temporarily my lover*

Eric felt his cheeks flush. "What is this, what kind of trick?"

"It's not a trick at all, Mr. Newman; just watch for a moment."

Then this was the magnometric something-or-other machine that Raven had thrown his life away for. Eric wanted to destroy it, but the guard was still behind him and trigger happy, so he didn't make any sudden moves.

"I'm not sure I understand what you are showing me. A machine which reproduces what you say?" he asked, hoping to stall for time while Don Enrique answered. Maybe a move would suggest itself. Heroes were required, and he detested himself for not being one.

Don Enrique looked at Eric with surprise. "Don't you see that this machine reads the mind? With this device attached to you, you don't lie. If you do, the readout screen will indicate the difference between what you say and what you think. YOU CANNOT LIE. WE WILL KNOW!" He was shouting, a crazed look in his eye. The man's mind was gone. Eric's literary conceit back at the house was reversed. In the presence of this machine, Don Enrique was like Ahab with the whale captured—only he was tied to it here at the end of the world. Yet Eric wanted to redeem him, reason him back in time, revise him into the great Raven!

"How does it read the mind?" Eric asked, hoping to calm Don Enrique. Rescue fantasies aside, the man was quite insane, and might in a moment of pique say the word to end it all for Odette and Eric.

Before Don Enrique could answer, the door opened behind them and Oswaldo shuffled in. The place was haunted with ghosts: Dr. Goldfeder looked more benign than his keeper.

"The maid told me you were all in here, and I wanted to see what was going on," he said. "I thought all the testing was over, Enrique. Why are you doing this?"

He seemed irate, as though a promise had been broken. Yet Eric saw the scientific genius who had spent half of his life to develop a monstrous apparatus, all in the name of science, as a Dr. Frankenstein. Eric felt as if his sanity were going. Fantasy was becoming real, and all that had been real was transformed into fantasy.

Don Enrique stepped across the room to Oswaldo and spoke to him in a low tone. Eric couldn't make out the words.

"It's my business, Oswaldo," he said with finality, moving away. "You can leave us alone; but if you stay, don't interfere:

just sit over there,"—he pointed to a chair in the corner—"and observe our triumph, for one last time."

Oswaldo grumbled something, but did as he was told.

Eric was dumb with horror, helpless, impotent before the power of death in the hands of this urbane and sophisticated, yet clearly desperate man. His need to *prove* betrayed his philosophy of self-sufficiency. No doubt he had the power he boasted of, but it only worked in isolation. His demonstration scared Eric, but altered his awe.

"Ah? So you are fascinated, eh?" He seemed quite pleased. "It is a combined electroencephalograph, alpha brain wave scanner, and a computer. It translates the brain waves into legible thought patterns expressed in language, and projects those thoughts—the alpha waves—onto the readout screen. No matter what is said verbally, the truth of what the subject is thinking shows on the screen. YOU CANNOT LIE TO THE MACHINE AND YOU LEARN EVENTUALLY THAT THERE IS NO POINT IN DOING SO: WE HAVE ACHIEVED COMPLETE CONTROL." He was screaming now, caught up in the idea, the fixation with the machine. "Watch this!" he ordered. "Adjust the dials, Walter, for disjunctive response—not lethal."

Walter fiddled with two dials. Odette lay quietly, as though asleep, while the guard tapped a drum roll on his gun with itchy fingers.

"Who is this man?" Walter asked her again.

"Eric Newman," she answered. The screen read: *Eric Newman.*

"He is your husband?"

"Yes," she answered. The screen read: *My lover only while on this assign—*

Eric was surprised again by the answer, but even more surprised and horrified when Odette's body suddenly arched upward, her torso lifting off the table as she screamed in pain. He started forward, but the guard grabbed him around the neck and had his gun jammed into Eric's back before he could take a step.

"Why did you do that to her, you sadistic . . ." Eric shouted at Don Enrique, Raven, whoever the hell he was.

"I didn't do it at all," he said, a cruel smile flickering across his hard mouth. "I don't have to hurt people myself. The machine did it because her verbal response was in disjunction with what she was thinking. After a few nonlethal shocks like that, *nobody* lies anymore. As long as what they answer is what they think—and whoever asks the questions *always* knows, just by looking at the screen. Imagine." His eyes blazed with fervor. "No one will ever lie to the authorities again. Crime will cease, and revolutions and subversions stop, and the world will live in peace. It is truly omniscient, like God!"

"You're mad," Eric screamed in his face, "absolutely crazy—a monster!"

"Perhaps so, my young friend," he answered unruffled, "but you are a fool not to recognize where power lies. The recognition of real authority is the only sanity. Refinements of this mechanism with the new electronics can put a device like this into a telephone receiver, or a portable radio. You can be questioned over the phone and not lie without the party, the *authority*"—he stressed the last word—"knowing the truth, and TRUTH will be everywhere, and this will lead to universal order. Freedom!!—is the recognition of necessity. That is from one of the communist sages, but he was right. Accept it and your mind is free for everything—even poetry." Flashes crossed his eyes as he spoke, and Eric thought he would see foam soon. Trapped in bedlam.

"Shall we continue our demonstration?" Don Enrique asked, and without waiting for an answer told Walter to continue.

"What are you doing here at Ultima Nidal?"

"Interviewing Don Enrique." The readout was just a jumble of letters.

"What is she doing?" he shouted at Walter angrily.

"She is probably thinking in French," Walter said.

"Well give her a jolt, show her who is in control!"

"I can't," Walter said. "Only for disjunction between the response and the thought—"

"Try it again, you idiot!" Don Enrique screamed at him.

"What are you doing here at Ultima Nidal?" Walter shouted at her.

"Je veux parler avec. . . ."

The screen was just a jumble of letters and lines, like a TV set with its vertical hold out of phase.

"SPEAK SPANISH," Walter yelled at Odette.

"Shock her," Don Enrique commanded.

"You don't understand?" Walter said, annoyed with the order. "The machine isn't programmed to—"

Don Enrique was furious. "Let her get up then, she's making you into more of a fool than you are already!"

Walter looked angrily at Odette and began to undo the electrodes, none too gently.

Odette sat up on the table after her hands and legs were released.

"What time is it?" she asked.

"Seventeen hundred hours," said Walter angrily, looking at the clock on the wall behind her, "as though that meant anything to you now, you French whore." He slapped her face very hard, and her left hand went up to protect herself against another blow while the right hand went towards her crotch, also an involuntary move to protect herself, Eric thought.

"Stop that," Eric yelled, and started forward, but felt the vice grip of the guard's arm around his neck, his submachine gun pressed into his back.

"You can do it again, Walter," ordered Don Enrique, and Walter raised his powerful arm, this time in a fist.

Oswaldo, who had been sitting in the corner all this time so quietly that Eric had forgotten he was there, shuffled across the floor towards the alphagraph, the gleaming monster. It was a familiar step, Eric thought. He had done this often enough before, dispassionately gone to make some minor adjustment after he had watched the interrogation of some helpless creature strapped to the table and mentally raped, privacy violated beyond all imagination.

Then suddenly Oswaldo's cane was a blur in his hand as he raised it above his shoulder and cracked Walter over the back of his head. The German went down silent and solid as a stone.

Odette jumped off the table quickly and pulled the pistol from its holster on Walter's ample waist, aiming it at Don Enrique, while Oswaldo moved to the control panel of the machine.

"Oswaldo! What are you doing? Betraying me?" Don Enrique shouted, stopped in his forward lunge by the threat of Odette's weapon.

"Yes! Betraying! Enough is enough," the old man said. "Innocent victims now? This needed no more testing. It was bad enough with the prisoners! I spent my life to develop a method of research, a scientific tool, not an instrument of torture. You can't use it this way. I won't permit that, and would rather destroy it—as you know I can—by overloading these circuits, than see you make my life's work into a monster, a Moloch to which the innocent shall be fed.

"It has bothered me for a long time, especially when the testing began in earnest a few months ago. But in my weakness and desire to leave this prison—as you had promised me—I said nothing. Now you have gone too far, Enrique. I'm an old man and must die soon in any case: kill me now if you must, but if you fire you will damage it, and one turn of these knobs, my last act, will destroy everything for you too!"

"Let Eric go," Odette said to Don Enrique, "or I'll kill you!" She had already eased the safety catch off the automatic.

Don Enrique spoke to the guard in rapid Spanish, and Eric thought he would be released then, but instead, the grip tightened, and the muzzle of the submachine gun pressed into Eric so hard it hurt.

"You must think, Miss des Chavannes, that I am a great fool. If I let Newman go, what power do I have over you? No, you won't shoot me, and Oswaldo won't turn the dials in his sudden turn of religion," he said sneeringly, "his last gesture of doing good. Because Newman will die instantly if you shoot, or if Leo —Oswaldo"—He realized his error and corrected it, but not before Odette caught on. Eric saw the recognition in her face— "moves his finger. My guard will cut Eric in half with this machine gun, and your victory will be small."

Eric saw her hesitate, and frankly, was glad. He believed that the madman would have killed him on the spot, as he threatened, and preferred to take no chances.

At a signal from his boss, the guard backed Eric toward the door. Odette had missed the opportunity Eric was glad she didn't take, and Oswaldo stayed his hands on the control panel, immobile. Eric wondered if Oswaldo would have destroyed his life's work after all. His bluff was never called, thank God. Not that Eric gave a damn about the stupid machine, but Oswaldo was shooting craps with Eric's life. Walter began to stir on the floor, and Odette, her gun still trained on Don Enrique edging through the door, bent down and grabbed Oswaldo's walking stick and coshed the bulky form once again. He subsided right away.

Then, as the guard, Eric, and Don Enrique got through the door, she moved quickly behind the machine, pulling Oswaldo with her. If the guards were to fire, they would have to destroy the machine as well as their intended targets.

As Don Enrique slammed the steel door and bolted it from the outside, Odette shouted, "Get out, Eric. Nothing will happen to me. I've got his machine in here!" He heard the inside bolts clang home.

Another guard from the end of the corridor had come running when he saw them emerge.

"Stay here, until you get further orders. Now watch this man!" Again a submachine gun was trained on Eric as Don Enrique ran to a telephone and called for reinforcements. "At the emergency exit too!" he said.

He took this guard's pistol and pointed it at Eric, who was terrified, thinking that this was it; Don Enrique was going to kill him on the spot.

"Ahead of me, Newman, the way we came," and he nudged Eric toward the door at the end of the corridor, through it, and into the tunnel.

Once back in the house, he pushed Eric to a corner of the dining room, saying, "Stay there and don't move." The dry hacking sound of a helicopter grew louder. Don Enrique looked confused when he saw the aircraft hovering. "That was quick!" he said. "They'll have to wait, that's all! Until I clear it."

Then there was a lot of noise outside. Bursts of machine gun fire, a sound of explosive shells and the increasing clattering roar of a large helicopter. Across the field, near the low building they had just come from, men were running. Khaki uniforms were firing at others in black who had dropped from the aircraft.

The helicopter, a large Chinook, now rose twenty feet and then swooped onto the roof of the low building. Several men leapt onto the roof, carrying weapons. Eric saw the bursts of fire from the helicopter's guns and then heard the noise afterward. The air seemed to be filled with smoke and shouting as the peaceful Estancia Ultima Nidal turned into a bloody battlefield.

"All my life," Don Enrique screamed, "all my life I've taken precautions against something like this, and now you, you cause my ruination. Even Leon turned against me. You'll pay, you'll suffer for this. A bullet is too good for you." He slashed at Eric's face with the pistol barrel, catching him on the cheekbone, still sore from Buenos Aires. The pain was terrible, bringing tears to Eric's eyes. He felt blood on his face as a jagged cut opened. "Ahead of me, quick, march!" Don Enrique shouted, prodding with the pistol.

Eric didn't believe what was happening. His mind was beginning to numb, completely boggled by the events that had flitted past so quickly. He had actually found Raven, and Odette had found that thought translating machine, and the scientist who had invented it. With Odette, Eric had somehow stepped backward into time, and changed history. But they were caught up in it now: as far as he could see, all that remained was painful death. Odette had the machine and Goldfeder, but it was only a matter of moments before the guards would rush in and overpower them. Eric had Raven, or rather, he had Eric, but under the stress of the entire dream crumbling, the reincarnated poet had become a completely different man from the brilliant madman who had performed his one-act Promethean tragedy before Eric only moments ago. Mad, Eric had thought him, but not a raving homicidal lunatic! And now Don Enrique was ready to kill, to destroy anything in his way.

And who knew what the hell that battle was raging out there? Eric didn't. Was that why Nick had cautioned him to visit only in the morning? Did he know there was going to be an attack? If Eric could only tell Nick, tell him that they had found everything they were all looking for. . . . Don Enrique, now prodding hard with the pistol, angrily, furiously shoved Eric toward his study.

Maybe Eric could jump him and get his gun, the way they did in the movies—but he was too terrified. Don Enrique would shoot without hesitation. Eric hated himself for the trembling which shook his body, impotent with rage.

In the study, Don Enrique locked the door, walked to the table, hardly taking his eyes off Eric, and reached underneath. The windows went dark suddenly as thick steel shutters clanged down over the entrance from the veranda. Eric heard the clanging also from the east of the house and assumed that Don Enrique had sealed all of the exits to the veranda. At the same time, a section of bookcase swung open like a door, and Don Enrique pushed Eric ahead of him through a second steel door to a stair-well with a spiral ladder leading down.

Inside, at the top of the stairs, he pressed another button, and the bookcase closed after them. He shut the inner steel door with a clang, with the finality of the gates of hell.

It was like a fragment of somebody else's nightmare, and Eric was so frightened that he almost was in a trance, but the pain in his face, which had now started to swell into a long bloody welt, reminded him that it was all happening, no dream! Reality! Power was the gun and Eric's fear of pain.

At the bottom of the spiral stair was a tunnel similar to the one on the other side of the house and standing in readiness was a four-wheeled machine which looked like a golf cart.

"Get behind the wheel," Don Enrique ordered, "and start the engine." Eric fumbled for the key, found it, and turned. The engine roared in the confined space. Pressing the gun into Eric's side, Don Enrique said, "Now you are going to drive this and if you do anything, try any nonsense whatsoever, I'll blow your guts out." He poked Eric hard with the gun.

Where, the thought lumbered in Eric's fear-dulled mind, was the sensitive aristocrat, the writer of elevated, philosophic thoughts, the man who lived for art, the articulate reader of po-etry and philosophy, the man of the world? Here on a golf cart in a subterranean tunnel was a madman, a homicidal maniac who would stop at nothing to get his way.

Don Enrique flicked a switch under the dashboard to put on the headlights, and slipped into the backseat where he sat next to a suitcase Eric hadn't noticed at first. The gun was now pressed against the back of his neck.

"Drive!"

The golf cart was not as slow as Eric thought it would be, but moved at about twenty miles an hour. It seemed an eternity of driving, however, and only two feet of clearance on either side forced Eric to concentrate on steering. When would the bullet come, he wondered. Before or after they reached the tunnel's end?

Five minutes of eternity later, the bullet had not come and Eric stopped the cart at another steel door.

Don Enrique shut the engine, pulled out the key, and leaped off the cart to press a button on the wall.

The door swung open and revealed a ladder up. As the door opened the lights in the tunnel flickered and went out.

"They hit the power lines," he said to himself, and then he reached under the dashboard and brought out a long multicelled flashlight, and turned it on.

"Take that valise from the back," he ordered, shining the torch in Eric's eyes and blinding him for an instant, "and no funny stuff; my promise will be kept if you try anything. I've used pistols before with less provocation, so don't test me," he snarled. "You'll lose."

He pushed Eric ahead of him up the ladder. The valise was quite heavy, but fear gave him strength. He lifted it over his head and climbed rapidly.

At the top another steel door, then a wooden door, and they were in a peasant's cottage. No one there. Outside in the front was a road, and beyond the road, Lake Villarrica.

"Walk slowly and casually across the road. If you try to signal any passing motorists I will kill you at once," Don Enrique said. His voice had an edge Eric hadn't heard before. It was arrogant and sneering. He had the power in his right hand, and he knew that he would use it. Eric knew it too, and wasn't ready to do anything. His only thought was to do as told until he could get some thinking space. Maybe then he could do something to get away, if the madman didn't kill him first. But for the moment, Eric was his slave, and numbed into obedience by terror.

As they crossed the road there was a deafening explosion behind them. Both looked back and could see a cloud of smoke rising in the air. Eric realized that they were at the perimeter of the estancia, and the explosion must have come from a bomb in the house or the other building, because the air was soon filled with bits of debris.

"Keep moving," he said. "They haven't got me yet. I set off that bomb as we left. I've been prepared for years."

"But your library, your paintings, the manuscripts . . ." Eric said, halfheartedly hoping Don Enrique would run back and leave him alone.

Don Enrique laughed, without a hint of humor. "The paintings are fakes—everything is, except me! Did you think I would leave traces, proofs of what I told you, so that they could trace me to the ends of the earth? You are a great fool, Newman. You too are like the rest of them. I misjudged you. But that doesn't matter now. There will be no evidence that what I told you ever happened. And I shall yet carry out my plans; despite you, despite all of them, I won't be stopped. Damn you all! I'll get there as I intended. I can still write it all again!"

He pushed Eric with the pistol. A car was coming along the road. Eric averted his eyes, afraid that he would do something involuntarily to encourage this maniac to squeeze the trigger. He heard brakes squeal.

"Eric!" a woman's voice shouted. "Eric, where are you?" Both Don Enrique and Eric turned to see a woman in military coveralls step down from a jeep. It was Donna Harcourt! Eric opened his mouth to say something, but before a word could come out he heard the gun go off twice and watched helplessly as Donna screamed and fell to the roadway, her clothing suddenly bloody rags. Eric screamed too, overcome with anguish and rage, incoherent.

Don Enrique was indifferent to the murder. He looked pleased; he had proven something. "I warned you that I was not joking," he said, "and there is your proof." He seemed glad at having destroyed life like this, arbitrarily, willfully, as though it gave him his own life to do so.

"I'm only sorry it wasn't that French cunt of a spy. I should have killed her when she was tied down. The pain would have been greater," he said. "Now quick march!" He prodded Eric with the gun. The suitcase felt very heavy—and Eric felt hopeless: his prisoner, his slave.

An overwhelming nausea filled Eric's chest as he looked back, and saw Donna lying there. He thought he saw her stir. Tears came to his eyes. What was she doing here? Nick's fling, lovely, alive Donna, the American Embassy culture maven who had wanted to know all about the research into Harry Raven. "I majored in English," she had said with her superficially serious Bryn Mawr manner, only yesterday morning on the way to the airport—now lying on a road in the Chilean hinterland, her life destroyed by two blasts from the gun of this lunatic. This power-crazed evil genius, whom Eric had dredged up from the dead, had returned at Eric's insistence on "truth" to bring death and destruction to the innocent. Here he is, Donna, Eric thought. You have met him now—the great American writer. He wanted Odette. Where was she? Alive?—or dead too? He cried like a baby, and stumbled across the road.

"Stop your blubbering and get aboard," Don Enrique poked him with the gun again.

A twenty-five-foot open speedboat lay at the dockside, its bow pointing into the lake with its two stern-drive inboard-outboard engines tilted up. It looked fast. Was there a way to get away? He thought he might jump overboard once they were moving away from the dock; Don Enrique would probably let him go in order to escape. But Eric didn't get the chance to work out strategy.

"Turn around," Don Enrique said.

"Are you going to shoot me in the back?" Eric shouted. "You rotten bastard!" He felt a sharp pain at the back of his head and the lights went out.

* * *

Pain. Gray and then lighter in color, bluish, then orange and the roar in Eric's ears was deafening. So he had wound up in the inferno after all, even though he fasted last Yom Kippur, he thought. That was God's justice? Eric opened his eyes to see what Satan looked like, but all he saw was Don Enrique Cuervo–Immerman–Krähe–Raven . . . Eric didn't know who the apparition really was standing at the controls of the boat, framed in the setting sun. The bright orange glow blinded Eric's eyes.

Like a captured animal, he was trussed up in ropes, hands tied in front so tight that he could hardly feel his fingers, feet also lashed together. The throttle was wide open and the boat was slicing fast through the water, making a large bow wave and a turbulent wake. Eric could see that it was used for fishing sometimes. There were poles and nets in racks under the gunwales, and in the stern, where he was unceremoniously dumped, was a heavy Danforth anchor and a large coil of line.

He raised his head above the gunwale. They must have been about two miles from the shore.

"Oh, you are awake," Don Enrique said, turning around as if to a guest who had just nodded off for a bit. He seemed changed, almost cordial. Maybe he felt safe, Eric thought, and wouldn't kill him.

The roaring noise increased as Don Enrique opened the throttle a bit more, and locking the wheel in place, he walked back to where Eric lay and said, "I think I am safe now," sharing his sense of success. "Soon I will get to Villarrica, where a plane is ready to take me to Argentina where I shall disappear, until my friends think it safe enough to get me to Paris. And then the Louvre, the Tuileries, the bookstalls on the Seine, the cafes, the picnics at the Forest of Marly . . ." He was rhapsodic in his romantic dream. Eric could only marvel at the total craziness of this man who thought nothing of what he did, except how it affected his own dreams, his own real or imagined pleasures.

"Enrique Cuervo shall disappear, and in his place will appear Henri Corbeau, who has made his fortune in South America, and returned home at last to a life of ease. Not exactly the way I planned to leave, but I know I shall succeed now." The use of the first person singular began to come through to Eric's fuddled mind. But he didn't need to ask what Don Enrique had in store for him. It was announced, unbidden.

"Long before that, Eric Newman shall disappear as well," Don Enrique continued, laughing at his own little joke.

"When we get out into the middle, beautiful Lake Villarrica will welcome you for a short swim. And you can watch me speed off into the setting sun. That's how I will repay you for your interest in me, for interfering with my life and plans. Too bad about the book. I'll miss it."

Don Enrique stepped back to the controls, unlocked the wheel and continued toward the orange disk hung up in the sky above the distant horizon. Ironic, Eric thought, how beautiful the sunset was. He was terrified and hopeless. The roaring engines droned louder and louder, but loudest in his ears was his heart banging fear to every part of his body.

The roaring increased and looking up, Eric saw the helicopter, the same Chinook above them. It dropped to fifty feet above the boat and veered off to the right side.

"Don't get your hopes up, my young scholar," Don Enrique shouted over the noise. "They won't attack me while I have you here."

He waved the pistol at the helicopter as though to say, "Look! See!" and then he pulled out a rifle from under the dashboard and pointed it at Eric.

The helicopter edged a little closer, and Eric could see the pilot at the controls and behind him at the open jump doors a man in a dark green coverall, turning and gesturing to the pilot. The man was waving his hand.

The movement looked familiar—Nick Burns! Maybe, Eric thought, he really was dead and was being ferried across the River Styx. These were spirits of his life, his evaporated imagination, the fantasist at work! No! Eric Newman was here, in a speedboat being driven by a maniac across a lake in Chile, and as soon as Don Enrique could do so, he was going to push Eric overboard, as he had promised, for revenge, tied and helpless to drown. Nick couldn't save Eric either, because if he tried, Don Enrique would shoot Eric first.

Don Enrique raised his rifle and aimed it at the helicopter; Eric saw the puff of smoke and watched the recoil. The sound was drowned out by the roar of the engines. The helicopter suddenly veered away and increased its altitude.

"Your friends can't save you, my little professor," he said gleefully. "I'll just wait till dark out here, dump you and then continue. They won't even know where I am. I know this lake like the back of my hand."

Eric's feeling of hopelessness grew, and numbed him in a sinking despair. The wreck of his own dreams would sink with him in the black water, and he would float downward, a corpse. Eric, this time—not Raven—the body floating away in the wake. The huge form of the witness to Raven's "death," Manuel Becari, swam up into his consciousness—Becari, who survived a shipwreck because he willed it, because he had the strength to resist despair. But how could Eric? Becari's hands weren't tied, but Eric was going to be drowned like a helpless kitten in a sack. Oh, but to live— He had to, he had to want it. Not to die in the splashing darkness—to live!

"Now we'll confuse them about my direction," Don Enrique shouted crazily, like a child playing a deadly game of cops and robbers, and he turned the wheel to port, putting the boat into a long turn away from the aircraft. At the speed he was going the craft banked sharply, and the heavy anchor came sliding toward Eric.

He saw the smallest opportunity for delaying Don Enrique if he didn't kill Eric outright. At least he could stall the time, he thought, and grabbed for the Danforth anchor with his tied numb hands. It took all his strength to lift it, but he put his back against the gunwale and pushed down hard with his feet against the cockpit sole.

The anchor went over with a splash and the nylon line began to run out of the boat very fast, smoking as it burned its way across the wooden rail. Don Enrique was too startled to react instantly by shooting, and with a shout of "What the hell are you doing?" left the controls and ran aft to grab for the line.

He stepped onto the coil and reached for the nylon line which was running out behind the boat almost as fast as the boat was moving forward.

The rope burned his hands severely as soon as he grabbed it, and he jumped back with screams of pain and stood for a second, staring at his seared, burned palms, howling with agony.

Then he started for the controls to do what he should have done in the first place, cut back the throttle, and he began to step back across where Eric had thrown himself in the center. Eric knew he had to try something else, now: to act, to will his own being, to save himself because no one else could.

With a surge of strength born of desperation, he hit Don Enrique with his tied hands, swinging them as hard as he could into his captor's crotch. Don Enrique screamed again and doubled over in pain, falling onto the quickly running coil of anchor line.

Suddenly the coil, which had been running free, had some resistance against it, but the momentum was too much for Don Enrique's weight to resist. With a quick jerk the line wrapped around his leg and then an arm as he struggled with his pained hands to free the leg. A splintering crash ripped the boat as he was pulled overboard by the line, the weight of his body breaking through the wooden transom.

The line ran out quickly after that and Eric heard nothing but another crunch of wood as the end of the coil, the bitter end, pulled out of the wooden rib it had been tied to, and disappeared. They had probably only used the anchor off the stern when fishing, and never taken the trouble to fasten it properly. The weight of Don Enrique's body and the speed of the boat did the rest; the frail hull couldn't withstand the sudden force!

Eric struggled to his feet, holding tightly to the rail for fear of going over himself, and looked back to see where Don Enrique was. He wanted to go back and throw him a cushion to float with, yet keep him off the boat, at gunpoint if need be, until the helicopter could come and pick him up.

But there was no head bobbing in the water. Eric looked in all directions and could see nothing but the distant shores. The boat was almost in the middle of the five-mile-wide lake, having traveled at least half of its eighteen mile length.

"Ra-a-a-ven!" he yelled. "Ra-a-a-ven!" Then, "Don Enri-i-i-i-que!" But there was no answer. Nothing above the roar of the engines.

Eric lowered himself to his knees, crawled forward to the controls and knocked the throttles back. The boat slowed down instantly, and the backwash of the wake came over the transom, soaking Eric. He stood up again and looked back, but saw nothing, and called again: "Ra-a-a-a-ven! Cue-e-e-e-rvo!"

Only the sun was behind him in the large circle they had made, its rim dipping quickly into the west. Eric turned the wheel back toward where they had just come from with his now completely numb hands, locked it in place and then groped in a tackle box until he found a knife.

The legs were easy, but the hands were difficult. He had to hold the knife between his feet and saw his hands back and forth, until a couple of strands were cut through and he could pull the rest free.

He increased the speed then until he thought he was roughly in the area where Raven had gone over the side, but there was nothing. He zigzagged back and forth, calling all the names he had learned, all the identities, but only the deep blue of the vast lake met his eye wherever he looked.

A roaring of engines overhead and the helicopter was back, hanging off in the distance. Eric didn't think they saw what had happened in the gathering twilight, and now it was getting too dark for them to see who it was at the controls, so he waved wildly and flashed the large flashlight Don Enrique had carried from the tunnel, and then headed toward them. They turned on glaring spotlights, and then closed the distance until the copter hovered thirty feet above, its blades kicking up a whirlpool as a ladder dropped from the open hatchway to right above the speedboat. A few seconds later, a man came scrambling down and jumped on deck. Nick Burns, his face smudged and clothes torn.

"Boy you look a sight," Eric said.

"You should talk," he answered, and in the middle of the darkening lake, the helicopter's rotors deafening, splashing them with waves driven over the side, Eric grabbed Nick and hugged him as though he were life itself.

The searchlights flashed on again adding blindness to the deafness and a voice called down through a loudspeaker:

"You lovers okay?"

Nick waved his arms to indicate that they were, and the helicopter rose into the night, leaving them in a sudden silence and darkness.

"Odette?" Eric asked.

"You'll see her in a little while. Oh man, I thought it was all over for you!" He turned to the controls and flicked on the dashboard, running lights and a headlamp.

"And Donna?"

Nick looked down, and turned his face away, but in the faint afterglow of the twilight, Eric could see the tears running down Nick's cheeks.

"Dead," he said, with a soft finality.

Eric felt drained of everything. Nick took the controls and moved the boat forward easily into the darkness. Lying spent on the floorboards, Eric watched the stars brightening overhead and drifted into sleep.

21

THE DIRECTOR made a cathedral with his fingers and whistled his breath through the nave. Then he stood up and walked to the bookcase-lined wall, opened a low cabinet, took out liquor and glasses, and poured two large measures of scotch over ice. He returned to the library table where Nick sat.

"It's not often that I drink during a working day, Nicholas, but your report warrants it. Cheers!"

Nick sipped his drink, but did not feel so cheery. The assignment was over, the mission was accomplished, and the casualties were light, officially. But Donna's death, her pointless, accidental death he took upon himself. Ironically, he had wanted her out of firing range, out of the way. Her experience had not trained her for battle, and he felt she had come far enough. So he didn't let her go airborne, but sent her out in a jeep to meet them when the action subsided. A pickup detail. It was almost as if he had killed her. His mistake for letting his professional judgment be swayed by sentiment.

The director's face watched Nick's face. "It isn't your fault, Nick. It was a fluke. Mine. The girl never should have known about your presence in Chile other than the official reason. But I thought you might—" He stopped. "I asked for blanket coverage and shouldn't have. It was all yours and not mine to set up. Perhaps I'm too paternalistic."

Nick swallowed his scotch in a hard gulp and gritted his teeth. Neat technique. Absolution by God. Home free. He rejected it: the responsibility was his. Love kills. He had known it, yet was weakened and gave in. Never again.

"Now we can build a bigger and better ETT. We control it. Do we win this round?" Nick's tone was sarcastic.

"In strategic thinking, yes," answered the director, ignoring

Nick's tone of voice, "in reality, who knows? By the way, you know Goldfeder won't work for us. He's gone to Jerusalem. So we'll muddle through on our own with our own scientists."

Nick couldn't blame the old man—why shouldn't he know some peace? But to the director, Nick said, "Then the chess game goes on as before. They lost a knight and we only lost a pawn, so I guess we're ahead, right?" Nick studied Barnwell's face and wondered if he himself would think like a chess master—if he would have to or want to—one fine day.

"Right, in terms of metaphor," said Barnwell, as yet not piqued, "except nobody ever wins. We go to a draw, or a stalemate. Now we control the board."

And those are the usually unspoken rules, Nick thought. Keep the game going and stay in business. No unemployment is this union's goal. But he kept his thoughts to himself. Still learning the game. Against an opposition he had thought of as an ally: ICO, the multinational conglomerate. He didn't want to discuss the implications now and risk a lecture from professorial Barnwell.

"Raven wove quite a nest," said Nick, shifting the subject, he hoped.

"Well, there's no doubt that the man was a creative genius, really a great literary mind, is there?" asked the director. "When he turned his talents to espionage, he was equally adept at creating. Or should I say destroying: that's really like reverse creation. At the root, the force is the same, merely guided by a different impulse."

"Why do you think Raven wanted all the copies of the manuscript as well as the original?" Nick asked.

"Because he assumed at first that if he destroyed the evidence, your friend Newman would be stymied, but didn't give Newman credit for being as excellent a researcher as he is; Newman was able to use his fine mind to track down what dozens of professionals have failed to do."

Nick finished his drink and got up to take his leave. "By the way, what about the hushed-up reports that Winkler submitted thirty years go. Why were they buried?"

The director gave him a wry smile. "Look at the international corporate structures, the interlocking control patterns of the multinational conglomerates, and you'll understand."

Nick pressed the issue; he had to risk the lecture because the question was preoccupying him recently. "So, it's them we fight for? It's them we struggle to protect? The rest is theater?"

"Not quite," answered Barnwell, avoiding what Nick both wanted and hated, shaking hands at the library door. "When you direct OMEGA beginning next month, you'll have a better grasp of the whole picture."

"So soon?" Nick was surprised. "I thought it would be a few years from now."

Barnwell smiled wistfully. "No, I'm past my prime. The job needs younger force, more agility than I have; and besides," he laughed, "I want to read some books I've missed. Enough of reports. The official letter will be in Paris."

* * *

The next morning Nick sat on a bench in the Tuileries, throwing crumbs to the pigeons. It was a cold day, but a weak sun poked its way through the haze and gave the bare gardens the look of an impressionist painting. He had saved the roll from the plastic breakfast on the TWA flight just for this purpose. He knew it would keep him occupied while he waited for his staff meeting, the new beginning which he had wanted. How he would shape OMEGA had kept him awake on the flight from Washington last night. It was still early and he wasn't ready to go home, so he hefted the suitcase he had brought with him and walked slowly toward the American Embassy on the Champs-Elysées, to finish business—and clear out his desk. He was ready to take on whatever came, sad that the separation between what he felt and what he had to do was becoming so distinct. For him, the ETT episode was closed, and time would move forward. He never looked back, at least not professionally. He remembered Eric quoting Hegel in the Santiago airport, "Everything is figured out—except how he himself is to live a life," and kept walking.

EPILOGUE

Paris, April 1974

SOME SCHOOLBOYS watched from the embankment as Eric stood on the Pont Neuf and dropped something into the Seine. He saw it float, caught by the rapid current, swirling over and under in little circles until it was out of sight. Being French, the boys didn't wonder for very long what the man on the bridge was doing, but shrugged their shoulders and continued to throw rocks into the water, competing for the biggest splash.

"Fact returns to fiction. The Raven manuscript is where it should have been thirty years ago," he said to Odette, who stood beside him in the raw April afternoon, the collar of her camel coat turned up against the wind on the bridge.

"And so is Harry Raven," she said, "but you and I are here, and for us the past is over. The only time is now, my love, now."

"Are you speaking to your 'lover, temporarily while on assignment,' or your pretend husband?" he teased her.

"I am speaking to my only lover, and perhaps someday, if he doesn't get scared and run away, my only husband."

She smiled at Eric, and he kissed her face, both cheeks, and watched the color of her deep blue eyes glow like sapphires as the light of the sun reflected in them. Arms linked, silent, they walked home along the embankment of the Seine as the last testament of Harry Raven drifted off into the tide and then, hopefully, into the vast ocean. Eric watched the river, the bateaux mouches, and the bare trees whipping in the wind. He felt empty, with nothing left to do.

"Why don't you do *that?*" Odette asked, as though he knew what she was thinking.

"Do what?"

"Write fiction. A novel about what happened and how. Invent

the parts you didn't experience directly, or whatever else you want—the characters, the conversations you didn't overhear; even the details can be made up. Whatever you want. Just tell the story."

The thought hadn't occurred to him. How could he marshal the murky chaos of history into the transparent order of myth? His own re-creation? Impossible!

He frowned. "That's crazy. I think you're crazier than I am, and that's saying a lot. I've never tried to write fiction."

But he liked the idea! Whether he could do it was another question. Yet there was no pressure to produce. Success would be in his own terms, only satisfying his own need to create. It was certainly acting on the present, not the past, and that was what he wanted, he thought.

"At least," she laughed, the bell sound echoing off the sides of the Seine embankment, "at least, to use a Newmanism, 'it will keep you off the streets'!"

The next morning, after Odette left for work, Eric armed himself with a packet of Gauloises and a large cup of café au lait, and started to type out the truth as he saw it. Only the facts were changed in his afterword, his postscript at the end of time:

Raven stood on the afterdeck of the *Libertador* and watched the phosphorescent wake. He looked at the time. Almost midnight. Stars but no moon, and the sea an infinite expanse of black. . . .

Schwartz, A.

No country for old
men